Mary Jane Staples was born, bred and educated in Walworth, and is the author of many bestselling novels including the ever-popular cockney sagas featuring the Adams family.

LOVE FOR
A SOLDIER

Mary Jane Staples

CORGI BOOKS

TRANSWORLD PUBLISHERS
Penguin Random House, One Embassy Gardens,
8 Viaduct Gardens, London SW11 7BW
www.penguin.co.uk

Transworld is part of the Penguin Random House group of companies
whose addresses can be found at global.penguinrandomhouse.com

Penguin
Random House
UK

First published in Great Britain in 1985 by Severn House Publishers Ltd
as *The Hostage* under the name Robert Tyler Stevens
Bantam Press edition published as *Love for a Soldier* 2012
Corgi edition published as *Love for a Soldier* 2012
Corgi edition reissued 2021

A CIP catalogue record for this book
is available from the British Library.

ISBN
9780552178198

Typeset in New Baskerville by Kestrel Data, Exeter, Devon.
Printed and bound in Great Britain by Clays Ltd, Elcograf S.p.A.

The authorized representative in the EEA is Penguin Random House
Ireland, Morrison Chambers, 32 Nassau Street, Dublin D02 YH68

Penguin Random House is committed to a sustainable future
for our business, our readers and our planet. This book is made
from Forest Stewardship Council® certified paper.

To Wendy and Jeffery

Chapter One

It was March 1918, and in the heart of the agricultural countryside that lay between Valenciennes and Douai, an open black Bugatti car was moving steadily along a winding dirt road. Like other byways of its kind in this part of northern France, the road was of little importance except to farmers and their carts.

At the wheel of the Bugatti was a young lady of exemplary background. The day was a challenge to her, the morning fine and cloudless, the sky blue, the air almost springlike after a crisp frost. From the west came the intermittent, murmuring rumble of guns; guns that had known few periods of silence since the far-off days of 1914. But apart from those uneasy murmurs of war, the countryside seemed placidly quiet. Fields patterned the landscapes. Some lay fallow, and some, richly furrowed, were hopefully awaiting the spring seed.

The young lady had passed German Army

vehicles earlier, on major roads, but since taking to the winding byways she had seen only the occasional farm cart. She wondered how far she was from Douai. Had she kept to the main roads, she would have been more certain of distances, but even so, and despite the wandering nature of her preferred rural course, she felt she could not be more than fifteen kilometres from the town. And the rural quietness was reassuring. It told her she was alone; that no one was in pursuit of her. She drove on.

Then the quietness was broken by a sound from above. She heard a low, fretful noise that quickly turned into an urgent buzzing. She slowed down and stopped. She was very much alone, with no other human being in sight. She looked up. Something came out of the clear sky. The sun caught it, flashed light over it and etched it into shape. A plane. It was in steep descent. She stood up in the car to stare at it out of huge blue eyes.

It was a machine of war, a biplane. And there above it, screaming down on it, was another. The two planes split the sky apart. The air vibrated and the grass in the fields rippled. A machine gun opened up, and the rat-a-tat of its fire reached the young lady's ears like the cracks of a whip. Tracer bullets, streaming light, burst from one of the planes.

A gasp escaped her. She realized the colour of the plane could only mean it was the war machine of the indestructible ace of the German Air Force, Baron von Richtofen. There was no one, friend or foe, who did not know that every Albatros in his squadron was painted predominantly red, but that he alone flew a machine wholly scarlet.

Spellbound, she watched.

She could hardly believe it was happening. That out of the tranquil sky had come two opposing machines of war, one in deadly pursuit of the other. Above her and to her left, the hunted plane, a British Sopwith Camel, seemed in its screaming descent to be aiming itself directly at the Bugatti. She froze. For one horrifying second she thought she and the car were going to be engulfed and obliterated.

But a miracle happened. The Camel levelled, rushed, stood up on its tail and soared to execute a high backward arc of escape. The roaring, flame-spitting red Albatros swept under it and made a wide fast turn that brought it back between the Camel and its homeward route to the British lines in the west. The Camel veered, drifted, slipped and buzzed. Richtofen dropped from the sky above. Scarlet flashed as the Albatros screamed at the Camel. The machine gun opened up again. The Camel shot upwards on surging power. The captivated young lady, heart hammering, saw a puff of smoke dart from beneath its engine. She trembled. Richtofen had maimed it. His Albatros, coming out of a climbing turn, rolled its wings and went in new pursuit as the Camel roared away. The German machine, faster than the British, was on its tail in seconds. But the Camel, more manoeuvrable, deftly slipped under another zipping stream of tracer bullets.

She felt for the British pilot, who needed every flying skill he possessed to escape Richtofen. Richtofen, she knew, was Germany's hero of the skies, and every Allied fighter pilot acknowledged him as the supreme master of aerial combat. She felt there was little chance for the Camel. It buzzed, flipped and fell away from the path of the bright red Albatros. Flying low, it roared over her head, and the noise of its engine deafened her.

The chase continued. The climbing Camel emitted another spurt of oily smoke. Its engine coughed and faded, and its wings dithered. Wide-eyed, the young lady stared in stricken pity at what she thought was its approaching destruction. Desperately, the pilot put the nose down and searched the pastures for a crash landing. But the engine picked up, and strongly, and the plane roared over the fields attempting another climb. The Albatros, securely stationed above and behind it, flew fast towards its tail. Again the Camel stood up, looped out of Richtofen's gunsight, and turned westwards, climbing. As the Albatros came round once more, a long ragged plume of smoke belched from the Camel.

She heard the roar of its engine die to a stutter. Her gloved hands tightened. The machine was crippled. It drifted out of its climb, wings faltering. The stuttering engine coughed, picked up once more, and the pilot straightened out to rush on a line parallel with the road. She saw it skimming fields and hedges, its shadow flying fast over the ground. And she saw the Albatros poised to strike, circling almost lazily above the crippled Camel. The oily smoke became thicker and blacker. The pilot sought height and landing space, but his machine began to cough itself to death. Its nose came down and the fields flew fast beneath it. The young lady saw it pass her, forty metres to her left, the helmeted head of the pilot visible. It was rolling and floundering, and he was fighting its urge to commit suicide. A tongue of flame darted out, licking at the engine. The plane flew crazily on, dipping and flipping above a high stone wall encrusted with briars. It dropped, disappearing from view, and came to grief in a field two hundred metres away. She shuddered and winced as she heard it crash.

Richtofen's Albatros rolled its wings and flew away.

The young lady stood with her heart pounding. From beyond the screening hedge of stone and briar, she heard the Camel explode.

A sheet of flame ripped high and nauseating smoke billowed. She plunged down into her seat and set the Bugatti in frantic motion, crashing the gears hideously, something she rarely did. She drove fast until she reached a gate on her left. There she stopped, for she saw the Camel, standing on its nose and burning furiously. Flames scarred the earth and seared the air. Smoke polluted the bright morning. She felt the heat of fiery destruction, and her breath caught in her throat. Richtofen may have earned his victory, but the British pilot had fought desperately and bravely, and now the fierce, terrible flames were consuming him. There was no chance, none whatever. Everything was engulfed in fire and smoke. Nevertheless, she jumped from the car and opened the gate. From her left, inside the shelter of the roadside hedge, someone spoke in French.

'C'est la guerre, mademoiselle.'

Chapter Two

Chateau St Alain, near Valenciennes, northern France, March 1918.

At the chateau, the headquarters of the 15th German Army Corps commanded by General Paul von Feldermann, a moment of confessional humiliation was taking place for Captain Erich Vorster.

The general, having received the confession, placed his hands on his desk, leaned back and said, 'You have managed to deliver to me the unbelievable.'

'I'm sorry, Herr General.' Captain Vorster stared fixedly at the portrait of the Kaiser that hung on the wall above the general's head.

'Sorry?' General von Feldermann, noted for his self-control, a quality as inherent in a Junker as stoicism in a Spartan, was unusually close to raising his voice. 'You've lost my daughter and you're sorry?'

'I did not expect Fräulein Sophia to be quite so agile.'

The general eyed the unimaginative captain a little pityingly.

'As I remember it,' he said, 'my orders contained the injunction to watch her with the utmost care.'

'That is so, Sir, but there was a moment – a few moments – when of necessity she was out of sight.'

'Necessity?' The general's blue eyes were bleak. 'State precisely what happened.'

'To ensure I had enough petrol for the journey, Herr General, I stopped at the 23rd Company Supply Headquarters to have the tank filled and to take extra cans aboard. At this juncture, Fräulein Sophia stated she wished to change her dress for a warmer one.'

'You were taken in by that?'

'She had begun to shiver, Sir.'

'With a leather coat on, she had begun to shiver?'

'Visibly, Sir,' said the unhappy captain. 'She—' He stopped, for the general's icy stare was numbing.

'Go on.'

'She assured me that on no account was I to think she would not return.'

'You did not suspect that her request and her assurance were in the nature of a deception?'

'I did suspect that, yes,' said Captain

14

Vorster, 'particularly in view of your warning. Therefore, I accompanied her to the officers' quarters, where a suitable room was put at her disposal, and where I waited outside the door. I respectfully submit, Herr General, that I could do no more than that.'

'What you are saying,' the general said caustically, 'is that despite my telling you not to take your eyes off her, almost the first thing you did was to allow her to place a door between the two of you.'

'But the situation, Sir. Her need of privacy—'

'The situation was one you should not have permitted. I imagine I know the rest. Using what you call her unexpected agility, she climbed out of a window and disappeared.'

Captain Vorster cleared his throat.

'With the car, Sir,' he said.

General von Feldermann sighed.

'I see,' he said. 'She made her promised return to it and drove off while you were still waiting outside the door in the officers' quarters. Is that it?'

'Unfortunately, yes, Sir.'

'Very unfortunately,' said the general, although for a moment a little gleam of paternal pride brightened his eyes. His spirited daughter's penchant for the audacious and unconventional commended itself to him, if not to his wife. His wife would be furious. She had mapped out Sophia's life from birth, and nowhere along the chosen path was Sophia scheduled to run off and marry a young flying officer who was a middle-class anonymity. The general had met the young man and thought him likeable, but quite without the character or background that would make him an acceptable suitor for Sophia. Sophia's infatuation was undoubtedly born of a perverse defiance of her ordained role. She had been only too ready to fall for a handsome face and dashing uniform. To her, Captain Fritz Gerder, as a flying officer with Richtofen's squadron, was irresistibly dashing, and quite different from the men her mother recommended. She was making a mistake, of course. Marriage to Captain Gerder would be a disaster. Within six months, if he survived the war in the air, she would discover his appeal to be that of an irresponsible youth. At twenty-three, he was too young for her, for she herself would soon be twenty-one. Wayward, she needed a man of strong character, not a callow boy, however well he handled a fighter plane.

Baron von Richtofen's squadron was stationed near Douai, and Sophia would almost certainly head for there. She had made it quite plain that if Fritz proposed she would accept him, and in two weeks or so she would be twenty-one. It was imperative to return her to her mother.

'Herr General,' ventured Captain Vorster, 'may I suggest I notify various units to keep an eye open for the car?'

'Out of the question. Every unit in this area is committed to General Ludendorff's new offensive, due to be launched very soon. You know that. Captain Vorster, having lost my daughter, yours is the responsibility for finding her. Take a car and go after her.'

'Yes, Sir,' said the young officer. 'But where?' he asked.

General von Feldermann sighed again. After almost four years of crippling conflict, Germany was not only short of manpower, it was short of the right kind of field officers and staff officers. Men of flair and imagination were harder to come by. Captain Vorster was keen and competently methodical, but had few inspired moments.

'I imagine that there will be people who've seen the car and its driver. Answers to common-sense questions should help you find the route she's taking. I think you'll find most of the answers will point you towards Douai.'

'Douai? That's only about twenty-five kilometres from our front lines, sir.'

'So?' The caustic note was there again. 'My daughter won't be intimidated by that. Find her, Captain Vorster, and carry out my original request to escort her home to her mother. One more thing. On no account are you to divulge to anyone, anyone at all, the identity of the young lady you're looking for. I don't want the larger part of the 15th Army Corps to know that its commander has lost his daughter.' The general's little dig did not escape the uncomfortable captain. 'Do you understand?'

'Perfectly, Herr General. But my work—'

'Ah, your work, yes. It's important, of course, but not as important as mine. General Ludendorff expects something more of me than running around in search of Sophia myself. Therefore, I must ask you to do so. Start at once. The morning is still young. Keep me informed, but not directly. Through Major Kirsten.'

'Very good, Sir.'

Captain Vorster departed in haste, though without relishing his assignment. General von Feldermann sat in thought for a few moments. With Ludendorff's well-planned offensive due to begin in a few days, he had worries enough and could have done without the personal problems posed by Sophia's waywardness. He must telephone his wife and give her the news of Sophia's disappearance. On the other hand, if Captain Vorster succeeded in finding her fairly quickly, nothing need be said, except to Major Josef Kirsten, a trusted confidante.

He summoned the major, an executive officer and aide of distinction. Major Kirsten, as a casualty of the Somme, had lost his left arm and his empty sleeve was tucked neatly in his jacket pocket. A further wound caused by a small but red-hot piece of shrapnel had left a scar puckering the skin of his temple, close to his right eye. It slightly distorted the eyelid, giving the impression of a squint. He was iron-grey though not yet forty. He listened to the general outlining a purely domestic problem.

'One has to admire Sophia's initiative,' he said. 'Are you expecting results from Captain Vorster?'

'I'm hoping,' said the general.

Major Kirsten, who knew Sophia quite well, said, 'Are you sure she'll go to Douai?'

'I'm sure she'll head straight for the arms of Captain Gerder, and Douai is their most convenient meeting place.'

'Allow me, Herr General, to contact Colonel Hoffner, the commandant at Douai,' said Major Kirsten. 'He's an old colleague of mine. I'll describe Sophia to him and ask for some of his men to keep an eye open for her. I shan't tell him she's your daughter, merely that for certain reasons I'd like to be advised if she's spotted. Allow me to also contact the young flying officer, Captain Gerder.'

'Is that wise?' The general frowned.

'I think,' said Major Kirsten, 'that if Sophia does land in his arms, I must persuade him to persuade her to return to her mother.'

'If you can do that, I'd be grateful,' said von Feldermann, who had a mountain of work to get through. 'Go about it in your own way, Josef.'

Returning to his office, Major Kirsten got

through to Colonel Hoffner in Douai. The colonel, advised that the major was interested in the whereabouts of a certain young lady, took down details of her appearance. The major said she was not to be apprehended, only located. The colonel promised to do what he could and to call the major back the moment he had any information to impart.

Major Kirsten then telephoned Richtofen's squadron headquarters and asked to speak to Captain Fritz Gerder. He was told that the captain was in Douai; his plane had been shot up two days ago and he had crash-landed. He had suffered no real injury, apart from some bruises, but was badly shaken up. He had spent a day in hospital and was now on a week's rest in a Douai hotel. He would be recalled at the end of the week, when a new machine would be available.

Major Kirsten telephoned the hotel. The hotel paged Captain Gerder while the major held on. After some minutes, Captain Gerder came on the line. The major proceeded to talk.

Captain Gerder listened for a while, then broke in to say, 'I'm unaware of the relevance of all this.'

'I'm aware you're unaware,' said Major Kirsten, 'but perhaps you'll permit me to finish. It's suspected that Fräulein von Feldermann is heading for Douai. Herr Captain, in the event of her making contact with you, may I have your word as a German officer that you'll persuade her to return home?'

'As a German officer, I'm required to obey orders and to fly my plane against Germany's enemies,' said Captain Gerder. 'I am not required, Herr Major, to influence the wishes or actions of private citizens.'

Impudent young devil, thought Major Kirsten.

'Nevertheless, Herr Captain, your cooperation is requested,' he said, 'and General von Feldermann would be extremely grateful for it.'

'My first consideration will be to respect Sophia's wishes,' said Captain Gerder.

'Very laudable,' said Major Kirsten, 'but I hope your consideration would also embrace her parents' natural anxieties. That isn't an unreasonable comment?'

'No, not at all,' said Captain Gerder, but sounded indifferent.

'Would you at least be good enough to inform me if Fräulein Sophia does arrive?' asked Major Kirsten.

'You mean that if I put Sophia's wishes above her parents' anxieties, you would at least like me to tell you exactly where she is?'

'Precisely, Herr Captain – if that is also not too unreasonable. Thank you.' Major Kirsten hung up, deliberately giving Captain Gerder no time to argue a refusal. There, he thought, was a young man as unconventional as Sophia herself. What was it he had said? *My first consideration will be to respect Sophia's wishes. Will be?* Not *would be?* One could infer from that, perhaps, that Sophia knew he was in Douai and had been in touch with him. One could also infer that he knew Sophia intended to go to him.

The major called Colonel Hoffner again and asked him if an eye could be kept on the movements of Captain Fritz Gerder, a pilot in von Richtofen's squadron presently staying at the Hotel Avignon in Douai. It was possible that the young lady in question might meet him there or somewhere else in the town.

'My friend,' said Colonel Hoffner, 'I presume you know the war is still on?'

'Even in a war like this,' said Major Kirsten, 'there are times when small favours have to be asked of old colleagues.'

'Are we dealing with spies and traitors, perhaps?' said Colonel Hoffner.

'I'm not permitted to answer that,' said Major Kirsten.

'Ah, so.' said the colonel. 'Well, I'll do what I can, Josef.'

'Thank you. I'm not asking for the young lady to be detained, only to be advised of her whereabouts.'

'You've already made that point.'

'I'm getting old,' said Major Kirsten, and put the phone down.

*

The winding country roads of agricultural Nord were indifferently surfaced, but Sophia von Feldermann handled the powerful Bugatti belonging to her family with the confidence of a young woman who had benefited from the expert tuition of the family chauffeur.

She had gone to her father to seek his understanding and help, although neither she nor her mother were encouraged to appear at the Corps Headquarters unless invited. She went because she knew he was not quite the autocrat he sometimes seemed, but her mother forestalled her. By the time she had reached the chateau late the previous evening, a parental phone conversation had taken place, and as soon as she mentioned her wish to marry Captain Fritz Gerder she was up against a prearranged opposition she could not break down. Further, to thwart any intention she had of eloping with Fritz, whom she knew to be in Douai, her father commanded Captain Vorster to drive her back to her mother first thing in the morning, her mother at present being in Baden-Baden. From there, Sophia knew, she would be taken home to Lissa in South Prussia and kept there until the war ended and certain young flying officers could go back to being clerks. Her mother believed that although many girls might look romantically at any airman, no discriminating girl would look even casually at a clerk. But Fritz was not a clerk. He was the son of a Bavarian professor, and he was also a university graduate. In addition, he was an excellent fighter pilot. He had to be, or he would not be flying with Richtofen's squadron.

The war would soon end. With the Russians beaten and in the throes of revolution, General Ludendorff was planning a gigantic offensive that would tear the French and British apart. Captain Vorster had confidently said so.

Sophia motored at a steady speed. She knew her father would send someone after her, and would probably pick on Captain Vorster, giving the poor man a chance to remedy his mistake. Her father commanded thousands of men, but it was her elegant and aristocratic mother who commanded the family. Both sons were with von Mackenson's army and on his staff. That was due as much to her mother's influence as her father's. Her mother was of very ancient and noble Prussian lineage, and considered it her duty to secure the proudest of futures for her children. Sophia had wanted to enlist in the Women's Army Corps when it was formed, but her mother would not hear of it and insisted she continued with her voluntary work for the German Red Cross. In the meantime, it was to be hoped that Sophia would favourably consider attaching herself to Count Frederick von Menckenburg. To Sophia, however, this scion of Prussian nobility was so austere and correct that she felt he would expect his wife to give formal notice whenever she desired to speak to him. She had no wish whatever to marry any man as humourless as that.

Fritz was very different. Correctness and convention, he said, were designed by the sour to suffocate the sweet.

He had just had a narrow escape from death in one more aerial combat with British fighter planes. His engine was on fire when he landed, his damaged machine pancaked and he was pulled out with his body a mass of bruises. He had refused to be hospitalized. Instead, he was resting in an hotel in Douai and had telephoned her from there. She desperately wanted to join him.

They had met in Berlin during a reception for newly decorated flying officers. Introduced, they at once found it easy to talk to each other. Fritz, young, handsome and amusing, captivated her with his cheerful disregard of formality. He had a reckless air that excited her. He was very different indeed from the stiff, monocled Junkers of Prussia.

Before the reception was over, Fritz found an opportunity to kiss her. It was an act of bold outrageousness, and she found herself breathless when he planted the kiss full on her lips. She affected indignation. It did not work, and Fritz laughed at her.

'Delicious girl,' he said.

'Impudent boy,' said Sophia.

'Let's both refuse to grow up,' he said.

'Apologize,' said Sophia, fair and brilliant in her gown.

'Apologize?' said Fritz. 'For kissing you?'

'Yes.'

'But how absurd,' said Fritz. 'We've met and soon we'll part. A single meeting with a beautiful girl and a single kiss. What's wrong with that?'

'Do you kiss every girl with whom you have a single meeting?'

'Only if they're like you, haughty and beautiful. But of course, a single meeting with you is also absurd. I shall write to you out of the sky, Sophia von Feldermann, and end every letter with a thousand kisses.'

'A thousand?' said Sophia.

'Give or take a few,' said Fritz.

'Am I expected to answer such letters?'

'I shall be very put out if you don't,' said Fritz, 'for every one will contain a declaration of love.'

'Ridiculous,' smiled Sophia.

'Very,' said Fritz, 'but there it is, you've swept me off my feet and must take the consequences.'

Sophia laughed.

'You're crazy,' she said.

'So is everyone else. Haven't you noticed the whole world's insane?'

She looked at him. He wore his brittle recklessness as carelessly as he wore his new Iron Cross.

'If you're serious about writing to me,' she said, 'I'm staying at the Hotel Bristol with my mother for a while.'

He did write, and his letters were as amusing as he was. They met again three weeks later when he was given leave. She introduced him to her parents, her father also being in Berlin at the time. Her mother was gracious but cool, a sure sign she disapproved. It had no effect on Fritz. Life for him was in the balance, and social nuances of any kind were of no importance to him whatever. The long battle for air supremacy was going against Germany. The improved fighter planes of the Allies were causing an alarming increase in German fatalities, even in Richtofen's squadron. Fritz wasted no time trying to impress Sophia's mother. He concentrated on the conquest of Sophia, who came dangerously close to giving herself to him, understanding instinctively his need to experience all he could while he could – without in her innocence realizing he had already experienced the ultimate bliss in the arms of several women looking for wartime escapism of their own. For all her dislike of stuffier conventions, Sophia was naturally cautious. She could, in her spirit of independence, reject her chosen path, but she could not wholly reject her sense of morality. That upset her, making her feel she had a prudish streak. If Fritz had mentioned marriage, she might have risked the consequences and yielded. She was close to doing so at times, when Fritz's kisses and caresses were demonstrably ardent.

Her mother hoped the association was no more than a little flutter in the storm of war. But when they had moved from Berlin to spend a month in Baden-Baden, Hildegarde von Feldermann discovered her daughter was still communicating regularly with Fritz, not only by letter but also by telephone. Gently, she advised Sophia to end the relationship. Sophia asked to be allowed to make up her own mind. Her mother asked if she could make it up sensibly. Sophia, defiant, said if Fritz proposed, she would accept, at which her mother said she would not allow her to make such a fool of herself. Knowing what this would mean, Sophia took to her heels a few days later, having received a telephone call from Fritz to say he had been shaken up by a crash-landing and was resting in Douai. Using the family car, she drove to France to seek her father's support. Her father, surely, would not disapprove of one of Germany's heroes of the air. Her mother guessed what was in her mind, which was why Sophia's case with her father was already lost before she arrived.

But it was not completely lost once she had given the talkative Captain Vorster the slip. In a few weeks she would be twenty-one and an independent woman. Then, if Fritz was willing, she would marry him, with or without her parents' consent, and when the war was over – and it had to be over soon – she would dance in the Bavarian cornfields with him. In Douai, she could see him, talk to him, and somehow let him know that if he would only ask she would gladly be his wife.

She used the rural byways, even though some of them were quite awful, in order to avoid being caught and taken back. The front, she thought at one point, could be no more than forty kilometres away, the rumble of guns spasmodic. She did not think about the hazards that might confront a young German lady travelling alone in the occupied area of France. Hers was a fearless spirit, and she never retreated from a challenge.

It was then that the biplanes of war came out of the clear blue sky.

'C'est la guerre, mademoiselle.'

Sophia jumped and turned. There he was, the pilot of the burning Camel, his goggles up over his flying helmet, his face oily. A scarf was around his neck, and below his thick flying jacket were khaki breeches, tucked into brown boots. Khaki. He was as British as his plane. His legs were long, his frame sinewy, his face rugged beneath the smears of oil. His eyes were quick and flickering, a sign of nerves still stretched to the limit. He regarded her with interest, and a smile showed, as if in acknowledgement of the fact that her arrival was far more pleasurable than the significance of Richtofen's triumphant departure. Her long black leather coat, belted, was not designed merely to keep out the cold. It was expensively styled, and it paid its tailored tribute to her curving figure. She was taller than the average woman at five feet nine, and carried herself with the pride of every Prussian aristocrat. The coat reached to her calves, partly hiding her knee-length, lace-up black boots. Her hat, a soft velour, was black with a white band, an onyx-topped pin keeping it securely in place. Beneath the brim, her pale blonde hair lay softly over her forehead, and her eyes were a bright blue because of the clear air and the sunshine. Sophia Erica Marlene von Feldermann was considered a highly desirable Prussian beauty.

Recovering from the shock of finding the British airman almost at her elbow, her thoughts ran quickly. It was natural for him to think she was French. No one would expect young German ladies to proliferate in occupied France. And the family car was not a German make, but a Bugatti.

She made up her mind to go along with his mistaken assumption – for the time being.

'Oh, such a gallant escape,' she said in fluent French.

'Gallant?' His laugh was self-derisive, his

flickering eyes darting around to come to rest on the car. 'I was beaten into the damned ground, and quite literally.' His own French was as good as hers, for it had been perfected during his months of service in France. He looked up at the sky. Richtofen and his red Albatros had disappeared. Nearby, the Camel was a fiery, crackling furnace. 'I must get out of here before the Germans arrive to inspect Richtofen's latest kill.'

'Richtofen?' said Sophia innocently.

'Yes, that was the Baron who knocked me out. Mademoiselle, do you live in this area?'

While relieved in all humanity that he had not perished in the flames of his crashed plane, Sophia felt a natural and distinct coldness towards him and his country. England had gone to war against Germany quite unfairly and quite unnecessarily. And it was the British Navy's harsh blockade that was causing starvation amongst the German people.

'I'm from Valenciennes,' she said, which was not wholly untrue.

'Valenciennes?' He thought about it. 'Is that your car?'

'My family's,' said Sophia.

'I'm Captain Peter Marsh, Royal Flying Corps,' he said, 'and I need to move fast and to find an escape route. Could you drive me to Valenciennes?'

'I could,' said Sophia, simulating a sympathy

she did not feel, 'but wouldn't advise it, *mon Capitaine*. Valenciennes is a restricted area and full of Germans. You must run for cover somewhere, of course. To a village, perhaps, where the people will hide you until you can get back to your squadron.'

Captain Marsh, eyes searching the unbroken quietness of the countryside, said, 'Mademoiselle, you know this area, obviously. I'd like you to drive me somewhere fast, somewhere safe.'

Sophia did not think that even a genuine Frenchwoman would take too kindly to the peremptory nature of that demand. She herself wholly disliked it. Nor was she very keen on a situation that had her face to face with a man who was at war with her country. She lowered her eyes to hide her reaction, and noted then that his left glove was off, his hand resting on his right elbow.

Opting for delaying tactics, she said, 'Your hand is hurt?'

'I gave it a nasty knock, yes,' he said. 'But I was lucky. I was, by the grace of God, allowed just enough time to scramble clear before the plane blew up.'

Without thinking of her reaction, Sophia said coolly, 'God is on your side?'

'Mademoiselle?'

Correcting herself, she said, 'I am sure He is, *mon Capitaine*, I am sure He is on the side of all our brave men. Shall I look at your hand?'

'Not now.' He seemed a little impatient. 'Mademoiselle, would you oblige me by getting me as far from here as possible, and as quickly as you can?'

Sophia, trapped by her adoption of a French identity, felt a surge of dislike. She was by no means disposed to help him escape. Men from the German Luftwaffe would not be long in arriving once Richtofen reported his victory. If she could keep the Englishman talking, things might resolve themselves conveniently for her.

'*Mon Capitaine*, I really think—'

'I'm sorry, there's no time for a conversation,' said Captain Marsh. 'I'd like to depart immediately.'

'You are insisting?'

'Insisting?' He looked surprised. 'You'd rather I waited for the Germans to arrive, or a crowd of farmworkers? Or both? I'd be gobbled up by the Germans, and I'd be an embarrassment to the workers.'

'The car is very noticeable,' she said.

'Not as noticeable as Poppy the Third,' he said.

'Poppy?'

'That's Poppy.' He indicated the still-burning Camel. 'She's the third flying bird I've mismanaged. Two in the Middle East. Your car will get me out of here faster than my legs, or would you prefer not to be involved? I'll understand, naturally.'

She thought him impatient rather than understanding. She supposed most French-women would do something to help a shot-down British pilot, but if she decided to be the exception, there was little he could do about it.

Politely, she said, 'I'd prefer, if the Germans stopped us, not to have you feel responsible for them shooting me. People who assist Germany's enemies do get shot. It's quite legal. If it happened to me, I'm sure you'd be most unhappy, yes?'

His expression hardened. He frowned.

'Then I'll drive your car myself,' he said. 'I've given my hand a knock, but I'll manage. You can stay here, and when the Germans arrive, as they will, simply tell them I made off with your car. They won't shoot you for that.'

That proposition, brusquely delivered, did not suit Sophia at all. She needed the car for her own purposes, to get to Fritz, a man who in his reckless disregard for convention might in the happiest way help her to break free from the possessive dominance of her mother. She would have to compromise, she would have to bluff this pilot. He was not only the first enemy fighting man she had encountered, he was also the first Englishman she had met. She was not very impressed.

'Very well, *mon Capitaine*, I'll drive you,' she said. 'I'm on my way to Douai. I'll take you there. It will be safer for you than Valenciennes. You can wait outside the town until it's dark, and then I'll come to meet you again and take you to people who will help you.'

What she must actually do was tell Fritz. As a loyal German citizen she had no alternative, and Fritz would know how to deal with the man.

Captain Marsh's inspection of the open Bugatti was brief. She got in, and he took his place beside her.

'Your arrival, mademoiselle, at the critical moment and in this car, was very fortuitous. To Douai, then, and thank you.'

'Thank me only if we meet no German patrols,' she said. 'For if we do, they'll stop us, and I'll be able to do nothing for you then – or for myself.'

She started the car and moved off.

Captain Marsh said, 'It needn't be as bad as that for you – I have my service revolver.'

'Oh, my God,' she said in sudden shock, 'you don't mean to open fire on any patrols – you can't.'

'Suicidal, I agree,' he said, and laughed. 'No, let's look at it differently. Let's give the impression, if necessary, that a man on the run wouldn't hesitate to commandeer your car and your services as driver. Your case would be that I threatened you with my revolver.'

'A flying officer would be as ungallant as

that?' she said, as they left the smouldering Camel behind.

'Not ungallant. Practical. Drive on, mademoiselle.'

Chapter Three

Sophia drove with self-assurance, negotiating the gear changes firmly as the family chauffeur had taught her. Captain Marsh watched the winding road and the vistas of rural France. He was quiet but alert. His silence suited her, for she had no wish to converse with him. He had taken off his flying helmet and buttoned his thick jacket to hide his khaki uniform. His dark brown hair, whipped by the wind, lost its brushed look. His bruised left hand lay in his lap. With his right hand, he used his handkerchief to wipe the flyer's telltale oil marks from his face, revealing a skin tanned by exposure to the elements.

He was relaxing, she thought. He was less edgy. His brush with Richtofen and his near escape from death had shaken him, but he was obviously recovering. And the fact that these rural lanes and byways were so quiet and empty must be a relief to him. She still hoped, however, that he would not attempt conversation.

She had no qualms about letting him think she was French or about what she really intended to do when she reached Douai, for he was at war with her country. All the same, she did not want to be asked questions she could not truthfully answer. She would lie if she had to, but she preferred silence to further deception.

They passed through a little village called La Calle. It was obviously too small to be considered suitable as a refuge for him, and too close to the scene of his crash-landing. How odd. Fritz had crash-landed last week. They were both fighter pilots, Fritz and her unwelcome companion. But Fritz, she thought, would have laughed at his narrow escape. This man had been short-tempered and edgy.

A small girl, playing outside a house at the end of the one street in La Calle, stared in awe at the big black Bugatti and its occupants. Strutting chickens, feathers threadbare from a long winter of meal scarcity, flew squawking from the path of the automobile.

Beyond the village the land lay rolling and open. Farmhouses dotted the countryside, and here and there Captain Marsh sighted elderly peasants and young women working in the fields. The French had mobilized their young men by the million, and farmers called upon their daughters or aged labourers to help them, although much of their produce was destined for German stomachs.

Captain Marsh broke his silence.

'You said Douai, mademoiselle?' He sounded slightly sceptical.

'Yes,' said Sophia, sensing he was somewhat suspicious of her.

'But you seem to be heading north. From where Richtofen brought me down, Douai lies west. Slightly north-west. Shouldn't you have turned left before you reached that little village, La Calle?'

He was a pilot. He had been operating, no doubt, in the skies above Douai, Arras and Lille, and the whole area probably existed as a permanent map in his mind. A new shock hit her. She was lost. She had thought herself to be driving in a predominantly western direction since giving Captain Vorster the slip. She had made guesses, yes, but confident guesses. The winding rural byways had deceived her. She was definitely lost, and definitely suspect if, as a Frenchwoman from Valenciennes, she could not find her way to Douai, about forty kilometres only by road. Here was another challenge, but she met it. She looked at Captain Marsh and gave him a little smile and a shrug.

'I must confess, *mon Capitaine*, that in attempting to reach Douai by all these country lanes it's quite possible, yes, that I'm failing myself. I usually take the main road. But on the main road one is always being stopped by the military police of Germany. One needs to have German permission to travel by car.' Sophia slowed to take a tight bend. She gave Captain Marsh another smile, simulating ruefulness. 'One can get permission, if one's father is the mayor of Valenciennes, yes – '

'Your father's the mayor?' said Captain Marsh.

'Although Valenciennes is full of Germans,' said Sophia, 'the mayor is still of some importance. *Mon Capitaine*,' she went on, the bit between her teeth, 'I must tell you that the reason I was a little reluctant to involve myself with your misfortune was because I'm in an emotional crisis.'

'I've a little crisis of my own,' he said, 'and although it's not an emotional one, it could mean we're on some common ground. Mademoiselle, we're heading for the Belgian border and, if I'm not mistaken, into the arms of German reserve divisions. I think it might be a good idea to take a left turn as soon as we reach one. Meanwhile, if you wish, you can tell me what your own crisis is all about.'

'I'm happy to be guided by you,' said Sophia, 'and just as happy to explain why I'm avoiding main roads.' Distinctly on her mettle now, she embarked on an impromptu story. She was, she said, in constant argument with her parents concerning a French flying officer who had been shot down and seriously injured. His injuries had caused his discharge, otherwise he might have been made a prisoner of war. As it was, he had made a gradual recovery and was now working in the Hotel Avignon in Douai. He was very much in love with her, but because of her parents' opposition she was being forced to consider the only alternative, an elopement. She had decided today to drive to Douai, to see him and to discuss this with him. She had no permission to travel. Therefore she had chosen the quietest possible route. She had never used these byways before, and she was quite prepared to believe that Captain Marsh was right that her navigation was faulty. 'It is most emotional, my crisis, do you see, and that hasn't helped me in finding my way.'

'Elopements, I believe, are very emotional,' said Captain Marsh, 'and I hope to avoid any such thing myself.'

'You are not a romantic, *mon Capitaine*?' she said lightly.

'At the moment, mademoiselle, I'm concentrating entirely on survival. That isn't at all romantic. Nor is the prospect of a prisoner-of-war camp. That I mean to avoid like the plague. May I ask your name?'

Sophia hesitated. Then she said, 'It would be better, don't you think, if—'

'Pull up!' Captain Marsh interrupted her in English. Sophia, who knew only a few words of English, kept going, but shot him a startled glance. 'Stop,' he said in French, and added, 'Look there.'

Sophia slowed to a halt, and followed his pointing finger. Two hundred metres ahead the lane was intersected by a minor but well-surfaced road. One side of the road was lined by fir trees, planted many years ago to provide the adjacent farmlands with a windbreak stretching many miles. Marching steadily along the verge, beneath the cover of the trees, were German troops in long endless columns. At intervals were officers on horseback.

It was a movement of troops that surprised Captain Marsh. Among the Allies, the feeling was that at last Germany was a drained force, and that the advent of the Americans into the war meant the Kaiser's cause was hopeless. But even from this distance, the pilot could see that the marching troops gave no indication that defeat was only a matter of time. Their heads were up, their march was strong and steady, and they were well equipped. And they were heading west, towards the front.

There were no vehicles, only men. Infantry-men. They were moving up under the very effective cover of the evergreens. Sopwith two-seaters, the British reconnaissance planes, flew the skies frequently in spotting missions, but their observers were unlikely to spot these German columns with the men marching in single file.

Sophia felt she knew what this troop move-ment meant. One of her father's divisions was sending infantry battalions up to the front in daylight, such was the pressure General Ludendorff was putting on his Corps commanders in respect of zero-hour dispositions. Daylight meant the exercise of care and caution. That, of course, was why there were no vehicles. They would move at night, with the guns.

She sat quietly in the car, one hand on the gear lever. A quick thrust into starting gear and a surging drive up to the crossroads would mean an early end to the escape bid of this British pilot. But she doubted if he would let her get far.

'Shall we go on?' she asked. 'I'll proceed slowly.'

'To proceed at all would be very foolish, mademoiselle,' he said. 'Those troops are moving up. There'll be no vehicles of any kind allowed on that road, nor any kind of observers. We're uncomfortably close to them as it is. Kindly turn back.'

'I can't turn in this road,' said Sophia, and thought again about slipping into forward gear and making a charge for the crossroads and her marching compatriots.

'Reverse, then.' Captain Marsh was peremptory once more, and Sophia recognized him as a man of dangerous determination. 'Reverse back to that farm opening and turn there. We can find another road.'

'*Mon Capitaine*,' said Sophia in very clear

French, 'I am willing to help, I am not willing to take orders.'

Captain Marsh, eyes on the scene at the distant crossroads, said drily, 'Oh, yes, your emotional crisis – it's of a kind that makes one highly sensitive, of course. You must forgive my impatience, but I'm not at my best this morning. Richtofen has made a monkey of me. Mademoiselle, would you please be kind enough to get us out of here? I'm a bag of nerves at the moment, for I feel like a sitting duck.'

Sophia's smile was genuine as she began to reverse.

'To be made a monkey of and then to feel like a sitting duck must be an extraordinary experience,' she said.

'Uncomfortable,' said Captain Marsh, still watching the crossroads.

Sophia, reversing competently around a bend, took the scene from his sight and sensed him relaxing again. In profile, she noted, he looked very resolute, and she wondered if there would be any unpleasantness before she reached the outskirts of Douai and parted company with him. Since she was a patriotic German and he was an enemy fighter pilot, it was impossible to dissociate some unpleasantness from their temporary relationship, even though he thought her French.

She backed the car into the farm opening, then began to drive back the way they had come. After a little while, she pointed.

'There's a fork ahead,' she said, 'a right-hand one.'

'Take it,' said Captain Marsh, 'and let's hope it will point us at Douai. I'm still unsafe in this area. When the Germans find what's left of my plane, they'll discover nothing of me. So they'll search every farm and village around. Accordingly, I'll be grateful if you'll drive fast.'

'Just as fast as these inferior roads permit, *mon Capitaine*,' said Sophia, taking the right-hand fork. It was another dirt road, another winding way, and her speed was governed by its hazards.

Captain Marsh, turning his eyes on her, said, 'I must say you're extremely blonde for a Frenchwoman. I've met none as blonde as you.'

'My grandmother was a Scandinavian,' said Sophia in a moment of inspiration. 'That is why my name is Sophia. Sophia Descantes.'

'I'm delighted to meet you, Sophia Descantes,' said Captain Marsh, and his smile lightened his ruggedness. 'You're a welcome gift on a day like this. God, this is a foul road.'

The lane widened then, and provided Sophia with better conditions. She drove very steadily, the moving car encompassed by the ubiquitous fields of agricultural France. They motored through a tiny village of half a dozen houses. Captain Marsh, stationed at Estree-Blanche Farm, searched his memory maps in an attempt to get a fix on his present location. His aerodrome was twenty miles west of the front line, and Douai lay a little over fifty miles south-east. He knew Richtofen had chased him far beyond the front line and brought him down somewhere between Douai and Valenciennes, well inside German-held territory. He reckoned now that he and this French girl were some twelve to fifteen miles east of Douai, perhaps slightly north-east. There were few villages of any size in the area, and certainly none large enough to offer a secure refuge. It would have to be Douai. He needed shelter, he needed civilian clothes, and he needed the help of some brave French people in order to get back to Estree-Blanche Farm or to England. He needed this girl to find such people for him. But she had problems of her own, it seemed. An emotional affair of the heart. An elopement. Elopement? In wartime and at this exhausted stage of the conflict? Well, that was the way some girls were. They could conjure up mirages of romance in the middle of a desert.

She looked very aristocratic, he thought, and much more the daughter of a French count than of a town mayor.

An elopement?

He smiled to himself.

Sophia stiffened, glimpsing movement ahead. Captain Marsh, spotting it too, put his injured left hand on her arm in warning, wincing a little at the pain that resulted. A hundred yards away, two German soldiers walked through an open farm gate, wheeling bicycles. They looked up as they heard the approaching Bugatti.

'This could be tricky,' murmured Captain Marsh in English, his right hand moving.

'I speak very little English,' said Sophia, her heart beating rather fast. The two soldiers were armed, their rifles slung. She could deliver this British airman into their embrace.

'If they stop us, mademoiselle, leave things to me,' he said calmly. 'I shall make out a case for you.'

Sophia decided to simply let events take their course.

The two Germans stood in the middle of the road as she drove towards them. One man held up a hand. She slowed down and came to a stop. The man lowered his hand and said in fairly good French, 'Your papers, your travelling permit – show them.'

'Show nothing, mademoiselle,' said Captain Marsh, 'they can look at this.'

The two Germans did look. They stared at the revolver that was pointing at them.

Sophia, who had forgotten his mention of his service revolver, was momentarily at a loss and could only gasp, 'Don't fire – don't.'

'Be quiet, mademoiselle, do only as I tell you to,' said Captain Marsh, thus establishing, he hoped, that the daughter of the mayor of

47

Valenciennes was as much under threat as the two Germans. 'Get out and relieve these gentlemen of their rifles.'

'No, I can't do that,' said Sophia, while the soldiers, supporting their bicycles, eyed the hatless man in the thick, buttoned-up jacket, with anger tightening their mouths.

'Do as I say,' said Captain Marsh, his revolver very steady.

'You are asking, Frenchman, to be shot,' said the first German.

'So will you be, if either of you move,' said Captain Marsh. 'Mademoiselle, get their rifles.'

His expression was one of fixed determination, but Sophia said firmly, 'No.' It surprised her to see a little smile flicker.

'You're a trial to me, mademoiselle.' To the first German, he said, 'Throw your rifle down, my friend.'

'I am not a friend to you,' said the soldier. His bicycle fell across the road as he used his hands to unsling his rifle. He dropped it next to his bicycle. It clattered. Captain Marsh gestured at the second German, who gave him a look of fury, but followed the example of his comrade. The pointing revolver was very steady indeed, and very deadly.

'Walk,' said Captain Marsh, gesturing at the road behind him.

'You are a French swine,' said the first German.

'Walk,' repeated Captain Marsh, and the man said something to the other.

Silently the two began to walk, passing the car. Captain Marsh turned his head to watch them. Sophia sat furious with herself and with him. When the soldiers had walked a distance of fifty yards, they stopped and turned, fully aware that the revolver was now much less of a menace.

'Go,' said Captain Marsh to Sophia.

'But the bicycles, the rifles,' said Sophia, tight-lipped.

'Drive over them.'

'Over them?'

'Yes, I think so, don't you? It will put the bicycles out of action.'

'Is that the cleverest thing to do?'

'I don't know, but it's the best we can manage. Put your foot down and go.'

Sophia stared at him. The revolver, plain to see, was pointing at her.

'You're mad,' she gasped.

'They're watching us,' said Captain Marsh, 'and what they can see is for your benefit, mademoiselle. So open the throttle.'

'You are very considerate,' said Sophia bitterly. She slipped into gear, put her foot down and the Bugatti roared forward over the rifles and the bicycles. Mangled metal shuddered in protest, and the rifles clattered.

The German soldiers shouted in fury. The

Bugatti surged on, Sophia driving with her mouth compressed. She had put herself in a stupidly awkward situation by not correcting Captain Marsh in his assumption that she was French.

Aware that she was angry about things, he said, 'Don't be disturbed, young lady, it was all done to give the impression you're a reluctant accomplice and, of course, to immobilize them. It will take them some time now to get back to their unit and report.'

'It was absurd,' she said, driving fast because she was angry.

'I thought it necessary. Could you have shown them a travelling permit? I could certainly not have shown them the right kind of papers.'

'I must be frank,' said Sophia, 'I really did not want to become involved in such an alarming way.'

'Oh, it need not be too alarming,' said Captain Marsh. 'I'm sure your father, as Mayor of Valenciennes, could speak up for you. The Germans have a natural respect for a mayor – he has chief responsibility for a town's orderliness, and the Germans are addicted to orderliness.'

'Really? You are acquainted with Germans and their addictions?'

'I'm acquainted with their martial ardour. This is the second time they've knocked me out of the sky. To return to the risk you're taking in being such an invaluable help to me – the thing to do, I feel, is to declare you were coerced. As a combatant on the run from Germans, I'm allowed by the rules of war to exercise reasonable coercion. So on to Douai, Sophia.'

At this familiarity, this unwelcome use of her name, Sophia shot him a look of disdain.

'I'm not sure we'll ever get to Douai,' she said stiffly. 'I'm quite lost on these silly little roads.'

'Never mind, keep going,' said Captain Marsh, 'and we may find a signpost. If not, we'll ask at the next village we come to.'

'I really think it would be better if I stopped to let you get out.'

'I'd rather not, if you don't mind.'

'Very well,' said Sophia coldly.

It was clear to him that she resented his presence. But he was determined not to spend the rest of the war in a prison camp. It might be only a month or two before the Allies, strengthened by the newly formed American divisions, brought the Germans to their knees, but he was still disinclined to give himself up.

The index finger of his left hand throbbed, and the middle finger was painfully sensitive. Both fingers were badly swollen, but the discomfort was nothing compared with the fact that he'd survived.

It was coming up to eleven in the morning when Major Kirsten re-entered General von Feldermann's office. The general looked up. He was quite alone. Few generals operated without some staff members around them, even at a desk. General von Feldermann called for them only when he needed them. At the moment, with a pile of papers in front of him, he wanted no other mind but his own to concentrate on the problems they posed.

'Well, Josef?' he said.

'First, the quartermaster's estimates, Herr General,' said Major Kirsten, offering more papers. 'They're the final figures, fully summarized and quite complete.'

The general took the papers, though he smiled a little tiredly. Everyone at Headquarters was under strain. Ludendorff was a hard and demanding warlord.

'Thank you, Josef,' he said, 'particularly for the fact that they're complete. That's your work finished at least. Myself, I've still to consider the ifs and buts. Ludendorff has confirmed he'll be here tomorrow. Have you been up all night?'

'I've burned a little midnight oil,' said Major Kirsten, looking as if he had missed out on sleep lately.

'I'm sure you have,' said the general, who knew Major Kirsten gave a great deal of himself when faced with staff work of unusual importance. It probably eased his frustrations, for he was more at home in the field than behind a desk. The major, actually, had come to terms with his loss of an arm and the slightly impaired vision of his right eye. He hoped now for a quick end to the war and for early retirement to his little estate in Saxony.

'There's no word from Captain Vorster yet,' he said.

'He's a man of method, not inspiration,' said the general, scanning his quartermaster's estimates. 'It will take him time— God in heaven, where are all these extra guns to come from?'

'I thought General Ludendorff said every divisional requirement will be met.'

'So he did,' said the general, 'but I'd still like to ask him exactly when they'll be met. Josef, take a rest – go off duty for two days. I shan't need you tomorrow.'

'Herr General – '

'That's an order.'

Major Kirsten returned to his office. Two days off duty while Ludendorff was master-minding the coming offensive had little appeal for him.

The telephone rang when he was drinking a welcome cup of coffee. He answered it. Colonel Hoffner was on the line from Douai.

'Yes, my friend?' said Major Kirsten. He and Kurt Hoffner had been cadets together.

'I've news of the young lady you spoke to me about.'

'What news?'

'From reports I've received, she appears to

have been abducted, and by a man who may be a British flying officer.'

'I think I'd like you to repeat that,' said Major Kirsten.

Colonel Hoffner repeated it and enlarged on it. Earlier that morning, a report had mentioned a British fighter plane being shot down east of Douai by Richtofen, whose squadron was stationed near the town. The crashed plane, burned out, had been investigated. The pilot, apparently, had scrambled free, for there was no trace of him, nor any semblance of a charred corpse. A search was going on for him. As to the other matter, the colonel said that two of his men on a routine country patrol had stopped a car containing a young lady and a man they took to be a Frenchman. The young lady answered to the given description. When questioned about the man, the soldiers had described him and the leather jacket he was wearing. One of them had said it was like an airman's jacket. The man had produced a revolver and threatened to shoot the soldiers unless they dropped their rifles and retreated. He had then compelled the young lady to drive her car over the men's bicycles, ruining them. She and the man, who was almost certainly the pilot of the destroyed Sopwith Camel plane, had disappeared, together with the car. The incident had taken place not far from La Calle, a tiny village slightly northeast of Douai.

At this point in his narrative Colonel Hoffner said, 'You're taking this in?'

'I am,' said Major Kirsten, 'but not without shock and disbelief.'

'I think we must both accept it's true. My two men were questioned separately, and each told an identical story. Each said the man was very determined, the young lady angry, and that she refused his order to relieve them of their rifles.'

'I'm to believe she has managed to get herself mixed up with a man as desperate as this?'

'I imagine she couldn't help herself,' said Colonel Hoffner. 'I've detailed a number of men to conduct a search, and they'll work in conjunction with the search party from Jagdstaffel II. Is all this interesting to you, Josef?'

'Beyond expectation,' said Major Kirsten. 'It's also damned serious.'

'Who is this young woman?'

'That's an awkward question, Kurt, and I can't answer it at the moment. I'd very much like your men to find her.'

'I'll let you know as soon as they do, but you understand, of course, that in the changed circumstances my men can't merely follow her. They'll have to pick up the desperate gentleman and separate her from him. Are we to hold her here in Douai or let her go?'

'I'd appreciate it if you'd give her some coffee while you report to me,' said Major Kirsten.

'I'm at your service, naturally,' said Colonel Hoffner drily.

Major Kirsten put the phone down and sat thinking for a while. His office had the same lofty grandeur as all other rooms in the chateau, and one could not complain of lack of space. He felt pressurized, all the same. Desk work could be more debilitating than field activities.

There was a light knock on the communicating door, and Lieutenant Elissa Landsberg entered. Lieutenant Landsberg was his immediate assistant, and a very efficient one. An officer of the Women's Army Corps, she was a first-rate typist, a genius at figures and a paragon of willing endeavour. Twenty-five years old, her slim but shapely figure was uniformed with tailored precision, and permitted the eye a pleasurable view of her silk-clad calves. Her crown of brown hair was neatly braided, her elegant feet neatly shod. A woman of excellent character and unswerving loyalties, she had worked with Major Kirsten for six months. Five weeks ago, with a tact that prevented anyone taking offence, she had declined an offer of a position on the quartermaster's staff and the promotion to Captain that went with the job. She told Major Kirsten she did not feel up to it; that its demands would be too much for her. Major Kirsten did not argue.

'Major,' she said, 'the draft of Directive Number Four has been typed. May I have the distributive list to check on how many copies will be required?'

'You've reached that point on top of everything else?' The major gave her an appreciative smile. 'Lieutenant, although my every nerve twitched at the thought of receiving women into the army, I'm now at peace with the High Command's fateful decision. You're a model of efficiency, and so is your office. If there are other young ladies of your quality sitting at home and knitting socks for soldiers, kindly go and recruit them.'

'I'm a little busy at the moment,' said Elissa. 'Do you have the distributive list?'

'Yes. There. Take it.' Three separate lists lay on the right-hand side of his desk. He indicated the first one. Picking it up, she looked at it. It embraced a whole spectrum of recipients down to company commanders.

'It's a long list,' she said.

'Is it?' Major Kirsten seemed abstracted. 'Are you tired?'

'Not yet, Herr Major,' she said. Her voice was always pleasant and even.

'Well, I am.'

'Yes,' she said, regarding his drawn look with concern. His sound left eye showed the light of amusement at her little frown. 'You've been working all hours, Herr Major.'

'So has everyone else.' He leaned back in his chair. He felt mentally fatigued. The war and its problems were draining his mind of its vitality. He felt old. He also felt he looked old. He thought about his little estate in Saxony. He was not much good for anything except walking around it, nor did it hold the completeness it had when his wife was alive. All the same, it was a peaceful place. It would provide him with all the interest and pleasure necessary to enjoy his years of retirement. 'Elissa,' he said, again a little far away, 'this is our last chance.'

Elissa's delicate flush at this, his first use of her Christian name, went unseen by the reflective major, for which she was grateful. Because she was regarded as cool and efficient, few people knew how shy she was and how much effort it had cost her to volunteer for the Women's Army Corps. The daughter of a Munich civil servant, she had been a bookshop assistant for several years when a totally foreign impulse to join the Corps took hold of her. She wrestled with it for days before finally making her nervous way to the recruiting centre. But she was glad now she had made the effort. She was gradually being cured of the worst of her shyness, while serving the war effort in the most direct way she could.

'Major, you're thinking of General Ludendorff's offensive,' she said.

'Is there anyone here who isn't?' said the major. 'You've seen as many figures as I have, you know the manpower and armament required. This could be our last offensive of any importance. If we fail, we're kaput. The Americans will be in the field by then. Millions of them, all healthy, fresh and eager. War to them will be what it was to us in 1914, a great patriotic adventure.'

'Was it that, Major – an adventure?' Elissa knew she ought to return to her work, but she was always prepared to listen to Major Kirsten. He could be ironic about some things, and withering in the face of stupidity, but she thought him a fair and just man. 'Could war ever be considered an adventure?'

'It was a rousing, roaring, exhilarating adventure for our armies in 1914, a mighty blow struck for the Fatherland.' Major Kirsten smiled and extracted a cigarette from his chased silver case, using his one hand dexterously. He fumbled just a little in his striking of a match. Elissa, watching him, did not attempt to strike it for him. 'That adventure, Lieutenant, fell to pieces after only a few weeks. It turned into a conflict crucifying for Germany. We're close to exhausting our manpower. We can't replace losses. If General Ludendorff's offensive fails to make the breakthrough, I think that will signal the beginning of the end. Clemenceau of France, their tiger, will then tear off what little meat is left on Germany's bones. I hope, however, he'll leave my bones alone. I've a little country house in Saxony, with some land, that will suit me very well to grow old in.'

'General Ludendorff doesn't like losing battles,' said Elissa.

'Who does?'

'I mean, he's reputed to have a very positive approach, and to regard setbacks as a challenge, not a prelude to defeat.' Elissa made the comment like a citizen who still had faith and belief. 'Herr Major, are you being pessimistic?'

'I thought I was merely being candid. But candour, I suppose, can sound like pessimism.' Major Kirsten sat up. 'Lieutenant, a matter unconnected with the offensive requires my attention. I'm taking a car and driving to the Douai area. I may be away a couple of days.'

'Yes, Major,' said Elissa in her unquestioning way. 'Shall I ask Corporal Hirsch to report to you?'

'Corporal Hirsch?' The major, deep in new thought, sounded as if she had tossed in an irrelevance.

'He's your usual driver, Herr Major.'

'Corporal Hirsch?' said Major Kirsten again. 'No, I shall drive myself.'

'Major?' said Elissa gently.

He came to.

'Heavens,' he said, 'what an idiot I am. Would you think I could forget the Somme was my Trafalgar?'

'Major,' smiled Elissa, 'the English Admiral Nelson did not lose his arm at Trafalgar.'

'Quite right, he didn't. He lost his life. End

of Admiral Nelson.' Major Kirsten reconsidered things. 'Very well, I can't drive the car myself, but I don't think I'll call on Corporal Hirsch.' He regarded Elissa with an interest that aroused her sensitivity. 'Tell me, can you drive a car?'

'Of course, Herr Major. I was among several recruits who took driving instruction. I have my certificate.'

'Good.' Major Kirsten became brisk, his tired look vanishing. 'Lieutenant, you and I are going on a little hunting expedition. You shall drive and I'll explain as we go along. Pass that distributive list to your sergeant. She's quite capable. Be ready to leave in five minutes.'

'Five minutes?' Elissa's manufactured calm was slipping away. 'But I've so much work – '

'Hand it over to your staff. I've General von Feldermann's authority to take two days off. You've my authority to accompany me.'

'Two days? We are to drive about on an unscheduled exercise for two days?' Elissa was distinctly flushed. 'But – '

'But?' said Major Kirsten.

Her colour deepened. She was not sure if he knew precisely what he was about after weeks of overwork. And there were WAC regulations to be considered. They did not permit her to spend two days alone in the company of a male officer unless the circumstances were of a kind that made the situation unavoidable. And two days could not pass without two nights intervening.

'Major, the irregularity of such a thing – I really don't know – that is, I'm not sure – '

'Good heavens.' Major Kirsten looked at her flushed face in mild surprise. 'Action of a very confidential nature is what you and I are about to undertake, Lieutenant, and it will clear away our cobwebs.'

'But the regulations – '

'Regulations are sometimes unimportant,' said Major Kirsten cheerfully. 'Whatever our own opinions are of our worthiness, against the present background of the war we are both figures of monumental insignificance. At least, I am. I need you to drive the car for me, and I need your intelligence. Five minutes, Lieutenant. Bring what you feel you must, although with any luck we'll be back here perhaps by tonight, or tomorrow morning. I'll meet you outside.' He smiled. 'Jump to it, Elissa.'

Excitement flooded her. Her hazel eyes grew bright.

'Yes, Major.' She almost flew from his office.

Captain Vorster was in Douai. Douai offered him nothing, for all his searching and questioning. But then, it did not occur to him to call on Colonel Hoffner, the commandant of the town. Captain Vorster was methodical, but not brilliant. He felt he would have to drive back to

Valenciennes and begin his questioning search all over again. He was not enjoying his role. He had failure on his mind. He also felt that chasing after a runaway girl in wartime was not the kind of thing any staff officer should have to engage in, even if she was his general's daughter.

Chapter Four

At a moment when they had left the infuriated German soldiers well behind, Sophia broke her cold silence to say, 'You're making grave mistakes this morning.'

'Unfortunately, mademoiselle,' said Captain Marsh, eyes constantly searching the road ahead, 'I'm a man of many imperfections and accordingly make all kinds of mistakes. I made one today in letting Richtofen cut me out.'

Sophia knew this situation could not go on. She drew a deep breath and said, 'I am going to tell you something that I hope will bring you to your senses and help you avoid making your worst mistake of all. I am not French, I am German. I am the daughter of General von Feldermann.'

'Oh, my God,' said Captain Marsh.

'Perhaps I should have let you know that at once, but perhaps I did not because I wished to escape being shot.'

'Shot?' Captain Marsh, startled by her revelation, sounded as if he was being left behind in the dialogue. 'Shot?'

'Yes. Knowing something of you now, I'm sure that if I'd said I was German you would not have hesitated to shoot me and steal my car.'

'Is this real?' asked Captain Marsh in English.

'Excuse me?' said Sophia, taking one more of countless bends.

'You really think I'd have shot you?'

'I think you perfectly capable of doing so.'

'What good would that have done me? I can't drive your car at the moment – my hand's crippled. Are you telling me the truth about yourself?'

'I am telling you I'm the daughter of General von Feldermann.'

'Oh, my God,' said Captain Marsh again. 'May I ask who General von Feldermann is, besides being your father?'

'He is one of Germany's most distinguished Corps commanders,' said Sophia. 'I hope you understand the seriousness of your position. As you said yourself, you are coercing me. If you're caught, which you will be, you'll be shot for it.'

'I'm to be on the receiving end now, am I? Because you're a general's daughter?'

'Yes,' said Sophia calmly, 'I think that would make it worse for you.'

'That hardly seems fair,' said Captain Marsh.

'How was I to know when I first saw you that you weren't a baker's daughter? It was damned ridiculous, anyway, a German general's daughter joyriding about occupied France. And let me tell you, Miss von Feldermann, that was a culpable piece of trickery, passing yourself off as a young French lady. And I think you mentioned that the mayor of Valenciennes was your father. I'll find it hard to forgive that kind of deceit.'

'You are not going to be asked to forgive me anything – you are the one who is in trouble, not I.' Sophia, having come to the truth, no longer felt in moral discomfort. 'I did not actually say I was French.'

'You said you were the daughter of the mayor of Valenciennes.' Captain Marsh was sarcastic. 'What is he, then, a Turk? I'd like to remind you I'm in uniform and entitled to use whatever reasonable means I can to avoid being bundled off as a prisoner of war.'

'I hope you are not going to be unpleasant,' said Sophia. 'I am willing to put you down, to leave you to make the best of things while I go on.'

'We'll stick to our previous agreement,' said Captain Marsh. 'We'll go on together until we reach Douai. Then you can put me down.'

'That is ridiculous,' said Sophia, face tingling in the slipstream of air. 'The moment I report what has happened, every house in Douai will be searched for you. If you'll allow me to stop now, if you'll get out, you have all this countryside in which to hide yourself.'

'Well, I don't fancy all this countryside, I fancy a bolthole in a nice large town. Keep going.'

'I will not,' said Sophia.

'What difference can it make to you whether you put me down here or just outside Douai? You'll satisfy your German conscience either way when you report me.'

'I am going to stop,' said Sophia.

'I beg you won't,' said Captain Marsh, 'for I've no chance running around the countryside, and I think you mean to get to Douai. I think the reason why you were alone in this car was because you really do have an emotional attachment. The atmosphere's thick with dreams of elopement. And if your father is who you say he is, I further think he'd move heaven and earth to stop you. I might do myself the world of good by helping him. Where are his Corps Headquarters?'

'You are the most detestable man I've ever met,' said Sophia icily. Very deliberately she pulled up. There was not another being in sight. There were only the fields and a few farmhouses. 'Get out,' she said.

Captain Marsh smiled.

'It's Valenciennes, isn't it?' he said. 'Your father is at Valenciennes. Very well, let's go to Valenciennes.'

Sophia stared. His revolver was pointing at her. His expression was so hard and resolute that her eyes grew huge.

'You wouldn't dare,' she breathed.

'Wouldn't I? I thought you said five minutes ago that I was perfectly capable of shooting you. Naturally, I should be full of regret, explaining that you tried to get hold of it and that it went off.'

'I cannot believe that any flying officer, even an English one, could be as cowardly and depraved as that. Fritz would never—' She broke off.

'That's his name? Fritz? He doesn't sound like a French hotel clerk to me. Why would he never do what I would?'

'Because he's a gentleman,' said Sophia, 'and you're a swine.'

'An officer and a gentleman, perhaps?' Captain Marsh smiled. 'A German flying officer?' He thought. 'And he's in Douai? I see. Richtofen's squadron operates not far from Douai. Yes, I think I do see. Only the best airmen fly with Richtofen. You're in love with a dashing young marvel, Sophia, but your parents aren't. Drive to Valenciennes.'

'I will not!' Sophia felt a sense of sickening outrage. To drive back to Valenciennes, to have this despicable man, a disgrace to his uniform, hand her over to her father and give himself up, would send the whole of Headquarters

68

into convulsions of silent laughter. Even Major Kirsten, whom she admired very much, would smile about it. If there was one thing Sophia could not endure it was ridicule. 'Shoot me if you like,' she breathed. 'I will not drive to Valenciennes.'

'Then let's go to Douai and get you to your Fritz. You are sure I'll be caught in the end?'

'Very sure,' said Sophia. 'God is not on the side of men like you.'

'Have I asked Him to be? I've asked help only of you.' Captain Marsh slid his revolver inside his jacket. 'And I'm quite willing to help you. The fact that we're on opposite sides need not lead to too many quarrels. Let's help each other. Since I'm going to be caught, why worry about it? You drive the car to my instructions under all circumstances, and I'll see to it that at least neither of us is caught between here and Douai, you by the long hand of your father and me by your soldiers. And whenever necessary, we'll emphasize you're the helpless victim of coercion. Shall we go on?'

Sophia said nothing but put the car in motion again. She obeyed his suggestions and directions in regard to their route. He took no chances of running into military traffic; he kept hopefully on course over lanes and byways, his eyes forever searching for landmarks. He frowned at times because of the seeming waywardness of unsurfaced roads and winding tracks. Sophia thought he was simply running nowhere, that he had no more idea of exactly where they were than she had. It occurred to her that he must know that when they reached Douai, if ever, she would have to do her duty and advise the military of where she had put him down. That made her wonder what he might be capable of to prevent this disclosure. A cold tingle of apprehension disturbed her, and there was a feeling that she was driving around in circles. The rural scenes hardly varied, and there was a similarity about every vista in which farms, fields and woods predominated. The atmosphere was still strangely peaceful, although twice she heard the hum of invisible planes high in the sky.

The land looked rich and untouched by war. If it had been devastated by the German advance in 1914, it had recovered. She knew it was along the line of the Western Front, from the coast of Belgium to the border of Switzerland, where she would find the earth ravaged by the guns and the trench system. Germany had lost so many men, and could not afford to lose more. General Ludendorff's offensive must succeed, it must. Fritz must be given the chance to enjoy the peace.

A faint trail of smoke became visible away to their left. Captain Marsh squinted at it. It was a creeping trail.

'It's a train,' said Sophia.

'Will you stop, please?'

Sophia brought the Bugatti to a halt on a rough dirt road running between ploughed fields. Captain Marsh studied the faint trail of smoke and listened intently. The rumble of the guns had ceased for a while, and there was only silence, but Sophia said again, 'It's a train.'

'Yes,' said Captain Marsh. He slid his right hand inside his jacket and pulled out an aerial map. He opened it up and peered at it. She saw his left hand, the fingers blue and swollen. The index finger was crooked. He glanced up from his map and again studied the trail of smoke, very faint now.

'That, I'm sure, is the railway line from Valenciennes to Douai,' he said. 'Let's see, it's on our left and the sun's over there – my God, we're pointing ourselves at Valenciennes.'

'It's not my fault,' said Sophia, 'you have been giving directions.' She wondered if he could bear a little pain. 'Let me see your finger.'

'Sophia?' He was suspicious as she took hold of his left wrist. Before he could react, she gripped the index finger and gave it a sharp pull. He let out a hiss. But the finger was straight again, the pain subsiding to an aching tenderness.

'It was dislocated, that's all,' said Sophia.

'Frankly, I thought it was broken.' He flexed the finger. He flexed others. The middle finger alone refused to bend. It protested painfully. 'Thank you,' he said.

'That other finger, that is probably the broken one,' said Sophia. 'See how angry the swelling is? All you can do is tear a hem off your handkerchief and bind the two fingers together.'

'You're very kind,' said Captain Marsh pleasantly. 'Are you a doctor or a nurse?'

'I've had a little Red Cross training,' she said, 'but haven't done very much except sit on committees. Committees are an occupational necessity for the female members of my family. Captain Marsh, might I suggest again that you get out of this car and find a farmhouse where someone will help you? If you do that, then I promise to say nothing until I reach Douai.'

'I thought we'd settled that argument. The fact is, your car is a chariot of speed. It will outrun any German Army vehicle. I need it to prevent your military bloodhounds catching me up, and I need you to drive it. And you need me to navigate, as I will, now that I know where we are. You'd like to reach your lover before the day's out, wouldn't you?'

'That is none of your business, and I would prefer you not to—'

He stopped her voice by putting a hand over her mouth. He was listening, his eyes quick and darting. She realized he was living on his nerves no less obviously than Fritz was. It was said that the average life of a fighter pilot could be measured in months, unless he was a Richtofen. But there was only one Richtofen. Fritz sought escape from his nightmares in his extrovert pursuit of pleasures. This British airman wore a mask different from Fritz's. Fritz was infectiously outrageous; Captain Marsh was dangerous. He was dangerous now, his hand hard over her mouth, his lips compressed and his eyes flickering.

She heard then the faint grinding noise of a motor engine in low gear some way behind them.

Colonel Hoffner's men were scouring the area. The colonel meant to catch the man, a suspected British airman, who had held up two of his soldiers and gone off with the young lady in whom Major Kirsten was so interested. Catch one, catch both, that was what was in Colonel Hoffner's mind. He would be satisfied, and so, he thought, would his friend Major Kirsten.

'Drive, Sophia,' said Captain Marsh, taking his hand from her mouth.

He had touched her, roughly, and her blue eyes were furious.

'I will not,' she said.

'Then when they catch us up,' he said, producing his revolver again, 'a little war will take place,'

'If they're German soldiers,' she said, 'they'll fill you with bullets.'

'You'll catch a few,' he said.

She stared at him. He was quite calm now, quite ready to use his revolver. It filled her with horror, the thought of bullets maiming and killing. She was sure it would happen.

Captain Marsh was sure it would not, but refrained from saying so. The bluff was enough to make her do as he wanted. The noise of a heavy motor vehicle was louder as she drove off at speed, her anger and contempt inducing a crazy recklessness. The Bugatti rocked and shuddered over the rough, pitted road. Captain Marsh turned in his seat. He saw them, two vehicles, a car and an open truck, four hundred yards away. Distinctly, he heard the noise of accelerating engines. They had seen the Bugatti.

'You are stupid!' Sophia shouted the words angrily.

'Faster, if you please.'

The big car spewed dirt, slewing as Sophia braked hard at bends. In a dip, farm buildings flashed by, and an old man, working in a field, looked up to watch the roaring black tourer. He looked up again a minute later. Another car, with a lorry thundering behind it, appeared. The lorry was full of soldiers.

The chase was furious. It was one thing to hunt down an Allied airman. It was another thing altogether when he had made fools of comrades and taken a girl as hostage.

Sophia drove with her lips clamped in anger. Speed was a compulsive outlet for the fury she felt at the way he had closed her mouth with his hand. She saw a village ahead, with a few flat-fronted houses on either side of the cobbled street. She slowed down for the cobbles.

'Don't do that,' said Captain Marsh, 'put your foot down.'

'We'll wreck the suspension – '

'Risk it,' he said, wanting to get through the village before the chasing Germans had them in sight again, 'and if there's a junction ahead, be ready to make a fast turn.' The car bounced, juddered and shook as she took it as fast as she could over the cobbles. Two children, a boy and girl, were bowling large iron hoops with the aid of propelling sticks. They ran for a doorway at the sight of the charging black car. The deserted hoops weaved drunkenly on before keeling over and rattling to rest. Sophia ran over the edge of one. The hoop sprang up and clanged against the fender. Captain Marsh, looking back, watched for the pursuing car to round the bend into the village. Sophia, driving very fast, saw crossroads approaching. Captain Marsh, eyes front again, told her to turn right.

Again he looked back. The chasing car was still not in sight. It was over a minute behind them now, an interval that paid tribute to the German girl's handling of the Bugatti. If she could turn at the crossroads before being seen, the Germans would not know which way they had gone. Sophia slowed for the turn, and he muttered impatiently.

'Do you want me to crash the car?' she shouted. She felt she was crazy to take such risks, and crazier still to take them on his behalf. All the same she made the turn at dangerous speed. The back wheels slewed, going away from her. She slammed into a low gear and gave the engine an open throttle. The car came out of its skid and burst forward in an excess of roaring power. Changing up, she reached a governable speed, and the Bugatti raced along a gently winding lane with uncut verges and low hedges on either side.

'Sophia, full marks for your driving,' said Captain Marsh. She had brought the car into the right-hand turn at the crossroads before the hunters had seen her. 'True, had you really been French, our relationship would have been more comfortable, but I couldn't have picked a better driver.'

'I should prefer it if you did not speak to me,' said Sophia.

'Oh, I think we ought to get to know each other.'

'I know as much about you as I want to, and none of it is a consolation to me.'

The man was unbearable. She thought of Fritz and the love she was prepared to give him. Fritz was a delight compared with men whose austere sobriety made them old before their time, and adorable compared with this arrogant pilot from England.

'Look out!' It was a sharp warning from Captain Marsh as the back of a farm cart, which had just turned into the lane from an open gate, loomed up horrifyingly close. It blocked the lane. For the fraction of a second Sophia had a vision of a crash, an immobilized car and a trapped enemy. But it did not affect her instinctive reflexes. She swung the wheel hard to the right. The Bugatti careered on to the verge, missing the cart by a whisker and scraping the hedge. With her foot rammed down on the brake pedal, the car jerked to a halt and the engine stalled. The cart continued on, the horse plodding, the driver undoubtedly as deaf as a post, for he neither looked back nor lifted his nodding head.

High above, at twenty thousand feet, immune from the guns of any Allied fighters, two German reconnaissance planes, Rumplers, headed west on a photographic mission over British lines. The Rumplers had been unusually active of late.

Sophia sat rigid, hands still on the wheel. Captain Marsh looked up at the sky, his own theatre of war. Just a few small white clouds disturbed the canopy of blue. He heard the noise of a car, and the heavier tones of the truck. He listened. The sounds faded. The vehicles had stopped.

'They're at the crossroads,' he said, and smiled. The German girl had outdriven her compatriots. She reached for the starter knob. He at once closed his hand around her wrist. 'I think not, not yet.'

'If I'm not to restart the car, you should have said so.' She wrenched her wrist free. 'I dislike you touching me.'

'I'm sorry, but your friends will hear you if you fire your engine. So please don't send them the signal.'

'I have no intention of doing so,' she said. 'I don't wish to have my head blown off.'

He watched her and he listened. The Germans had the choice of three routes – left, right or straight ahead. Would they separate, the car and the lorry, to give themselves the choice of two out of three? It would depend on the thinking of the officer in charge of them.

Sophia sat in silent contempt. Could he not face up to a prisoner-of-war camp? However unpleasant that might be, the millions who had died would have rapturously opted for it.

The engines of the stationary vehicles back at the crossroads came alive. Captain Marsh tensed, and Sophia burned with hopes and wishes. Two events meant far more to her than anything else. Victory for Ludendorff and Germany, and the right kind of reunion with

Fritz. Much as she wanted Captain Marsh to be taken, she did not want bullets to fly, bullets that would rob her of the chance to celebrate Germany's victory and marriage to Fritz.

But wait. Bullets would not fly, not from the Germans. They would not fire at Captain Marsh, not with her beside him. They would know who she was, for by now her father would have advised local commanders that she had gone missing in the Bugatti. He would have asked for help in finding her. Almost certainly the two soldiers whom Captain Marsh had threatened would have long since reported the incident, and described her and the Bugatti. The soldiers in the car and the lorry at the crossroads were probably looking for her, as well as for the man beside her. No, there would be no bullets if the soldiers caught them up. They would surround the Bugatti and Captain Marsh would have to surrender.

She reached quickly and pulled the starter knob. The engine kicked, fired and purred into life. Captain Marsh did not move, nor did he say anything. He was listening to the sounds of the Germans' car and truck, sounds that lessened in volume. The vehicles had either turned left or gone straight over the crossroads.

He gave Sophia a smile.

'I don't think they heard you,' he said.

'I am ready to continue,' she said flatly.

'Thank you. Proceed, then.'

79

The sun was beginning to dip westwards, but the day was still bright. There were some hours of light still left. Sophia, reversing off the verge, saw his right hand slip from inside his flying jacket. He had been in touch with his revolver, his instrument of blackmail.

The farm cart had disappeared and Sophia coasted along. Another Rumpler, making height from the direction of Valenciennes, climbed into the sky to head west. Captain Marsh watched it.

'Busy as bees,' he murmured, half to himself.

Sophia kept quiet. He looked at her, curious about her. Her profile was faultless, the smooth outline of determined chin matched by the firm shape of her lips. The lashes of her visible right eye flickered in awareness of his survey. Her lips became firmer.

The countryside was a patterned blanket of silence, the sounds and signs of war absent, the guns quiet. Sophia, sensitive to atmosphere, experienced a feeling of vulnerability that was unpleasant. She knew she was regarded as an attractive woman. She saw herself going on and on with this man, driving in endless, wandering circles until night fell and there was nowhere to rest without him being frighteningly close to her.

'Turn back.' The German lieutenant in charge of the search party was convinced they had made a wrong guess. They had heard and seen nothing of the Bugatti containing the man and the young lady since deciding to go straight ahead at the little crossroads.

The car driver turned into an opening, then backed out and brought his vehicle round. He backed further to let the lorry enter the opening, then drove forward to return to the crossroads, the lorry, containing a platoon of soldiers, following on.

Chapter Five

In the village of La Calle, Lieutenant Elissa
Landsberg was speaking to the one person
visible, a little girl who, while playing, had
looked up at a big black car with shining brass
lamps a few hours ago. Major Kirsten remained
in his staff car, leaving Elissa to do the talking.
Little girls might not like answering questions
from a man with a puckering scar that gave his
right eye a slightly villainous look.

'Yes, madame, yes,' the little girl was saying.
She was fascinated by the gentle-faced lady in
a grey-green military greatcoat. She was not
old enough to think about what the greatcoat
represented.

'A big black car?' smiled Elissa, her French
softly accented.

The little girl spread her arms wide.

'Big, yes, like that.'

'And a lady and gentleman were in it?'

'Yes, madame,' said the child.

A house door opened and a woman emerged. She hastened up to the child, took her by the hand and said, without looking at Elissa, 'Come, Marie, your face must be washed.' And she walked the little girl briskly into the house, shutting the door positively. Elissa smiled wryly. The French were still unfriendly.

She returned to the car.

'I saw the innocent snatched from your claws,' said Major Kirsten, as she slipped into the driving seat. 'Did it distress you?'

'It discomfited me a little. She was so sweet.'

'What did she say that was sweet?'

'She said, Major, that the car came through here two or three hours ago, and that it contained a man and a woman.'

'Good.' Major Kirsten seemed rejuvenated. 'Go on, Lieutenant. Stop whenever we see a French citizen who looks talkative.'

'Talkative?' Elissa, a less experienced driver than Sophia, was so intrigued by events that she drove out of the village in the wrong gear. The engine laboured somewhat. Elissa, sensitive about her mistake, made a hurried adjustment. The gears ground noisily.

Major Kirsten, considerately declining to comment, said, 'Talkative citizens might also be informative.'

'Major, we shall be lucky to get information out of the French.'

'I shall leave it to you to unlock their tongues. Your French is superior to mine, and your manner far more charming.'

'Major, I'm painfully reserved, especially with strangers.'

Major Kirsten spared a few moments from his survey of the rolling countryside to turn his sound eye on the trim Lieutenant Landsberg. She sat correctly upright at the wheel, with not an eyelash out of place or a button unpolished. She was handling the staff car with the precision of a young woman who had paid keen and conscientious attention to her instructor. One would have thought that by now any of the eligible staff officers would have been courting her, for she did not lack physical appeal. Her features were attractive, her figure feminine, and with the skirts of her coat parted to give freedom to her legs while driving, her shapely calves presented the prettiest picture.

'I was shy myself as a boy,' he said, eyes on the road again, 'and was cured in an entirely practical way by being thrown in at the deep end, as it were. A cadets' school. Well, whatever our feelings, we're now in pursuit of a man who appears to be singularly reckless and dangerous. We need some help, and I've no doubt you may be able to charm a few answers out of likely informants. If we come up against objectionable characters and you suspect them to be deliberately withholding information, make it clear to such people that I'll shoot them.'

'Shoot them?' Elissa was shocked. 'You aren't serious, Major?'

'Indeed I am. Don't you know this is expected of us?' Major Kirsten was ironic. 'You must have heard that we roast babies and outrage widows.'

'That's just dreadful, obscene Allied propaganda.'

'To you and to me, yes,' said Major Kirsten, peaked cap shading his searching eyes, 'but not to the British and French. So, naturally, if you tell a French citizen I'll shoot him unless he speaks up, he'll believe you.'

'Major,' said Elissa, gloved hands firm on the wheel as she took a bend with care, 'I'm quite incapable of telling anyone that, and I really can't believe you expect me to.'

'Treat it as a means to an end,' said Major Kirsten. 'Let's accept that General von Felder-mann's daughter is in the hands of an aggres-sive lunatic – an English airman shot down by von Richtofen this morning. He may be using Sophia in order to secure some kind of immu-nity for himself. We have to find them. This is quite the wrong time for General von Felder-mann to be burdened with the more unpalat-able facts. Ludendorff has given him worries enough without him being told his daughter has been abducted. We must find her, and be-fore she's lost her honour to a young German pilot who thinks he's the only man facing a hero's death. Such young men consider themselves entitled to enjoy forbidden fruits on their way to Valhalla.'

Elissa, who had already been apprised by the major of everything concerning Sophia, said, 'Perhaps they are entitled.'

'Perhaps, but not at the expense of the general's daughter. Sophia is a delightful young lady, and worth saving from her misguided impulses.'

'Yes, Major,' said Elissa, wondering if his affection for Sophia was the motivating force of this venture.

The vistas were bathed in light. Rolling fields and pastures offered only the inoffensive promise of nature's bounty. Smoke rose from the chimneys of distant farmhouses. Two elderly French peasants bent to their work of pulling winter root crops in a far field. Narrow lanes showed no trace of traffic. Everything was as quiet as if the war had permanently retreated.

'I wonder now,' mused Major Kirsten. 'Where would our British lunatic head for? He'll keep off the main roads until dark, that's certain – unless he's completely mad. But where is he now, and what dark design does he have in mind concerning Sophia? Is he holed up somewhere? In a wood? In a farmhouse? Men on the run favour farmhouses, which provide dark little corners in which to hide. But he'll also need to hide the car and to drag Sophia into any shelter with him. He must know he's made himself a target of unusual importance. Colonel Hoffner's men will be searching every farm and village. He'll suspect that, because of Sophia. He'll also know men from the Luftwaffe will be looking for him. He belongs to them, since it was Richtofen who brought him down.'

'Do you think our participation unnecessary?' asked Elissa, steering a cautious course over a road uncomfortably afflicted with muddy potholes. 'Should we return to Headquarters and wait to hear?'

'Certainly not.' The major was in no mood to give up the stimulation of the chase. 'What our man doesn't know is that you and I are also after him. Colonel Hoffner's men and the Luftwaffe search party are much more likely to advertise their manoeuvres than we are. You and I are going to proceed with care, not charge about like agitated giraffes. It's very quiet. There's not even one likely informant in sight. Nor any searching men. Stop a moment, Lieutenant, while I examine my map again.'

Elissa stopped. She looked around while Major Kirsten consulted the comprehensive large-scale map of an area bounded by Henin-Lietard in the north, Cambrai in the south, Arras in the west and Valenciennes in the east. Every road, byway and lane, every village and wood, and every river and canal, were clearly drawn.

Elissa thought how quiet it was, although Valenciennes was only sixty kilometres from the front, and she and Major Kirsten midway between. With the passing of the noon hour, it seemed that peace had descended on France. That reflection was interrupted by the murmurous drone of planes climbing into the sky. She looked up. She could just see them, two of them.

'Rumplers,' said Major Kirsten, 'on reconnaissance for the Corps.' He put his finger on the map. 'We'll try this place, the village of Lutargne. There's a very useful wood close by. Our friend, the mad Englishman, will begin to need food and drink soon, and a place where he can get the car out of sight. That car is important to him. It gives him speed of flight. I've a feeling he's trying to reach Douai. According to our information, Douai was the town he was closest to when he held up the two soldiers. Only in a town will he be able to lose himself and to find people willing to help him escape. I'm firing shots in the dark, I know. What we really need is the light of inspiration, for I'm worried about what he may do with Sophia once he decides she no longer offers him security for his safety. He won't want to leave her free to inform on him.'

'Major,' said Elissa, startled, 'we're to assume he might kill her?'

'It will do our nerves no good at all to assume he's as mad as that. Let's find our way to Lutargne. That's a definite shot in the dark. I'll read the map for you.'

'Yes, Major. Thank you.'

He smiled. Elissa Landsberg was a very civilized young woman and quite the most engaging army officer it had been his pleasure to meet.

Elissa drove on. She looked admirably composed. He was not to know how warm and alive she felt, or how exhilarated.

Chapter Six

It appeared in the middle of the afternoon, sailing serenely through the lower reaches of the sunlit sky. Caressed by the touch of a light wind, a playful child of the prevailing westerly, its basket swung gently at a height of eight hundred feet. Its gas-filled cylindrical bag trailed the long anchoring cable that was attached to the slow-moving open lorry foraging its way into the countryside. Through the cable, telegraph wires enabled two-way communication to be conducted between air and ground. The dipping sun was behind it, blinding the eye. But Captain Marsh, heading east with Sophia, saw it clearly, hanging in the sky, and knew precisely what it was – a Drachen observation balloon, a German make known as a 'Sausage'. It was far distant, but moving slowly towards them.

The RFC man knew where he was now. His constant references to his map had eventually keyed him in on his location, and he had made up his mind to cross the main road when darkness fell and head for Douai by night. He could disappear more easily in Douai than in the countryside. He meant to get back to England. His aerial action today, although a disaster, had brought him closer to the end of his tour of combat flying. Two more missions and he could expect to take command of a training squadron back home. He had lost his plane to Richtofen because he had been careless in his feeling that the gods who had brought him through so many dogfights would see him safely through to the end. The gods did not like being taken for granted, and had laid their perverse hands on his plane. His determination to get back was edgily fierce.

That observation balloon was not on course for the front. It had come from its depot not to do some artillery-spotting for the Germans, but to look for a Bugatti car and its occupants. Captain Marsh could not assume otherwise. His eyes darted around. A haystack, big even though only half its original size, stood bulky and massive in a field ahead, its eastern side dark with shadow.

'Sophia, do me the favour of parking the car alongside that haystack,' he said.

'Why?' Sophia, after hours with him, was as edgy as he was. Her nerves and emotions were ragged

'Please just do it. Turn into the field and

drive the car up against the open side of the stack. Quickly, now.'

Sophia saw the observation balloon then, well west of them, and she too guessed why it was sailing slowly in the sky. She decreased speed. She fumbled the gear change and the cogs tangled and grated. She lifted her left foot, the clutch pedal came up and the engine stalled.

'I'm sorry,' she said, hiding the satisfaction she felt at the convincing way she had achieved the stall.

'Are you playing games, Sophia?' Captain Marsh knew it was not a genuine blunder. 'Don't fool around. Get this car off the road.'

The longer she took to do as he wanted, the better was the chance she gave the balloon observer to spot them. It was still far off and needed time, she thought. She restarted the engine, slipped into first gear and headed slowly for the gate that led into the field. She stopped as she turned the car to face it. Captain Marsh jumped out and ran to the gate. On an impulse, her fierce dislike of the man prompting her, Sophia pressed the accelerator. The engine roared and the car leapt forward. Captain Marsh, flinging the gate open, jumped sideways and backwards. Sophia, turning white at what she was doing, rammed the brake pedal with a frantic foot. The car shuddered, the chassis vibrated, and the bonnet came to a stop within a few inches of Captain Marsh's chest.

He looked up at her. Through the windscreen he saw her face, tense and pale. Her eyes were huge. The balloon dallied in the distance. Sophia, seeing the grim, tight mouth of the man she was beginning to hate, said quietly but clearly, 'You are English, I am German, and that is all that needs to be said.'

'Drive the car in and park it alongside the stack.' He spoke quietly too.

She drove over the field to the haystack. The car bounced. She spun the wheel and planted the Bugatti so close against the open side of the stack that the dark hay smothered the offside fenders. Captain Marsh came running.

'Why are we doing this?' she asked.

'Sophia, sweet innocence sits on you with its wings showing,' he said. 'Get out.'

'I prefer to stay where I am.'

'Get out.' His flickering eyes, watching the balloon, now moving again, turned to her. Apprehension again darted at her. He looked very cold and very dangerous. She got out. He told her to sit up against the stack. She did so. The hay-littered ground, in shadow, was cold. A tarpaulin cover, folded back along the top of the stack, had its ropes hanging. One touched her shoulder. Captain Marsh sat down beside her. The balloon was now hidden from them.

Sophia, aware of a shoulder close to hers, shifted her position, her nerves taut.

'Why are we sitting here?' she asked.

'Waiting for that balloon to disappear.'

'Balloon?'

His laugh was deep and unexpected.

'Oh, descend you shades of darkness and make the eyes of woman invisible to mine, for by day they show deceitfully bright and man is a child before them.'

'Is that a quotation from a French cynic?' she asked.

'No, it's one of my uncle's sayings. He's convinced that all women, except his wife and mother, are born of the Devil, their penchant for deviousness inherent and incurable. He's quite harmless, however, and confines himself to wandering monologues on their abominations. When he's actually in the company of women, he's charm itself.'

'You share his opinions without inheriting his charm?' said Sophia.

'Not at all. I find most women very likeable. You saw that balloon, didn't you?'

'Was that a balloon, that thing in the sky? I really had no idea.'

He laughed again. He seemed very cheerful about the way they had masked themselves from the hovering spotter. The worst of Sophia's apprehension eased away. He rose to his feet and peered around the haystack for a quick, furtive search of the sky. The balloon was sailing away, back the way it had come.

'Damn,' he said, for there was only one

conclusion to reach. The observer, equipped with field glasses, had spotted them. He would not otherwise have ended his search so quickly. Sophia von Feldermann had kept the Bugatti in sight just long enough for it to have been seen. Her lashes lifted as he looked down at her. 'They saw us,' he said.

'Really?' she said coolly. 'They are waving to you?'

'They're on their way back,' he said, 'and that towing vehicle will rendezvous with a waiting platoon of ground searchers any moment.'

'Your situation has always been hopeless,' she said, getting to her feet. 'I advise you to run if you're to have any chance. I'll stay here with the car. I'll give you a good start. No one could arrive here immediately. I'll say nothing about your more unpleasant behaviour – '

'Or about your attempt to murder me by running me down?'

Sophia compressed her lips.

'You are complaining about that after having threatened to shoot me?' she said. 'We are even, I think. I should like there to be an end to this situation now, so please go. I promise to tell the authorities that you did not treat me badly, that you only—' She broke off, hearing the sound of motor engines.

Captain Marsh was all quick nerves again. The vehicles were some distance away, the noise of their engines distinct but faint.

'Take hold of that rope,' he said, 'we'll pull the tarpaulin down over the car.'

'You are ridiculous!'

'Sophia, do as I say, please.'

She gave him an angry, bitter look, but because she was not sure exactly what he might be capable of, she took hold of the rope. He took hold of another and they brought both ropes round over the car. Standing on the far side of the car, they pulled. He pulled hard with his right hand, his left hand of little help. Sophia pulled lightly with both hands, determined not to be too cooperative. The heavy, folded tarpaulin cover scarcely moved. He turned, hoisting the rope over his shoulder and told her to do the same. His fierce determination had a compulsive effect on her, and although she could have wished him dead, she did what he wanted. With their backs to the car and the stack, they pulled. Sophia, quite strong and supple, did her part. The tarpaulin moved, slithering down, heavy and damp. It landed with a soughing plop on the car. Captain Marsh turned and began tugging, using both hands, although he winced a little. Sophia resignedly lent her own hands to the task of dragging the tarpaulin right over the car. They heard the oncoming vehicles moving steadily. The tarpaulin, in place, reached from the top of the haystack to cover the Bugatti completely. Captain Marsh took Sophia by the arm and pulled her under the tented tarpaulin out of sight. He stood with her against the bonnet of the car.

They heard the approach of the searching vehicles.

'They'll stop,' said Sophia quietly. 'They'll see this stack and they'll investigate. They are bound to be searching every likely hiding place. Give yourself up. You must know it's only a matter of time.'

'I'll give up only when there's no alternative,' he said, 'and I don't think you're too keen to be escorted to Valenciennes, are you? Now stay quiet, please.'

The Germans were close, travelling at a speed which gave them time to observe and speculate. Captain Marsh was perceptibly tense at the sounds of the vehicles slowing a little. It was all too easy to read what he could not see, the turning of heads and the questioning look of eyes taking in a haystack covered by its winter tarpaulin. They would be looking for the car, as well as its occupants. He felt Sophia quiver and sensed she was tempted to shout. She was no frightened creature, she was a young lady of spirit. At the sound of the car and lorry close to the gate of the field, he clapped an involuntary hand over her mouth. He felt her lips and teeth move in a fury of outraged resistance. His hand tightened. Her own hands came up to wrench at his wrist. The Germans drove on, slightly increasing speed, and Sophia was writhing in fierce anger. She kicked, and the toe of her boot struck the front of a fender. A dull metallic clang echoed under the tarpaulin, but the noise of the lorry's engine prevented the sound reaching the ears of the Germans, and they continued on. Captain Marsh waited a little longer, then took his hand from Sophia's mouth. She turned on him and struck him, stinging his jaw with the flat of her hand.

'Never touch me again!' she stormed, her eyes glittering, and then she was away, darting out from under the tarpaulin and running over the field towards the gate. He was quick and fast in his pursuit. She heard him behind her. An arm swept around her waist. She at once stood still. Stiff and proud in her refusal to engage in the humiliation of a struggle, she said, 'Let me go.' He released her and she walked back with him, her face flushed, her teeth clenched.

'We'll leave,' he said. She made no comment. She helped him uncover the car. 'I apologize,' he said, when they had the tarpaulin clear. She did not respond. Instinct made her turn her head. A man was walking towards them. Captain Marsh slid his hand inside his jacket. The man, mud caking his boots and a flat cap on his head, his clothes dark with age and daily wear, advanced with plodding deliberation. He regarded the car from beneath bushy brows. His chin was bristly, his eyes enquiring.

'What are you doing here?'

'This man – ' Sophia stopped. There was little to be gained in complaining to a French farmer that she was a hostage in the hands of a British airman. On the other hand, it would do a Frenchman no good to help any Allied airman if a German citizen was witness to it. Unless between them they killed her and buried her.

'The fact is,' said Captain Marsh pleasantly, 'we're parked in your field only because the engine has been overheating, not to give you offence, m'sieur.'

His French was excellent, but while it had no fault in Sophia's German ears, it had an accent in the ears of the French farmer.

'My friend,' said the farmer, 'go on your way. Birds fly and swallows call. It's all over the Douai arrondissement, the news that the German Army and Air Force are looking for a British flying officer. Take your car and your helpful mademoiselle and go.'

Sophia wanted to laugh. So that was the news. A British flying officer on the run with a helpful French girl. Was that because those two German soldiers had heard her speaking only in French? Had no one realized, because of the Bugatti, that she was the daughter of General von Feldermann?

'The birds gave you the news, m'sieur?' said Captain Marsh.

'And the Boche,' said the farmer. 'They have called too. I've just had a visit from some.' His expression wooden as he looked at Captain Marsh's flying jacket and khaki breeches, he added, 'If you'll wait here, I'll bring you a German greatcoat and helmet.'

'I can't wait, m'sieur, I must get out of here quickly.'

'Then take me down the road in your car, stop at the house and I'll bring the items out to you,' said the farmer.

Captain Marsh glanced at Sophia. She was German, and it would be her patriotic duty to remember this Frenchman.

'Thank you, m'sieur,' he said, 'but it doesn't matter.'

Sophia drew him aside and whispered, 'If it will help you get away, then accept what he's offering.' Which meant, he knew, that she would remain silent about anything which would hasten their parting.

They arrived at the farmhouse five minutes later. The farmer got out, walked sturdily into the house and returned fairly soon. He handed a German greatcoat and helmet to Captain Marsh.

'They were left by a German deserter,' he said, 'who took a hat and coat of mine. It's all I can do for you.' He hesitated a moment, then whispered, 'Go to Lutargne, to the auberge there. Pierre Gascoigne, the proprietor, will give you food and drink. And perhaps a little advice. His mother is English.'

'Thank you, my friend. Is Lutargne on the way to Douai?'

'It's not too far out of your way. Good luck.' The farmer went back into his house.

'We're going to Lutargne,' said Captain Marsh, struggling into the greatcoat and putting on the helmet. Sophia looked at him. He was quite ridiculous, posing now as a German soldier. Her dislike for him intensified.

'Where is Lutargne?' she asked.

'On the way to Douai – and Fritz,' he said, taking out his map. He found the village of Lutargne, some way south-east of Douai, but not very far from this farm. The point was, how long would it be before a mass of Germans descended on him following the report made by the balloon observer? He decided to risk a quick drive to Lutargne. He was starving. The wandering drive around the countryside had baffled the searchers so far. A run to Lutargne was no less risky than all that had gone before. The car had been a godsend. At Lutargne he could wait for nightfall, a matter of a couple of hours now. 'Would you oblige me by going on, Sophia?'

'Only if it will bring us to a parting of our ways,' said Sophia.

'Of course,' said Captain Marsh pleasantly.

Sophia started the car and listened to his

directions. Captain Marsh, after a while, assured her they would reach Douai, where she could join her gentleman flying officer and he could go to ground. Sophia said nothing. She drove, he thought, with the fierce silence of a young woman obviously disgusted by the role he had forced on her. But he could not drive the car himself. His damned finger hurt and the bruised hand was as stiff as the devil. Her Bugatti was a liability in one way. It was very recognizable. But it was still a godsend. It gave him great mobility.

'Turn right at the next fork,' he said.

Sophia, nerves on the edge of an emotional precipice, said nothing.

At Jagdstaffel II Headquarters, Baron von Richtofen washed his hands of the matter of the missing British pilot. He had placed his finger squarely on the map at the spot where the Camel had crash-landed, but the men who had been searching most of the day for the pilot had had no success, and the army commandant of Douai had advised that he too had so far drawn a blank.

Richtofen, informed that the observation balloon had spotted the quarry, and that a new detail was being rushed to the area in question, only said, 'What does it matter? It's an absurdity, using scores of men to find one airman. Finish with it, and he'll walk into our arms sooner or later.'

'But the young woman mentioned by Colonel Hoffner – '

'Even more absurd,' said Richtofen. 'No flying officer of any nation would harm a woman. I want to hear no more about it.'

Chapter Seven

In the afternoon sunshine the rural roads were dry, although a little muddy wetness still lay in ruts and potholes.

'Stop a moment,' said Major Kirsten. He and Elissa had made slow progress en route for Lutargne, halting on occasions to ask questions of farmworkers near enough to be hailed. None had been of any help. Elissa had drawn only negative information from them. No one had seen an open black car, a man wearing a thick leather jacket or a fair-haired young lady.

Elissa brought the car to a stop. Ahead were ruts deep and muddy. Major Kirsten got out and inspected them. His look was thoughtful as he got back into the car. He nodded and Elissa resumed the journey.

'You noticed something?' she said.

'Only confusing tyre marks,' said Major Kirsten, 'but they looked fresh. I wonder if Colonel Hoffner's men were in hot chase of our man along this road?'

'Major, is it important that you find Sophia Feldermann before anyone else does?'

'It's her safety that's most important, but yes, I'd like to return her to her father before he and the whole German Army know she's been foolish enough to land herself in the clutches of this mad airman, and that on top of her foolishness in running away like an infatuated young girl.'

'She may not be infatuated, Major,' said Elissa, 'She may be very much in love.'

'She may. Well, you are young yourself and can understand her better.'

'I'm not quite so young,' said Elissa, not wanting to be seen as a mere girl.

'Or so headstrong – ah, slow down, please.' Major Kirsten put a hand on her arm as they approached fields lying fallow. On their right was a tarpaulin-covered haystack. 'Stop, Elissa.'

She braked and stopped. Major Kirsten surveyed the field containing the haystack. The gate was open. There were no cattle, but it was unusual for a French farmer to leave a gate open. French farmers were careful in their husbandry. The major descended. Elissa thought him easy in his movement, despite his loss of an arm, and she liked his air of maturity. He examined the approach to the gate and its entrance. He raised his head and looked at the stack, at the loosely hanging tarpaulin.

'What is interesting you?' called Elissa.

'Come and see,' he called back.

Elissa joined him. He pointed to depressions in the ground. They were tyre marks. He walked towards the haystack, Elissa beside him. He pointed again. In the rough grass of the field were more depressions, faint but perceptible. They led to the stack and finished adjacent to it.

'Sophia von Feldermann's car?' said Elissa.

'Or the farm cart?' Major Kirsten pointed yet again. In the next field a man was driving a lumbering, horse-drawn farm cart, piled high with turnips.

'A cart journey to the haystack?' said Elissa. 'For fodder? Yes, but I think it was the car.'

'So do I,' said Major Kirsten, and together they peered at the faint depressions showing amid scattered straw. 'One occasionally makes a hit. Well, let's go and talk to the French gentleman on the cart.'

They walked into the next field. The cart was coming towards them.

'I am to ask the questions, Major?' said Elissa.

'If you would. He'll like your smile better than mine. I'll walk up and down, having nothing to do with the interrogation unless it's necessary for me to shoot him.'

'Major, I simply can't take that seriously.'

'But he might. Very well, just talk to him.'

The farmer, flat-capped and boots caked,

106

stopped his horse as the German woman officer approached his cart.

'Good day, m'sieur,' said Elissa politely.

'What is it you want?' asked the farmer, observing the strolling major in the background.

'A car has been on your land today,' said Elissa.

'Has it?'

'A large open black car, carrying a man and a young lady.'

'That is so, is it?' said the farmer.

'Quite so,' said Elissa with a smile.

'Then it escaped my eyes,' said the farmer, 'but then I'm a busy man, with no help and no time to go around watching cars arriving. Some of your soldiers called earlier, asking questions, but I'd seen nothing then and I've seen nothing since. You'll excuse me, but I must get my turnips stored.'

He was really very talkative, thought Elissa, in his insistence on the negative.

'A moment, please,' she said, 'the matter is of some importance to us.'

'I believe you,' said the farmer, 'but there it is, everything is of some importance these days.'

'The man and the young lady, please describe them,' said Elissa, sticking to the positive in an attempt to undermine the negative, 'and also tell me which way the car went when they left in it.'

The farmer pushed his cap back and scratched his grey head.

'Is the impossible expected of me?' he asked. 'I'm to describe people I didn't see, and point out the direction of a car I wasn't aware of?'

'I'm afraid that unless you tell me the truth, m'sieur,' said Elissa, seeing the need to exercise the major's bluff, 'the Major will shoot you.'

The farmer's expression became stiffly impassive.

'Now?' he said.

'It's possible, m'sieur.'

'I'm to be shot because my eyes did not observe what you think they did?'

'No, not because of that,' said Elissa. 'Wait there, please.' She walked away to interrupt Major Kirsten in his strolling. 'Major, we're faced with a man of exceptional obstinacy. He's so adept in his evasiveness that I'm sure he's lying.'

'I see. What next, then?'

'He's waiting, Major, for you to shoot him.'

'Shoot him?' Major Kirsten raised an eyebrow. 'Do you think that wise, Lieutenant?'

'No. And he doesn't think much of it himself.'

'If you believe him a liar,' said the major, 'then we can both believe our runaways were here, and not all that long ago. Excellent. Back to the car, Elissa.'

They retraced their steps. The farmer watched them. He grimaced, talked to himself and flipped the reins. His horse began to plod.

'Major,' said Elissa when they had reached

their car, 'I'm relieved to have found you won't shoot anyone.'

Major Kirsten smiled. 'We'll continue on the assumption that our lunatic is definitely heading for Douai. We'll go via Lutargne as already agreed. That's a little out of our way, but it's the most promising village between here and the town. Had he left this place in the reverse direction, we might have met him and Sophia bonnet to bonnet.'

'Major,' Elissa said when she had the car in motion, 'if we don't find them, shall we return to Valenciennes for the night?'

'I'm not considering a return to Valenciennes until they are found. The night, I think, is going to be cold.' The sun was in full retreat, the air crisp with the hint of frost. 'Why, I wonder, did they drive up to that haystack? What was the point? They could have been seen from the road. But they saw the farmer, perhaps, and asked him for food? They've both been on the run since early this morning. It can't be pleasant for Sophia. Consider it, Elissa, a large black car containing our man and his hostage, and we can't find them.'

'Others may have by now, Major.'

'If so, we're chasing shadows. But I've a feeling we're not. Proceed at your own speed. Are you hungry?'

'A little,' said Elissa. They had brought some plain but wholesome rations with them and eaten them in the car just after midday. They had had nothing since.

'We might get some food in the auberge at Lutargne,' said Major Kirsten.

'Yes,' said Elissa.

'We should reach there before dusk,' said Major Kirsten.

Lutargne was not a village of great importance, but it did boast a fifteenth-century church, some seven hundred inhabitants and a little textile factory that produced fine linens like batiste from the local flax. There was also a pleasant, well-kept auberge situated in the middle of the sloping, cobbled main street, with a spacious carriage yard at the rear. The only Germans resident in the village were those whose duty it was to ensure maximum output at the factory, and to see it correctly packed for dispatch to the Fatherland.

It was dusk when Captain Marsh, wearing a German Army greatcoat and helmet, walked up the street accompanied by Sophia. They had left the car tucked out of sight in a small wood fifty metres outside the village.

'You are carrying this to impossible extremes,' said Sophia, whose body felt tired and whose soul felt bruised.

'I need your car, Sophia, and you to drive it. With it, we'll both get safely to Douai. I thought we both understood that.'

'I've understood nothing,' said Sophia. 'All your actions have been incomprehensible to me. You are actually going to the bistro?'

'Yes. I'm starving, and you must be too.'

She was. And in her weariness, she was also in need of a bed. Food was possible, perhaps, but not a bed. She was sure Captain Marsh meant to drag her on through the night.

'When are you going to release me?' she asked, as the village inn came in sight.

'After we've crossed the main road late to-night and reached the outskirts of Douai. That's not so bad, is it?'

Sophia breathed in relief.

'I'll make a bargain with you,' she said in her tiredness. 'If you'll promise to keep your word, and if we can get some food at this place, I'll say nothing while we're there.'

'I give you my promise. Your offer is very agreeable.'

'I don't feel at all agreeable, only tired and disillusioned. I thought all flying officers were honourable men.'

'Sometimes, survival is more important than honour. Here we are. Let's go in.'

They entered the wine bar of the inn. It had a welcoming air with its tables and chairs. On the left of the serving counter was a door. Behind the counter was another one, shelves on either side full of bottles and glasses. The counter was polished and the tables were clean, a sign of the proprietor's respect for his establishment and his customers. There was only one customer, an old white-haired man sipping a glass of cognac diluted with soda water. He was muttering to himself and did not raise his eyes to the newcomers. Looking inwards, his muttering was directed at the ingratitude of his family.

'Sit here,' said Captain Marsh, guiding Sophia to a table at the farthest point from the old man. As Sophia sat down, the door behind the counter opened and the proprietor appeared. Captain Marsh approached him. The proprietor, middle-aged and with a dark moustache, had the friendly eyes of a man naturally receptive to customers. They became curious at the sight of the disguised British pilot. Captain Marsh smiled.

'*Bonjour*,' said the proprietor politely.

'*Bonjour*, my friend,' said Captain Marsh, and leaned over the counter to murmur. 'I'm a British flying officer on the run, and I think you're Pierre Gascoigne. I was recommended to you.'

'I am Pierre Gascoigne,' said the proprietor. 'I did not catch the rest. I'm hard of hearing. Wait, please.'

He disappeared through the door. Captain Marsh kept his eye on Sophia. She sat quietly. An elderly lady appeared, clad in high-necked black. She took a good look at Captain Marsh, her grey eyes shrewd.

'So,' she murmured, and he smiled. Sophia saw the smile. It made him look warm and friendly. She was unable to hear the soft-spoken conversation that followed, with English being used.

'I'm Captain Marsh of the RFC. I was shot down this morning.'

'So you are the one the Boche are chasing,' said the elderly lady, whose hair was grey, soft and bunned. 'They've been here, men from the German Air Force, and German soldiers too. The soldiers are most anxious to catch you, and the young lady with you. She's French?'

'Yes,' said Captain Marsh.

'My son tells me that's a German private's coat you're wearing.'

'Yes. A farmer gave it to me. He recommended I call here.'

'My son also mentioned you were wearing your brown boots.' She smiled. She was satisfied. His speech was undoubtedly that of an Englishman. And his description tallied with that given by a German Army lieutenant who had called earlier with his men. So did the young lady's. 'You must go to Douai. We'll give you an address. But you'll need black boots. We'll find you a pair. What else do you want?'

'Food, if possible, Madame.' Captain Marsh glanced at the old man.

'We can manage a little food,' said Madame

Gascoigne, 'and you needn't worry about old Henri.'

'Is there a room you could let us use?'

'There are rooms we have for guests,' she said. 'One can be made available, and we'll serve the food there. Go through that door.'

'Thank you,' he said warmly.

'I love France, which has been my home for many years, but I haven't forgotten England.'

Captain Marsh turned and beckoned Sophia. She rose and accompanied him through the door to the left of the bar. They entered a passage and waited.

'What were you talking about?' she asked.

'About food and a room we can use.'

'I shan't complain.' She was still proud, still very cool, but willing to make no fuss on the promise of being released.

A girl appeared, a white apron front over her neat black dress, her smooth black hair parted down the middle, her eyes full of darting interest. Captain Marsh, the helmet off, smiled at her.

'If you please?' she said, her voice soft and lilting. She led them through the passage, then turned and climbed a narrow flight of stairs. They followed her. On a long landing, with doors on either side, she entered a room. It looked cosy with its low ceiling and small windows. The girl lit a candle lamp. Sophia saw an iron and brass bed, two chairs, a mahogany wardrobe, a small table, a washstand and a fire-place.

She said, 'The bathroom, mademoiselle?'

'This way, if you please,' said the girl, daughter of Pierre Gascoigne.

Captain Marsh could only watch as Sophia followed the girl out to the bathroom at the end of the landing. He heard them exchange a few words. He went to the door and looked. Sophia was disappearing into the bathroom. The girl returned.

'The food will come in a few moments, m'sieur,' she said, and eyed him with quick interest again. He looked bravely strong to her. 'Oh, many good wishes,' she whispered breath-lessly, and walked to the stairs. He thought, coming from a French girl, the remark could be related as much to his romantic prospects with the ravishing young German lady as to his chances of escape, especially as everyone thought her French.

He waited in the room leaving the door open. The girl came back again carrying a towel. He heard her knock on the bathroom door. It opened, and Sophia took the towel with a murmur of thanks. The girl went downstairs again. Captain Marsh sat on the edge of the bed feeling drained. He had been living on his nerves from the moment he found Richtofen's red Albatros on his tail and impossible to shake off. The crash-landing and the long hours of flight that had followed had taken their toll. But he needed to stay alert. The spirited German girl would vanish, given the smallest chance, and pay him out by informing extensively on him. Douai as the objective could be discounted then.

It was some time before he heard the bathroom door open and the sound of her footsteps on the landing. Not putting it past her to head for a rapid flight down the stairs, he tensed for action. But she came in through the open door of the bedroom, her tired look lifted by her ablutions and new make-up. Refreshed, with her coat over her arm and her hat in her hand, she was a creature of bright fairness, her hair a mass of pale gold. A dress of fine silver-grey wool draped her curving figure.

His eyes flickered. He could not deny she was beautiful.

Sophia, who had examined the bathroom window and found it too small to allow her to climb out, placed her hat and coat on the bed and sat down on a chair beside the fireplace. Outside, dusk was turning to darkness. A lamp cast faint light over the carriage yard.

Captain Marsh rubbed a hand over his chin and felt the oncoming bristles. He looked at his hand. It was grubby. His other hand was swollen, the broken finger painful.

'There's no need to sit watching me,' said Sophia, 'you can wash too, if you like. The girl brought a razor as well as a towel, saying you might wish to use it.'

Someone had been shrewd enough to recognize that German soldiers did not go around with an unshaven look. But he distrusted Sophia's cool tones. He could not afford to let her vanish, not yet. Not until he had made contact in Douai with the kind of people who could outwit a German search for him in the town. Madame Gascoigne had said she would give him an address. And that address he had to reach before Sophia von Feldermann helped to ring the alarm bells. No, he could not yet afford to let her go. Running around on his legs was not his idea of elusive mobility. He saw a key in the room door.

'I'll wash, then,' he said. He extracted the key and locked the door from the outside. He enjoyed a quick shave and wash, listening the while for the sounds of someone coming up with the promised food. When he rejoined Sophia she spoke coldly.

'You locked me in.'

'It's the circumstances.'

'I might have climbed out of that window,' she said, 'did you think of that?'

'It's too far from the ground.'

'But I might have risked it,' she said. 'After all, you might not keep your promise to release me. Has it occurred to you that I have parents and friends who care for me? Has it occurred to you that in forcing me to stay with you, you must be causing them worry and distress?'

'The fortunes of war affect us all, Sophia. I don't doubt that the news I've been shot down will distress the people who care for me.'

Sophia, at her coolest, said, 'Are there people who care for you? You are hardly the most like-able of men. Even your wife must have discovered that.'

'She hasn't, not yet. I'm not married.'

Footsteps sounded, followed by a knock on the door. Captain Marsh, still in his greatcoat, opened the door, and the French girl, Josephine Gascoigne, entered with a smile and a laden tray. On the tray were two large bowls of hot onion soup covered with melted cheese, a dark-grained loaf and a little pot containing extra cheese. Bone-handled cutlery lay on snowy napkins. Josephine set the tray down on the little table.

'It isn't very much, but is all we can supply,' she said.

'It's splendid,' said Captain Marsh.

'Thank you, mademoiselle,' said Sophia, to whom the smell of the soup was heavenly. She brought her chair to the table. Pierre Gascoigne appeared outside the door, and Captain Marsh quickly approached him. The proprietor handed over a pair of black boots and a small slip of paper, containing a name and address in Douai.

'Read it, remember it and destroy it,' he murmured.

'I'm very grateful,' said Captain Marsh.

'*Bon appetit*,' said Josephine, coming out of the room. She and her father left, Captain Marsh closed the door, put the boots down under the bed and drew up the second chair to join Sophia at the table. He slipped off the greatcoat before sitting down.

Sophia silently distributed the food and put the tray aside. Captain Marsh carved up the loaf. Hungrily, they attacked the bread and soup. Again there was a knock on the door.

'Just a moment,' called Captain Marsh. He stood up and put the greatcoat back on. To appear before any of the family in his RFC uniform and to have them make no comment, would tell the German girl they were aware he was British. That might mean she would advise German authorities that the Gascoigne family collaborated with Allied servicemen on the run. They could be shot for that. Sophia von Feldermann could not be expected to behave other than as a loyal German. At the same time, he could not disclose to the Gascoignes who she was. The fat would be in the fire if he did. 'I'd better not let anyone know I'm British,' he said casually as he went to the door. Madame Gascoigne, the proprietor's mother, was outside. She entered with a bottle of wine and two glasses. She placed the glasses on the table.

'Mademoiselle?' she said to Sophia.

Sophia was tempted to tell everything then. But she had made a promise, and although she had made it in a moment of weariness, it was still a promise. So she only said, 'Thank you, madame.'

Madame Gascoigne filled both glasses, then looked at Captain Marsh. He hoped she would make no revelations.

'You may use the room to rest for a while, if you wish,' she said, and made her exit silently, leaving the bottle of wine on the table.

'Rest? What did she mean?' Sophia was both curious and suspicious. 'Doesn't she think it strange, a German soldier coming here in search of food and a room?'

'Oh, she looks upon you as my French lady friend. She understands, naturally, that we need to be discreet because the citizens will disapprove of your affection for me.' And Captain Marsh resumed his meal.

Sophia regarded him with cold contempt.

'These people here, they really think you're a German soldier?' she said.

'They haven't said they think I'm not,' he said, and she noted how he had kept the long greatcoat buttoned to the neck. It showed nothing of his flying clothes. Only his boots were visible.

'You can't face up to telling them the truth, can you? You can't face up to the disgust they'd feel at your behaviour, even though they're your allies.'

'I'm worried, Sophia, that you'll be tempted into telling them yourself,' said Captain Marsh.

'I am very tempted,' said Sophia, 'but I made you a promise. In any case, these people are being very kind. They have found us food and given us this room. If I told them who I was and why I arrived here with you, I should place them in a terrible position. I prefer to rely on your promise to release me.'

'Thank you. Finish your food.'

Sophia went back to her bread and soup. He observed her. He saw the faint spots of colour on her cheeks, indicative of the anger that had persistently simmered all day. He took a piece of the dark bread, applied soft cheese to it and devoured it with relish. The lamp cast its small amount of light. Sophia drained her glass of wine. He refilled it.

'When do we leave here?' she asked.

'We'll wait a while,' he said. 'We'll wait until the Germans, apart from their patrols, are in their barracks.'

'It will make no difference in the end, you know, whether you escape or not,' she said. 'You will lose the war. Germany will drive you and the French into the sea. We did not ask for this war, nor did we want it. You are the aggressors and will finish up as the losers.'

'What am I hearing, a cry from the heart of

the innocent and the aggrieved?' said Captain Marsh. 'How upsetting to be so misjudged.'

'You will never conquer Germany,' said Sophia firmly. 'General Ludendorff will break your armies apart.'

'Oh?' Captain Marsh looked interested. 'Will he? When?'

Sophia, instantly regretting her words, said casually, 'I'm simply speaking of the inevitable. You have no leaders to equal Field Marshal Hindenburg and General Ludendorff. Nor,' she added pointedly, 'have you any flyer to match Baron von Richtofen.'

'Don't remind me of that, Sophia.' He watched her sipping her wine. 'You and I will never come to any agreement about the war, of course. But how will Ludendorff break the French and British Armies apart? Has he confided in you? You are, after all, the daughter of a general.'

He was smiling at her, and Sophia became distant.

'I'm tired,' she said, 'and shall lie down until you are ready to drag me back to the car.'

"Do that, by all means,' he said. 'I'll wake you when it's time.'

She got up and stretched out on the bed. Her body became languorous with the comfort of rest. Her lashes drooped. She eyed him sleepily. Seated at the little table, he was pouring himself more wine. She wondered just how safe she was from him. Her eyes closed. Instinct made them open again a moment later. He was standing beside the bed, the greatcoat in his hands, his expression speculative as he gazed down at her. Her limbs froze at his sudden movement. The greatcoat descended, covering her.

'To make up a little for my unpleasantness,' he said.

The room was cold now and the coat was warm.

'Keep away from me, please,' she said.

He retired to a window, taking a chair with him. The lamp candle burned steadily. Sophia's eyes closed again.

Chapter Eight

It was dark and cold. Elissa parked the staff car in the carriage yard at the rear of the inn. She and Major Kirsten alighted.

'Excellent,' he said. 'You deserve what I hope is available here, some food and wine. But shall we start with a cognac to warm our noses?'

'Major, is my nose pink?'

'I can't say. The light is too dim. However, cognac would be welcome, don't you think?'

'Thank you,' said Elissa.

'We'll ask no questions, not at first.' Major Kirsten glanced around the yard. There were no other vehicles. He surveyed the rear of the establishment. A faint light showed at a curtained window. 'I wonder if they have a telephone here? I'd like to contact Colonel Hoffner, to find out if the English lunatic has been caught yet with Sophia. If not, we are on our own, Elissa. The official search parties will have retired until morning. Come along.'

They walked to the front entrance and went in. Lamps were alight and several tables occupied. The villagers looked up, then returned, blank-faced, to their wine and dominoes. Major Kirsten smiled. Elissa looked composed, hiding the sense of excitement that had been with her all day.

Behind his counter, Pierre Gascoigne received the new customers politely, and answered Major Kirsten's enquiry regarding cognac with a courteous nod. He poured two measures. Elissa and the major took the glasses gratefully. She sipped hers. The major let a little of the cognac linger for a moment on his palate, then drained his glass.

'If it's possible, m'sieur,' he said in his tolerable French, 'we should like some food.'

'There's onion soup, cheese and bread,' said Pierre Gascoigne, wise enough never to take up an attitude that might become difficult to defend.

'Almost a feast in these difficult times,' said Major Kirsten, given to carrying the game to the opposition. 'Lieutenant?'

'That sounds excellent,' said Elissa cordially.

It was something to have two German officers speaking French at his bar, and Pierre Gascoigne noted it. The man was battle-scarred, the woman trim. One could not approve of the Boche, but there were always some one need not actually dislike.

'M'sieur,' said Major Kirsten, 'dare I enquire after wine?'

'We still have a few bottles of Chablis,' said the proprietor.

'You are offering us one? Thank you,' said the major. He smiled. 'May I use your telephone? I need to make a call. You have a telephone?'

'Yes,' said Pierre Gascoigne, 'but as you know, we're forbidden to use it ourselves.'

'One of the restrictive nuisances of war, m'sieur,' said Major Kirsten without embarrassment. 'Where is it?'

'Go through that door, if you please,' said Pierre Gascoigne, 'and I'll come round to meet you.'

'You'll excuse me?' said Major Kirsten to Elissa, and went through the door into the passage. On the wall was a neatly framed, handwritten notice containing information for guests. Pierre Gascoigne appeared and opened a door on the left of the passage, disclosing a small room he used as an office. There was a roll-top desk, a chair, and a telephone on a shelf next to the desk. 'Thank you,' said the major. Entering, he shut himself in. He picked up the receiver. The operator, a German, came on the line. Major Kirsten informed him of his requirements, and a minute later was talking to Colonel Hoffner in Douai.

He rejoined Elissa when he had finished his conversation, by which time she had seated herself at a table, from where she was able to observe that every customer had managed to turn his back to her.

'I fear we aren't too welcome here,' she murmured.

'You're surprised?' he said, removing his cap and sitting down with her.

'No, a little sad, that's all.'

'The French,' he said, 'produce excellent painters, witty satires, moderate opera, fussy chefs and fine champagne. I'm unacquainted with their other contributions to life, which they appear to keep to themselves, including their conversation.'

'Their lack of communication, Major, is probably due to the fact that we're at war with them.'

'Very tiresome,' said Major Kirsten. They talked. He told her that Colonel Hoffner's men had had no luck, nor had the Luftwaffe search party. 'Only you and I are still on the prowl, Lieutenant.'

'We're going to prowl tonight?' asked Elissa, but the proprietor brought the food and wine then. Behind the counter, his grey-haired mother noted the German customers.

'That looks delicious,' said Elissa, surveying the bowls of piping hot onion soup.

'It's the best we can do,' said Pierre Gascoigne.

'We shall enjoy it,' said Major Kirsten. 'By the way, you have guest rooms here?'

'We have no guests these days. Visitors no longer come.'

'It's this wretched war,' said the major casually, and Elissa kept her eyes on the aromatic, cheese-topped soup. 'How many rooms are there?'

'Four,' said the proprietor, turning to go.

Detaining him, Major Kirsten said with a smile, 'Would you please prepare two for my colleague and myself? We are staying over-night.'

Pierre Gascoigne was not the kind of man to make the mistake of arguing, or of suggesting a hotel in Douai would be more suitable for German officers. Below the surface of the major's pleasantness was the glimmer of Teutonic steel, or so Pierre Gascoigne thought. He was up to something, with his request coming so soon after his telephone call. Either he meant to stretch German military ethics by bedding his female colleague, or he too had a nose for a missing British airman.

'The rooms will be ready in an hour,' he said.

'They're upstairs?' said Major Kirsten, tack-ling his soup.

'Yes. Two overlook the back, two overlook the street. I'll let you have the front two. They're more pleasant.'

'Thank you, m'sieur,' said Major Kirsten, and the proprietor nodded and left them.

The villagers departed in ones and twos, perhaps to go home to their own meals, or perhaps because they did not wish to linger in the presence of German officers enjoying the food and wine of France. Elissa and Major Kirsten were soon alone. They enjoyed their meal.

'Major, we're actually to stay here?' Elissa ventured the question a little uncertainly.

'We might as well. We'll take a walk first. It's a fine evening, and the rooms won't be ready for an hour. You brought an overnight bag, I believe.'

'Yes,' said Elissa, wishing she could sail through life in the same easy way as the major seemed to.

Telling the proprietor they would be back later, they left the auberge. Major Kirsten conducted Elissa back to their car.

'Search it for your gloves,' he said.

'I have my gloves,' said Elissa.

'Look for something else, then, and while doing so, cast your eyes upwards. There's a light in one of the rooms. One of the guest rooms. Don't be too obvious. Someone may be watching us. There is a light, isn't there?'

Elissa, groping around in the car, took a quick glance upwards. She saw a curtained window. It was visible because of a faint light behind it.

'But is it a guest room, Major?'

'What else? Two rooms overlook this yard, and although our accommodating proprietor was at pains to tell us they have no guests, would they light a lamp in an empty room?'

'The French are very thrifty,' said Elissa.

'A perceptive observation. However, for the moment, let's take our walk.'

They left the carriage yard and began to stroll down the cobbled street, which was without lamps.

'It's a very fine night,' said Elissa, 'but cold and frosty. One would not want to sleep out of doors if one could find a room.'

'Which means our man may have found a room here?' said Major Kirsten. 'If so, is Sophia there too? But how did he get her in?'

'By threatening to shoot her?' suggested Elissa, the heels of her shoes clicking on the cobbles.

'In front of the proprietor? What, I wonder, does a long day in the hands of a lunatic Englishman do to the nervous system of a young German lady? What would it do to yours? Might it make you compulsively obedient?'

'It would make me run,' said Elissa. 'Will you consider asking the proprietor to let you inspect that room?'

'Would I get my head blown off when I walked in? I can manage without an arm, I can't manage without a head.' At this, Elissa smothered a laugh. 'Was that a comment, Lieutenant?'

'Not a comment, Major. If I made a comment, it would be to say I'd prefer you to put sense before heroics.'

'The war has gone on too long, Elissa. I've finished with heroics. Now, assuming our man, with the help of the proprietor, is taking a rest before making his run to Douai in the middle of the night – which is what I would do – what has happened to the car? And what has happened, or might be happening, to Sophia?'

'I beg you, Major, not to increase my alarm.'

'You are envisaging a fate worse than death?' murmured the major, walking briskly beside her.

'Major,' said Elissa delicately, 'my imagination isn't carrying me as far as that.'

'Nor mine. But what have they done with the car?'

'Hidden it outside the village?' said Elissa.

'You are right.' Major Kirsten sounded in fine spirits, as if he found animation in Elissa's companionship. 'They would then have walked into the village as soon as it was dark. In his uniform, he wouldn't have shown himself by daylight.'

'I think he may have gone to the back door of the auberge and spoken to the proprietor there.'

'Very possibly. But what Frenchman would have given help to a British airman who had a young German lady with him? Do you have the torch?'

'Yes,' said Elissa, 'I brought it from the car.'

'I commend you, Lieutenant, for your aptitude.'

'My aptitude?'

'Charming,' murmured the major, talking to himself, apparently. 'Charming.'

The darkness hid Elissa's warm flush. They came out of the village. She produced the torch and flicked it on. Its beam cut through the darkness, revealing trees and untidy patches of briar. She walked slowly with the major, using the light of the torch to search for gaps.

Captain Marsh, nodding in the chair beside the window, jerked his head up at the sound of a low, insistent knocking. He rose to his feet and glanced at Sophia. She was deeply asleep. He unlocked the door and opened it. Madame Gascoigne came in, a tray in her hand. She smiled briefly on seeing he had changed his boots.

'You must go, and at once,' she whispered. 'There are two German officers here, a man and a woman. They have asked for rooms. It may mean nothing, but it's still too risky for you. The man has only one arm, and a scarred right eye, but his left eye is as sharp as a needle. They've just gone for a walk. Go before they return. My son has told them there's no one here, no guests. Wake your young French lady.'

'Yes, immediately. Thank you for all you've done.'

Madame Gascoigne looked at the sleeping Sophia, covered by the greatcoat.

'She's very brave wanting to help you. She'll guide you safely to Douai, I'm sure, but the less I know of her, the better. I must tell you that the German officer who called here with some soldiers was as much interested in her as you.'

'Did he know who she was?' Captain Marsh, his voice low, saw Sophia stirring.

'He said nothing about who she was, but described her very accurately. She is far too easy to identify with that golden hair of hers. So you must both go, and quickly. I'll clear up the room.'

'Give us a few more moments together before you do that, please,' he said, and Madame Gascoigne smiled and nodded. When she had gone he woke Sophia. She opened her eyes, looked sleepily up at him, came to and compressed her lips. 'I'm sorry, Sophia,' he said, 'but we're leaving.'

'I can trust you, I can rely on you to let me go when we reach Douai?' she said.

'Yes,' he said. He could not leave her here. She would be bound to discover the other guests, the German officers. She would talk to them, and that would be the end for the Gascoigne family. Their only chance would be if they could plead total ignorance. This German girl might, in charity, confirm the Gascoignes had reasonably accepted him as a German soldier and her as his French lady friend. She had said she would not repay their kindness with ingratitude. All the same, it would be a mistake to let her come face to face with the other Germans. 'Will you get up, please? I'm in need of the car.'

'Very well,' said Sophia dispassionately, and threw off the greatcoat. He picked it up and put it on.

'Might I mention the proprietor and his family have no idea I'm not German?' he said. 'I wouldn't wish—'

'Is that a joke, showing consideration for them when you've had none for me?' she said bitterly, and her mouth set tight again at the odious position this man had put her in. Her sense of justice was always acute, and she was angry at realizing that when questions were eventually asked of her she might have to lie to protect the kind and courteous proprietor and his family. 'You are entirely detestable, but I'll come with you.'

'Well, I shall end up as the fates decide, but you'll end up safe in the arms of your Fritz,' he said smiling, and this piece of impudence made her want to hit him. Hearing footsteps on the landing he opened the door. Josephine Gascoigne caught his eye. He went out to her and whispered, 'We'll say nothing at all about our stay here. Say nothing to us when you see us out except that I'm a good German.'

'Oh, that is for any ears that might be listening,' said Josephine. 'There are always ears in some dark corners.'

'Sweet girl,' said Captain Marsh and kissed her warmly. Being French, Josephine kissed him back.

Going back into the room, he found Sophia ready. She eyed Josephine silently as the girl opened a landing door that led to the back flight of stairs. They went down with her and emerged into the carriage yard.

Josephine said, 'It is a pleasure to have met a good German. *Au 'voir.*'

Captain Marsh pressed her arm, then hurried through the yard with Sophia. They saw a car.

'Why not take that?' said Sophia mockingly.

He looked at the car. The faint light was enough to show him it was a German Army staff car.

'I favour yours, Sophia.'

They turned out of the yard and began their walk back to the wood in which they had left the Bugatti. Captain Marsh strode quickly, and Sophia, despite everything, kept pace with him, concentrating on the moment when she would at last be free of him.

His thoughts were on the fact that Madame Gascoigne had said the two German officers, a man and a woman, had gone for a walk. What kind of a walk? It was hardly a night of high summer. The temperature was very cold, the air sharply frosty. In the darkness, he kept his ears pricked, and his eyes were feverishly alert as they became used to the night. Sophia stiffened as he took her arm to hurry her along.

'Don't touch me!'

'Hurry, please.'

'You are a wretched man. Hurry, hurry – drive, drive – run, run – this way, that way – stop, stop – go, go. How disgusting it all is, and how purposeless.'

'Sophia, be quiet, please.'

Her hatred of him was a fire inside her. Her teeth clenched. She went on with him, passing no one. They reached the end of the village, leaving the cobbles behind and walking close to the rough, grassy verge of the road. Captain Marsh, wearing the German greatcoat and helmet, kept his eyes to the left, searching for the opening into the woods. Tall plane trees loomed up. They turned in after the second tree, groping their way until they reached a wide gap in an old brick wall, at which point Sophia was seized and drawn forcibly to the left, inside the sheltering darkness of the wall. Old ivy festooning the brickwork rustled for a second against her back.

'You—'

'Don't move!' His voice was a whispered hiss, his body in such close contact with hers that she felt newly outraged. In her fury Sophia could have killed him. She heard a light thud as he dropped the helmet. She heard people, the sound of their movements and the sound of their voices. They came out of the darkness, the beam of a torch lighting their way. It was steady and direct, that beam. The people, whoever they were, were heading for the gap in the brick wall. A fractional change in the direction of the beam, and Sophia knew she and Captain Marsh would be seen. Her every instinct, because of the outrage of the close physical contact, was to violently kick and struggle. But the oncoming people must be French, and the French were more inimical to her than to him. Her body heaved. He pressed suffocatingly closer. She heard, amid her fury, the voice of a woman; a German voice.

'But it's a very critical situation now, Major.'

'One could say so, Lieutenant.' That was the man's voice, and one not unfamiliar to Sophia. Major Kirsten! Her constricted body writhed. 'Am I to contemplate heroics, after all?'

'I beg you won't. He has a revolver and seems very ready to use it.'

The beam advanced. It cut through the gap. Behind it came Major Kirsten and Elissa. They were so close then to the pinned, stifled Sophia and the determined RFC officer, that only the length of an Uhlan's lance separated one pair from the other.

'I must take a few risks.' Major Kirsten's voice was thoughtful.

There was a hand over Sophia's mouth and a body smothering her own. The circle of light played over the ground as the major and Elissa passed through the gap.

'You can telephone Colonel Hoffner again.' The woman's pleasant, even tones were perceptible to Captain Marsh, although he understood nothing of the German-spoken dialogue. 'I'm sure he'll send a detachment of troops immediately.'

'While we hold a watching brief?' The beam halted as the major and Elissa stopped a little way beyond the gap. 'That's a more tempting tactic than heroics to an aged soldier looking forward to peaceful retirement.'

Sophia, trapped by brute force in her well of darkness, was sure no sensation could be worse than that induced by physical intimidation. It was being applied by a man whose nerves were on the brink again. His disgusting indifference to her feminine modesty repelled her. Major Kirsten, a friend, was only a short distance away. A fierce impulse made her bite at the hand stifling her. Captain Marsh, feeling the ripple of fury running through her, took no chances. As she drew breath to scream, he kissed her, aborting any sound. A dog in the village began to bark. Sophia, her lips imprisoned, the kiss compelling silence from her, shuddered from head to foot. Her head swam and her blood coursed wildly through every vein. Only dimly was she aware of Major Kirsten and his companion moving on, leaving her on fire in the arms of Captain Marsh.

Oblivious, Major Kirsten and Elissa took the road back to the village and the establishment run by the Gascoigne family.

Sophia heard nothing except the sounds of her hammering heart. Release came suddenly. Captain Marsh stepped back. The crisp, frosty air was an intoxication to her starved lungs. She gulped it in, tears of humiliation stinging her eyelids. Fury welled, and she struck him across his mouth. Following up instantly, she placed her hands on his chest and thrust with all her strength. He was not expecting that. It sent him staggering backwards.

Sophia ran, coughing breath torturing her. She ran free of the woods, her flight impelled not by thought, but by blind anger. It sent her haring across the road. Only a moment's thought might have made her turn in an attempt to catch up with Major Kirsten. As it was, she simply ran in a straight line. Over the verge on the other side of the road and on to open ground she went, her eyes familiar with the darkness now. There seemed to be nothing ahead but the land at night, the grass thick beneath her feet. She heard the small thumping sounds of a man in pursuit, and only then did she wonder why she had not headed into the village to catch up with Major Kirsten. With Captain Marsh in pursuit of her, she was beyond the point of no return now. Before her was a formless void that might offer her a precious avenue of escape.

Hitching her coat and skirt, she committed herself recklessly. She ran fast, the thick winter grass kind to her feet. But he was closer. She could hear him more clearly. He was pounding the ground. It began a slight descent which helped her increase her pace. It was so dark, the night, but she flew. Panting, she veered to outmanoeuvre him. But seconds later he was still behind her and gaining. The small thumping sounds made by his booted feet seemed to change to rushing thuds. She ran harder and the slight descent suddenly became alarmingly steep. She could not check her impetus. She pitched and tumbled, sprawling sideways, and panic struck her as the ground fell away from her feet and legs. She slithered, her feet hanging below her, her clutching hands raking the grass of a bank as she struggled to hold on. With horror, she saw the dark, dull glimmer of water below her. Clawing frantically at the turf, she strove with her feet to find purchase. But she was sliding, sliding, the grassy bank steep. The waters of the Lutargne canal, which provided power to the little textile factory, were running fast. Cold wetness enveloped her boots and she felt the drag of surging tide. Her hands dug madly in. It was German that rushed from her lips then, not French.

'Herr Hauptmann!'

The darkness had become terrifying, the nearness of the running water horrifying. Her body was steeply angled against the high bank. Her hands scrambled and clawed, but she was slipping, still slipping.

'Herr Hauptmann!'

He was there, kneeling at the top of the bank, and he could smell the canal. He turned and quickly lowered his feet.

'Take hold of my legs!' They were beside her head, his long legs, and she hurled herself at them and wound her arms around them. Captain Marsh, elbows digging in, hung from the bank, steadying himself against the drag of her weight. He began to draw himself up, bringing her with him. Her weight felt dead. 'Hold very tight, and stay still for a moment.'

She held on while he drew breath and dug his elbows rigidly in. He used them to lever himself slowly up until the top of the bank was level with his waist, Sophia hanging from his legs. He held his position for a moment, then threw himself forward and down, digging in his hands to anchor himself. His broken finger endured sharp, angry pain. He heard Sophia gasping words.

'I can hold on – it's not too difficult.'

'Good. Take a breath. Good. Now, climb up over me. Take your time.'

Strong and active, she hauled herself up over his legs and body while he maintained clamped contact with the cold turf. She scrambled to safety and he heaved himself clear. She stood trembling but thankful. She knew she could not have fought those icy, surging waters for long.

'Thank you,' she said.

Bareheaded, he stood before her, looking formidable in the darkness.

'You owe me no thanks,' he said. 'Everything is my fault. Accept my regrets, but you're at war and so am I. I don't intend to give myself up, and I'm afraid all my behaviour has been governed by that. I need your car, Sophia, because I know that any man's chances on foot in this kind of countryside are frankly dismal. That doesn't mean I don't understand your feelings, and I like the way you've put up with things. Whether I could drive the car myself now, I don't know. Shall we go and see? That is, if your fall hasn't hurt you. Are you all right?'

'My boots are wet, that's all,' said Sophia quietly. 'Yes, we are at war, but I will drive you. I think you wrong in all you've done, and I don't think you'll escape, but I wish to be submitted to no more violence.'

He ran an uneasy hand through his hair.

'I'm sorry I was so rough,' he said, 'but those people were German.'

'But you did not know that, not at first.'

He could have told her what Madame Gascoigne had told him.

'I felt you were going to call out to them who-ever they were.'

Sophia, still shaken by her narrow escape from the icy canal, said, 'I told you I would go to Douai with you, I told you I would do that as long as you promised to release me outside the town. There was never any need to almost suffocate me. You've just saved me from the canal, but I shall never forgive you for what you did to me back there.'

She turned and began to retrace her way back to the road. He followed, caught up with her and walked with her. They were both silent. They reached the road, crossed it and entered the woods. He retrieved the dropped helmet, and they made their way to a little clearing in which the Bugatti had been parked out of sight. They got in. Sophia started the car.

'Which way?' she asked.

'Through the village, please. Try to do with-out the headlamps for a moment, and stop a little way past the auberge.'

'Stop?'

'If you would.' Captain Marsh was very polite.
'We must immobilize that car we saw.'
　'You mean you must.'
　'I should like you to help me, Sophia.'

Chapter Nine

Pierre Gascoigne, on the return of his German guests from their walk, showed them up to the rooms which had been made ready for them and wished them a good night. Since this did not necessarily mean to others what it might have meant to a Frenchman, Major Kirsten permitted himself a smile.

Elissa, who had brought her small case from the car, inspected her room. One could not always say the French gave quite the same attention to domestic details as they did to cooking, but having looked around Elissa could not fault the cleanliness and tidiness of the room. And a little hump in the bed indicated the presence of a stone hot-water bottle. Major Kirsten took it upon himself to also inspect her room, and this solicitous gesture intrigued Elissa. She felt it heralded a paternal phase.

Seemingly satisfied with the amenities, he quietly closed the door he had left open. At once, Elissa was sensitively aware of being alone with him, and any thought of him being paternal was displaced by something quite different. A nervous pulse beat.

'What are you going to do?' she asked, and realized immediately the question was embarrassingly incomplete. 'About this man, I mean, and Sophia von Feldermann. Do you think they really are here in that room?'

'The room which showed a light, the room directly opposite this one?' Major Kirsten reflected. 'They have to be somewhere in this village, or they wouldn't have left the car where they did.'

'That light was out, Major, when we returned,' said Elissa, opening up her case and closing it again as neatly folded underwear cast a shimmer.

'A sign that they've retired to bed for a while?'

Elissa thought he could sometimes be very disconcerting.

'Major, you can't believe Sophia von Feldermann would actually consent to that – you can't.'

'If she is here with him, her silence is incomprehensible to me.' Major Kirsten drew his hand over his mouth. 'But certainly, I can't imagine the daughter of one of our outstanding corps commanders forming a romantic attachment to a mad English airman who has abducted her. But it's a strange and complex world we live in, and most of us reflect its complexities in the curious way we behave at times.'

'Major, I thought Sophia was romantically attached to a German flying officer.'

'True,' said Major Kirsten.

'What are you going to do? Telephone Colonel Hoffner or ask questions of the proprietor?'

'First, I'd like to find out for myself if that room is occupied. I might simply knock and walk in—'

'Please don't do that.'

'I have my own revolver.'

'Major, is there to be a shooting match, with guns going off?'

'You don't favour that?' said Major Kirsten, intrigued by her concern.

'I don't favour anything wildly dangerous. We must be more subtle.'

'I agree. Will you volunteer, Elissa?'

'I'd like to help Miss Von Feldermann in any way I can,' said Elissa.

'It need not be at all dangerous. Your overnight things – do they include a negligee?'

'Yes.'

'Then remove your uniform, don the negligee, go to the bathroom, and on your return make the not unusual mistake of a guest just arrived. Go into the wrong room. Apologize with a blush and some confusion – '

'Major?' Elissa opened her eyes wide.

'The appearance of a charming young lady in her negligee will arouse anything but suspicion, and the last thing even a certified lunatic would do is shoot you.'

'Major, I'm to casually walk into the wrong bedroom?'

'Not subtle enough?' said Major Kirsten blandly.

'The door may be locked,' said Elissa.

'But you'll try?' He was sure she would not be at risk. He was sure it was the right way, the most innocent way.

'Yes, I'll try,' said Elissa, excitement tingling and butterflies in her stomach. 'And if the door is locked?'

'It's then that we'll begin to ask questions of the proprietor.'

'Major, you had no real intention of risking a shooting match, did you?' said Elissa with a little smile. 'You're thinking of Sophia, aren't you? You don't want Colonel Hoffner's soldiers here. You want to resolve the problem quietly, don't you?'

'If it's possible,' he said.

'I will gladly help,' said Elissa.

'Permit me to retire while you get ready.'

Elissa composed herself and undressed. Major Kirsten, standing behind the slightly open door of his own room, heard her go to the bathroom. He waited, listening the while for other sounds. The room opposite hers was quiet, very quiet. It was not difficult to imagine Sophia, tired and weary after a traumatic day, resting on the bed and asleep, perhaps, with the man watching her from a chair and taking his time for the night to advance until it was safe to continue his flight. That was when he would make his dash for a town, in the middle of the night.

The bathroom door opened. Major Kirsten heard the soft sound of Elissa's slippered feet advancing along the landing. She passed his door. She stopped. He did not want to show himself and put her at risk, and could only visualize her next move, her turning of the door handle and her entry into the room. He listened with care, poised for instant action, if necessary, acknowledging the while that in Elissa Landsberg he had discovered a gem. He heard nothing, nothing at all, until the faint swish of her negligee reached his ears. Then came a light knock on his door. He pulled it wide open. Elissa stood there, her expression wry.

'The room is empty,' she said.

'Is it? Quite empty?'

'Yes,' she said, and the major was conscious of two completely different and unrelated facts. One was the fact that expectations had come to nothing, and the other was the fact that Lieutenant Landsberg looked entirely delicious. Her negligee was of rose-pink satin that graced her figure with shimmering softness.

Elissa coloured. Major Kirsten smiled philosophically.

'Let's take a look,' he said, and she followed him to the empty room. The bed and furniture conveyed a nothingness. He moved to the mantelpiece and placed his hand on the lamp globe. It was not hot, but nor was it quite cold. There was the faintest suspicion of retained warmth. And the curtains over one little window were drawn too. 'Our birds have flown, Elissa.'

'You're sure they were here?'

'Quite sure. The lamp isn't yet cold, and those curtains are closed. Our good proprietor has tidied up.'

'You think he warned the Englishman we were going to stay overnight?'

'I think the lunatic would have disliked bumping into us.' Major Kirsten drew Elissa back to her room. Over the bed lay her nightdress of pink silk. He eyed it as if it presented new problems. 'How is one to get the truth out of an honest-faced proprietor without subjecting him to the thumbscrew? But is that important, when the truth is already obvious? They were here, and for some reason Sophia accepted the situation as it existed at the time. Now they've gone. Now they're running again, the man keeping Sophia with him to use her as a lifeline if he's cornered. Is that a reasonable assumption?'

'Very reasonable,' said Elissa.

'They'll drive through the night, they'll reach—'

'Major, they may not get very far. Whichever way they go, they'll find every surfaced road impossible to use. All those roads will be alive tonight, with our divisons moving up.'

The major's sound eye gleamed.

'My dear Lieutenant, what a treasure you are,' he said. 'I ask you now to dress yourself and to go down and bring the car round to the front, while I study our map, which is in my room. We are going after them, and I'm making a guess they'll definitely be trying to reach Douai.'

Elissa said, 'In the dark, Major? We're going to try to catch them up in the dark?'

'In the dark, Elissa, the light of headlamps is visible for miles.'

Elissa dressed quickly, then hurried down to the carriage yard. She returned ten minutes later looking perturbed as she informed Major Kirsten that the car simply would not start. The major went down with her to investigate the cause. Not until the bonnet had been lifted and the torch had illuminated what was exposed, did they find what was wrong. The distributor head was missing.

'Our lunatic is no fool,' said the major, 'he's several steps ahead of us. I must telephone our transport depot.'

'Direct me, please,' said Sophia, after she had been crazy enough to help Captain Marsh sabotage the German staff car.

'If I remember my map correctly – let's see – Lutargne – yes, there should be a right-hand turn a little way out of the village. Take it, and then at some point we should reach a junction with a road on the left. I think that will eventually bring us to a main road. We can't use it – too risky – so go straight over at the crossroads there.' Captain Marsh paused and reflected. 'Take your time. We're starting much earlier than I wanted to.'

'I hope you don't feel inconvenienced,' said Sophia with quiet but candid sarcasm.

'I feel the day's been a trial to both of us,' said Captain Marsh, 'but thank you for your help.'

'Don't say that. Do you think it's something I want to hear?'

'No, of course not. I'm sorry. Shall we move off?'

Sophia turned her coat collar up against the cold night air. She started the car and switched on the headlamps. The beams pierced the darkness. She set the Bugatti in motion and left Lutargne behind. The frosty air became a cold breeze. She thought of Douai and the waiting Fritz. It did not linger, that thought, for her mind had been unable to dislodge pictures of the nightmarish incident on the bank of the canal ever since it had happened. If Captain Marsh had not been so close behind her, if he—

She shivered.

'Are you cold?' He sounded concerned.

'Yes.'

'If you'll stop, I'll put the hood up.'

'Thank you,' she said, and stopped. He got out. The engine ticked over, a low purr in the silence of the night. She had a chance then to slip back into gear and to leave him floundering in the bleakness of dark and frosty March. Her lack of will confused her. The rising hood creaked and was pulled blackly over her. It fully enclosed her, separating her from Captain Marsh. And she sat there, the engine running, doing nothing while she waited for the hood to be anchored and for him to rejoin her. Because of his crippled left hand, he made an awkward job of the fixing, and she bit her lip because of her inaction.

He slid in.

'That should make you less cold,' he said, and she thought how well he spoke French, how fluently they conversed together in the language that was foreign to both of them. She drove on and the car lights picked out what they were looking for, the right-hand turn about a kilometre beyond Lutargne. She took it and motored without haste through a long, winding lane.

'The road on the left of a junction is next,' said Captain Marsh.

'Yes, you said so.'

'Tell me about Fritz,' he said.

'He is nothing to do with you.'

'Only in that I want to help you reach him.'

'Help me? You are insufferable. Help is a word that has nothing to do with anything you have done to—' She stopped, and her teeth clenched as the nightmare obtruded again, the nightmare of his precariously hanging body and her own hanging even more precariously, her arms wrapped around his legs. 'It is so stupid,' she said.

'What is?'

'To suggest that two people who are at war with each other should have a cosy conversation about their private lives.'

Captain Marsh laughed. He had a warm and quite infectious laugh, but it did nothing to make Sophia feel better.

'You're really a very engaging young lady,' he said.

'Don't you dare speak to me like that. That is a familiarity I won't endure.'

'So sorry,' said Captain Marsh.

The beam of the headlamps reached out to illuminate the winding way, to pierce the darkness of that part of France which lay frostily prostrate under German occupation. Sophia wondered why a little rim of sadness had begun to edge all her other emotions. The night was even quieter than the day. The guns of the Western Front lay silent, although in the far distance the faint light in the sky told her of searchlights playing over the deep trench systems, the Germans watching the Allies and the Allies watching the Germans. How terrible was war, how profligate the slaughter.

'Is that the junction?' she asked, peering ahead.

'Yes. There, take the road on the left.'

Sophia turned and found herself motoring over a fairly reasonable surface. The steel braces of the hood creaked a little, but the wheels ran smoothly. Captain Marsh became conscious of light at his back. He slewed round in his seat. Through the malleable window of the risen hood he saw two small beams, coming up fast.

'What is it?' asked Sophia.

'Traffic. Pull off the road as soon as you can.'

Sophia saw them in the mirror, the chasing lights. She opened the throttle and the Bugatti burst forward.

'We can outdrive them,' she said, then wondered at her crazy self. Why should she think of outdriving anyone, whoever it was? Could it be Major Kirsten? Had he put his car to rights so soon?

'Don't try speed, Sophia, not on a night as dark as this and on a road we don't know,' said Captain Marsh, urgent in his need for her to do as he wanted.

But Sophia, bitten by impulses incomprehensible even to herself, rushed on, her gloved hands tight on the wheel, right foot active on the accelerator. What was she doing, driving at this speed, careering into bends that leapt at the headlamps? The tyres scurfed at her intermittent use of the brake. She was trying to keep this man out of the hands of her countrymen. She was driving like a maniac and behaving like one. The lights brought into view an opening ahead, an opening to a farm track. She slammed into low gear and swung the wheel hard to the left. The car slewed round, the tyres burned and the back wheels skidded. Sophia, maintaining power, straightened the roaring Bugatti and burst through the opening. The car bounced and jolted over the rutted track. She braked and stopped. She switched off the engine and the lamps. She sat with Captain Marsh in darkness, her hands trembling on the wheel.

'You handle this car as if you built it yourself,' he said.

'I am good with cars,' she said numbly.

They heard the noisy roar of motorcycles. The machines, two of them, shot past the farm track. Their roar faded. Two more followed a moment later. Captain Marsh, turning, heard a steady, growing whine and knew what it was. It was the sound of a long column of motorized vehicles. The first of them appeared – infantry lorries carrying troops. He saw them passing, black moving shapes with masked headlamps. The steady, driving noise of engines was indicative of a column stretching far down the road.

Sophia, feeling disorientated, watched silently. She knew what it meant as vehicle after vehicle passed the farm opening. Another of her father's divisions was moving up to join the growing concentration of troops which were to form the spearhead of General Ludendorff's gigantic offensive.

Captain Marsh was mesmerized by the endless stream of packed lorries. It made him think of the long infantry columns he had seen moving so cautiously during the day. What he was seeing now was a huge effort of transportation, taking place under the cover of darkness. Every army on the Western Front made its more important troop movements at night.

'There's something brewing,' he murmured.

'There's always something happening in war, isn't there?' said Sophia. 'Something that means more slaughter.'

'One only comes to that conclusion when it's no longer credible to wave our flags.'

'Whether our German flag is being waved or not, it is still flying,' said Sophia.

They sat in the car, watching the lumbering, motorized troop carriers thunder by. They could not move. They were trapped by the endless procession.

As a diversion, Captain Marsh said, 'How did you come to drive a car so well?'

'I was taught by our family chauffeur. He would not have liked the way I made that turn.

He would have said however self-satisfied I felt about it, it was an abuse of a car.'

'It was magnificent, even if it was an abuse, although it didn't do my nerves much good.'

'Your nerves?' Sophia flashed him an angry look. 'What do you think mine are like?'

'Yes, it's been a long day,' he said, 'and it's going to be longer waiting for this traffic to clear.'

'Longer even than you think,' she said. 'We'll never get back on the road tonight.'

'Why not?'

'It will be too busy. Can't you see?'

'I can see.' Captain Marsh, eyes on the lumbering shapes, was thinking. 'But all night?'

Sophia shook herself.

'Perhaps,' she said, and shrugged.

'Is this a new German Army, Sophia?'

'How should I know? All I do know is that Germany will win.'

She was very impressed, he thought, by the weight and strength of the motorized column. A staff car appeared, and he tensed as it pulled over to park sideways on to the opening. It was quite clear in the dim lights of each oncoming lorry. Four officers alighted. They lit cigarettes and stood to watch the progress of the vehicles. They were only about thirty-five yards away from the Bugatti. Sophia saw them. One of them turned about. Captain Marsh knew the man was looking into darkness, but the way he was looking conveyed an impression of curiosity, as if the Bugatti was visible. He took a few steps forward, and perceptibly he was peering.

Captain Marsh whispered, 'I think he's going to take a closer look. That means I must run. You're free now. My sincere apologies for being so rough, and my deepest admiration for your courage and endurance – and your driving.' He could not resist the impulse to kiss her warmly on her cheek. Then, as the curious officer took further steps, he slid swiftly and silently from the car. Bending double, keeping his line of retreat shielded by the bulk of the car, he moved fast down the rutted track to let darkness swallow him. A gate loomed up, and a hedge. He went over the gate and pressed himself flatly into the hedge. He waited and listened. There was still the continuous whining rumble of the countless lorries, but above it he heard the gate creak as someone else climbed over it. The next moment the German girl was beside him. He was astonished but said nothing. He felt her shoulder close to his. She was trembling and breathing fast. He essayed a cautious look back. Against the vague outlines of the passing vehicles, and against the faint patches of light cast by the masked headlamps of each successive lorry, he saw moving silhouettes. All four German officers were advancing on the standing Bugatti.

Sophia also essayed a look. She saw a torch

flash on. It moved about, then hovered, its light playing over the farm track. The four officers conferred. The torch moved again, beaming light into the car. One man opened the luggage compartment. In it was her travelling case.

Knowing the Bugatti was lost to them, Captain Marsh whispered, 'Time for me to definitely run, but for God's sake, you didn't need to.'

'Yes, that is easy for you to say,' whispered Sophia. She drew a breath. 'You are somebody's son. I am only somebody's daughter. Do you know how difficult it is for a daughter to be a free being compared with a son?'

The German officers were obviously both curious and suspicious, and Captain Marsh delayed his answer to Sophia's question as he watched them moving around, the torch sweeping in a search of the dark surroundings. The discovery of a Bugatti car, with its engine still warm and its driver missing, parked close to a road forbidden to all traffic except that which was part of the German military machine, was causing activity and discussion among those officers.

He said, 'Parents consider their daughters more vulnerable than their sons. Go back to your car.'

'No.' Sophia was in emotional confusion, quite unable to understand herself. 'I'm running too.

What I told you was true. I do want to get to
Douai to see Fritz. If I go back, my mother will
smother me with a surfeit of protection, and I'll
end up marrying the man of her choice, not
my own.'

Frost lay over the furrows of ploughed fields,
and the stars in the sky were jewels of crisp
light.

'Sophia, you must make your own decisions,
and I must make mine. I'm going to run before
those officers begin a thorough search of this
place.'

He moved quickly along the hedge, keeping
close to it. Sophia, hesitating, drew another
breath and followed him. The field was
ploughed, the ridges crumbling beneath their
feet. She stumbled in her effort to catch up with
him. He turned at once and steadied her. They
walked on together, putting distance between
themselves and the Bugatti. Enclosed by the
night, they were invisible to the prowling,
searching German officers.

Breathless because of her hurried stride,
Sophia said with an effort, 'My mother is very
loving. She's also very strong. I shall soon be
twenty-one and wish to live my own life, not
my mother's. It's so very difficult, because how
could one not love one's mother?'

It struck a strange note, this breathless, murmured little outburst, and he wondered what
his demands on her had done to her nerves

and emotions. In the darkness, he grimaced at himself.

'Sophia, to their children, most mothers are irreplaceable, whatever their faults. Even their possessiveness can be an endearment. But our own way of life means much to all of us. We all know when it's time to leave the nest.'

'Yes, you are right,' said Sophia. 'I know it's time for me to leave.'

They were entering the silent realms of France again, the sounds of the motorized column no longer discernible to their ears.

Captain Marsh said soberly, 'I'm afraid I turned your escape from possessiveness into something of a disaster. Very unfortunate, but I wasn't in the best of tempers this morning. The complicated situation is now more complicated. What am I to do with you?'

Sophia, totally bemused by the mad impulse which had made her scramble out of the car to go after him, said, 'You can make up for the results of your bad temper by helping me to reach Douai on foot now that we have no car. You mean to get there, so I will go with you. My father, I know, will have men looking for me. I don't wish to be caught. Therefore, we shall still have to put up with each other.'

Her father, in fact, had sent only Captain Vorster to look for her, and Captain Vorster had long since returned to Valenciennes to report failure. He had received a brusque order to try

162

again, starting at dawn tomorrow. He was to go direct to Douai.

'I've no wish to offend your mother,' said Captain Marsh, deciding that this ploughed field was a damnably extensive one, 'but I'll be only too pleased to get you to Douai. It's the place for both of us. It holds Fritz for you and hope for me. I want to find a way of returning to my squadron.'

Sophia, hurrying with him, caught her foot on a hard, frosty ridge of earth and stumbled again. He swept an arm around her. She wrenched herself free, her hat falling off. She let it lie.

'Don't touch me!' she breathed.

'I'm sorry – I thought you were going to fall.'

'I keep hoping I'll find you're only a bad dream,' she said, 'but you aren't – you're real.'

'Shall we go on?' he asked. Silently, she continued on with him. 'Ours is an awkward relationship,' he said, 'but I mean you no harm and should like to avoid fractious moments with you.'

'I'm sorry,' said Sophia, 'but I'm not at my best any more than you have been.' She bit her lip. There were clouds in her mind, clouds that obscured rational thought and reasoning. It was becoming so difficult to conjure up clear pictures or to call on the angry hostility that had burned so brightly and naturally for most of the day. The one unclouded picture now was the welcome Fritz would give her when she finally arrived. And even that could not be sustained.

They reached a gate at last. He climbed it. She heard him wince a little because of his broken finger. He turned to give her a helping hand. Pride and confusion made her ignore it. Then there was the necessity of lifting her coat and dress in order to freely negotiate the high, barred gate. She thought how ridiculous it was to worry about him seeing her legs when the whole world was anxious about the magnitude of this awful, never-ending war. Aware of her pride at least, Captain Marsh moved on. He disappeared in the darkness, and she was shocked at the way his disappearance panicked her. She hitched her clothes and climbed the gate with long-legged and supple agility. She landed safely and as she straightened up the panic increased because there was only darkness ahead. She could neither see him nor hear him. She ran, frosty grass beneath her feet. A gasp escaped her as she collided with him. Momentarily, the warmth of his hard body assailed her own body. She drew sharply back.

'We must turn right and keep the road on our right. It leads to Douai. We can't simply wander. Eventually, we'll have to cross that road. The river's somewhere in front of us, and we can't cross that. But we can get to Douai by using the little lanes on the other side of the road, and without having to cross the river. It'll be a long walk. Let's go on over the fields now and try not to lose contact with the road. It's our guiding line.'

'I am willing,' she said.

They went on at a steady trudge, through the darkness and over fields lying fallow and fields full of ploughed furrows. They climbed innumerable gates. He always climbed first and moved on in polite regard for her modesty. Sophia, very much a woman and owning her share of woman's endearing perversity, began to get angry with him, and this confounded her confusion.

Aware that her firm chin was up, Captain Marsh said, 'I feel I've upset you again.'

'Our relationship is awkward, as you said, but – ' She stopped, knowing her feelings to be quite ridiculous. 'It's of no importance.'

'What isn't?'

'I am used to men being a little gallant, at least. The gates are all very high.'

'Sophia?'

'It's not important,' she said, at which another gate loomed up. He climbed it. He turned, and she was angry with herself for her absurdity. She ignored the hand he extended. She hitched her skirts. Her silken-clad legs glimmered. She began to climb. He reached with both hands and, despite his painful fingers, took hold of her waist, swung her lightly upwards and over and deposited her feet gently on the ground. Flushed, she said, 'Thank you.'

'Look,' he said, and her eyes strained until the vague outline of buildings crept into her vision.

'A farmhouse?' she whispered.

'I think so.'

'Be careful of dogs,' she said. The dogs of French farmers were fiercely aggressive at the smell of intruders.

'Even the French farmers have been short of meat for their families. Most of their dogs have been eaten.'

'So have all our German dogs.'

'Touché,' said Captain Marsh with a smile. 'It's time we took a rest. We can't walk all night. We'll be dead on our feet at a moment when we might need to run fast. And if, as you say, that road is going to be busy all night, we may not be able to cross it until dawn. It'll be quiet then. My squadron will be over on patrol. Let's take a look at these farm buildings.'

He advanced cautiously, reaching bare, trodden ground. Sophia followed, the same question hammering at her mind. What was she doing? She could have been free of him, so what was she doing?

The blank wall of a brick building loomed darkly. They skirted it and turned at the end of it, feeling their careful way. They smelled farm animals. They reached a sturdy door, its top half open. A stable. Captain Marsh felt for the latch, lifted it and opened the lower half. In a stall, a plough horse stirred, lightly shaking the mane of its drooping head. Against a wall, piled straw offered primitive comfort. Sophia sank down. The banked straw rustled and yielded beneath her body. Tiredness returned then.

'Will it do?' whispered Captain Marsh, peering down at her dim form.

'Yes.'

'We must be awake and away before dawn.'

She was languid. The stable smell was a warm one. She was almost murmurous as she said, 'If there are chickens here, the cock will wake us up.'

He smiled and took off the greatcoat. He hesitated, knowing her capable of rejecting it, but she had said something about gallantry. He smiled again and placed the coat over her. Its extra warmth was a physical luxury to her, and she closed her eyes. Her body sought sleep and her confused mind sought oblivion.

He came down beside her after a while, sharing the bed of straw with her at a modest distance, and in the darkness he pondered on the fact that life was unpredictable and events took their own course. His feelings towards this unbowed German girl were a sign that man could not govern the consequences of his acts or equate emotions with reason.

Sophia slept. Captain Marsh listened. There

was not a sound except for her even breathing and the occasional little scurry of field mice. The farm buildings were locked in by the night, and the farmer and his wife were no doubt sleeping the sleep of the just, the deserving and the hardy.

His heavy lids fell. He slept. They both slept. The hours slipped away. Sophia did not move. Neither did he.

Chapter Ten

In the east the dawn was beginning to break, the dark horizon showing a streak of grey. The chickens rustled on their perches. Outside, the cock strutted. When Sophia woke up, grey light was penetrating the stable. She felt warm and dreamy. She saw a figure beside her. The dreaminess rushed from her. Reality took over. She sat up, throwing off the greatcoat. Her sudden movement brought Captain Marsh awake, and he was at once on his feet, his eyes darting as if the enemy was on his tail. Sophia stared up at him, at his set face and stiff figure, outlined by creeping grey dawn.

'You are not in the sky,' she said.

His face relaxed and was warmed by a smile, and Sophia, who felt the night had dispelled her clouds, was shocked as confusion returned.

'I was dreaming,' he said, and ran a hand through his thick, untidy hair. He looked around. The seeping light was spreading, painting the whitewashed stable walls a pale grey.

The implications of retreating darkness aroused him to urgency. 'We must go,' he said, 'or the farmer will kick us out and pepper us.'

'I am ready,' she said, avoiding his eyes.

Seeing the tumbling mass of her bright hair, he asked, 'Where's your hat?'

'Lost,' she said.

'Where?'

'How do I know?' She forced herself into hostility. She stood up, brushed past him, went to the door and looked out at the encroaching dawn. He came up beside her. He saw the strutting cock, proud in the new light.

'There may be an egg or two we can take,' he said.

'If there are eggs, there must be chickens,' she said, 'so why take only the eggs? Why not wring one poor creature's neck and take that too?'

'Yes, why not? I've some French francs we can leave in payment.'

She looked at him, her blue eyes searching.

'How very considerate of you,' she said.

'It seems only fair,' he said as they emerged into misty grey. He made his way towards a tumbledown chicken house. Entering, he saw four eggs nestling in the straw-lined boxes, laid overnight. He put them carefully into the pockets of the greatcoat. The chickens began to squawk, hop and run about. The cock, mottling with anger, crowed in hoarse rage. A gate banged. Sophia called out.

'Quickly! Run!'

He came out at the double, and they ran, both of them, into the spreading dawn light and into the fields. The farmer, out of his house, shook a furious fist at them.

It was seven-thirty in the morning before two mechanics from the transport depot arrived at the Lutargne auberge with a new distributor head for Major Kirsten's car. It had been impossible to make the journey overnight, they said. However, it did not take long to fit the new head. Major Kirsten then collected Elissa from her room. They went downstairs to settle their small bill with Pierre Gascoigne. He was polishing his counter. He accepted the settlement courteously.

Major Kirsten smiled.

'By the way, m'sieur,' he said, 'I believe you had other guests here last night.'

The proprietor, ready for this, shrugged philosophically and said, 'Am I to understand he was one of your men, *mon Commandant*?'

'Tell me about him,' said the major, while Elissa stood by. She had had a good night's sleep and felt very refreshed. The excitements of yesterday had given her a lively anticipation of what today might bring forth.

With another shrug, Pierre Gascoigne said,

'I must betray a confidence, it seems. Yes, there were two other guests, a German soldier and his lady friend. They asked for a room and a little supper. They also asked for nothing to be said, he being only a private, and a German one, you understand, and she being obviously of good family.'

'Of good German family?' enquired the major.

'German? I thought her French,' said the proprietor truthfully. 'She spoke in French, and so did the soldier.'

'Ah, so?' said the major with a lift of an eyebrow.

'I felt, *mon Commandant*, that he had absented himself without permission and hoped to return to his unit before his absence was noticed. They were only here a few hours and seemed most attached to each other. So I kept quiet about them, which in my trade is often part of the service guests expect.'

'Describe them, if you would, m'sieur,' said Major Kirsten, and Elissa wondered if his appreciation of his opponent's finesse was good or bad for the proprietor.

Since Pierre Gascoigne had received descriptions yesterday from a German lieutenant in charge of a search party, and would therefore have been expected to recognize and report persons who fitted, he embarked on specious descriptions of his own. Major Kirsten listened admiringly.

'So that is how you saw them,' he said.

'I'm not an unobservant man,' said the proprietor with a straight face.

'Some are gifted in this respect, m'sieur, and some are not. I've known several people describe the same man in a way that indicated they all saw him differently. However, thank you for your information, and I quite understand the discretion you exercise on behalf of any guests in need of it.'

'We have a good reputation as hosts, *mon Commandant*,' said Pierre Gascoigne, without the flicker of an eyelash. 'May I ask, am I right in thinking you to be the man's commanding officer?'

'If I am, and if he was indeed a man whose presence here was suspect, I came very close to catching him out.' Major Kirsten looked as if that amused him. 'I think we can say – ah, you didn't give me his name.'

'I didn't ask him for it, *mon Commandant*.'

'Or the young lady?'

'Neither of them,' said Pierre Gascoigne.

'Extremely discreet of you, m'sieur.'

Recognizing the major as a man who could respond to equivocation with satire, Pierre Gascoigne smiled politely. The major nodded, and he and Elissa left.

'He was very plausible,' said Elissa on their way to the car.

'Had the war been in its infancy, we might

have found the time and inclination to knock a few holes in his story,' said Major Kirsten. 'As things are, we can let him rest. We've at least discovered that our thinking lunatic has acquired a German uniform. That's in addition to a beautiful young German lady and the distributor head of our car. How has he managed so much with Sophia as his prisoner? Heavens, one might suppose she's been more of a help to him than a burden.'

'With a revolver in my ribs, Major, I should be a weak creature myself,' said Elissa.

'A point,' conceded the major. 'Now – wait, I think before we leave I'll telephone Colonel Hoffner. He may have some new information, and he at least needs to know the quarry now looks like a German soldier.'

Elissa sat in the car to wait. When Major Kirsten returned, he took his seat beside her looking very intrigued. He informed her that Colonel Hoffner had received a telephone call late last night from Captain Vorster. This concerned a Bugatti car containing a luggage case with a label bearing the name of Sophia von Feldermann. There was no one in the car. It had apparently been abandoned some ten kilometres from Douai, close to the road leading from Denain, forty kilometres southeast of Douai. A dispatch rider had arrived at Headquarters in Valenciennes with a scribbled report for General von Feldermann. The general had passed it to Captain Vorster and told him to deal with it. Captain Vorster had telephoned Colonel Hoffner, no doubt because he had been told to as a first step. The colonel had sent two men to mount a watch on the car in case the general's daughter returned to it. So far she had not.

'Colonel Hoffner now knows who she is,' said Elissa.

'Yes. A pity. It's an embarrassment for the general.'

'Major, why didn't Colonel Hoffner telephone you with this news last night?'

'Because at the time when I spoke to him from this place in the evening, I told him I'd be moving on. A little later, when I decided we should hang around, I omitted to let him know.'

'The car is still where it was left?' asked Elissa.

'It is. I have the location. We'll go there.'

'Yes, Major,' said Elissa and started the staff car. 'Do you think the Bugatti was abandoned because the Englishman suddenly found the road far too crowded and therefore far too risky? Last night four divisions were due to move up. Many roads would have been busy for hours.'

'You have such information at your finger-tips?' Major Kirsten smiled approvingly at her. 'You're a remarkable young lady, Elissa. And you're right. Our man was forced to leave the car and run for it, taking our suffering Sophia with him. Let's get going. I'll read the map for you.'

'I hope I shall be up to coping with new events,' said Elissa.

'You will,' said Major Kirsten. Lieutenant Landsberg was indeed a gem, he thought. She was also rather appealing. 'Colonel Hoffner, by the way, has dispatched a new search party.'

As she drove away from the auberge, Elissa said, 'But you would still like us to find Miss von Feldermann?'

'Yes, I would.'

Captain Marsh put a finger on his map.

'We're somewhere around here,' he said.

He and Sophia were sheltering just inside a wood, facing a terrain of rolling, undulating fields, and he had made a guess that the Nord river was a few kilometres to the west, with a main road in between. He felt he and Sophia were about eight kilometres from Douai.

Sophia, sitting beside him, her back against a tree, looked at the spot he was indicating on the map. Hatless, her long fair hair was loose and flowing.

'I imagine you're right,' she said.

It had been some time since they had left that farm at a run. They had trekked across country, avoiding using roads of any kind, and had gone to ground more than once when sighting farmworkers. Once they had heard the noise of slow-moving vehicles that reminded them of yesterday's pursuers. Today, Captain Marsh knew the hunters were undoubtedly aware of Sophia's abandoned Bugatti, and Sophia knew her luggage case would have been inspected. Also, Captain Marsh had left the German helmet in the car.

'We might consider making a dash across this other road,' he said, 'and using the river as our guide to Douai.'

'Swimming?' said Sophia. Her nerves were on edge, and she was sensitive to every movement he made beside her.

'I don't think either of us would care for that. But I'd very much like to get close enough to Douai so that we could slip into the town by dark. I suppose I might have to find a boat, while you could simply use the bridge.'

'You've agreed to help me reach Douai,' she said. 'That doesn't mean I want to be delivered into the arms of the guards on the bridge. Because of my father, every German soldier in Douai is probably looking for me. You had better think of something better than depositing me on the bridge.'

He laughed. He thought her very droll in the way she had put that. Sophia, affected by so many confusing emotions and so many nerve-racking incidents, felt a rush of temper so wild that she slapped his face. Jaw tingling, he stared at her in astonishment, then shook his head and laughed again.

That sent her out of all her senses, and she went for him. Because of all her humiliations and inexplicable actions, she launched herself at him in an uncontrollable desire to scratch. He caught her wrists, holding her off. She wrenched them free. Then they were locked in impossible confrontation, rolling over leaf mould and twigs, he in shock and she like a provoked tigress.

'Sophia, for God's sake – '

'How dare you laugh at me, how dare you!'

He held her, for her own sake, pinning her arms, and she stared fiercely up at him, eyes glittering and body twisting and heaving. Her hair was all about her head and face, her mouth exhaling tortured breath. Hating him, she brought one knee sharply up. It punched his stomach hard. It hurt. What with that and the pain of his broken finger, there was no help for what he did next, not in his own mind. He kissed her, pressing his lips firmly to hers. Her involuntary cry was smothered. The craziest sensations of suffering engulfed her. Her writhing body stiffened and sagged. Shudders travelled through her, tormenting every limb. Her imprisoned lips tightened as she clenched her teeth, resisting the kiss, only for incalculable reaction to take such a hold of her that her teeth parted and her lips yielded.

The kiss, prolonged and hungry, stupefied them both.

He lifted his head and looked down at her crimson face, his expression that of a man confronted by the unimaginable.

'Sophia – I'm sorry, desperately sorry – forgive me. That was unpardonable – I'm sorry.'

She turned her face away, her body hot and clamouring, her senses reeling. Her dizzy eyes took in movement, the movement of an approaching man. He wore the thick blue blouse and black trousers of a French peasant, and over his shoulder was a spade. He was walking towards the wood, straight towards them.

'There's a man,' she gasped.

'Quickly, we must move.'

'No – it's too late – we must do this.' She wound her arms around his neck. He came out of stupefying incredulity and played the game of pretence with her, his mouth moving lightly over her cheek. For all the pretence, Sophia's body shivered. They heard the man enter the wood, his booted feet turning winter leaves. He saw them. Sophia, lying on her back, with Captain Marsh beside her and leaning over her, stared up at the Frenchman in simulated shock. Sturdy and weatherbeaten, surprise slowing his trudge, his eyes opened wide. To him, the picture was of a man in a German greatcoat enjoying a tender moment with a lovely young lady whose face was deeply flushed and whose magnificent blonde hair was dishevelled. He said nothing. He walked on, going through the wood to the farmland beyond.

Sophia sat up, trembling, her face averted. Captain Marsh, aware that his behaviour had been unforgivable, was at a loss for the right words.

'Sophia – '

'You should not have laughed at me,' she said, her voice husky.

'I know that now.'

'I have never behaved like that before, like an uncivilized Russian peasant. I am ashamed of myself.'

'I'm hardly proud of what I did. You must forgive me.'

Sophia, face still averted, every emotion indefinable, said, 'Do you always cure hysteria in a woman in that way?'

'No, and I've never had to. And you weren't hysterical, only very angry.' Captain Marsh was intensely penitent. 'Believe me, I wasn't laughing at you, I simply thought that what you said about not wanting to be deposited on a bridge – and the way you said it – was irresistible.'

'Do you mean ridiculous?' She sounded cold.

'No. Delicious.'

'That is not a word that should be used between two people at war with each other,' said Sophia, and forced herself to think again of Fritz. Fritz was so necessary to her; they had so much in common concerning the absurdities of the high and mighty. She knew he wanted them to become lovers. And they would, yes, they would.

'Sophia, I must—' Captain Marsh broke off as the sky, full of scudding March clouds and stretches of blue, erupted with sound. It was a sound familiar to him, an aerial dogfight. They were far in over the German lines, the British or French planes up there, and it had to be a flight from Richtofen's squadron that was engaging them. He came quickly to his feet and walked to the edge of the wood. He looked upwards, searching the sky. The planes were high, too high for him to distinguish between Allied and German, but there they were, those that were out of the clouds. They seemed invisibly linked in the flowing pattern of their manoeuvres. From the ground, there was no impression of speed. Rather, they seemed to float, to drift, or to lazily dance. The noise of their engines was like a power-charged buzzing, with a varying pitch intermittently interrupted by the sound of machine-gun fire. On the rim of the deadly dance, the pattern broke as two planes angled in descent. Noses down, they plunged. Other planes followed in diving pursuit. Unidentifiable shapes gradually materialized into recognizable machines. The first two were German – Fokker triplanes. Chasing them were four Sopwith Camels. The

Fokkers screamed and the Camels whined. Out of the high blue descended another formation, a flight of Albatros planes which had been lying in wait while the Fokkers dallied to bait the Camels.

The Fokkers came out of their dive, their paint as blue as the sky, and began to fly fast to the north. The Camels held to the chase, roaring after them in reckless unawareness that they had been lured and tempted. The Albatros formation closed in on them from above.

The Fokkers and Camels streamed northwards. The Albatros machines, red markings vivid, split formation to attack the Camels from the rear. The Camels, pilots suddenly alerting to the trap about to be sprung, stood up, left the Fokkers alone, and soared towards the clouds in fast ascent. The Albatroses followed. The sailing clouds received the Camels. The red machines of Richtofen's squadron veered, skirting the white to climb high into the blue and into the sun.

The sounds were lost and the planes became invisible.

'The war is going on up there?' Sophia appeared beside Captain Marsh, her face lifted, her eyes straining in search of the unseen planes. A brisk eddy of wind caught her hair and tossed the strands around her head.

'Yes, it's still going on.'

'And I have a few scars of my own now,' said Sophia, hands thrust into her coat pocket and her eyes turning to scan the countryside.

He felt unable to comment on that. He listened to the distant rumbling of British batteries near Arras. The Allied armies had been relatively quiet of late, taking something of a rest after four years of devastating conflict. The launching of a new offensive awaited the arrival of General Pershing's American forces.

He searched his conscience. Early yesterday morning, which now seemed ages ago, the unexpected appearance of a car and its lady driver at the scene of his crash-landing had seemed entirely fortuitous, especially as he had assumed she was French. Should he have let her go when he discovered she was German? He had not been in the mood to, and her car had been too valuable to him. And he had, after all, been shot down by a mercilessly persistent Richtofen, a hero to her. He had not felt disposed to play the gentleman. Unwilling though she had naturally been to cooperate with him, her usefulness had become important, and the complex challenge she presented as a spirited German girl had never been less than intriguingly mettlesome. She was undeniably beautiful. That fact had merely been noticeable at first. Now it was disturbing. He had said theirs was an awkward relationship. From the moment he had compulsively kissed her, it had become an impossible one, especially for her.

'I was wrong in forcing you to help me,' he said, 'and I made things far worse by my moment of insanity a little while ago. If you wish to see me hanged, I'd not blame you.'

'No?' Sophia was doing some searching of her own. Not of her conscience, but her emotions. And she was discovering nothing comfortable about any of them. She should have killed him for his assault on her lips. It was the second of two such assaults. She had the means to kill him, her long and deadly hatpin, taken from her hat yesterday evening. It had caused her to lose the hat, but that had been a small thing compared with the gain to her defensive strength. But she had not used the long steel pin when he had kissed her. It had been to hand, threaded in the skirt of her coat, but she had not even thought about it. Instead, her lips had betrayed her, clinging to his in crazy response. Worse, immediately afterwards, she had acted to give a French farmworker the impression that she and Captain Marsh were a harmless courting couple, and that he was not the English airman everyone in the area must know was wanted by the Germans. The act had no rationality at all to it, for no one, in any case, would expect a Frenchman to run to any Germans with his suspicions loud on his tongue. What was she doing, what was happening to her? With an effort, she said, 'Yes, it was unforgivable of you, but I would rather you said nothing more about it.'

She could not help the bitter note, aimed as much at herself as him. He had in a single day brought her to the edge of a strange darkness and made her foothold perilously insecure. She recalled the moment when he had saved her from the icy canal. She knew that that had its own association with her sense of insecurity.

Her eyes, still fixed on fields and pastures, failed to register the implications of distant movements until she heard Captain Marsh draw a quick breath.

Then she gasped, 'Look!'

He drew her back into the shelter of the trees. From there, they peered into the distance. The crisp March sunlight played its revealing part. The movements resolved into the definable figures of soldiers on foot, an extended line of them, advancing steadily in an obvious and methodical search of the terrain. Captain Marsh felt his chances were narrowing. The Germans had to know by now that he was on foot.

'They'll reach us. They'll surround this place,' said Sophia. Why she felt sad she did not know, unless it was because they would take her as well as Captain Marsh, and escort her back to her father. But was it so desperately vital, her assignation with Fritz? Her mother could not, in the end, stop her marrying him. She would never literally chain her up. Even so, she felt inexplicably sad as she watched the long line of soldiers advancing.

'We'll be surrounded if we stay here,' said Captain Marsh. 'They know we've no car now. They probably think – ' He paused, and she saw a faint smile. 'They probably think I've a gun to your head.'

'In effect,' said Sophia quietly, 'you have had a gun to my head from the beginning.'

'Yes, and that's what you must tell everyone. On no account must you admit to anyone that there was a time when you weren't under duress.'

'What do you mean?' she asked.

'There's no time for a discussion now. If you're still determined to get to Fritz we must move. If we break out on the other side of this wood, we'll at least be shielded while we make a run for new cover.'

'I will come,' she said.

They cast a final glance at the oncoming searchers, then turned and made a quick way through the wood. Emerging, they were faced by the familiar vistas of farmlands, wandering hedges and a few wooded areas. Away to the left was a barn, large and isolated. Everything looked very quiet. Not a single person could be seen. As far as northern France was concerned, Sophia was beginning to believe that all but a few of its men were in the trenches.

'We shall be seen,' she said. 'There's nowhere we can hide except behind hedges.'

'We can't stay here,' said Captain Marsh, and they began to move over the open ground. 'Do you see that copse down there beyond the barn? If we can get to it, and then to that other patch of trees farther on and to the left, we'd have the barn between us and them, providing we made our dash at the right moment. Then we'd have to think about circling back to get behind them. It's the one way to escape them. Run, Sophia – that is, if you want to.'

She ran with him. He headed fast for the first objective, Sophia behind him, picking up her skirts and freeing her supple legs. He was going away from her, and she had a feeling he was ready to separate himself from her, to give her the freedom to choose her own way. If he thought to ease his conscience by doing that, he was not allowing for her bitter determination to see he did not. She lengthened her stride. As they began to pass the open end of the high barn on their left, he pulled up so sharply that she almost ran into him. He turned very quickly and plunged into the barn, Sophia following.

'We're in trouble,' he said.

'But those soldiers haven't reached the wood yet.'

She stiffened as he took her by the arm and drew her cautiously forward to the opening.

'Take a look to the left,' he said, 'but don't show yourself. If they're moving fast, they've seen us.'

She peered out. Rising from a dip in the distance, in line with the second copse he had pointed out, she saw more men. They were strung out in much the same way as the soldiers, and they too were advancing on the wood, but from the opposite direction. They were Luftwaffe men. She did not, however, think they were moving fast. She drew back.

'All this is because my father is not a man to sit and do nothing,' she said. 'Even at a time like this, he has managed to organize a comprehensive search for me.'

'A time like this?' said Captain Marsh. 'What does that mean?'

Sophia, angry with herself at her new indiscretion, said, 'It means you've turned my absence into a crisis. It means my father will find me, and you too.'

'I don't think I want to stay here and make it easy for him.'

'You can't run any more,' she said. 'You'll be seen as soon as you leave this barn.'

'I'll risk it,' he said.

'No, wait.'

'Sophia, it's time we parted.'

'No, wait,' she said again, and looked

around the barn. There was a large hayloft, pitchforks and, hanging from a hook, an old leather apron. 'We've a few minutes before anyone gets here. I still want to reach Douai. Give me your scarf and boots. Where did you get those boots?'

'I found them.'

'Never mind. Give them to me, and your scarf. Quickly.'

'Sophia – '

'Quickly!' Sophia was agitated but insistent. 'Do you want to get away or not?'

He unwound his flying scarf from beneath the collar of the greatcoat. She bound it around her head, tucking up and hiding her hair, and it became a good imitation of a peasant woman's scarf. He took off the black boots given to him by Pierre Gascoigne. She unlaced her own boots, rather more elegant than his, and put the black boots on. She removed her coat and gloves, lifted the large leather apron from its hook and donned it. It hid most of her dress. She stooped, swept her hands over the dusty floor of the barn and rubbed a little of the dirt into her face. He watched in amazement as she turned herself into a farmworker with a dust-marked face and very dirty hands.

'For God's sake, what are you doing?' he asked.

'Making myself presentable – in a way,'

she said. 'When the men arrive, I'll speak no German, only French.' She pointed to a huge pile of loose hay beside the barn ladder. 'That's your only chance, not the loft. They'll search the loft. Take my coat and boots. Put my coat over yourself, because when they come in I shall stick a pitchfork into the pile of hay. With my coat and that greatcoat, the prongs shouldn't bite you. I must make them think that whoever might be hiding in the loft, there's no one under that hay on the floor.'

'Do you know what you're doing?' said Captain Marsh.

'No – I don't,' said Sophia. They listened. The wood they had left was alive with the sounds of men. 'I don't know what I'm doing at all, or why, except that I'm as determined to live my own life as you are to escape. We are reluctant partners. Bury yourself under that hay, lying flat, or stand there and do nothing and be of no help to me or yourself.'

He spent a few precious seconds trying to understand her, but Sophia did not even understand herself – or if she did she closed her mind to it.

'Sophia, for God's sake, if this doesn't work, do you realize just how suspect your part in it will look?'

'Hide yourself,' she whispered.

Taking her boots, gloves and coat, he moved to the pile of fallen hay. He could hear the German soldiers clearly now. They were breaking out of the wood. He made a deep rift in the hay, uncovering the floor. He lay on his back and put her coat over himself. Quickly, she began to pile the hay thickly above him, using a pitchfork. She massed the hay high. She heard them coming, the soldiers, she heard their voices. She heard them at the entrance to the barn. She turned, the black boots feeling big and clumsy on her feet.

Five soldiers were looking at her, their rifles slung and their faces in shadow beneath their low helmets. She heard others outside the barn, moving around it. The five men entered and glanced about them, noting the loft. Sophia wondered how the situation would develop if a farmworker arrived, or the farmer himself. Her heart, beating fast, beat faster. She knew herself to be quite mad.

The dry barn smelled sweetly of fodder. Its size interested the soldiers. Sophia's ragged nerves became raw, but she said nothing. The men wandered about and looked. She stood motionless, eyeing them as she supposed a Frenchwoman would, impassively and without welcome. She knew she must be distant and un-helpful. That was how most French people were towards Germans, although it was the French who had declared war.

Eyes were on her. They were seeing her, she hoped, as the hard-working daughter of a

French farmer, or simply as a French peasant. The madness of her role hammered at her mind.

One man broke the silence.

'Miss?' he said.

Chapter Eleven

Elissa and Major Kirsten had reached the abandoned Bugatti in good time. Elissa, turning off the road into the farm opening, drew up behind Sophia's car. There appeared to be no one about, but moments after they had alighted a corporal materialized out of thin air. He came to attention and saluted.

'Corporal Haussen of Garrison A Company, Major.'

'Have you been here all night?' asked the major.

'No, only since seven-thirty this morning, Major, when I relieved Corporal Weiss of B Company. Also present is Private Kreik. He's—'

'Yes, somewhere about.' Major Kirsten waved an airy hand. With Elissa, he inspected the Bugatti. The ignition key was there. So was a German helmet. And in the luggage compartment was a case. 'Corporal, anything to report?'

Corporal Haussen, impressed by the bearing

of an officer with a scarred eye and a missing left arm, drew himself smartly up and said, 'Nothing, Major, except that a platoon from Douai garrison arrived here at eight-fifteen, and the officer in charge questioned me. I informed him I had noticed nothing, nor had Corporal Weiss who was on duty during the night. I was then told to advise you that a search of the area was to be commenced.'

'It commenced from here?'

'No, Major. The platoon drove off, intending to proceed until they were in a position to begin a sweep over the fields from west to east.'

'There was no search of this immediate locality?'

'No, Major.'

'Thank you, Corporal Haussen. You may resume your hidden watch in company with Private Kreik.'

Corporal Haussen saluted and disappeared, thinking Major Kirsten somewhat luckier than he was. He only had Private Kreik, a morose comrade, for company. Major Kirsten had a very nice-looking WAC officer.

'I should have thought Colonel Hoffner's men would have spent a little time here,' said Elissa.

'And they no doubt thought that would be time wasted, that the quarry would not have lingered. But you have a point.'

Elissa saw a gate a little way down the rutted

farm track. It led into a long ploughed field. She felt she could read what had happened. Although the road was fairly quiet now, it had been jammed with moving infantry last night. The Bugatti, which was pointing at the gate, had obviously been driven off the road in order to avoid being trapped or stopped. Just as obviously, it had been noticed. That would have been the moment when the RFC pilot abandoned it, taking the unfortunate Sophia von Feldermann with him. Regrettably, that seemed to indicate he really did mean to use her as some kind of hostage when the last of his luck ran out.

'Where are they, I wonder?' she asked in concern.

'Yes, and why did he take Sophia with him when he left the car?' mused Major Kirsten, making his own survey of the gate and the ploughed field. 'On foot, she would have been twice the burden, making her value as a hostage a very wearisome responsibility.'

'He would think her worth the effort, Major, if he means to try to exchange her for his freedom. Is there no honour among men of war?'

'I'm afraid this kind of war drains most of us of our finer feelings,' said Major Kirsten, beginning a walk to the gate and taking Elissa with him. 'Millions have died. Those of us who are left have few illusions.'

That disturbed Elissa.

'Major, if you were on the run behind Allied lines, would you consider forcing a French-woman to help you escape?'

'I'd regard my escape as more important to me and the Fatherland than the sensitivities of a hostile Frenchwoman. Yes, I'd consider it.'

'Is soldiering a brutalizing thing?'

They halted at the gate, and Major Kirsten said, 'Soldiering is a career based on the high ideals of defending one's country against its enemies. It's war which is brutalizing, Lieu-tenant. Now, where is our audacious friend and his hostage? I doubt if they moved very far during the night. They'd have wandered in circles, exhausting themselves. I've a feeling he'd be wise enough to avoid that. Let's assume he sensibly went to ground and began to move again about dawn. Have you thought about the fact that if he's making for Douai, his objective would suit Sophia? Her own objective is certainly Captain Fritz Gerder, who's there at the moment.'

'I can't believe she would be a willing com-panion to an English pilot,' said Elissa. Amid the vista of farmlands far to the right, she picked out a huddled cluster of buildings. 'Is that a farmhouse? Shall we enquire there?'

'It's quite a walk, but why not?' said Major Kirsten. 'I make assumptions which are entirely improbable, and you make suggestions entirely practical. Together, we may come to make a perfect team – acting, of course, on the practical.'

'I'm modest in my hopes,' said Elissa.

They opened the gate. It squealed on its grinding hinges. They made their way along the edge of the field, a hedge on their right. Another gate showed in the distance. The major looked with interest at crumbling depressions in ploughed ridges. Midway, Elissa pointed. Just ahead, between two ridges, lay a lady's black and white hat. Elissa picked it up. Its pin was missing. A pin was very necessary if the wearer was driving an open car. She explained that to Major Kirsten.

'It's Sophia's hat, I can tell you that,' he said, his sounder eye glinting. 'Is the missing pin significant except to tell us that's why the hat fell off? How did it fall off and why did she leave it?'

'Major, did she attempt to resist here? I'm sure these are their footmarks.'

The furrows looked trampled, the crisp ridges broken in parts, though all that Sophia had done at this point was to wrench herself free from Captain Marsh's supportive arm.

'You're suggesting,' said the major, 'that Sophia felt either her life or her virtue to be in such danger that she had to attack him or resist him, and pulled out her hatpin to do so?'

An entirely unpleasant picture presented itself to Elissa.

'Major, no, I can't think he'd have actually attacked her, not for any reason. He's desperate, perhaps, but still an officer.' Elissa noted Major Kirsten's raised eyebrow. 'I think she probably refused to go any further with him and made an attempt to escape him.'

'Certainly, it doesn't look as if her hatpin drew blood. If these are their footmarks, they continue on.' Major Kirsten smiled, looking as if his sabbatical in company with his trim assistant was proving even more stimulating than he had expected. 'Assuming there was some kind of struggle, we can further assume he came out none the worse for it. I hope we can say the same about Sophia.'

They reached the second gate. It was padlocked. Elissa climbed it, and the major experienced a moment of frank pleasure at the shapeliness of her legs. The familiar faint pink touched her face. Alighting on the other side, she said, 'Do French farmers lock many of their gates?'

'I hope not, if there are others to climb,' said the major. He took his turn to climb. Elissa, aware of his handicap, was pleased when he sensibly said, 'May I borrow your hand? I'm still a little clumsy at some things.' She reached out. Their gloved hands gripped and he swung himself over. 'Thank you, Elissa.'

It was a long walk to the farmhouse and its adjacent buildings. There were other gates, most of them locked. Elissa negotiated them quite athletically, the major with a little help. They found the farmer, a typically earthy and insular Frenchman who, in response to questions put by Elissa, complained bitterly that all he knew was that as he was dressing at first light, his chickens set up the kind of screeching row he could only associate with an intruding fox. He rushed out, but there was no fox. There were only disturbed chickens and no eggs. Usually, this time of the year, there were a few overnight lays to collect. There were none this morning. Someone had stolen them. But that was how it was these days, the trials of war making thieves of everyone.

'This was at dawn, you say?' said Elissa.

'Yes, I did say that.' The farmer was growlingly irritable. He was never happy, anyway, when Germans in field-grey appeared. 'Don't ask me who they were. They were too slippery for me.'

'They?' Elissa's smile was encouraging 'You saw more than your disturbed chickens, then?'

'Not at first,' said the farmer. He had to answer, however hostile he felt. German field-grey commanded answers of some kind. 'Then I saw them. Over there.' He waved an irritable hand towards his pastures. 'They were running, a man and a woman. Am I to be interrogated because I didn't catch them? Name of a thief, was I at my age expected to chase after them with my boots still unlaced? I've enough to do as it is without—'

'We are not expecting anything of you, m'sieur, except the truth,' said Elissa in her quiet way. 'Could you describe them?'

'No, I couldn't, they were already too far away. With my eggs. And a chicken or two as well if I hadn't come out. But whether you like it or not, one of them looked like a German soldier to me.'

Major Kirsten interposed.

'Why did he look like a German soldier?'

'He was wearing a German greatcoat.'

'I see. And they were running together?'

'Together?' The farmer stared sourly at Major Kirsten.

'Side by side, like thieves who were comrades?' suggested the major.

'How else would two thieves run off?' The farmer was heavily sarcastic, conceding nothing to German omnipotence except the necessity of answering. 'They were together, they ran off together, and that's all I know. Except,' he added on a note of growling satisfaction, 'one of them was a German thief.'

'In that case, allow me to restore our good name,' said Major Kirsten blandly, and dropped a little French silver into the farmer's large hand. 'And thank you for your help.'

The farmer's expression was one of indifference. To him, all Germans were intruders, and a few coins could not change his mind about that. All the same, he pocketed them.

Major Kirsten and Elissa began the walk back to the car.

'Very intriguing,' murmured the major. 'They ran off together. Is it possible that Sophia has now accepted they've a common interest and might as well run hand in hand?'

'Major, you can't be serious,' said Elissa. The March sky was again a mixture of cold clouds and blue patches, and somewhere a plane's engine was droning. 'How could they have a common interest? Sophia must hate the man by now.'

'No doubt. But they're both in flight; he in the hope of vanishing, and Sophia in the hope of landing in the arms of what she thinks is love.'

'Perhaps it is love,' said Elissa, who had made much the same comment before. 'You are saying flight is their common interest?'

'We know they spent the night together, and we know they didn't leave until dawn. We've guessed they're heading for Douai. Now we can be certain of it. Elissa, there was no suggestion from the farmer that Sophia was under coercion. In fact, if they did snatch some eggs, I've a feeling they'll have managed to cook them together and eat them together. We human beings are very unpredictable, and frequently behave in a way our friends don't expect us to.

We can even puzzle ourselves. Could any of us be certain of how we would react to a situation we had never envisaged?'

'With all due respect, Major,' said Elissa, 'I'm certain I would never run hand in hand with an enemy of my country.'

'You might if you were in a disoriented state. Consider this particular situation.' Major Kirsten paused while Elissa climbed a gate and he followed. 'Two people, a British airman and a German general's daughter, have been indivisible since yesterday morning, mainly because he has seen her as useful to his purpose. Together, they've travelled in a car, shared a room, stolen a distributor head, slept in a farm building and raided a chicken house – from which they ran together. What effect has all that had on a traumatic relationship? Has it made them strange allies?'

'You're worrying me,' said Elissa.

'I'm worrying myself. It's my guess now that they're on a cross-country wander to get as close as they can to Douai in order to try to enter it after dark, which is what I'm sure they were attempting last night, but by car. They were trapped on that road to Douai. So, we'll use our car to make up the time they've gained on us and decide at what point to take to our legs ourselves. If we can, we'll try to get between them and the town.'

'Yes, Major.'

'Miss?' said the German soldier again, since Sophia had not responded.

'You are speaking to me?' asked Sophia in her fluent French.

His own use of the language was laborious as he said, 'We are looking for a man and a young lady.'

'Excuse me?' she said. She saw other soldiers outside the barn, watching the approach of the Luftwaffe search party.

'A man and a woman,' said the spokesman, just as laboriously. 'Have you seen them?'

'You are looking for a French couple?' said Sophia, and stuck the pitchfork into the pile of hay. She felt the prongs strike solidity, but there was no movement. The pitchfork, buried deep, stood up.

'Not French, no,' said the soldier, while his comrades, rifles unslung, began to prowl again. One poked at the pile of hay, disturbing the pitchfork, which fell sideways. Sophia, nerves screaming, picked it up and made a resentful gesture with it. The man grinned and moved away. Simulating irritation, Sophia thrust the pitchfork back into the pile.

'You're asking if they're here?' she said.

'I ask, have you seen them?' said the spokesman impatiently. He was not in the best of tempers. None of them were. This business of chasing an elusive fox was exhausting and unrewarding. All day yesterday, and probably all day today. It wasn't as if they were young. They weren't. Germany was in no position to supply young men for garrison duties. Mangling his French, he said, 'Tell me who you have seen.'

'I've seen only my father and Jacques,' said Sophia. 'Jacques is the only one we have to help us, and even he is too old to be of much use.' She slid loose hay across the floor with her booted foot, towards the pile.

An officer arrived, a middle-aged lieutenant. The soldier spoke to him. He gave Sophia a look, then gestured to the loft. Two soldiers climbed up to it. Using their rifles and boots, they began to search the large mounds of hay. Sophia shrugged and continued clearing the floor of fallen straw, adding it to the pile with her pitchfork. The officer watched her, a frown on his face. He seemed no more enthusiastic than his men. Sophia, heartbeats erratic, thrust the fork into the hay yet again, but this time used it to lift out a heap.

'Are they going to be long poking about?' she asked the officer. 'I've got to get all this up there.'

The officer ignored her complaint. In the loft, the two men kicked at the hay. Sophia tossed her forkful back on to the pile in seeming disgust. The scarf kept her bright hair hidden. The black boots on her feet, obviously men's, would, she hoped, be accepted as practical.

'Mademoiselle.' The officer spoke sharply.

'Yes? Yes?' She looked at him. He did not seem to think much of her dirty face. She prayed her nerves weren't showing. Heaven help me, what am I doing, what am I doing? The man they want is under this hay, and I must say so.

'Have you seen any strangers, any strangers at all?' The question was put in German.

'What is it you're saying?' she asked.

The officer conjured up a few words in French.

'Have you seen a man and a woman on your land today?'

She wanted to cry out, to tell him to look instead of asking questions.

'I've seen no one except my father and old Jacques. I've already said so. Search all over if you want to.'

'Even if you'd seen a thousand British airmen, you're not the kind to say so,' said the officer, but in German. 'You're a dirty-faced French slut.'

'Excuse me?' said Sophia, fighting a surge of hysteria.

'You're an unwashed peasant,' said the officer, and his men grinned at Sophia's look of mystification.

'Excuse me?' she said again.

'Nothing,' he said, and looked bad-tempered

as the two men came down empty-handed from the loft. 'Nothing, mademoiselle.' He accorded her the favour of using French.

'If it's nothing,' said Sophia, 'perhaps your men would help me get this spilled hay back to the loft instead of standing about.'

The officer understood enough of that to take instant offence.

'That's work for you, not German soldiers!' He glared at her, and Sophia wondered if he had been given a detailed description of her, including the colour of her eyes. Her heart was sick and tortured, the soldiers were watching her and the officer shouting at her. Then he turned and strode from the barn. A soldier spoke to a comrade, and Sophia heard herself described as a French ratbag in need of a good wash, and that she had feet as large as an elephant's.

Outside the barn, the Luftwaffe search party had arrived. The two groups mingled and conferred. Sophia, knees perilously weak, stuck the pitchfork into the hay once more and leaned on it. Beneath the pile, Captain Marsh lay still. A hovering soldier said, 'What are you like when you're washed, are you pretty?'

'What are you saying?' asked Sophia, racked with nerves and guilt and self-contempt.

The soldier, close to fifty, gave her a smile that was not unkind.

'You're pretty,' he said. And although he

assumed she could not understand German, he added for good measure, 'Yes, under your dirt that's what I think you are – pretty.'

She put on a look of incomprehension. He wandered away. Another soldier appeared beside her and stirred the pile of hay with a lazy boot. Sophia lifted the pitchfork and shook it at him.

'That's it, make a mess of it,' she shouted.

The soldier, being the one who spoke painful French, laughed at her. He took hold of the pitchfork and wrested it from her, and Sophia knew he was going to scatter the pile. At that moment his officer shouted an order for reassembly. The soldier threw the fork down and vacated the barn with his comrades. The two search parties joined forces and moved away to take up the hunt on a new line, towards Douai. Sophia did not stir, and not until two minutes had passed did she speak.

'Can you hear me?'

'Yes.' The voice was muffled.

'Well, I am telling you not to move, not yet.'

'Haven't they gone?'

'Yes. But I think they may come back. I think the officer wasn't very satisfied.'

I am completely mad, she told herself. Sanity, in conflict with emotions, had disintegrated. She had betrayed Germany and herself.

She went to the entrance, the boots so heavy on her feet. She experienced no surprise when two soldiers came towards the barn from the left, walking quickly. One of them was the man who had taken the fork from her. They passed her without a word and entered the barn. Sophia went in after them.

'Now what do you want?' she asked.

There was no answer. They climbed smartly up to the loft. Sophia knew why. Their officer, dissatisfied, had thought he might catch her out. Of course, he had been looking for two people, not one. In accepting her for what she looked like, he had retained his picture of a British airman and a young woman in a black leather coat. Two people could not have hidden in that pile of hay, but there were possibilities about the loft.

The two soldiers rooted around, talking irritably. They spent little time on the disturbed hay, seeming more suspicious of the boarded walls. They hammered at them with their rifles, and searched for a section that might open. Sophia waited silently until they gave up and came down. Ignoring her, they investigated the lower walls. Finding nothing , they left abruptly, hurrying to catch up with their comrades. They had been looking for a place where two people could hide, not one. Yes. She could have helped them. She had chosen not to.

In a mood of bitter self-dislike, she prodded with the pitchfork and called to Captain Marsh. The large pile of hay heaved and broke apart.

He came to his feet and brushed off clinging straw. He looked at her, his expression very concerned.

'Is Sophia your real name?' he asked.

'My name is for my friends to use, not you,' she said.

'I understand. You've put yourself into a very uncomfortable situation.'

'That worries you?' she said coldly.

'Yes,' he said. 'I'm not an authority on your country's laws in wartime, but I'd say you'd have been put under arrest if your soldiers had found out I was in that hay, no matter whose daughter you were. It was a risk you shouldn't have taken.'

'Then you should have stopped me, shouldn't you?' she said agitatedly.

'Yes,' he said, 'I should have.'

'You could have struck me down and made your run.'

'Struck you down?' he said in astonishment.

'Yes. You're very quick to use violence.'

'Not to that extent.'

'If that means you'd hesitate to actually strike me, I'm grateful.'

Captain Marsh, having spent a nerve-racking time under the hay marvelling at the incredible risks she was taking for him, shook his head at her. It was not difficult to understand that her nerves had been stretched even tighter than his.

'All your feelings are very natural, and you're entitled to relieve them.'

'I'm quarrelling as much with myself as you,' said Sophia. She took off the leather apron and put it back on its hook. She sat down on the pile of hay and removed the clumsy army boots. She unwound the scarf and her bright hair sprang free. He took the boots and scarf, and handed her own boots to her. She put them on, laced them up and rose to her feet. She brushed straw from her dress. He helped her into her coat, his expression still concerned. She refused to meet his eyes. 'Are we to go on our way now?' she asked.

'First, thank you for what you did,' he said. 'It was damned uncomfortable under that hay, but I don't think I suffered half as much as you did. Second, do you want to go as you are, with your face still dirty?'

'Oh.' That vexed her. A charade was a charade, but when it was over what woman liked to be told her nose was still painted red?

'Allow me,' said Captain Marsh, and gave his handkerchief to her. She cleaned off the dust and dirt, using her handbag mirror to inspect herself. Her lips grew tight, for he was smiling at her. 'You're really quite beautiful, aren't you?' he said.

Colour suffused her, angry colour.

'Oh, that is almost indecent!' she cried.

'It was said, Sophia, without—'

'You've no right to say things like that at all!' She was stormy and fretful. 'If you can forget you're at war with my country, I can't. You sided with France for your own ends. Now you're trying to ease your conscience about your treatment of me by telling me something I don't wish to hear – not from you.'

'It was nothing to do with my conscience.'

'I don't care. I'd rather have your incivilities. Go away from me, go away!'

'Yes, that would be the wiser thing to do now. Goodbye, and good luck.'

Quite sure she was mad beyond recovery, she called out as he walked from the barn.

'Come back! You promised me – come back!'

But he went on. She ran after him. He gave her a slightly exasperated look.

'Sophia, this is becoming absurd.'

'You promised to get me to Douai – you know this area far better than I do – you've seen it all from the sky – and there are soldiers looking for me as well as you.'

'But we shouldn't go together, not now,' he said. They were out in the open, recklessly exposed and he was striding fast, Sophia finding it difficult to keep up with him. 'There'll be too many questions asked of you, and no one must suspect you aren't a completely loyal German patriot. You risked too much back there. We must separate.'

'You promised to get me to Douai,' said

Sophia again, 'and that's all I'm concerned about.'

Captain Marsh slowed up and looked at the view. It was still rural, with its dips, its meadows, its farmlands and its patches of woodlands. Douai was only a few kilometres away. The search parties were out of sight. In the distance, where evergreen copses prevailed, he caught a glitter of reflected light. It was too far off to define its source, but he thought there were outlines foreign to the surroundings. He did not like being out in the open. It made him feel vulnerable. He had sold too much of his soul to throw away his chances now. Any moment one search party or the other might reappear. Where were they? Scouting well ahead in the direction of Douai? He began to stride out again.

'Must we go so fast?' asked Sophia.

'It's my nerves, Sophia,' he said with a smile, but he slowed, and they trudged over fields, Sophia suffering guilt and despair because of her inexplicable need to share this journey with him to its bitter end.

What kind of a fighter pilot was he? Skilful and deadly, probably, although he had not been a match for Richtofen. Fritz in an air battle would be a reckless cavalier. That was why she must marry him. He might have so little time left before he was shot down, and while she could she must as his wife give him love and make him happy.

It disturbed her then, that what should sound so right to her now actually seemed naive and even adolescent.

It was adolescent because it was sickly and prudish. If Fritz wanted her, she must not run around looking for a pastor who would marry them. What could marriage mean to him when his chances of survival were so limited? If he wanted her, she must simply give herself to him.

But the decision did not make her feel less disturbed.

'Two centimes for your thoughts,' said Captain Marsh.

'My thoughts are not your concern,' said Sophia.

'We must do better than that, or we'll come to blows again,' he said, intent on reaching the shelter of the evergreens. 'We can improve on meaningless chatter, I hope. I find you very interesting—'

'I don't want you to talk to me like that,' she said, newly agitated. The guns began to rumble ominously, and she wondered if they were German guns, heralding a major bombardment of that sector of the British lines which Ludendorff meant to smash on the opening day of his offensive, according to the conversational Captain Vorster. Captain Vorster had also said Ludendorff was planning to drive a huge wedge between the British and French Armies. Thinking of that, it was curious to hear herself say, 'What is so interesting about me?'

'Everything. Fritz must find you quite endearing.'

'I won't have you say things like that! It's a disgusting familiarity—'

'Sophia – drop down!' Captain Marsh sank fast to his knees, then lay flat out. Sophia flung herself down beside him, then wondered in new despair why every response was so compulsive.

They bedded their bodies in thick, cold pasture. The guns seemed to be rending the sky with thunder. It was a heavy, rolling noise from far off. And somewhere, planes were in the sky. Sophia wanted to put her hands over her ears. Captain Marsh was squinting. She followed his gaze. The pale grey ribbon of a farmland road split the earth, and on that road a car was travelling slowly, an open car. It was not possible to pick out its individual features, but Sophia had a feeling it was not unknown to her.

'Is that – is that the car we immobilized last night?' she whispered.

'You mean the car I immobilized?' he said pointedly.

She realized he was sincere in his concern for her, genuinely worried about the questions she might be asked.

'Yes – is it?'

The little road snaked and wound, and the car seemed to crawl like a beetle. It passed them well to their right and disappeared as the road was lost in the terrain.

'Yes, that was it, I think,' said Captain Marsh. 'Did you notice how slowly it was moving?'

'Yes. With two people in it. Are they looking for us?'

'They were German officers, one of them a woman. We almost bumped into them, you remember.'

'They are looking for us, particularly for me,' said Sophia. 'The man is on my father's staff. I recognized his voice last night.'

'I'm beginning to think that you've elected to go through fire and water for Fritz. Are you so madly in love?'

'That is between Fritz and me, and no one else.'

'I'm intrigued, that's all,' said Captain Marsh. 'I think we'll wait a while before we move, then I suggest we get to those woods and hide there for the rest of the day. I did think of going by the river, but I'm certain we're so close to Douai that we can cross the main road when it's dark and be almost on top of the town. But what's that?'

He squinted again. He made out what had been indefinable before. A clearing between two stretches of woodland. There were buildings like tiny boxes on either side of the clearing. His searching eyes strained. Everything was in miniature at this distance, but he thought that what he was looking at on the clearing itself were three aeroplanes. He could not be sure, but he thought that was what three little objects might just be.

'It's an aerodrome, isn't it?' said Sophia, the same thought in her mind.

'No. The layout isn't right. And it's a little too small.'

She looked at him. His head was up, and his face in profile was strong and vigorous, his expression intrigued. He was a man of warplanes, she supposed, rather than of social graces. His mouth was very firm, very definite, and he was far removed from adolescence or boyishness.

Abruptly, Sophia looked away.

Chapter Twelve

Time was passing, and Elissa thought the day would run away from them all too soon.

'Major,' she said, gloved hands gripping the wheel as the car bounced over the death-defying surface of a road that had nothing good to offer the traveller except its eventual end, 'the morning has gone and I feel we've achieved little more than part of a circular tour.'

'Yes, it's chastening to discover that keen endeavour can lead us nowhere,' said Major Kirsten. 'Apart from finding Sophia's hat and a farmer who growled at us, we've drawn nothing each time we've stopped but a large, discouraging blank. We've no idea at all whether or not we've put ourselves between Douai and our quarry.'

'We did at least make contact with Colonel Hoffner's search party.'

'Comprised of old and grey men, wandering about with an old and grey officer. I'm going to suggest our elusive pair have gone to ground again, that they're hiding somewhere and waiting for darkness. Yes, of course.'

'Of course?' said Elissa, negotiating potholes with care.

'I'm not yet completely discouraged by my inadequacies,' said Major Kirsten, drawing in lungfuls of the cold, healthy air. The car was open to allow them maximum observation. 'I think they're so close to Douai that that's the obvious thing to do. They won't want to scuttle about like rabbits.'

'You're quite convinced they're acting in collusion?' said Elissa.

'I've a feeling, that's all. Look, do you see that wood up there?'

'Yes,' said Elissa, 'we passed it on its other side an hour ago. There's a barn, too. That must be the barn Colonel Hoffner's men told us they'd searched.'

'They also told us there was a girl working in the barn, a dirty and impudent French girl. Elissa, have you ever seen any kind of a French girl parading dirt?'

'Not all over her face,' said Elissa. 'The officer said she looked sluttish with dirt.'

'I'd have liked to see under the dirt myself,' said Major Kirsten. 'Pull up and we'll take a walk.'

'Another one?' said Elissa. They had been pulling up and taking walks frequently. But she came to a halt. 'Major,' she said, as they alighted, 'if we leave the car here, is it possible we shall lose the new distributor head?'

'If that happens, Elissa, I shall dig a hole for myself and leave you to erect a suitable headstone. We'll risk it. In fact, should our mad friend be around, let's tempt him. We can keep the car in sight. If he does appear, we might then discover if he and Sophia are running for the car together, or if she's being dragged.'

They walked to the barn over fields lying fallow. There were a great many fields lying fallow. Everything farmers needed, including seed, was in short supply, and despite the amount of pasture available they had seen nothing in the way of livestock.

Major Kirsten startled Elissa by asking if she had a service revolver.

'No, we aren't issued with weapons of any kind, Major – '

'Don't be alarmed. I've my own revolver in an emergency. In my coat pocket, not my holster.'

Elissa was alarmed, however. She hated the thought of shots being exchanged. But the adrenalin was still flowing, and a sense of excitement still prevailed. She had not yet experienced a really close relationship with a man. She supposed she had been courted once, by a customer who visited the Munich bookshop regularly. He was a friendly and talkative intellectual, she a painfully shy woman

of twenty-two. He was just a little too friendly
at times, always contriving to touch her when
there was no one else in the shop. She began
to dislike it, together with his assumption that
she could not wait to be kissed. Her reactions
worried her. She confided in her mother, a
warm and companionable woman.

'Do you look at men, Elissa?' her mother had
asked.

'Mama, of course I look at them.'

'Do you like what you see?'

'I like what I see in some men. I dislike what
I see in others.'

'Then don't worry. You're discriminating,
that's all. There's nothing wrong with that.
Society expects a woman to behave in a set way,
to be grateful to any man merely for noticing
her. Be discriminating, my dear, rather than
in a hurry. It's better to wait until you're forty
before you marry than to take the wrong man
at twenty-two.'

'Forty? Forty? Mama, who would marry a
woman of forty? Why, even at twenty-two I'm
already an old maid.'

Her mother laughed.

'What you think is a problem, Elissa, is only
a sensitive instinct for what you know is right
and what you know is wrong. Too many women
marry the first man who asks them. You'll
marry the man you know to be right for you.
And you aren't an old maid. You're very nice.

So take your time. The man you eventually choose will have no cause for complaint.'

Elissa came to as Major Kirsten, walking beside her, brushed her arm with his. It was the lightest of contacts, but it made her say something to herself. Forty? I can't wait until I'm forty. I'll wither.

'Lieutenant, you're far away.'

'Yes, a little, Major.'

'Ah, some young man, I suppose, at Headquarters. Preferable to a mad British airman. Now, the barn.'

They reached it and he entered without checking his stride, his hand in his coat pocket. Elissa followed. The barn was empty. She was not too happy when he climbed the ladder to the loft, but she thought perhaps he did things like that to give his handicap something to think about. He climbed down again.

'Nothing, Major?' she said.

'Nothing. We've drawn another blank.' He smiled ruefully, and she liked him very much for his maturity. Outside, the day was cold but fine. The clouds were brisk in the sky, the patches of blue sharp. Elissa was aware of the warm pleasure of companionship.

'There's no French girl here now, is there, with or without a dirty face,' she said.

'She's gone. Back to the farmhouse, or simply gone? Simply gone, I think.' Major Kirsten's thoughtful look appeared. 'They're not far from here, our fugitives, I'm certain. Not unless they've risked a bold entry into Douai, and I doubt that. They're waiting. But where? Shall we take a look inside that wood?'

They took a look. The wood was not far from the barn. The trees reached upwards in search of the light they partially denied to the haven, which seemed full of shadows. Elissa was a little wary, a little on edge, the wood enclosing them in silence. She had a feeling for atmosphere, and there was an atmosphere. Were they here, the English pilot and Miss von Feldermann? Major Kirsten scoured the place, hand in his coat pocket. Elissa called softly to him.

'Major,' she said, as he came up, 'I think they were here, but I think they've gone now. Look.'

On a little patch of ground between trees were eggshells and the remains of a fire built of twigs. The ashes were grey. Major Kirsten's unblurred eye gleamed.

'Ah, so?' he said.

'So?' said Elissa.

'Well, you and I know, even if others don't, that our pair of flying pigeons stole some eggs. You've found what's left of them. Now we must find the pigeons themselves.' Major Kirsten gave her shoulder a light pat. She was proving a very intelligent assistant. It was a pity, he thought, that he was not young and handsome and whole, for she was also proving delicious in her appeal. She even blushed at times. Very delicious. 'Come along, Lieutenant.'

Elissa wished he would not call her that, not when he called her by her name so often. They left the wood and scanned the rolling fields in the direction of Douai. Nothing disturbed the view.

'We'll use the car to retrace our route and put ourselves closer to the town,' said Major Kirsten. 'We must find them, Elissa, and take Sophia back to her father. That's as necessary as getting our lunatic locked up.'

On the way back to the car, Elissa said, 'You don't think we should take her to the man she loves?'

'General von Feldermann has reservations about that young gentleman. He considers him socially irresponsible. That might do for the first six months of a marriage, when irresponsibility seems like lovable gaiety, but it won't do for a lifetime.'

'The war has given a very short lifetime to some marriages,' said Elissa.

'It has not allowed some to even begin.'

'That is a sadness,' said Elissa. 'Miss von Feldermann's marriage is important to her parents, of course?'

'It's important to them that she marries a man they consider suitable. Parents have an excessive interest in that sort of thing. Fortunately, my own parents not only approved of the choice I made, but considered my wife Anna to be far too good for me.'

'I am so sorry about her,' said Elissa, who knew his wife had been killed in a road accident several years ago.

'The worst is over,' he said.

The car awaited them on the crumbling road.

'You will marry again, perhaps?' said Elissa.

'I hadn't thought of it,' he said.

They boarded the car.

Elissa said, 'I wouldn't like to be responsible myself for preventing Miss von Feldermann from marrying the man she loves.'

'Nor I,' said Major Kirsten.

'You'd like, then, to help her reach Captain Gerder?'

'I didn't say that.'

'Major?'

'I'd like her to give herself time to think more objectively about him. She may then change from an impulsive young lady into a thoughtful and discriminating one.'

'Discriminating?' said Elissa, reminded of her mother's words.

'It can happen. Women do become discriminating, although it takes time.'

'Men are discriminating from birth?' smiled Elissa, starting the car.

'Heavens, no,' said Major Kirsten. 'Most men are idiots from birth and remain so. The ordained task of women is to make what they can of them.'

'Major, that isn't true.'

'Indeed it is,' he said, 'as you'll discover if you're rash enough to marry one. You'll need all your feminine intelligence in making a passable adult of him. I think you'll manage. You must, for the world relies a great deal on the improving and civilizing qualities of women.'

'If I were to accept all that as true,' said Elissa, 'it would mean, Major, I believe myself to be a superior being and you to be an idiot. I'm sure there's something in the German Military Code which forbids any such belief. Which way are we to proceed on this road?'

'The way we came, so turn round, please, Lieutenant,' said Major Kirsten. He was smiling.

Chapter Thirteen

The broad copse, nestling in a dip, was thick with bush, shrub and tree. Winter had stripped the deciduous members, but not the evergreens.

'I'm hungry,' said Sophia.

'So am I,' said Captain Marsh, examining his aching finger as if he could put it out of its misery by eating it.

They had shared four eggs after frying them in a discarded tin lid in the wood where she had lost her temper and earned the assault on her lips. Their new shelter lay a hundred metres from an old, neglected dirt road. Away to the right, some three hundred metres away, was what Captain Marsh had picked out from afar, a small Luftwaffe repair establishment, its workshops humming with activity. Its perimeter, a succession of posts supporting a high wire-mesh fence, was built inside a boundary of fir trees, which provided a camouflaging effect. The sheds lay on each side of a grass runway. Three planes were visible. They had been moved, Captain Marsh thought, since he had first spotted them. Each was standing just inside sheds. Since Richtofen's squadron operated not far away, the repair facilities probably supplemented its on-the-spot amenities, no doubt currently overloaded. Captain Marsh squinted from just inside the copse, picking out what details he could at this distance. He could see no guards. But he thought he could make out a sentry box at the near end of the perimeter, where there was a wide gap with no trees fronting it. That, obviously, was to allow planes to take off. He thought two of the machines were Fokker triplanes. The third looked like an Albatros D5a, the latest and best from the manufacturers.

'I'm also not very warm,' said Sophia, but it was mainly her restless nerves that had her stamping about.

'I'm sorry.' He turned from his concentrated scrutiny and joined her, taking off the greatcoat and placing it around her shoulders, adding its warmth to that of her snug-fitting leather coat.

'No, I'm not as cold as that,' she said, and gave the coat back to him.

He regarded her worriedly. She turned away. 'Sophia?'

'Don't concern yourself,' she said.

'I have to,' he said, 'I'm responsible for the situation.'

'We're both responsible now,' said Sophia. 'In

any case, I think that in your place I might have acted just as you did. It would have almost been a challenge, and challenges can provoke one. So don't feel too concerned.'

'That's very generous of you, but you worry me. Are you becoming uncertain about your decisions?'

Uncertain? How could she be uncertain, she thought, when she knew that the alternative meant she would finish up under the close and confining protection of her mother? Her mother would guard against what she would consider future flights of fancy. Flights of fancy were not in accord with the traditional behaviour of her class. They were mistakes, and mistakes of that kind were all to do with giving in to impulses without considering the consequences. She could hear her mother now, understanding but disconcertingly analytical.

'Sophia, my dear, you have never known what you really want. Your wishes relate only to passing enthusiasms. You wished to paint, did you not, when you fell in love with the genius of Monet? Nothing else mattered except an arrangement which enabled you to study art. It proved boring all too soon, I believe.'

'No, not boring. I never said it was boring. I only said I felt inadequate. In acknowledging that, I acquired humility. That's not such a bad thing in a person, humility.'

'It isn't, as long as you know when to show

it. Humility before God exalts a woman. Before man, it diminishes her. You fell in love with some forgettable Austrian count, did you not, and showed him a deplorable amount of humility in your desire to be all things to him.'

'Mama, I was seventeen and impressionable, and he was wickedly fascinating.'

'Even at seventeen, I thought you intelligent enough to see through a man like that at once. But your feelings, as always, ruled your head, dearest.'

'Mama, my feelings are important to me. My feelings tell me I don't want to marry any of the men you've suggested to me. They're all old men.'

'Old? They're all comparatively young.'

'I mean they're old in their behaviour. They're all stiff, pompous and correct. I'd rather marry an artist, or a poet.'

'Yes, I think there are times when every girl would. But artists and poets, like actors, are all reincarnations of Narcissus. They take wives, but are all firmly married to their own genius. Don't you think I had dreams and feelings at your age? I too visualized Siegfried at my door. Fortunately, my parents made sure my door was kept shut, and instead of allowing me to be swept off my feet by a dreamlike hero, persuaded me to marry your father. It was a dutiful ordeal on my part. As a bride, I was haughty, disgraceful and unforgivable. Your father, a practical man, left me to my sulks in Baden-Baden and went fishing for a week.'

'Mama, on your honeymoon? He went fishing?'

'He's clever as well as practical. He gave me time.'

'Mama, you are you and I am me. I love Fritz. I want to marry him.'

'Has he proposed?'

'No. But he will.'

'I hope he won't. He's quite wrong for you. He'll never grow up. He's a likeable boy, and that's all he is.'

'He's what I want him to be.'

'He's what you think you want him to be.'

'You're forgetting, Mama, that he's one of Germany's finest flying officers.'

'I'm not forgetting that at all. I'm grateful to him and all others like him. But that doesn't make him a suitable husband for you.'

'It would if his family were Junkers.'

'Yes, it might, for he'd be a different kind of man then. One who would accept all the responsibilities of marriage. Sophia, good marriages are not made in heaven, but in drawing rooms.'

Sophia thought about that conversation now.

'No,' she said to Captain Marsh, 'I'm not becoming uncertain.'

He sighed. He was faced with the consequences of an act stupid at best, dangerous at worst. Dangerous for her. If it was ever proved that she had gone willingly with him to Douai, her people would not forgive her. And her father, quite probably, would have him shot.

'I shan't like that,' he said.

'What do you mean?' she asked, watching him. She felt that her eyes could not leave him alone. The recurrent agitation was beginning to be painful.

'I was thinking your father might have me shot.'

'Don't be silly,' she said, flaring up.

'Yes, gruesome thought,' he said.

'You haven't been caught yet, and even if you are, you'd speak up for yourself, wouldn't you?'

'Not without becoming hopelessly confused,' he said, smiling at her.

'Don't be silly,' she said again. She looked around. The copse seemed thick and lush. Her blood erratic, she said, 'Is there no way we can get something to eat?'

'Do you like rabbit?' he asked, pointing, and she saw the long ears and quick hop of a furry creature.

'If you can make it edible, yes, I shall like it. Could you catch that one?'

'A man running after a rabbit is a clown. The rabbit always makes a fool of him.'

'Well, try,' said Sophia, 'or we'll starve before the night comes.'

The creature was nibbling not more than twenty paces from the edge of the copse.

'Sophia – '

'I think you should try,' said Sophia. 'It would make our relationship a little more agreeable, even if our countries are still at war.'

Captain Marsh studied the rabbit. She watched him.

'I could shoot it,' he said.

'Then please do so. I'm famished.'

'The shot will be heard,' he said, gesturing towards the repair shops.

'Then why did you suggest it?'

'If they'd only do some engine testing, the noise would be loud enough to smother the sound.'

'I am willing to wait for that to happen,' said Sophia, 'but is the rabbit?'

Captain Marsh laughed.

'Sophia, you are really very likeable,' he said.

'Likeable?' Her mother had said Fritz was likeable. For some reason, it seemed such a luke-warm word. One's postman or stationmaster was likeable. 'I'm likeable, Captain Marsh?'

He looked at her. Her loose, flowing hair was a bright cascade, and the lashes that framed her eyes were dark and soft. Her mouth, slightly parted, was warm and kissable. He shifted his gaze to the nibbling rabbit again.

'I'm sorry if that's offensive too,' he said.

'Oh, likeable is hardly cause for a quarrel,'

she said, and the rabbit hopped, whisked away and disappeared. 'There, it's gone. We've lost it through your indecision. Are you happy that you'll end up starving me to death?'

It was a bitter little question, born of so much guilt and so many disturbing facets. It made him wince, and Sophia wished she could take it back.

'Sophia, I must point out the situation isn't what it was – you're here of your own free will – '

'Oh, I'm to be blamed for what has developed, am I?' she cried.

'I've no intention of blaming you for anything – damnation, look at that.'

She turned to follow his pointing finger. Along the road, seen from the shelter of the copse, an open car was moving. Clearly visible were its occupants, two German officers, a man and a woman, the woman at the wheel. The man was looking around, searching and peering. Sophia knew who he was. Major Kirsten. He had his eyes on the copse now. He spoke to his companion. The car travelled on.

'They're after us,' said Sophia.

'They were after us last night,' said Captain Marsh.

Sophia was a little pale. Their eyes met. Hers dropped at once. They both knew the situation was impossible. She was German, he was British. Each knew they should be going their separate ways.

'My father seems very determined,' she said.

'He's probably very concerned. I'll risk staying here until it's dark, then make my own way into Douai. You must go now, you must get away from me, or those questions we mentioned will be very difficult for you to answer.'

Her every emotion was in agitation. All clarity of her mind disintegrated. She shook her head wildly, and her hair flew.

'No,' she gasped, 'I'm going to Douai with you.'

'Sophia – '

'Don't argue!'

A sudden roar startled them both. The new 160 h.p. Mercedes engine of the Albatros had come alive. The rabbit reappeared, jumping wildly, but finding a clump of sweeter grass, set to again. Captain Marsh drew his revolver and moved out of the copse. He sighted the revolver, both hands clasping it, with one finger stiffly angled. Sophia watched. He was very steady, very deliberate. The rabbit cocked its ears. The plane engine roared louder and then ran powerfully at test speed. Captain Marsh fired. The sharp crack was followed by sudden death. The rabbit, bowled over by the bullet, did not even twitch. It lay still and inert.

Two people in a car looked at each other.

Captain Marsh was not to know the car had stopped three minutes ago, at a little distance beyond the blind side of the copse.

Chapter Fourteen

Major Kirsten said, 'That, I think, was a shot.'

'I heard something too,' said Elissa, 'just as the noise of that plane engine changed.'

The major had told her to pull up adjacent to a broad patch covered with firs and rhododendrons. They had sat for some minutes, making new guesses and sharing the feeling that the fugitives were always well ahead of all guesses. The major got out of the car now.

'What are you up to?' asked Elissa.

'If you'll stay here and look after the car, I'll take a little walk.'

Elissa tensed.

'I should come with you, I think, Major.'

'If that was a revolver shot,' said the major, 'it's possible our mad flyer has finally put a bullet into Sophia. In which case, he won't hesitate to put one into you.'

'Or you.' Elissa alighted. 'Please let me come with you.'

'On the other hand, Sophia may have

managed to put one into him and so dissolved an alien partnership.'

'I think we should investigate together, Major,' said Elissa, gently firm.

'True, three good eyes are better than one,' he conceded. 'I must say, this place makes a very convenient starting point for a final hop into Douai.'

'I'm worried that the man has his eyes on you now,' said Elissa.

'True again, someone fired that shot. Why, I wonder?' Major Kirsten eyed the copse sombrely. 'Damned if I feel at all comfortable about the reason. I think we'd better give the impression we're looking for seclusion, not for him.'

'I'd like clarification of that,' said Elissa.

'You're an attractive lady, out for a drive with an admirer. It would be quite natural for us to wander into a wood to seek a little seclusion.'

'Major?' Elissa was startled and pink.

'I assure you, nothing ruinous will happen to you. Forget my age and allow me to simulate harmless courtship. An arm around your waist, a kiss or two—'

'Major? A kiss or two?' Elissa was very pink. Major Kirsten's blandness seemed totally un-related to the tenseness of the situation. The man he was resolved to take and the young woman he was determined to return to her father as discreetly as he could, might well be in that copse, but here he was spicing the moment with whimsy. 'You're not serious?'

'Only with your permission, Lieutenant. A courting couple seeking seclusion should arouse no suspicion.'

'But if Miss von Feldermann is there, she'll recognize you.'

'Oh, I hope she'll think my arm around your waist the significant factor. I shall look as if I'm in romantic pursuit of you, not in alarming pursuit of her. We shall talk, of course, and in romantic terms, while keeping our ears and eyes open. If you see them, pretend you haven't.'

Elissa drew a long breath.

'Yes, Major.'

'You're ready for your part?'

'Yes.' She sounded fairly composed.

He put his arm around her waist and they began a slow walk towards the copse. Elissa felt they might be walking into bullets, that the gun was already sighting on them. But Major Kirsten seemed quite unworried, taking on the attitude of a lover without any awkwardness. He was full of surprises. She could not imagine any of the other officers acting like this. He seemed to have put the war aside, and to have forgotten General Ludendorff's imminent offensive. General Ludendorff was actually at Headquarters today, but Major Kirsten was completely absorbed in his search for Miss von Feldermann. He must care very much for her.

Their pace was leisurely, his arm still around her waist, and everything was quiet except for the powerful hum of the distant plane engine. Suddenly it stopped. Its cessation created a peculiar sensation of floating lightness.

'If they are here,' she whispered, 'what will you do?'

'Ignore them, unless the situation is such that I can point my revolver at him and get you to take his. If not, then I shall continue being your ardent admirer. With your permission, I shall kiss you – '

'Major,' she breathed 'it will be rather like enacting Offenbach when the audience is expecting Wagner.'

'Well, if we are aggressively confronted, we must improvise in what we do and say. Have no fears.'

'I'm all fears,' said Elissa, 'and my apprehension is indescribable.'

'Shall we turn back?'

'No,' whispered Elissa as they neared the copse, 'for I'm sure this is the only chance I'll ever have of playing Offenbach when the atmosphere calls for thunder and lightning.'

Major Kirsten smiled and his arm gave her waist the lightest of squeezes. They entered the copse. A little stream, running over a pebbled bed, glittered in the filtering light. Elissa's heart tightened. The copse was a place of silence.

*

Captain Marsh was skinning the rabbit when Sophia, who had wandered restlessly away for a while, returned in a rustling rush.

'They're coming,' she breathed.

'What?'

'Their car is on the other side. They're walking this way. He has his arm around her waist.'

'How charming,' said Captain Marsh.

'Charming? What do you mean, charming?' Sophia's whisper was edged with alarm and impatience.

'Well, in a few words you've drawn quite a nice picture of them. They're not on honeymoon, I suppose?'

'What are you doing, sitting there skinning the rabbit? You must hide – we both must – or it's all been for nothing.'

'I am hiding.' Captain Marsh, sitting with his back against a tree, indicated screening shrubs, thick with glossy leaf. 'But there's no need for you to. Why don't you go and meet them?'

'You know why, and I've gone too far now to turn back.' Sophia, hating herself, dropped to the ground beside him. 'And you've gone too far to be careless now. They'll see you. Get down. Look, we must lie flat, close to these bushes.'

He moved, and they lay flat.

They heard a rustle of sound then. They slightly lifted their heads and peered through gaps in the leaves. They glimpsed the figures of a man and woman in field-grey slowly

239

meandering, passing through light and shadows, the skirts of their coats brushing shrubs. Captain Marsh noted the man did indeed have his arm around the woman. That was his only arm. His left sleeve was empty, and neatly tucked into his coat pocket. He stopped and the woman turned to him, her face flushed beneath the peak of her cap. He bent his head and kissed her. Sophia, recognizing Major Josef Kirsten, drew a silent breath, but relaxed a little as the kiss became prolonged. Major Kirsten, a man she liked, had found consolation for the loss of his arm, and perhaps for the loss of his wife too. Was that why he was in this place, just to enjoy its seclusion in company with the attractive WAC officer? It was a very pleasant haven for lovers.

Captain Marsh did not relax at all. His suspicion was acute, his hand inside his jacket and gripping his revolver. Something tugged at his memory. Madame Gascoigne's words: *The man has only one arm, and a scarred right eye, but his left eye is as sharp as a needle.*

They were the same Germans, the same officers, who had been at the auberge and had come so close to discovering him while he was keeping his hostage forcibly quiet in the shadow of that brick wall.

The earth was unsteady beneath Elissa's feet. Major Kirsten was kissing her. Her blood was racing nervously because of someone who had fired a shot, and riotously because of Major Kirsten. Was kissing really necessary to the act? Could they not have wandered hand in hand, smiling at each other? But whether kissing was necessary or not, participation was a giddy sweetness, despite everything else. His lips were firm on hers, but without being demanding, as if he felt the pretence of courtship was an effort for her. If kisses of pretence rendered her so giddy, she thought, what would it do to her if Major Kirsten kissed her in love?

He released her. Her face was fiery. It perturbed him a little, the realization that because she was so painfully shy, this kind of nonsense was an ordeal to her.

In a light murmur, however, he said, 'I wonder, was that convincing? Do you feel eyes, Elissa?'

'I feel giddy,' confessed Elissa faintly.

'My deepest apologies,' he whispered. 'But give me your hand and smile at me while we romanticize. Look as demure and happy as you would if I were young and handsome and about to propose. Tomorrow you can laugh about it.'

She gave him her hand and a nervous smile. The silence of the copse intruded on her consciousness, and little goose pimples rose. Major Kirsten talked to her about Munich, her birthplace, and told her he had more liking for it now that he knew it was her home. Elissa raised a light laugh at that.

Sophia, lying beside Captain Marsh, observed the uniformed lovers and heard the murmur of their voices. Her body was stiff and tense. Captain Marsh was as still as if he had been sculpted out of stone. Was Major Kirsten actually proposing to his companion? She looked very flushed.

They were hand in hand, walking slowly towards the group of screening shrubs. Sophia trembled. Captain Marsh put a hand on her arm. His touch agitated her. Wildly, she felt cramp was about to seize her limbs. She heard Major Kirsten's voice.

'You must be back at what time, Elissa?'

'We must leave in fifteen minutes.' The woman's voice was a little unsteady, as if she was suffering the nervous excitements of love.

'It's been delightful, our time together,' said Major Kirsten warmly.

'Yes – lovely – I shan't like going back a bit,' said Elissa.

They came on, skirting trees, and cramp took hold of Sophia. Her limbs jerked convulsively, creating a whisper of sound, at which moment Major Kirsten laughed.

'That squirrel – those antics,' he said.

'I see no—' Elissa stopped as his hand tightened around hers. 'Oh, yes,' she said. He had heard the slightest of sounds, as she had, and she knew he had laughed to cover it up and to make a non-existent squirrel his reason. The sound had come from behind a clump of bushes, just to their left. Without a pause, they walked on. But then Major Kirsten stopped, put his arm around her and, in quite audacious fashion, kissed her again. She was far too tense to feel sweetness this time. Apprehension turned her cold, for Major Kirsten had his back to the concealing bushes, his body sheltering hers. If a revolver was being pointed, it was at his back, yet he was kissing her very tenderly.

Sophia's cramp eased, and she and Captain Marsh lay frozen. There they were, Major Kirsten and the WAC officer, and as close as they had been once before. Sophia almost stopped breathing, and Captain Marsh had his revolver out. Her eyes dilated and she put a hand on the gun, silently begging him not to use it.

Major Kirsten and Elissa broke apart and strolled on. In the way of lovers, they stopped again. He put his arm around her shoulders, and once more they strolled on. They disappeared. Captain Marsh and Sophia did not move or speak. He was dark with suspicion, she pale and tense, toes tightly curled to ward off the cramp.

After seven or eight minutes, Major Kirsten and Elissa reappeared. Making their way back through the copse, they were still unhurried in their walk, still talking in a light and affectionate way, and they passed the screen of shrubs without any change of pace or attitude. A couple of minutes later they had left the retreat.

Captain Marsh finally spoke.

'What the devil was that all about?' he said.

'A lovers' walk,' said Sophia, her breathing painful.

'You think so? What were they talking about?'

'Nothing that was of any importance except to themselves.'

'And when they almost bumped into us last night? What were they talking about then?' Captain Marsh sounded edgy.

'What does it matter?' said Sophia, then remembered the conversation last night had been very different. But wanting no trouble, no exacerbation of a situation already painful enough, she added, 'They are obviously only interested in each other.'

'Well, I wish they'd indulge their mutual interest a lot farther away from me,' said Captain Marsh, getting to his feet. 'It's too much of a coincidence finding them at the auberge, then that place just outside Lutargne, and now here. Damned if they don't seem to be sitting on my tail. They've been riding around in that car all day.'

'Isn't that what lovers like to do?' asked Sophia, rising.

'In March? With the hood down?'

'What difference does that make to people in love?' Sophia was as edgy as he was.

'If I were in love, I'd prefer a cosy fireside and a warm sofa.'

'Perhaps you've never been in love,' said Sophia stiffly. 'Have you?'

'Once or twice,' he said.

'Once or twice? Once or twice?' Sophia smiled mirthlessly. 'That couldn't have been love.'

He looked sombrely at her. Their eyes met again. Hers were very blue, his were dark grey. The agitation seized her, and she averted her face.

'No, it wasn't,' he said. He frowned. 'I'm going to check on your friends.'

He walked to the west side of the copse, Sophia following. They stood in shelter and from there they watched. Sophia saw Major Kirsten and the woman he had called Elissa. They had just reached their car. They got in, and after a few moments drove away.

'They're going back to Headquarters,' said Sophia. 'I heard the woman say she had to be on her way soon.'

'If Major Kirsten had been given the chance, would he have escorted you back to your father or helped you reach Fritz?'

'He would have been loyal to my father and I'd have quarrelled with him. That is why I'm still with you, even though we both dislike the situation. What are you going to do now?'

Captain Marsh gave her a faint smile. She was an enduring young woman. She was neither haggard nor limp, despite so much discomfort. Nor was she complaining. But she was hungry.

'Well, since there's nothing much else to do while we wait for evening,' he said, 'I'll finish skinning that rabbit, then make a fire and cook it. We can clean it in the stream on the other side of the wood.'

'You have your better moments,' said Sophia.

'Are you sure about that?' he asked with another smile.

She turned her back on him.

'I'll collect some kindling,' she said.

Captain Vorster, sitting in Douai, was out of the hunt, and the combined search parties were miles away. Major Kirsten and Elissa alone had prospects of success.

After driving away from the vicinity of the copse, they had stopped immediately they were out of sight of it.

'I'm relieved we came safely out of the place,' said Major Kirsten.

'You were worried?' said Elissa, putting it mildly.

'I was when I realized they were actually there.'

'You did not seem worried.'

'I shouldn't have placed you at such risk,' he said.

'Major, I volunteered,' said Elissa.

'And played your part excellently. I must apologize, however, for all the embarrassment it caused you. But we had to investigate and I thought that was the only way of doing it innocuously.'

'Please don't apologize,' said Elissa.

'You've earned a decoration,' said Major Kirsten. 'Of flowers. Did you actually see them, by the way?'

'No. I only heard them. It was a very small sound.'

'Yes, I heard it too, and glimpsed feet.'

'Feet?'

'Two pairs,' said Major Kirsten. 'And a half-skinned rabbit.'

'Herr Major, the shot we heard – '

'One dead rabbit, Elissa. They're hungry.'

'So am I,' said Elissa.

'We'll dine in Douai, perhaps. Do you think we deceived our lunatic into believing we were unaware of them?'

'I think we must remember that although he seems crazy, he's not an idiot,' said Elissa.

'I agree. So what I'd like you to do now is drive to Douai. Explain to Colonel Hoffner that I'd like the immediate assistance of a few men. I'll stay here.'

'You aren't intending anything rash, I hope,' said Elissa.

'I intend only to walk back far enough to keep an eye on the place. If they leave, I'll mark their direction, but I don't think they will leave until it's near to dark. You should be back well before then. Be charming to Colonel Hoffner, but not so charming that he'll prolong your stay. Tell him six or seven men will be enough.'

Elissa smiled. One warmed very easily to Major Kirsten. He was enjoying himself, playing a game of cat and mouse against the background of war, escaping his desk and his weariness of the war. Whether he really believed Sophia von Feldermann had allied herself with the British fighter pilot or was under constant threat from him, she did not know. But he had found out where she was, and was determined not to lose her but to separate her from the man in the safest way he could devise. He would not send Colonel Hoffner's men in firing from all angles. He would be more subtle than that.

'Major, I've just thought, why not ask for help from those repair workshops?'

'I can't approach them without being seen, and I can't bring men out of there without so alarming our fugitives that they'll vanish again. No, let them sit where they are for the moment. I know you'll bring Colonel Hoffner's men close enough without one of them being seen. Make for the point where we stopped before.'

Major Kirsten got out of the car. 'Off you go, Lieutenant.'

'Yes, Major,' said Elissa, 'but I hope you'll take sensible care of yourself.'

'All old soldiers have an instinct for self-preservation,' said Major Kirsten, 'which means getting the other man before he gets you.'

He watched her drive off. The afternoon was advancing. He turned and began to circle back to a concealed position from which he could keep careful watch.

Chapter Fifteen

The fire became a heap of hot, grey-white ashes. The rabbit had been roasted and eaten, Captain Marsh having cut the meat free with a penknife. Sophia had dined ravenously. They had washed their hands in the stream and drunk from it.

'Roast rabbit is good,' said Sophia.

'Anything edible is good to the starving,' said Captain Marsh.

'You are a man who can survive, I think,' she said.

'If I am, then you have similar qualities. And what are we to look forward to? A better world, according to our prime minister.'

'Better for you or for us?' asked Sophia.

'Better for everyone, if you can believe politicians.'

'There was nothing very wrong with the one I was living in before you went to war against us,' said Sophia.

'But you were far more prepared for it than we were.'

'Are you proud that your sea blockade is starving millions of women and children?'

'No prouder than you are about bombing women and children from your Zeppelins.'

'That's a lie,' said Sophia. 'Our Zeppelins only attack your military installations.'

'Are you sure?'

'I dislike you,' said Sophia.

'I don't dislike you.'

'In the way you've acted, you've proved yourself very self-centred.'

'Is that a nice thing to say after I've just given you the best cuts and larger share of my rabbit?'

'I consider that remark petty and untrue. In any case, it was as much my rabbit as yours.'

'I shot it,' said Captain Marsh.

'But I was the one who saw it first.'

'Were you? I thought I was.'

'Are you enjoying this ridiculous conversation?'

'Yes, very much. And I don't think it ridiculous.'

'Don't be patronizing,' said Sophia, feverishly determined to keep a necessary gulf between them. 'That is as objectionable to me as your brutality.'

'You're not going to forgive me?'

'Never,' said Sophia, then remembered again

the dark, icy canal and the way he had risked sliding into it with her. She remembered the strength of his body and its life-saving firmness and warmth. She bit her lip. 'Captain Marsh, I'm sorry, I shouldn't have said that. Although there have been unpleasant moments which I'd rather forget, I think I understand what you are doing. Perhaps in the circumstances you were entitled to make your own rules.'

'I think I was entitled to take possession of your car,' he said, 'but not of you.'

Sophia looked at the ashes of the fire. There were no flames in which to draw pictures, pictures of Fritz. Fritz, incredibly, was a retreating image. Had he too been no more than a temporary enthusiasm of hers? Her mother would have said so. Were all her enthusiasms born only of instinctive rebellion against the lifestyles of the Junkers? Fiercely, she tried to conjure up a soul-saving picture of Fritz. All she achieved was a picture pale and meaningless. She glanced at Captain Marsh. Sitting with his back against a tree, he was making one of his many surveys of the fields and that pitted little road. His features were strongly masculine, his vigour apparent even when he was still. He did not have Fritz's gaiety or charm. He was a harder man than Fritz. Fritz was amusing. Captain Marsh was resolute.

'You're still going to wait until it's dark before you move?' she asked.

'No,' he said. 'I've been thinking, and I know I'm not too happy about your Major Kirsten and his lady friend. What was the point of them coming in here to make eyes at each other? Had it been to make love – '

'Don't be disgusting. Major Kirsten is not a man to act like a peasant.'

'Even so, it's wishful thinking to believe they weren't aware of us.'

'Then why didn't he try to arrest you?'

'Because he must know I'm armed.'

'You'd shoot a brave soldier like Major Kirsten, a one-armed man with a damaged eye?'

'I suppose he'd shoot me if he had to.'

'But would you have shot him?' asked Sophia in strange anguish.

'No. I'm not as desperate as that.'

'You had your revolver ready.'

'Yes. For the sake of advantage. Just the advantage, that's all. I'm going to get out of here very soon and cut across the road and the fields. There's a long belt of trees adjacent to those workshops. I'll risk that no one will think I'm sitting within striking distance of a Luftwaffe repair establishment. I'll stay there until it's dark, and then go on.'

In a strained voice, Sophia said, 'We'll both go on. I shall lose my way otherwise.'

'No, you won't. Skirt the far end of the work-shops' perimeter and keep going. You'll come to the main road – '

'I'm not going on my own. I have no confidence in the dark.'

'Are you sure of all this?' said Captain Marsh gently.

'Yes.'

'I'm not sure myself that you're really sure.'

'How many times must we argue about this?' Sophia got up, moved away, came back after a moment and said, 'Until you're ready for us to move, tell me what life was like for you before the war.'

'My father's a country parson,' said Captain Marsh.

'Yes?'

'Yes.'

'That is the story of your life up to the war?' said Sophia.

'More or less. Christian upbringing and rural pastimes. Grammar school in a Wiltshire country town, and holidays in the hayfields. Vicarage tea parties on Sunday afternoons.' Captain Marsh did not mind talking, although he remained alert. His two sisters entered the nursing profession and his brother, receiving the call, was admitted to a theological college to train for his orders. He himself, at seventeen, began to study farming. His father, recognizing he had a practical turn of mind, cajoled various Wiltshire farmers into paying him seven shillings a week to work from dawn to dusk. However, he became far more interested in the wheels of the industry than in the soil. The carts, the wains, the tools, the equipment and the machines of farming were his field.

He occasionally liked to handle a plough, but his bent was mechanical, and motorized farm machines fascinated him. Just before the war, when he was twenty-five, he had used some savings to purchase a blacksmith's business in a small market town, together with a derelict warehouse next door. The old blacksmith had died, and his assistant, Simon Tukes, did not have the money to buy the business for himself. Simon, however, had been given a quarter-ownership and a wage to run the forge, while the warehouse was to be converted into a workshop for the repair and maintenance of mechanized transport. Motor lorries and other vehicles were beginning to take the place of horse-drawn carts and wagons.

The development of the workshop had been halted by the war, but he was certain business would be there for the asking when peace arrived. The smithy would still be needed, very much so, and that and what would come to be an automobile garage, with a petrol pump, would mean that both the mechanical and horse-drawn trade could be catered for. He and Simon Tukes would run both businesses. He forecast an impressive postwar development of the automobile industry, and an increasing need for garages.

'Do you mean you will crawl about under broken-down cars as a way of life after the war?' asked Sophia in astonishment.

'As a way of establishing a profitable business. I'm certain I can't fail.'

'But will you like it?' Sophia had never heard any officer talk of running such a business as that. 'So much dirt and oil and grease?'

'Naturally, I'll like it. I wouldn't consider it otherwise.'

She stared at him in amazement. Repairing motor cars was work for people who were no good at anything else, or had no profession. One was aware of such people, and their usefulness, but she had never known any gentlemen take on that kind of work.

'But what would happen if you married?' she asked.

'You mean how would my wife like me crawling under cars and getting dirty?'

'Would she like it?'

'Not if I asked her to crawl under with me. But I hope she'd look at my prospects, not my overalls.'

'You don't have a fiancée?' said Sophia, studying discarded rabbit bones.

'I've been a little too busy these last four years,' he said. 'I was in Mesopotamia until late 1917, flying against your allies, the Turks, which I admit was not quite so hazardous as flying against Richtofen. I was transferred to

France a few months ago, since when I've died a death a dozen times, but I'm still hanging on. Richtofen kept after me yesterday, because he had me going the wrong way over his territory. You saw what happened. Does your Fritz fly with Richtofen?'

'Yes.'

'I thought so.' Captain Marsh was impressed. 'He must be very good, then.'

'All Richtofen's pilots are among the best,' said Sophia. 'Captain Marsh, are you sure you're going to be a blacksmith and a car repairer after the war?'

'You don't think much of it?' he said, watching the road through the trees.

'But you're a gentleman, aren't you?' she said.

He laughed.

'Have I behaved like one?'

'No,' she said.

'Then is your question answered?'

'No,' she said.

'I see. I suppose what you really want to know is whether my background entitles me to be classed as a gentleman. It doesn't. I'm simply known as a parson's son. That entitles me to be called respectable, like a farmer's son.'

'All German officers are gentlemen,' said Sophia.

Captain Marsh coughed.

'Are you sure?' he said.

'None of them would—' She stopped.

'Brutalize you?'

'I have told you – I would prefer to forget that.'

'Frankly, so would I. It's on my conscience. However, what's your life been like?'

'Unexceptional,' said Sophia, 'until I met Fritz. I've spent most of my years learning how to take my future place as a good German wife and mother.'

'I see. And that had no appeal?'

'I don't like being fitted into a stiff frame, I would like to be allowed to kick and scream, if I wished – '

'Kick and scream?' Captain Marsh looked as if she had pronounced the earth flat.

'Yes. I have never done so, of course. Such behaviour is as unknown among my family as cowardice among the Spartans, but as a wife I should like to feel I could do so, if I ever wished to, and that my husband would understand.'

'It could on occasions, relieve any monotony that might be hanging around. Sophia have you suffered repression?'

'No, lectures,' said Sophia.

'Then let me wish you a future free of all lectures, and a husband who'll encourage you whenever you want to let your hair down, which is what you mean by kicking and screaming, don't you?'

'Yes,' said Sophia, inspecting her gloves.

Captain Marsh climbed to his feet. She rose with him. 'It's time to go?' she said.

'I think so. I've asked a hundred times, I know, but I must ask again – are you sure it's right for you to come with me?'

'I know what I'm doing,' she said. She did know now, and the knowledge was crucifying her.

'There's still too much daylight left, but I wouldn't put it past your Major Kirsten to come back after he's dropped his lady love, and to bring a company of German grenadiers with him. We'll move out, cross that dirt road and make for the belt of trees on this side of the repair shops. Someone might spot us and take note, but we'll chance it. When we leave that belt of trees, we'll head for the main road. It should be dark by the time we reach it.'

'The main road might be very busy,' said Sophia.

'Again? Surely not. Not unless – ' Captain Marsh lapsed into serious thought for a moment, then began walking, Sophia beside him.

They emerged cautiously from their shelter and at once felt very exposed. The afternoon was fading, the light pearly grey, but it felt very bright to them. There was a tangible quality to the atmosphere, as if it could be touched. Now and again the ring of metal on metal echoed around the distant sheds. That was the only sound. The guns were silent, the concentrations of German batteries concealed and waiting, and there was not a plane in the cloudy sky. To Sophia, the atmosphere held its portent of gigantic battle. It was the great quiet before the great offensive.

Something began to disturb the quiet. Light breezes turned into a strong wind. Dead leaves began to lift and skitter over the grass. Sophia's loose hair whipped, smothering her face with strands of bright gold. She tossed them back. They reached the dirt road. They looked around. They saw no one, they heard no one. They crossed the road and walked rapidly. Sophia's hair danced and frisked. It was like a waving banner of light to the watching Major Kirsten, buried in a fold in the ground not far from the copse.

Captain Marsh, the field-grey greatcoat buttoned around him, lengthened his stride. Sophia quickened her pace to keep up with him. He was such a positive man, she thought. He would make mistakes at times, but never out of hesitation or uncertainty. He seemed as sure of himself as ever, even at this moment when he must be aware of their vulnerability. Away to their right, a German guard suddenly showed himself beside the sentry box of the repair establishment. He had his back to them, and Captain Marsh was making ground rapidly to put them out of sight of the man.

The long belt of trees lay ahead, separated from the enclosed workshops by a strip of ground no more than twenty metres wide. Captain Marsh sank down then, pulling Sophia with him. An open lorry had appeared on the dirt road, trundling to make a turn that took it on to a wide tarmac surface leading to the workshops. It stopped at the entrance beside the sentry box. The guard spoke to the driver. The lorry drove in after a few moments, the guard watching it. Captain Marsh and Sophia rose, and made for cover at a swift run. Their cover was the belt of trees, and they rounded the first trees and walked alongside the wooded stretch, quite hidden from the establishment.

Captain Marsh cast backward glances as they walked fast. The light was a deeper grey.

'Just right,' he said. 'By the time we reach the main road it should be dark.' He cast another glance behind him. 'Damn.'

'What's wrong?' asked Sophia. 'I thought we were going to wait here, inside this wood – '

'Walk on. There's someone behind us, in the lee of a hedge. He's in uniform. Don't look round.' He took her arm, pulling at her.

'Don't do that,' she said a little wildly.

'I must. Let me drag you. You mustn't be seen walking of your own free will. At times you must show resistance.' He continued pulling at her, and she understood. The situation never improved. It worsened every hour, because she knew why she was staying with him.

'When we reach the end of this wood,' she said, 'we'll have no shelter at all.'

'When we come to that point,' said Captain Marsh, hand firm on her arm, 'we'll angle around it to get ourselves out of sight, then turn and enter the wood. That might just fox whoever's behind us into thinking we've gone straight on. After all, if we were going to use the place as cover, we'd have entered it by now.'

Sophia wondered desperately how it would all end.

Major Kirsten was experiencing a self-critical stage. Lieutenant Landsberg should have been back twenty minutes ago at the latest. He had made no real allowances for a hold-up, no provision for what she should do in such an event. He had only said he would take a note of the direction of the fugitives if they made a move. They had. He had followed them for a while, then stopped in order to avoid losing contact with Elissa when she returned. She would leave the car at the point beyond the copse where he had parted from her before she began her drive to Douai. She would expect him to show himself then, to meet her and to take charge of whatever men Colonel Hoffner had sent with her.

He had seen the fugitives leave the copse, walking fast, and at a time when there was still no sign of her. If they got too far ahead and made all kinds of twists and turns, he would lose them unless his endearing colleague –

Endearing?

'You are a fool, Josef,' he said to himself.

The chase had become compulsive. Sophia could not be left indefinitely in the hands of the RFC pilot, and her father was too admirable a soldier to have his daughter's wilfulness made known to all and sundry. Major Kirsten hoped the general was still unaware that she was a hostage. It was enough that Colonel Hoffner knew it. But was she definitely that? She had left the copse with the man, without any sign of being dragged or threatened. True, as far as the major could make out, he had taken her by the arm in their progress adjacent to that wood, but exactly why? To hurry her on? To pull her on? To encourage her? They would be out of sight soon, for they were cutting across to the end of the long wooded stretch.

They were heading for Douai. That was absolutely certain now. The afternoon was going, the light very grey, but they were clearly visible. For some reason they had risked coming out into the open. Douai held something for both of them. A name and address for the British flyer, perhaps, and given to him by the pleasant and helpful proprietor of the inn at Lutargne? And for Sophia, there was Captain Fritz Gerder.

They disappeared beyond the wood. Major

Kirsten moved from the sheltering lee of a hedge and considered his next move. He could keep them in sight if he went after them now. He could even catch them up, but then what? A shooting match? Out of the question if the man kept Sophia close to him. Major Kirsten swore softly. He needed the soldiers Elissa should be bringing from Douai. There would be no shooting match then, but an encircling manoeuvre. He hoped to God that Colonel Hoffner would not send greybeards.

There were men available in that distant Luftwaffe repair unit, but whether the officer in charge would part with any was uncertain. He took another look back, standing on the second bar of a gate in the hedge to give himself extra height. He saw the car then, back beyond the copse, with a small military runabout van behind it. Both vehicles were stationary. Lieutenant Landsberg was out of the car and looking around. From the van came several soldiers. Steadying himself, Major Kirsten lifted his arm and signalled. Elissa saw him, a small figure in the distance. She waved and came at a run, the soldiers following.

Beyond the wood, out of sight of Major Kirsten, Captain Marsh and Sophia made a quick turn-about and dashed for shelter. On their left was the tree-lined west side of the wire perimeter. They entered the wood, and the effect of becoming enclosed was now a very familiar one. Captain Marsh stopped and patted the trunk of a plane tree.

'I hope we haven't jumped out of the frying pan into the fire,' he said.

'Be thankful the French farmers haven't cut all their trees down,' said Sophia.

'It's sound farming policy to look after standing timber. Have you seen what winds can do to young wheat?'

'I've seen what it can do to ripe wheat,' said Sophia, 'for I've faced the winds of East Prussia and almost been blown off my feet.'

'It's given you a very healthy complexion. Stay there a moment while I take a look.'

Sophia, however, was not disposed to accept orders, and she followed him to a point where they were able to make a survey of the area they had just left behind. In the distance, a man became visible as he moved away from a hedge. His cap and greatcoat distinguished him as a German officer. Sophia did not need to guess at his identity.

'It's Major Kirsten,' she said.

'Composing a poem to his love?' said Captain Marsh sarcastically.

'Perhaps,' said Sophia defiantly. She saw the distant figure move to a gate and stand on it. Perceptibly, he lifted an arm and signalled. Captain Marsh grimaced.

'What's he doing now? Waving goodbye or

bringing up reinforcements? I'll wager he'll be on our tails again in a moment. Can you climb a tree, and if you can, would you want to?'

His eyes were quick as he turned to scan the interior of the wood, picking out evergreens. His every reaction to danger, thought Sophia, was to immediately work out a countermove.

'I climbed every kind of tree with my brothers when I was young,' she said, 'until I was told it was not a recommended activity for growing girls. I protested. My mother spoke to me about ladies' legs.'

Captain Marsh glanced at her. For a brief moment, a reminiscent smile seemed about to break forth, but died almost stillborn. Her mouth twitched, that was all.

'We need not consider legs, except for climbing.'

It was a comment that appealed to Sophia's natural sense of humour, but it was not a time when she could react with a smile of any kind.

'I'm not expected to climb trees now, I hope,' she said. 'You must give up. We both must.'

'You can, if you wish to,' said Captain Marsh, 'and I recommend that as being in your best interests.'

'While you hide in a tree? How ridiculous. That is like playing a children's game in a house that is on fire.'

'I shan't hide in any tree if you want to give

266

up, since if you do you must inform on me. You must, for your own sake.'

'I'm not going to give up,' she said, her face set.

Captain Marsh pointed to a huge cedar tree, its branches laden.

'We could climb that easily enough,' he said, 'just in case they comb this place. Out in the open, there's still too much light.'

'But up in that tree, we could be trapped,' said Sophia.

'Yes, if they see us. But we'll climb high and make a sporting game of it.'

'Sporting game?' Her low laugh was bitter. 'This has never been a game to me, least of all now.'

'I know. However, they may not even enter this wood. On the other hand, they might. It's your decision.'

Captain Marsh took a final look at the distant figure of Major Kirsten. He saw other figures appear. He turned and made for the cedar tree, Sophia with him. The lower branches were easily accessible.

'Shall you go first?' he said.

'My mother would strongly disapprove of that,' said Sophia.

'I've never met your mother, and am never likely to, but she has an exceptional daughter, so rather than upset her, I'll go first.'

He began his climb. His stiff and painful

finger was a minor worry. He found easy footholds. Sophia followed, aware that she was in a despairing relationship with the impossible. Above her, Captain Marsh reached down with a long arm to give her a helping hand from time to time, pulling her up after him. Her limbs were supple, but her skirts hampering. The multitude of thick branches gave firm assistance to the climb, although the dense foliage plucked at her hair and coat, and the spiral leaf tufts yielded reluctantly to her upward passage. The tree was a massive giant, with a vast spread.

They climbed until the profusion of growth shut them off from the ground. They sat together on a solid branch, Sophia with her shoulder against the trunk. From where they were they had a commanding view of the ground they had covered all the way from the copse. The light was dimmer, but they made out the shapes of two vehicles, a car and a canvas-covered van. On the move were soldiers. There was also a woman.

'Your military Romeo and Juliet are leading the charge,' said Captain Marsh.

'We've been playing your game,' said Sophia, 'and they have been playing theirs.'

'And who, I wonder, is going to lose?'

'I am,' said Sophia.

Chapter Sixteen

Elissa reached Major Kirsten at a run, eight soldiers behind her.

'I'm sorry I'm so late – '

'Come along,' said Major Kirsten, and began to step out. Elissa felt that for once he was not too pleased with her. 'What happened?' he asked.

'A lack of cooperation, Major.' Elissa explained that Colonel Hoffner had been absent. His deputy was not at all helpful. He knew nothing of Major Kirsten and even less than nothing of the major's involvement in the hunt for a British airman and a young lady. Elissa had taken it on herself not to disclose the young lady was General von Feldermann's daughter. That fact Colonel Hoffner had kept to himself, apparently. His deputy made it plain that he did not like a junior WAC officer making demands on his time and attention. It took Elissa far longer than she expected to convince him that Major Kirsten and Colonel Hoffner shared an understanding of the matter, and that she and the major had located the missing pair. In the end, very grudgingly, a small party of garrison soldiers was detailed to go with her. It included a sergeant and a corporal.

'A triumph of perseverance,' said Major Kirsten. He turned and beckoned the sergeant to come up with him, and he beckoned the corporal too. The NCOs arrived at his side, saluted and marched briskly with him. The sergeant addressed him.

'Sergeant Lugar, Major.'

'Yes. Good. Listen.' Major Kirsten indicated the direction taken by their quarry. 'Your men are to go after them at the double. The moment they're spotted, one man is to double back to report to me. Corporal, you take charge. Do nothing except keep them in sight. Sergeant Lugar, please stay with me.'

'Very good, Major,' said Sergeant Lugar. He cracked a thumb and forefinger, and the corporal went off at the double with the men. Sergeant Lugar took up a position ahead of Elissa and the major, and marched at a steady pace, the tireless pace of a veteran.

'They'll stop at some point, our man and Sophia,' said Major Kirsten to Elissa, 'for I'm certain they won't try to creep into the town except at night. On the other hand, our man is capable of the unexpected. I thought him comfortably tucked up in that wood with

Sophia, and that he wouldn't move until dark. But out he popped, and they both moved fast. She seemed quite willing. He did take her by the arm at one point, but what that meant I can't say. If she had words with him, I was too far away to hear. I wonder why he took the risk of coming out into the open?'

'Perhaps we failed in our performance, Major?' said Elissa. 'Perhaps I was too much the nervous amateur to be convincing?'

'Don't be modest,' said Major Kirsten. 'Your performance was splendid, and you'll receive all the credit due to you, whether we were convincing or not.'

'Major,' said Elissa in alarm, 'you aren't going to submit a written report that I – that we – Major, I shall never live down such a report.'

'You think not?' he said, eyes on the disappearing soldiers and the unhelpful portent of failing light.

'With all due respect,' said Elissa, more alarmed, 'written details of such a performance will arouse incredulity and – and hilarity.'

'Damned if I'll stand for that,' said Major Kirsten, 'but I didn't intend putting in a written report, in any case. I merely thought of letting the general know how splendid you've been. Let's hurry. If we lose our pigeons, I'll blow my own head off.'

They quickened their pace in the wake of

Sergeant Lugar, and after a while passed the end of the extensive stretch of trees.

The twilight was turning to dusk. Captain Marsh and Sophia had heard the running German soldiers going on a line pointing directly to the southern environs of Douai. They kept going, the corporal in the lead, the men strung out behind him. Some way ahead was one of the main roads leading to Douai.

A little while after the soldiers had passed by, Captain Marsh and Sophia heard other people. Too many trees and too much foliage prevented them from seeing who they were. They had a view of the pastureland to the rear, a view which took in the distant copse, but they could see nothing ahead or to the side. But they heard Major Kirsten's voice, and then Elissa's. Captain Marsh gave Sophia a pointed look. She shrugged. They stayed silent, and they listened. The sounds of the voices faded. Periodically, muffled clangs travelled to their ears from the plane sheds.

Sophia, aware of the gloom of oncoming dusk, said, 'I think this quite farcical. It's absurd, perched up here like chickens or owls.'

'I don't think owls would consider it absurd,' said Captain Marsh. 'They sit purposefully all night, while more foolish creatures scurry about in the grass and get eaten. However, as the hounds have passed us by, I think we can climb down now.'

'Thank you.' Sophia was only too ready to free herself from her close physical contact with him, a contact that did nothing to ease her suffering soul. 'It will be a relief not to have to descend in the dark. My courage would fail me.'

'I don't think your courage would ever fail you.'

'Would you please spare me these unwanted compliments? Go down, if you will.'

'Yes, I think I'd better go first,' he said.

She knew this meant he intended to ensure she did not come to grief, that he was considerate of her welfare.

He began the descent. She followed. He did not hurry, timing his downward climb to coincide with hers. It was not easy, and he concerned himself with her safety, maintaining contact so that she was always just above him. Her booted feet reached for branches, and she sacrificed a good part of her modesty as her legs stretched downwards, one after the other. He extended an assisting hand from time to time. She took it, and there were moments when she held tightly to it. Their boots scraped bark or bruised the foliage, creating sounds noisy to their ears. Reaching the ground, Captain Marsh turned to receive her as she jumped from the final branch. She landed in his arms. For a brief second he held her. For a brief second each was a warmth to the other. Then she broke free.

'And now?' she said, a catch in her voice and her back to him.

'Not the way the bloodhounds went or we might run into their jaws,' he said. 'But let's take a look first.'

They moved to the end of the wood and took a look. Captain Marsh stiffened and Sophia drew a breath. Not far away, at no more than a hundred metres, three people were moving quietly towards the wood. One was a woman.

'They've turned back,' whispered Sophia. 'They've guessed where we are.'

'Their car,' breathed Captain Marsh, drawing back with her. 'They left their car.'

'We're to take it? But without the keys – '

'Most cars can be started without a key – come on.'

She went with him as he began a fast, raking progress through the length of the wood, heading for the open and the area in which the copse lay. They could not, in their hurry, command silence from their feet, and the rustle of every disturbed leaf and twig seemed betrayingly harsh. But they could not risk breaking their cover before they had to. Sophia thought the little forest twice as long as it had looked, and dangerously unquiet after a while. Indeed, by the time they broke out at the far end, she was all too aware of whispering sounds that told her the hunters were on to them.

Major Kirsten came to a halt at the main road. With Elissa and Sergeant Lugar, he surveyed the clear, open ground beyond the road. It was flat and quite without cover. He knew the quarry would not have crossed. That wide landscape of flatness would have been too revealing. At night, certainly, it could prove easy going, but the night had not yet arrived. There was still light. And the road was no rural byway. It carried German military traffic. The Englishman would not have risked being clearly spotted.

The corporal and his six men had crossed the road minutes ago. They were far ahead and almost indistinguishable. They would reach the outskirts of Douai in time, but with not a hair of the RFC pilot's head to show for their efforts.

The quarry had gone to ground again. But where? There had been no cover for them once they had passed that wood adjacent to the Luftwaffe repair shops. And unless they had run they would at least have been glimpsed by the corporal and his men, going at the double. So where were they?

'They've slipped us, Lieutenant,' he said.

'It seems so,' said Elissa, and silently reflected on how desperate Sophia von Feldermann must be to reach her lover if she could only do so by running in company with a man who was at war with her country. Elissa felt sad.

'Damn it,' said Major Kirsten, 'they can't be using the road, they can only – ' He paused. He looked back. 'I wonder now,' he said, 'have they hopped from one wood to the next? To gain a few hundred metres? But why do that in daylight, when they could have stayed where they were, waiting for dark? Any suggestions, Sergeant Lugar?'

'Yes, Major. Why not take a look?'

They retraced their steps, Major Kirsten asking for silence. When they reached the wood, the light was gloomy. Cautiously they entered, the major signalling to Elissa to keep to the rear. His hand was in his coat pocket, in contact with his revolver, and Sergeant Lugar held his rifle at the ready. They advanced as quietly as they could. Far ahead of them, a woken pigeon left its perch with startled slaps of its wings. Leaves stirred and whispered. Major Kirsten smiled wryly. Of course. The quarry had been here all the time. The moment they passed the wood, they must have seen the complete lack of cover in front of them and all around, and had retreated into their only haven to wait for the night.

They were up and moving now, beating another retreat. Physically fit, and impelled by purpose and dedication, the major began to run, Sergeant Lugar behind him and Elissa on the sergeant's heels. It had been wise to keep Sergeant Lugar with him. Between the two of them, they could pin their man down.

It occurred to Elissa, in an unreal moment, that the runaways were becoming as fond of woodland havens as lovers.

Sophia and Captain Marsh, plunging out of the wood into the dusk, picked up their feet and ran.

'Sophia – think – must you do this?'

'Yes – yes,' she panted.

'Then for God's sake, run ahead of me and run fast.' His revolver was out, pointing at her. 'This is to make you move – you understand?'

She understood. He was protecting her reputation as a proud patriot. When the hunters saw her running, they would also see Captain Marsh and his gesturing revolver. They might think there was nothing to stop her falling, nothing to stop her using some kind of delaying tactic like a tumble, but all the same it was reasonable to assume she was too frightened to attempt anything. And she had to run, she had to. It was all despairingly compulsive.

He urged her on. She hitched up her coat and skirts, and her long legs stretched out. She flew over the ground in the dim grey light, and heard him behind her, his booted feet a rhythmic thudding. And she heard the sounds of pursuit. From the repair sheds back there and away to the left, the other sounds began again, the muffled clang of metal on metal, with not one mechanic aware of the distant drama. She ran. Incredibly, her heart and mind and body were suddenly charged with exhilaration, as if pursuit was a challenge that sent the adrenalin racing and quickened every nerve. The speed of her flight was a wild infectiousness to herself. Behind her, Captain Marsh saw her go, gracefully athletic, her fair hair streaming. Oh, my God, she's beautiful, he thought. And she could run, by Jesus she could.

Major Kirsten was out in the open, Sergeant Lugar crashing through and Elissa threading her way with an economy of effort. The light was going fast, but she saw them clearly, the man and the woman, and for the first time. There they were, two hundred metres and more ahead, Sophia tall and agile, the airman at her heels. How they were running, the ground clear for them all the way to that copse, that place of leafy shrub and bush. The airman's left arm was swinging to the rhythm of his run, his right hand making gestures.

Major Kirsten, moving sparingly, conserving resilience and stamina, showed a brief, tigerish smile. Sophia was flying under the threat of a gun, or so it seemed. He had never seen so fleet a woman.

Sergeant Lugar, sturdy and barrel-chested,

rifle in his hand, pounded hard in a burst of speed. He passed Major Kirsten.

'Yes – go on,' called the major, 'and try a warning shot – over their heads – over their heads.'

Sergeant Lugar pounded on, but if he had gained on Major Kirsten he had not gained on the runaways. They were opening up distance.

'Major!' called Elissa.

'Stay back!' shouted Major Kirsten.

But Elissa, coat open, ran fast. The major, she knew, was as determined to corner the quarry as the quarry was to escape. 'He has a gun!' she called.

'Yes – so stay back!'

But Elissa kept on.

Sergeant Lugar, his burst of speed flagging, dropped to one knee, drew a breath and roared at the flying pair.

'Halt – or I fire! Halt!'

He aimed his rifle and fired. The shot cracked and echoed. The clang of metal on metal in the distant workshops kept the sound from the ears of the personnel there, and even from the ears of the guard. A bullet flew high above the heads of Sophia and Captain Marsh. Sophia, hearing the crack of the rifle, faltered in her stride.

'Stop if you want – Sophia, stop if you want – I'll give you a push as I go by and you can take a fall.'

The voice was strong and warm and understanding. It induced new compulsion. She ran strongly again. She knew all bullets would fly harmlessly over their heads. Captain Marsh was too close to her for anyone to try bringing him down. The thought of it happening, of him falling and dying, crucified her.

The car, there it was, to the right of the copse and beyond it. They must get to it. But would he have time to raise the bonnet and manipulate the ignition?

What am I doing? What am I doing? Oh, God.

Major Kirsten passed Sergeant Lugar. They ran together.

'Major!' Elissa shouted. 'The car!'

They were heading for it, the quarry; they were heading for the dirt road on which the car was parked, with the small runabout vehicle which had brought the eight soldiers.

'Try another shot, try several,' panted Major Kirsten, and again Sergeant Lugar dropped to one knee. He loosed off three bullets, all of which flew above Sophia and Captain Marsh, and none of which checked them in their race for the car,

Elissa, suddenly alarmed and discomfited, caught up with Major Kirsten.

'Major – the car key – I left it there – in the ignition!'

It had been a lapse caused by her worry over

the fact that Major Kirsten was nowhere around when she pulled up before reaching the copse.

'That's a blow, Lieutenant.' Major Kirsten slowed and called to Sergeant Lugar, who came on again. 'Sergeant Lugar, they're heading for the car. Get as close as you can and see whether you can hit the tyres. The tyres – by God, if you hit the young lady – go on – run.'

Sergeant Lugar drew on his physical reserves and began to pound. Elissa and Major Kirsten ran at a steady pace behind him. Elissa, eyes on the runaways, still flying, thought she had never seen so much purpose in a man and a woman. The woman's hair shone in the gloom.

What was she doing? Why didn't she stop? The airman would never dare to shoot her in sight of her compatriots. He would hang if he did.

Sophia ran on over the thick grass, reaching the dirt road and flying alongside it as she made for the car. The exhilaration was a strange wildness, lifting her and smothering her torment and guilt. The open staff car was nearer, nearer. She ran and ran. She glanced back. She saw the face of Captain Marsh, dark and almost fierce. She saw the revolver he still held.

'Sophia – stop – you must.'

'No – if you can start the car I will drive – I will, I tell you.'

They were passing the copse on their left.

They heard again the roar of a strong German voice.

'Halt! Halt!'

But they flew on. Captain Marsh, anguished for her, played the only part he could as they reached the car. He might perhaps have taken hold of her and flung her down. He might have done that and run on alone, leaving her to be taken care of by the persistent Major Kirsten. But so many of his actions were as compulsive as hers. He did not do what he might have done, what he should have done. Instead, he pointed the revolver at her and gestured with it, a gesture that demanded she get into the car. Sophia, panting and breathless, was so at one with him that she jumped over the open side of the automobile into the driving seat. Captain Marsh darted towards the bonnet. She cried out.

'Peter! The key! It's here!'

Peter? Her use of his name, which he had mentioned only once, compelled from them a moment of precious time in which to stare at each other. The resurgence of torment showed in her eyes.

The rifle cracked and a bullet smacked into the offside fender.

Captain Marsh leapt into the passenger seat. Sophia switched on and started the car, her hands shaking. She opened the throttle. The engine roared.

Sergeant Lugar was no more than eighty metres away, and down on one knee again, rifle steady in its aim. Major Kirsten and Elissa came up with him. The car was moving forward, towards the bend that fronted the end of the copse. It would bring the car sideways on to Sergeant Lugar's rifle. Sophia knew it. She slammed into intermediate gear and accelerated. The car burst into roaring speed.

Major Kirsten ran forward.

'Sophia! Stop!' His voice carried.

Sophia spared him one quick glance. His lifted arm was begging her. The WAC officer was behind him, and a soldier was kneeling, rifle pointed. Sophia powered into the dusk. Sergeant Lugar fired. The bullet nipped a spoke of the rear wheel. He fired again, striking the mudguard. The car rushed on, bouncing and rocking over the terrible road. It passed the line of the copse, dark now beneath a sky turning black. Major Kirsten sighed. It meant nothing, the revolver the British airman was visibly pointing at Sophia. In the major's mind, she had run like the wind of her own free will.

'Major.' Sergeant Lugar rushed up. He brought his rifle to his shoulder. The car was disappearing into grey murk. Sergeant Lugar again took careful aim.

'No.' Major Kirsten pushed the rifle aside. 'Have you got the keys of your wagon?'

'Yes, Major.' Sergeant Lugar grimaced. The car had disappeared.

Elissa caught up, and all three made for the runabout.

'Lieutenant, can you handle that kind of vehicle?' asked Major Kirsten.

'My certificate says I can.'

'Good.' Major Kirsten preferred to have her beside him. He could be frank with her. With Sergeant Lugar it was a question of remaining silent about the fact that they were in pursuit of the daughter of General von Feldermann.

Darkness had arrived. Sergeant Lugar handed the ignition key to Elissa and climbed quickly into the back of the van. Elissa, with Major Kirsten beside her, started the engine. She found the gears cumbersome after the smooth fluency of the staff car, but she gritted her teeth, thrust the lever home and moved off.

'I must redeem myself,' she said.

'You have sinned?' said Major Kirsten gravely.

'If stupidity is a sin, yes, Major. It was very stupid to leave the key in the ignition.'

She switched on the headlamps and the beams cut swathes of light through the encroaching darkness.

'All will be forgiven if you can get some speed out of this old iron,' said the major. A solid wooden partition cut them off from Sergeant Lugar, who was trying to make himself comfortable in the back of the shuddering van.

284

'The road is awful, but I'll try,' said Elissa. She was hot from the long run, and not without a recurring feeling of pity for Sophia von Feldermann, but the excitement of the chase and the mystery of the inexplicable bond that seemed to tie the two runaways closely together, prevailed over all else. She moved into top gear, opened the throttle and the van's sudden surge of speed was a blood-tingling surprise. But it rocked over the rough road like an awkward boat in an untidy swell. She gripped the wheel, kept her foot down and in the light of the headlamps saw the road running and rushing to meet her. The van was built for rough-riding. It tore along, and in a while she picked up the tail lights of the staff car. Sophia had had to switch on. Captain Marsh had agreed.

They had tried to effect a complete disappearance by doing without the headlights, but the swift descent of complete darkness made this impossible.

'You must give me directions,' said Sophia.

'Sophia,' said Captain Marsh, quietly, 'this is completely wrong for you, and I am completely the idiot in piling one mistake on top of every other.'

'We all make mistakes,' said Sophia, just as quietly, 'and I'm more concerned with making decisions, my own decisions. Give me directions. You are better at finding the right roads than I am. Major Kirsten is behind us. They're using the van.'

'Sophia – '

'I've burned my boats, don't you see that?' she said, face set and eyes fixed on the illuminated surface of ruts and ridges.

'Are you so much in love?' he asked.

'What is that to you? Such a question is not for you to ask.'

'I know.' He sounded very sober. 'Well, this road is no good – it's not a road at all, and you can make no real speed on it. But we need to keep within striking distance of Douai. It has to be tonight – I don't think either of us want another day like the last two. So take the first turning on the left that we come to, and we'll try to simply circle around this area. That means a second left turn. I hope we'll find a surfaced road. We must lose the van – and the persistent major. He's hanging on as if you were his own daughter.'

Sophia said nothing to that. She was frighteningly disturbed by every nuance of a relationship that was rushing towards bitter fantasy. She gritted her teeth, as Elissa had gritted hers, but for a different reason. The headlights picked out one of the little crossroads that abounded in the area, and which could send a traveller every way except the right one. Every way was a wandering rural course that farmers knew but which led everyone else nowhere. Except Captain Marsh, perhaps. He always knew where he was, what he was doing, where he was going and what the future held for him. Fritz was an over-bright fatalist, who laughed a lot. Captain Marsh was a survivor, who thought a man should contend with fate.

In a spasm of emotion, she rushed up to the crossroads and spun the car round in a grinding skid that brought its nose into the road on the left. She glimpsed the headlamps of the van in the distance as she powered the car forward. Major Kirsten would have seen her make the turn, because of her own headlamps. But the new road had a tolerable surface to it and she picked up speed immediately, running fast through her gear changes. All too soon, however, the road began to tiresomely wind and wander. Her lights were her lifesaver, picking out the bends for her, and she drove recklessly into every one.

'Do you like polkas, Sophia?' It was a quiet question from Captain Marsh.

'Polkas? Polkas?'

'I asked because at times you're very exuberant and dashing.'

'Stop it,' gasped Sophia. 'Don't talk to me. I wish I'd never met you, and I hope your country sinks into the sea.'

God help me, she thought.

*

Elissa turned left at the crossroads. The van's engine was a singer. It hummed an extraordinarily mellow note quite at variance with the vehicle's unlovely look. She was not at all sure, however, whether she could match the speed of the car or the remarkable skill of its driver. That was another strange facet, the expertise Miss von Feldermann applied to her driving. She did not have to drive as well as that, even under duress. More and more did it seem that she was in collusion with the RFC man. And she was outdistancing the van, for her rear lights were becoming smaller with every turn of the road.

'We're losing them,' said Elissa.

'They've nowhere to go,' said Major Kirsten. 'Persevere, Elissa, and we shall wear them down.'

'I'm afraid the reverse might happen,' she said, straight-backed, tense and concentrating, 'I've never before driven at night.'

It was an effort to brake at just the right time at every bend, to slip into the correct gear with every change in their speed and not to lose more ground.

'My confidence in you is unshakeable,' said Major Kirsten, peering to pick up the lights of the car. 'You have many gifts, and if the Women's Army Corps isn't disbanded after the war, it will offer you an exciting and rewarding career.'

'That isn't what I want after the war,' said Elissa, wrenching at the wheel as the van rounded the sharpest of bends.

'Ah, so?' murmured the major. 'There's a young man?'

'No, Major – are there any?'

'God in heaven,' he said, 'is that what the war has done to Germany and for its young women?'

Perhaps they both thought then that what did it matter, this relentless pursuit of a man and a woman? Compared with the afflictions and inflictions of war, how could it matter?

But the van raced on through the black night, its headlamps searching the dark way with beams of light.

'Left,' said Captain Marsh.

Sophia saw the approaching junction. She neither banked nor changed gear, but used the full width of the road to sweep round into the left-hand fork. Her front offside fender scraped a bank. The bank tore at it. A farmhouse loomed darkly on her right, and a dog ran out, barking furiously. It was caught by the lights in front of the car. Sophia's foot jammed hard on the brake, and the car slewed and ran its nose into the opposite bank. Sophia and Captain Marsh were jerked forward. The engine stalled and the dog leapt, snarling. Sophia came out of gear, restarted the engine and backed off.

The front offside fender jangled. The dog leapt again, like an animal ferociously determined to savage whatever it could reach. With a clenched right fist, Captain Marsh punched its snout. The dog howled and whirled about. Sophia swung the wheel and shot forward. The dog gave furious chase, snapping and snarling at the back of the car. Sophia put her foot down and the car raced away.

The chilly night wind gusted around her, but she did not feel cold. Her nerves were feverish, her blood heated. She and Captain Marsh had stolen a German Army staff car, and there was a new turn in the chase, a new challenge. The dark road flung its hazards at her, and lights shone behind her. The van was close. The dog had cost them seconds they could not afford. She awaited a comment from her companion, but he was silent.

'You are critical?' She spoke angrily. 'You should blame the dog, not me.'

The front offside fender was hanging and banging.

'I'm far from critical, I'm very impressed.' Captain Marsh turned in his seat, the wind buffeting his face and hair. He saw the lights of the van. It was no more than fifty metres behind them. 'Go on,' he said, 'there's no crisis, only a few lost seconds.'

*

Elissa had slowed at the junction, not sure which fork the car had taken. Major Kirsten peered:

'There they are,' he said. 'Elissa, you've gained on them. What a splendid young lady you are.'

The rear lights of the car were so much closer than expected that Elissa was astonished. Either she had performed minor miracles in her handling of the van, or the fugitives had suffered a minor hold-up. She drove in very purposeful pursuit, her blood tingling, her mind wondering at the actions and behaviour of General von Feldermann's daughter. A dog ran yapping and howling at the van as it passed a farmhouse. In the beam of light, Elissa saw its lips drawn back and its teeth gleaming. It was fierce enough to run beside the van, snapping and snarling, and Elissa winced at its fury.

'The dreadful creature,' she gasped.

'They're not dogs, some of these French farm breeds,' said Major Kirsten, 'they're savages on four legs. Keep going, Elissa.'

Elissa, aware of the fast-moving rear lights ahead, did her best not to lose them. The wind thudded against the tightly anchored canvas cover. In the back of the vehicle, Sergeant Lugar was jolted about as he tried to light what was left of a precious cigarette.

Along the winding country road, the two vehicles rushed, light piercing the darkness. The car burst out of every bend. The van swayed and shuddered. The skill and flair of the car's driver were fired by the challenge of pursuit and by other things. The driver of the van went resolutely by the book. Both women were entirely admirable to their companions. Only Sergeant Lugar had his mind on something that was unrelated to the outcome. He was thinking wistfully of his comfortable quarters in Douai and a French widow who had come to like his sturdy, straightforward manliness. Countries could be poles apart, but people were people.

The car forged ahead.

Chapter Seventeen

'Do something,' Sophia said.

The loose fender was shaking and banging, screaming at her nerves.

'I can't do anything unless we stop,' said Captain Marsh. 'Then I'll pull the damn thing off.'

'Yes, why not? It isn't our car.' Sophia was running out of self-control, every emotion under attack from the sharp dagger of shattered self-respect. 'Why not blow it up when we've finished with it?'

'Should we treat it so unkindly when it's serving us so well?'

'Unkindly?' Sophia's brittle laugh was a little hysterical. 'Are you crazy?'

'I'm worried about you.'

'I am touched.' Sophia was bitter. The realization of what she was doing and the strain of this wild night drive were diminishing the fevered excitement of the challenge. Her hands trembled on the wheel and the beams of the headlamps danced before her eyes. 'We are going nowhere, we are running in circles.'

'Are you suffering, Sophia, because you know you're doing the wrong thing?' The question was sympathetic and understanding, and her emotions swamped her.

'Oh, that is so stupid. I am doing what I want to do. I have said so, a hundred times.'

'I don't think Fritz would want you to—'

'He is nothing to do with you!' Sophia, tormented, skidded the car around a tight bend. 'You throw his name about as if you were his comrade. You are not his comrade. You have probably been trying to shoot him down for months.'

'It's how things are in war, Sophia.'

'You are not to call me Sophia!' It was a cry of despair.

'I'm sorry.' He looked at her, at her hair whipping in the slipstream, and at her profile. Her mouth was unsteady, her teeth biting on her bottom lip. She looked desperately unhappy, she looked vulnerable, and she was becoming an increasing worry to him. Some of her actions had been incomprehensible. She was having reckless moments at the wheel, and only her skill overcame the hazards she created for herself. He felt she was going to lose the road at times, but she never did. She could handle a car magnificently.

The van was far behind. Its headlamps

blinked and winked at intervals, and were lost in between. He judged they had almost half a mile on it.

A right-hand fork appeared, and he got Sophia to take it.

'Keep going now,' he said, 'I think we're facing Douai again.'

'You are sure?' she said edgily.

'Yes.'

He was always sure, she thought. He was that kind of man. He was like a Junker in a way. Yet he was also not like a Junker at all.

'What happens when we reach the road to Douai?' she asked.

'We'll decide that only if we've lost the bloodhounds.'

She drove on. The images that tormented her mind were black and shapeless, except one, which was paralysingly bright and clear.

It was impossible, but it existed.

The van was running bravely, its warm engine humming, pistons and cylinders a perfected harmony, and Elissa was more relaxed in her driving, despite knowing she could not catch the car. It was quite mad, this chase after the fugitives through the byways of rural France at night, but it was a mesmerizing madness. She escaped a little from what she thought her instructor would have called the limits of her competence, and began to take some bends at a quite giddy speed. The van threatened to leave the road once or twice and plant itself angrily in a ditch. Major Kirsten made no comment. He was intrigued by Elissa's adventurous moments, and asked only that they did not lose the car completely, despite it now being far ahead. They tracked it by the beam of its lights.

The farms were silent, the fields black and invisible. Only the road and the hedges came to the eye.

'We shall never catch them, Major,' said Elissa.

'Remember they'll stay off all main roads, Elissa. Every main road will be full again.'

'We are going to chase them around in circles?'

'We are going to wear them down,' said Major Kirsten, 'unless we lose them. I hope we don't. I'm already badly demoralized.'

Elissa coaxed herself into finding more acceleration. The vehicle scorched up to a bend, juddered as she braked, and careered drunkenly around the curve. The back nearside wheel hit the verge and hovered for a crazy second above a ditch before Elissa, foot down, snatched it from disaster. The van lurched and careered on. Elissa fought the road and the recalcitrant wheels, wrists aching as she brought the van on course and scorched on.

'I apologize,' she said breathlessly.

'Do you? Why?' Major Kirsten, a man not easily shaken, could find no fault.

'There was nearly an accident.'

'Nearly an accident is inadmissible. You are an adorable young lady. Drive on.'

'Major?' she said, colour flooding her.

'Put your foot down – don't get lost.'

Elissa wondered. Did he know what he had said? Adorable? She had not been called that before, at least not since she was a child of seven or so.

'They're well behind now,' said Captain Marsh, and Sophia wished he would not sound as if he had no weaknesses. She had a thousand of her own. 'Switch the lights off as soon as we come to the next farmhouse and run the car in.'

'If you say so,' she said, like a woman who was ill.

'Are you all right?'

'No.'

'Then I really think we should—'

'Don't talk, please.' There was no real conversation she could have with him. A dialogue polite or civilized or tolerant was meaningless. The extreme was preferable, a furious and blazing quarrel. That would have its own meaning. She drove automatically, so much so that she passed the entrance to a farmhouse before she was aware of it. She did not stop, she kept going, waiting for Captain Marsh to tell her she had missed her chance. He said nothing. Perversely, she felt resentful, and again her teeth caught her bottom lip.

She concentrated, but it was some while before the car lights picked out an opening that looked promising. It was a wide entrance that sloped a little. She made a slow turn into it, braked gently, came out of gear, switched off the lamps and rolled silently down the slight slope into a large farmyard.

Squinting into the darkness, Captain Marsh whispered, 'Keep going.'

Under the brake, the car eased forward past the side of a farmhouse and towards the looming bulk of a barn. Sophia had enough impetus to coast very slowly into the barn. There was a rustle as the bonnet nosed into hay. The car stopped.

'This is satisfactory?' said Sophia.

'Very. Well done.'

'I did not want to arouse any dog,' she whispered.

'No. Very wise. We'll wait now.'

They sat silently in the car and waited for the van. If it went by, if it continued on, they could assume the hunters would spend the rest of the night chasing shadows.

It was a few minutes before they heard the van. It approached quite fast, its lights whitely scouring the road, its engine humming. It passed the farmhouse entrance at a rush.

A little of the strange exhilaration returned to Sophia.

'They've lost us,' she breathed.

'We've diddled them,' said Captain Marsh in English.

'Excuse me? Diddled?'

He explained. Sophia laughed, shakily.

'And we can go now?' she said.

'We'll wait a little longer.'

Major Kirsten asked Elissa to stop. They had noted the disappearance of the far-off beams some minutes ago, and seen nothing of them since. Elissa, bringing the van to a halt beside the verge, said, 'Major?'

'Damnation,' muttered the Major.

'Yes, Major, quite so,' said Elissa.

'Either they've stopped and we've passed them, or they're driving without lights. But they can't be, not on a night as black as this. Did you ever encounter a more elusive gentleman?'

'I think encounter is the wrong word,' said Elissa.

'Have we passed any turns or junctions since we last noticed them about ten minutes ago?'

'I'm not aware we have.'

'Nevertheless,' said Major Kirsten, 'I'm convinced we must have passed them. That means they must have turned off somewhere.'

'Have you considered farmhouses?' asked Elissa.

'Ah. Thank you. Turn and go back, please,

and—' The major broke off as Sergeant Lugar appeared beside his door.

'Major?'

Opening the door, Major Kirsten said, 'Get back in.'

'I thought you'd found—'

'We haven't. We're about to turn round.'

Sergeant Lugar climbed back in.

'We're going to look for farmyards?' said Elissa, beginning the turn.

'Yes. Turn into each one we come to – no, don't do that. Drive past and pull up when I ask you to.'

'I am yours obediently, Major,' said Elissa, and with the panache of a young lady who had escaped from the confinement of painful reserve.

'How charming,' said Major Kirsten with a smile.

Sophia and Captain Marsh, buried in the barn with the car, made no move. There was no hurry, in any case. They still had many hours of darkness in front of them. Beyond the barn the farmhouse lay dark and silent. But there would be a light showing, thought Captain Marsh, on the far side of the house. A kitchen light. There might be a dog, perhaps, lying with its nose between its forepaws on the kitchen floor. Sophia's very silent coasting roll down to the barn had been perfect in its unobtrusiveness.

She stiffened in her seat. Out of the silent night came the humming noise of the van. It was on its way back. Captain Marsh grimaced in the darkness. The van went by, lights shining. They heard it going steadily until the sound died.

'I'm not sure I like that,' whispered Captain Marsh, 'I'm getting out. I don't want to be trapped.'

'But they've gone on,' breathed Sophia.

'Have they? How far?' He got out. Sophia hesitated. He had not suggested she should get out too. What was he going to do, disappear while she sat there? He was capable of doing that. He would not mind at all if Major Kirsten took charge of her. He was in favour of that. She felt desperately unhappy. 'Sophia?' He whispered her name. 'Are you going to stay there or do you still want us to go together?'

'Yes – oh, yes,' she breathed. She opened the door and slid swiftly out. He took her by the arm, and she did not object. They moved very quietly out of the barn and across the extensive, mud-caked farmyard to stand against the front wall of the house, close to the front door that faced the dark fields and pastures. From there, if necessary, they could make another run for it, into the black void of the fields.

They waited. Sophia felt she had endured an eternity of waiting moments with him, but she could not separate herself from his run for freedom. She was close beside him, their shoulders touching, and she could not separate herself from that, either.

The silence gave way to little sounds. There were footsteps on the road. Sophia tensed. Captain Marsh had read the mind of Major Kirsten. The van had gone on, yes, but not very far. They were coming, the three of them – Major Kirsten, the woman, and the soldier with the rifle. Anguish consumed her, and the images of guilt and weakness clarified to dance in fiendish brightness in her mind.

What did it matter, however, this single event among a million events in the execution of a terrible war? Against all that, she and Captain Marsh were as insignificant as seeds blown by the wind. Why could they not be left to run as free as the wind?

The darkness was cold and eerie. Huge cloud formations smothered the sky and hid the stars. The footsteps were clearer now. A hand touched hers. Warm fingers closed around her gloved ones. Sophia, suffering her realization of the impossible, did not know what was to become of her, for as the hand squeezed hers in encouragement, she returned the pressure.

Major Kirsten, Elissa and Sergeant Lugar turned in at the farmyard entrance, moving cautiously. They were there to check a suspicion, not to confirm a certainty. Major Kirsten went to the right of the extensive yard, Sergeant Lugar to the left. Elissa kept central. The place seemed empty of everything except black shadow. Elissa made out the side of the house and the vague outline of a high barn in front of her. She was primed for a quick retreat from danger, if necessary. She did not think the fugitives were here, but Major Kirsten and Sergeant Lugar were intent on making sure. It was unexpected and uncomfortable, a sudden tautening of her skin and a little dart of coldness down her spine, as if her subconscious was aware of unseen eyes watching her. Elissa moved slowly towards the great, dark barn. What was that, that dark outline against the faint paleness of heaped straw.

A light startled her. It illuminated the window of a room at the front of the farmhouse, to the right of the door. A lamp, just lit, was flaring. Elissa gazed at the window. The light spread and in its diffused paleness she stared into wide, stunned eyes. It was such a faint glow that light, but it was enough for Elissa to see the eyes were a deep, night blue.

And Sophia, transfixed, looked into the eyes of the woman, eyes that were shadowed by a peaked cap.

Sophia could only transmit a silent plea.

The lamp moved as it was carried from the room. The light went with it, and the front of the farmhouse presented a blankness once more. Elissa turned and walked away. Sergeant Lugar kicked at something, and inside the house a dog began to bark.

Major Kirsten made himself heard.

'Sergeant Lugar?'

'Nothing to report, Major.'

'Lieutenant?'

'I'm here,' said Elissa, by the entrance.

'We've drawn a blank?'

'Yes, Major,' she said.

'Well, now that we've disturbed their dog, let's get on. That car must be tucked up in one of these places.'

'What's happening to Corporal Fischer and my men, that's what I'd like to know,' said Sergeant Lugar, not without a slightly grumbling note.

'Back in Douai by now and resting their feet,' said Major Kirsten.

They left. The dog continued barking.

'She saw me,' breathed Sophia.

'Impossible,' whispered Captain Marsh, wishing the dog would shut up.

'She saw me.'

'Did she say so? Something was said.'

'She agreed with Major Kirsten that they'd drawn a blank – but she knew we were here – she saw me. We must go, we must.' Sophia's whispers were urgent.

'No, not yet. They'll hear us and jump on our tail again. We must lose them.'

304

'But don't you see, they'll come back – she'll tell Major Kirsten – she has to – they'll catch you if you stay – ' Sophia jumped as a door at the back of the house was noisily opened to let out the barking dog. Captain Marsh took her arm and they ran back to the barn to get to the car. The dog came fast from around the house. Bristling and hostile, it was at them, and Sophia, remembering the other dog, was paralysed. A dark, blurred shape, it leapt at her arm to pull her down. Captain Marsh knocked it sideways in mid-air with a blow from his right fist. It yelped, it snarled, and turned again on Sophia, its teeth savaging the skirt of her coat. Sophia kicked it. It leapt, jaws agape, and took her by her left arm.

Captain Marsh pulled out his revolver and shot it.

Back at the van, Major Kirsten, Elissa and Sergeant Lugar all heard the shot; a sharp, explosive crack.

'My God!' Major Kirsten, appalled, jerked the van door open for Elissa. Elissa, a guilty silence on her conscience, was even more appalled than he was. She slid in fast. Major Kirsten ran round and got in beside her. Sergeant Lugar tumbled into the back. Elissa began a quick and frantic turn. 'They were there,' breathed the major, 'my God, they were there, and we missed them – get back fast, Elissa.'

Elissa, completing the turn, put her foot down and the van vibrated as it raced back to the farmyard.

'Major – he couldn't have – '

'I assumed, I accepted, he wouldn't really use that pistol, that he and Sophia had found something in common – God in heaven, has he proved himself the complete madman, after all?'

It was in Elissa's mind too, the terrible suspicion that the man's nerves had snapped and that Sophia had been shot.

'Major – '

'He's away, Elissa – look!'

She saw the car. It came roaring out in reverse from the farm entrance, swung round and burst forward, going away from them. The roar of the engine died away as the gears were slammed through to top, and the sound became a hum of power.

'Shall I stop?' gasped Elissa, suffering a mental picture of an inert body and blue eyes closed in death.

'No,' said Major Kirsten in a suppressed voice, 'they're both in the car.'

Elissa, speeding past the entrance, caught a brief glimpse of a man with a lamp standing over the carcase of a dog.

'A dog – he shot a dog,' she cried in a rush of beautiful relief.

'He's done no service to the farmer, but he

has to unexpected callers,' said Major Kirsten. 'That kind of dog thinks the uninvited arrive to be eaten. And most French farm dogs are partial to Germans. That one may have been trying to eat Sophia. But where the devil were they hiding out in that farmyard, with the car? The three of us searched every corner.'

'It was very dark,' said Elissa, fighting the road in her attempt to match the speed of the car, which was already gaining.

'Even so – Elissa, foot down – never mind the road – foot down – stay with them, and when Ludendorff brings us into Paris I'll do myself the great pleasure of dining with you at Maxim's.'

Elissa, conscience pricking her again, did all she could to reach maximum speed over an indifferent surface. The van hummed and vibrated, its canvas cover, stretched over a rattling frame, noisy and resistant. She saw the rear lights of the car before it disappeared around the thousandth bend of the night. A little sigh escaped her. She was in the middle now. She had put herself between Major Kirsten and his quarry. She did not like the way it made her feel. But those wide, startled eyes – and the appeal in them.

It was impossible to accept what one felt, that the daughter of a German general had found she had so much in common with a British airman that she was running with him to help him escape. Her lover, the young German airman, must have become irrelevant.

To Elissa, the car seemed to be travelling at an incredible speed on such a road on such a night. It was pulling away from the van at an alarming rate. She was losing the rear lights, and only the beam of the headlamps marked its course.

'She's driving too well for me, Major.'

'The car is easier to handle than this old iron,' said Major Kirsten. 'Has it occurred to you that we've never seen him driving? There's just a faint hope that she is under coercion, coercion of some kind. That's something I must impress on Sergeant Lugar. He must not suspect there is no coercion.'

'It was wise to put him where he is,' said Elissa.

'It was also selfish. You have more appeal for me than he has.'

Elissa, bringing the van around a bend with its tyres protesting, said, 'That is an official comment?'

'A heartfelt one, Lieutenant – damnation, I've lost their lights.'

Their own lights picked out crossroads ahead. The lights of the car had disappeared. The black landscape was dead. Elissa brought the van to a halt.

'Which way?' she asked, and he was not to know she would not be unhappy if the car had given them the final slip.

'Straight on,' said the major. 'I think we'd have noticed the change in the direction of their lights if they'd turned left or right. Yes, straight on.'

But they slowed and stopped after ten minutes. There was only blackness on all sides of them.

'We've lost them,' said Elissa. 'Shall we take Sergeant Lugar back to Douai and then return to Headquarters? We have to be on duty tomorrow morning.'

'No, by God,' said Major Kirsten, 'we aren't returning yet. We'll get out, and we'll look and listen.'

'Very well Major.'

'Shall we give up?' said Captain Marsh. They were at a halt after turning left at the crossroads with their lights switched off and the car creeping along for five minutes.

'You don't mean that,' said Sophia. She was shivering. She had driven like a crazy woman since reversing fast out of the farmyard. That dog had been a nightmare.

'You're cold,' said Captain Marsh.

'You're worried about that?'

'I'm worried about everything.'

'So you want to give up? It is all going to be for nothing?'

He turned in his seat to look at her. Her lips compressed and her teeth grated.

'I was thinking,' he said, 'you take the gun.'

He offered it to her, its metal a dull gleam. 'Switch on the lights. That will bring them to us. You will have the gun. The turning of the tables, Sophia.'

'You will let me do that, let me hand you over? You won't mind?'

'It's the best thing – for both of us.'

'But will you mind?' Sophia was insistent, and shivering uncontrollably.

'No, of course not.'

But he would mind, she knew he would. He was not a man who would like being locked up.

She said, 'It's a terrible war.'

'Yes.'

'You and I, we are not really very important. Generals are important and big guns even more important. Armies are important. But you are only one of many thousands of airmen, and I am only one of many millions of women. If you fly against Richtofen again, will that mean the winning or the losing of the war? If I disappoint my parents, will that mean the collapse of Germany? You see, you and I are very insignificant. The gods of war don't even notice us. Captain Marsh – ' Sophia hesitated.

'Yes?'

'Why should we give up? You are at war with me, yes, but I – I think you a man of great courage, and I don't wish you to give up. You risked your freedom when you fired that gun and shot the dog.'

'I shot it because it was trying to eat your arm.'

'My leather sleeve saved me – how can people keep dogs as savage at that?'

'To prevent hungry people like me raiding their farms.'

'Don't make jokes, please.'

'No. The situation has never been one to encourage jokes. You're cold. I'll put the hood up. You're sure you don't want this gun?'

'No!' Wildly, she pushed it away. 'There are too many guns, too much killing.'

'Yes, I know,' he said, and got out.

Sophia sat quietly while he worked the hood into position and enclosed the shining cloud of her hair. The night was so silent, the war in the trenches dormant, the guns at rest. Suddenly, the silence was so absolute, the hood fixed, and Captain Marsh making not a whisper of sound. She jerked upright in her seat. He had gone. He had slipped away. She would never find him in this darkness. She flung the car door open and, in anguished panic, slid out and came frantically to her feet. She rushed around the car.

'Sophia?' It was a cautious whisper. She turned. He was leaning against the back of the car smoking a cigarette.

'Oh, my God,' she said, and turned away, trembling. When she had thought him gone, it was as if life itself had left her.

'What's wrong?'

'Nothing,' she whispered, 'nothing.'

'I thought this all a great challenge,' he said, 'but it's become a great strain, hasn't it?'

'But it has been a challenge, yes,' she said, facing him. 'Do you think events are too much for people? Do you think some events present such awful problems that people think they can only solve them by going to war?'

'Some people think that,' said Captain Marsh, eyes searching the darkness. 'What I think is that you were right; you and I are un-important in relation to everything else. As for being insignificant, I am, but you aren't. No woman can be called insignificant. Women are far more necessary to life and the future than men are. If you'll forgive me for throwing his name about again, I don't think Fritz considers you insignificant in the least.'

'He – I – I am not actually engaged to him.'

'I thought—' Captain Marsh stopped and listened. Out of the night came the small but distinct sound of a clang. It became repetitive.

High above the sleeping earth, clouds broke apart and the black sky was pierced by the brilliant silver crescent of a new moon.

Sophia said, 'That sound is familiar.'

'It's coming from over there,' said Captain Marsh, pointing. 'We've come almost full circle. It's that plane-repair works, and they're still busy. I think that road near the copse isn't far ahead of us. We'll drive there and then walk. We can take the route past that wood again and cross the main road.' He threw away his cigarette and gave Sophia a warm smile. 'Shall we do that?'

'We have lost Major Kirsten and the others?' she said.

'It seems so – I hope so.'

'Then why should we give up?' she said, and got back into the car. He joined her. She switched on the lights and fired the engine.

Sergeant Lugar was some way off in his looking and listening. Major Kirsten was standing on the square bonnet of the van, which Elissa thought practical in respect of elevated observation, but not quite what any disabled man should do for a living. He had been up there ten minutes, like a balanced monument of patience and hope. It was another minute before his act brought its reward. He picked up the sudden beam of light in the distance. The light began to move.

'Your hand, please, Lieutenant.'

Elissa reached up. He took a firm hold of her hand and jumped down. He buckled a little, then straightened up. Elissa regarded him with a certain wry wistfulness, wanting him to know that in her feelings for him as the man he was, she did not require him to behave like an acrobat.

'Major, you'll break a leg if you – '

'Bless you, young lady, you sound as my wife would have certainly sounded, but never mind. I've seen them. We'll go back to the crossroads and turn right. Sergeant Lugar!'

Sergeant Lugar, who had been wishing himself tucked up with the French widow, came hurrying up to take his place in the van. Elissa started up, turned the van round and headed for the crossroads. Reaching them, she took the right-hand road. She peered. She could see no lights.

'There's no sign of them,' she said.

'There will be,' said Major Kirsten, 'and we shall catch them in the end.'

Bravely, Elissa said, 'Must we?'

He did not seem to analyse the reason for her question, but simply said, 'Yes, Elissa, we must.'

For the sake of the major, and for the sake of her conscience, Elissa put her foot down.

Far ahead, a faint beam of light appeared.

It was very familiar, the rough road the van eventually found itself on. The clouds had parted again, and the new moon brought tolerable visibility to the night.

'Major, I think we're near that little copse,' said Elissa.

'The romantic Arcadia? Yes. It's down there, on our left.'

'Should we have turned right to join the road to Douai?' she asked, slowing down.

'They won't take the car on to that road.'

'But between them they're remarkably audacious,' said Elissa.

'I wonder? Elissa, make a turn somewhere and head for the Douai road. Even if they don't use it, they may leave the car and mark their direction for us.'

Elissa began a turn a little way on. Her headlamps threw light over field grass. Major Kirsten put a hand on her arm. She saw what he had spotted. The staff car, its hood up. It had been driven off the road and carefully parked out of sight of any pursuing vehicle. In making a turn at this point, Elissa had caught it in her lights. She sighed.

'We'll never catch them now,' she said.

'We'll see. They've returned to the same starting point for their final lap. It's easy to walk across country from here to Douai. They're probably making a night stroll of it at this precise moment. But how far will they get? That road runs west to the front.'

'Yes, I know,' said Elissa, 'and will be busy to-night.'

'I'll take Sergeant Lugar with me. You return to Headquarters now. I think you're tired. There's the car.'

'I'm not at all tired,' said Elissa, 'and would like to see it through with you.'

Chapter Eighteen

Having abandoned the staff car to complete their journey on foot, Captain Marsh and Sophia were now back at the point where, hours ago, they had turned about and retreated into the wooded belt adjacent to the repair sheds. This time, however, they continued straight on.

'The road shouldn't be far,' said Captain Marsh. 'We can either cross it and keep going, or risk walking some way along it before turning off. We need to make our final approach over common land on the outskirts of the town.'

'You know the area so well?' said Sophia. Physically she was not too fatigued. Mentally she was beginning to feel drained.

'I've flown over it a few times. It's easier to draw a picture of any part of France than it is any part of a desert.'

'Yes. Of course.' Sophia would have liked to blank out the images that danced so exhaustingly in her mind. Curiously, guilt had become vaguer than so much else. Among so much else was the thought that it would not be long now before they said goodbye to each other. What would that entail – a few awkward words and nothing about the fact they would never meet again? 'It isn't so dark now,' she said with help-less irrelevance.

'No. It's a new moon.' He was walking easily, unhurriedly, matching his pace with hers.

'I know there's still the war,' she said, her booted feet bringing whispers from the stiff, frosty grass, 'but we shall wish each other luck?'

'Yes, Sophia. I shall wish you a mountain of luck. And it won't mean winning or losing the war if you give my regards to Fritz.'

Fritz. Fritz stood outside the paralysing light of impossibility, for Fritz had become only the image of a likeable young man. She had been in love with escape, not with Fritz. Fritz, brittle and irreverent, was in love with escape too, escape from decimating war.

'Can you see the road?' she asked.

'Not yet. But I'm sure it's there. Just over the rise.'

The crescent moon bestowed its little light. Sophia felt she had been in flight with this man for weeks. He was still sure of his way, still one step ahead of Major Kirsten. She supposed that all fighter pilots had to be resourceful men. Imagine, this one was going to apply his resourcefulness to the extraordinary business of making horseshoes and repairing cars. He was not going to make himself a landowner or become a banker, he was going to help a blacksmith called Simon Tukes beat hot iron and crawl under oily cars. What was it like, the forge he had spoken about, with its fire and its hammers? What was the little country town like? It did not sound as if it bustled with people, as if it would provide him with enough business to make him rich. What kind of a woman would marry a man who, having been a fighter pilot, came down from the skies to repair broken-down cars?

Murmurs began to disturb the night silence. Silence, she had found, could be both reassuring and frightening, but never prolonged. Something always came to disturb it. The murmur grew. Captain Marsh stopped and put a hand on her arm. She stopped too. The plane-repair sheds were well behind them, the road to Douai was in front of them, and the murmur turned into the sound of marching men. Sophia's eyes grew wide. The sky, brightly garnished by the new moon, threw enough light to bring the moving columns to her sight. She and Captain Marsh dropped to their knees and watched.

The road was not a road, but a flowing river of shadowy field-grey. Darkened by the night, helmeted and greatcoated, with packs on their backs and rifles slung, the infantry of Germany tramped in step. They represented part of the final might of the Fatherland. Horse-drawn ammunition wagons appeared at intervals. There were thousands of men, their columns stretching far back. They were marching to the west, their objective that which had been determined by General Ludendorff.

'My God,' breathed Captain Marsh, 'in two days I've seen what looks like the best part of the German Army on the move.'

Sophia's blood was running fast. This tide of marching men was the ultimate in spectacle. With others, they were the men whom Ludendorff and his corps commanders were to use to smash the Allies apart. All that was left of Germany's effective manpower was to be concentrated on an offensive which Ludendorff hoped would give his country the victory it so desperately needed. Sophia watched spellbound, knowing the infantry probably belonged to one more of her father's divisions.

'How magnificent,' she whispered in German.

'Excuse me?' said the mesmerized Captain Marsh.

'We can't use that road,' she said, 'we can't even cross it.'

'I can see that.' He knew something far more important than a switch of troops from one sector to another was taking place. 'Your generals have been moving a million men, all to the west, all to the same area.'

Sophia, bitterly determined to give nothing

away, said caustically, 'Isn't that what all generals do? Ordinary people play chess and move a few pawns. Generals play war games and move millions of men.'

'I don't think your generals are playing any kind of game at this particular moment. There's a big offensive coming, isn't there?'

Sophia set aside all weaknesses and said firmly, 'I know only one thing: that it's time we finished the war; that it's time England and France were beaten. And it's time for you to go and for me to be true to my country.'

'Do you think I can argue with that?' he said, and shook his head and smiled at her. 'Join your soldiers, Sophia, while I find another way to get to Douai. In wishing you all the luck in the world, I mean it, and you know that, don't you? Two days have been a lifetime of— No, never mind. Goodbye.'

He rose to his feet and walked away, moving fast, going back the way they had come. Sophia, still on her knees, did not look up. Her head dropped and the anguish returned.

He went on, his mouth tight. He knew she was right. He had to go his separate way, and she had to return to being a loyal citizen of her country. He should have been firmer about that before, he should not have gone on delaying their parting. At no time could that have been anything but inevitable – and permanent.

He lengthened his stride. He must get back

to that dirt road. It could put him on another cross-country route to Douai. Much longer, but easily accomplishable during the night. It took him a little while to reach the long wooded belt, and he chose to keep straight on, selecting the ground that lay between the wood and the fir-lined fence of the Luftwaffe repair unit, now silent and in darkness. Had he chosen the previous ground, on the other side of the wood, he might eventually have walked into the welcoming arms of Major Kirsten and Sergeant Lugar.

He did not expect what happened next, what had happened before, the sound of Sophia running to catch him up. He had no idea of what motivated her. He was aware of his own feelings, but not aware of hers, or how self-tormenting they were.

She arrived at his side, her breathing noisy. He pulled up and turned to face her. She would not look at him.

He felt he could only save himself by being brutally frank, but it was beyond him to do anything except try to understand her.

'This isn't very sensible,' he said.

'I've—' Sophia drew a painful breath. 'I've changed my mind. We can wait until the road is clear.'

'You worry me,' he said. 'You worry me desperately.'

'Do you suppose I am not a worry to myself?'

He could not help a wry smile.

'I thought,' he said, 'that you were only a worry to your mother.'

She did not respond to that.

'We can wait until the road is clear, can't we?'

'It's a little difficult to understand you, Sophia.'

They stood there, lacking communication because of the barrier of the war, because they were on opposite sides. At this moment, Major Kirsten, Elissa and Sergeant Lugar, having finished an inspection of the deserted staff car several minutes ago, were advancing over the ground that led to the other side of the wood. They were retracing the route taken earlier by themselves and the soldiers.

Sophia said, looking into the darkness of the wood, 'Are you going back to the car? I will drive it if your finger is still bad.'

'I've forgotten my finger. And I'm not going back to the car.' Captain Marsh was gently firm. 'We've brought it as far as we dare. I'm going to walk a short distance along that dirt road, and then cut across country. Sophia, go back to your father. You must in the end, you know. There are ammunition wagons on the main road, and the driver of any one of them would gladly give a lift to the daughter of a general. He'll drop you off at Douai.'

'That is not true! Do you think that thousands of men on the march are all going to stop to

allow me to climb up into one of their carts?'
Sophia lost control. 'Oh, you are crazy with
your running about, this way and that way, and
with your mad dreams of escape! But you are
good at running and looking after yourself—'

'Sophia, not so loud,' he whispered. The
repair establishment might be silent and asleep,
but there was bound to be a sentry or two on
night duty at the entrance. 'We must separate,
you know we must.'

'Oh, yes, you are good at everything except keeping your promises,' said Sophia. She
knew she was being entirely impossible, but her
nerves and emotions were stretched to their
limits.

'This can't go on. I have to leave you. Sophia,
go back to your father.' And Captain Marsh
made another effort to go his own way. He
turned and resumed his retreat, striding out at
a speed that spoke of finality. Sophia, driven
by anguish, again went after him. She knew
herself out of her mind because of the certainty
they would never see each other again, and
there had to be something more to the parting
than this unbearable nothingness. She ran
blindly and wildly to catch up with him. She
stubbed her toe against a stiff, grassy hump
that was as hard and unyielding as the stump
of a tree. She stifled a cry at the dart of pain
that shot through her right ankle. She pitched
and fell. Captain Marsh turned back at once.

She was lying on her side, her right knee drawn up, her gloved hand reaching to feel her ankle. 'Sophia?' Concerned, he went down on one knee beside her.

'I caught my foot,' she whispered.

He listened for a moment. The pounding rhythm of the marching Germans could not be heard from here, but there were other people who might not be far away. Where was that van and Sophia's friend, Major Kirsten? But what did it matter? Only Sophia was important.

'Painful?' he said.

'I turned my ankle – yes, it hurts.'

'Then it has to be over now,' he said gently.

'No, it's not so bad – perhaps just a bruise. Oh, I am sorry I am being so difficult and stupid. If you please?' She reached up, he took hold of her hands and helped her to her feet. She gave a little hiss of pain as she put her weight on her right foot.

'It's not just a bruise, is it?' he said. 'You fell very heavily. If you've broken it – Sophia, stay here and I'll go and get help. There'll be a sentry at this place – '

'No!' she whispered. 'You can't – not after so much. It will make no difference to the war if you escape – we both know that – please, I shan't mind if you manage to get away, and you've tried so hard.'

'Let's think about you, shall we?' he said. There was no more running to be done. He could not leave her now. She had become very dear to him, and had worn her love for her country as brightly as a polished badge. He lifted her. She put her arms around his neck and turned her face into his shoulder. Her pale golden hair softly touched his cheek. He began to carry her along the rough, grassy avenue that separated the fir-lined perimeter of the workshops from the belt of trees.

'Please,' she said, 'I don't want – '

'I must take you to the sentry, Sophia. There may be a resident medical officer who can see what damage you've done.'

'No.' She was whisperingly distraught. 'No, don't do that. Please don't do anything that will mean giving yourself up. It will make me so unhappy.'

'Sophia, a broken ankle – '

'It isn't broken, I'm sure it isn't. A sprain, perhaps, that's all. We could look at it. Don't take me into this place.'

He hesitated, then carried her into the fir trees, thick and concealing. He placed her on the ground, beneath the low, covering branch of a tree. He took off the greatcoat, laid it next to her, then lifted her on to it, giving her extra protection from the cold grass. She was silent; so was he. Fifty metres away, on the other side of the wooded belt, Major Kirsten, Elissa and Sergeant Lugar were quietly passing by on their searching walk to the main road.

Captain Marsh knelt beside Sophia. It was not so dark that they could not clearly see each other. Fifteen metres away, the high wire-mesh fence looked like black netting stretched tightly between posts.

'Let's take a look at your ankle now, shall we?' said Captain Marsh.

Sophia nodded, and lay quietly as he unlaced her right boot and drew it off gently. The removal of the boot hurt her ankle, but she said nothing. She felt his hand lightly touching the joint and moving carefully over her stocking to her heel and then her instep. It was only the ankle that was painfully susceptible to his touch.

'I think I twisted it,' she said.

'I'm sure you did,' he said, 'but your boot may have saved you from something worse. Tell me if this hurts.' His hand lightly moved her foot. A little spasm of pain attacked her ankle, but it was not unbearable.

'A little,' she said. 'It's not so bad – it feels hot.'

'And it's a little swollen. But you'd know it, I think, if you'd broken it; you'd have felt real pain. Are you sure you didn't?'

'When you turned my foot? No, it wasn't the pain of a fracture, it was just a tender pain.'

'A tender pain?' He smiled. 'That's new to me, a tender pain. We'll settle for a wrenched ankle, then. I'll put a cold compress on it – if you'll release your stocking.'

He turned away to avoid embarrassing her, and Sophia drew up her coat and skirts, unclipped her grey silk stocking and rolled it down. She lay back again, watching him. He had his handkerchief out and was pressing it flatly to the cold, moist grass. He pulled long blades free from a thick tuft, gathering a large handful. He turned back to Sophia. She was still lying quietly. Her legs were partly uncovered. One glimmered in its silk stocking showing above her boot, and the other was palely naked. He placed the pad of frosty, damp grass on her swollen ankle, and its coldness brought immediate bliss to the joint. She emitted a sigh. He folded the handkerchief into a wide strip and bound it around her ankle to hold the grass compress in place.

'Thank you,' whispered Sophia.

'Sprained ankles are only supposed to happen to the heroines of Victorian novels, you know. It enables the villains to catch up with them and – let me see, what happens next?'

'Don't you know? The hero arrives just as the villain is about to carry the heroine away to his villa in Nice, and a desperate duel is fought. The hero is always victorious, which is rather unfair, I think, because some of the villains are far more exciting than the heroes, and I like the sound of a villa in Nice.'

Captain Marsh laughed softly. Sophia regarded him mistily.

'I'm afraid I've been the villain in this case,' he said.

'But you don't have a villa in Nice?' she said with a faint smile.

'I've nothing like that to offer any heroine. Has that compress made your ankle feel a little better?'

'Not a little, no. Much better, thank you.' She was emotional because of his concern, his attention and the compress he had so gently applied.

'Good,' he said. He drew the rolled stocking up from her foot and eased it over the bound handkerchief. 'If you fix your stocking again it will keep the bandage in place, do you see?'

'Yes,' said Sophia. She drew the stocking upwards and clipped it. She sank back again. He, acutely conscious that she had not covered her legs, covered them for her by adjusting her rucked dress and petticoat and folding the skirts of her coat into place.

'You need to keep warm,' he said.

'It doesn't matter that you don't have a villa in Nice,' said Sophia huskily.

'Sophia?'

'I love you,' said Sophia.

In shock, he stared down at her.

'Oh, my God,' he breathed.

'You need not feel too embarrassed, for my mother would tell you I'm a creature of passing fancies. She would also tell you I'll probably be in love with someone else tomorrow.'

'Would she be right?' he asked, not knowing what else to say.

'Sometimes she is right about me,' said Sophia, thinking of Fritz and how her mother had implied she could not be seriously in love with a young man who was merely likeable.

'We can forget, then, what you just said?' With the moment hovering on the edge of un-reality, he wondered if she had indeed actually said it.

'Only if you can believe my mother knows me better than I know myself.' Sophia was almost calm. It was out now, that which had given her so much torment from the moment when he had kissed her and she had responded in an excess of ardour both crazy and passionate. It was not the best thing that had ever happened to her, this shameless, shattering want for a man who was at war with her country, but there had been nothing she could do to smother it. It had taken hold of her so possessively that if he had asked her to, she would have run with him to the ends of the earth.

'Sophia, it's been an unendurable time for you, I've turned your life upside down. I've been mindlessly stupid and unforgivable – '

'You have already said that. It isn't relevant any more. I love you – '

'That can't be true. The situation has always

been such that in a way we could both say we've never really met.'

'I could not say that. Could you?'

'No. But wise people might.'

'You said a little while ago that for you two days had been a lifetime of – you didn't finish. Could you tell me now?'

He shook his head, but said, 'A lifetime of discovering how sweet and beautiful you are.'

'That is something to remember.' Sophia was quiet and sad. 'If you really think that of me, I shan't be completely unhappy. And tomorrow, perhaps, I'll be in love with a different man. I've been told, you see, that my enthusiasms are very transient.'

'That's what you've been told?' He felt intensely moved, and had forgotten the hunters, who were well on their way to the Douai road now. He wondered, guiltily, just how much responsibility he must accept for Sophia's strange sadness. 'Sophia, we all experience a hundred different enthusiasms when we're young, and few of them last with any of us. But that doesn't mean we're incapable of permanent loyalties and affections. Only promiscuous people are strangers to faithfulness.'

'But don't you see, I am German and you are English,' said Sophia, 'and I'm unfaithful to Germany in loving you.'

'That's very difficult, yes, but it's nothing to do with unfaithfulness.' He could not declare his own feelings, he could not kiss her or caress her, or love her. He could not do anything that would make an impossible situation far worse.

Sophia fumbled at her coat then. She drew out the secreted hatpin and showed it to him.

'That was to stab you with, if you touched me again,' she said, and she threw it away.

Her gesture made him produce his revolver and drop it into the grass.

'And that was to help my escape,' he said, 'but I'm trapped now.' He was trapped by the intensity of his feelings for her, but he was also torn by the necessity of finding someone in Douai who would know how to pass on to the Allies the information concerning gigantic German troop movements.

'You aren't trapped,' said Sophia, 'you can go when the road is clear.'

'I can't leave you, and won't,' he said, close to letting emotion displace wisdom.

'But you have to soon, one way or another,' she said. She seemed to be quietly wandering. 'I've been told many times I don't really know what I want. I think my mother was mostly right about that. What she would say about what I want now I can guess. I want to hear that the war is over; that our countries are at peace. I want to hear you tell me you love me – oh, that is very impossible, isn't it? I want to help you repair motor cars. I'm really not too bad with a motor car, am I?'

'The best, Sophia.'

'But you aren't in love with me? No, how could you be?'

'But I am, aren't I? And you know it. In just two days—'

'We are both in love?' Sophia was breathless. 'In just two days we have both lived a lifetime together?'

'Unfortunately, yes.' He smiled and touched her hair. Her lashes flickered and fell. Her body trembled. He touched her face and was shocked to feel the wetness of tears. 'I hope, on top of everything else, I'm not making you cry.'

'I want to know – you aren't saying you love me because I've hurt my foot and because you want to be kind?'

'No, I'm simply saying I love you because I can't help myself,' he said.

'That is something else to remember, something wonderful.'

'Aren't you forgetting Fritz?' he asked.

'Oh, you will forgive me about that, won't you?' Emotional, she caught his hand. 'You will forgive me that Fritz was my yesterday's wish? I don't want you to think you are today's – that I could only love you until tomorrow or next week – it isn't true. You must believe me.'

'Are you sad, Sophia, because you know it would be better if it were true?'

'I've only thought it would be better if I didn't love you at all,' she said, 'and anyway, what does it matter how much I love you and for how long? There's nothing for us, is there? Nothing.'

'There's the end of the war, my sweet, and what we can make of the peace.'

'But don't you see, when you leave me we shall never see each other again. All we have is now.' She reached to touch his shoulders. 'That is right, isn't it? We only have what we have now. Please?'

He bent his head and kissed her. Her lips were warm and feverish. She wound her arms around him and her sadness drowned itself in the surging, swamping tide of love.

She soared into the unknown.

The road was still a river of dark field-grey. Infantry divisions, newly made up to strength, were solid in their march. They would take hours to pass. Major Kirsten watched in company with Elissa and Sergeant Lugar.

'They couldn't have crossed, Major,' said Elissa. 'The road would have been blocked well before they got here.'

'So, what else can they do, then, but wait until it's clear?' Major Kirsten felt he was balanced very finely between success and failure.

'Major,' said Sergeant Lugar, 'my orders – '

'Yes, quite so. Return to your barracks, Sergeant Lugar. You can drive that van?'

'Yes, Major.'

'Give him the keys, Lieutenant.'

Sergeant Lugar, receiving the keys, saluted the major. He also saluted Elissa. She had given him a rare jolting in the back of the van, but he had no hard feelings, and he began his walk back to the van.

'A day of blanks and near misses,' said Major Kirsten, and looked up at the crescent moon. 'We almost had them.'

'Yes, almost,' said Elissa. 'They will have to wait, Major. Douai will be under curfew until dawn.'

'They may not realize that, but they'll wait until the road's clear, at least. Lieutenant, return to the car and drive yourself back to Headquarters. You need a meal and you need rest.'

'Major?' said Elissa in dismay.

'I shall stay,' he said. 'They're somewhere around. I know it; I feel it.' He looked back. The darkness was touched a little by the moon's light. 'I'm worried by the fact that they're in concert. Sophia can't know what she's doing. But they'll come this way again, as soon as they think the road is clear. Perhaps they're in that wood again. If so, they'll hear me before I hear them. I must catch them in the open, and this time I'll risk a confrontation.'

'Major, you'll allow me, please, to stay with you,' said Elissa. 'With respect, it's hardly fair to dismiss me from the exercise now. Indeed, I'll only go if you order me to.'

'With regret, Lieutenant, I must order you, then.'

He seemed so uncharacteristically severe that Elissa whispered fiercely, 'Oh, that's not fair.'

'Lieutenant?' he said, an eyebrow lifted.

'Well, it isn't.'

'I'm not aware of the relevance of that.'

'I'm afraid it's very relevant, Major, for you're placing me in the impossible position of having to refuse the order.'

'I don't think I heard that,' said Major Kirsten. 'Indeed, I'm sure I didn't. Return to Headquarters, Lieutenant.'

'I'm sorry,' said Elissa, 'but I'm not permitted to.'

'Not permitted?'

'As a WAC officer, I'm not permitted to be in charge of any army vehicle without a male escort. This regulation is strictly emphasized in occupied territory. By day, the escort must not rank lower than a sergeant. By night, not lower than a junior officer.'

Major Kirsten received this information with a sigh.

'Your regulations are terrifying,' he said.

'Major, I think you are well aware of them.'

'I am now. Thank you for filling me in.' Major Kirsten mused on the dark, flowing stream of Germany's unequalled fighting men, and thought of other great and mighty offensives.

They had all turned into bloodbaths. 'So, either we both return to Headquarters or we both stay, matching ourselves against our elusive pair. I prefer to continue the match, even if I have to prowl about here all night. Elissa, we must separate Sophia from this airman while we alone know she's not under duress. Do you understand?'

'Yes, I understand,' said Elissa, and felt uncomfortable.

'If she reaches Douai and elopes with her lover without a word of complaint or information about the Englishman, do you see how seriously that will harm her standing as a loyal German, and how that will reflect on her father?'

'I do see,' said Elissa. She could not explain her moment of defection, except to say she had acted out of a sense of compassion.

'Men are imperfect beings,' murmured Major Kirsten. 'We're imperfect both in peace and in war. We've no idea how to keep the peace or how to end a war.'

He walked with Elissa on silent patrol, the pastures shrouded by night, the moon a receding glimmer as clouds edged back over it. A blustery wind came to assert its claim on the month of March. Searchlights, fingering the western horizon, created their faint moving patterns in the sky. The day had been fairly quiet. The night was uneasy.

If the fugitives were around, thought Major

Kirsten, they would emerge eventually. Sophia, if not the airman, must be apprehended.

Elissa's thoughts ran on different lines.

It was after midnight when she took a walk to speak to the sentry on guard at the entrance to the Luftwaffe repair unit. Sleepily, he told her where to go to get what she wanted. She walked down to the sheds, passing an Albatros plane standing silent on the runway, and aroused the duty sergeant. Major Kirsten stayed where he was, pacing slowly about, watching the shrouded landscape and listening for the elusive, while Elissa arranged for the preparation of hot drinks and a little food.

Chapter Nineteen

The dawn was grey and cold. Captain Marsh awoke to the sound of an engine firing. Stiffly, he detached himself from Sophia's arms. She stirred and murmured. In the bleak light he saw the Albatros standing at the beginning of the lengthy runway. Its engine pitch increased. A mechanic throttled down, left it ticking over and descended from the cockpit. He spoke to a ground mechanic. The man gave the chocks a glance, then both men took the long walk to an airman standing outside a shed. All three entered the shed in search of some hot coffee, while the plane's new engine warmed itself up.

It ticked over very steadily.

Sophia opened her eyes. Captain Marsh, on his feet and keeping himself out of sight of German personnel, smiled down at her. Warm blood suffused her.

'We are going to Douai now?' she whispered.

'No, Sophia. I'm going over that wire fence. You're going to go back to your father. I've got my eye on that plane. They're letting the engine run for a while, and I think the pilot's drinking hot coffee. I can fly an Albatros. If I can get the chocks away before anyone sees me – Sophia, I must take this chance to get back to my squadron – '

'No, you can't,' she gasped, suddenly aware of what that meant.

'I must. But I'll write – somehow I'll get a letter to you – '

'No, you can't,' she gasped again. She was horrified, knowing that if he got away he would inform the British Army of the huge German troops' movements. She had forgotten, in wanting him to escape, all he had seen. He would rob Germany of the chance of ending the war, he would alert the British and the French.

'Sophia, my sweet, I have to go,' he said, and bent to kiss her. Stricken by what he would do and by her own part in helping him to avoid capture, she twisted away. He winced, but he went. She saw him run to the wire fence and make his leap. His hands clamped around the top of a supporting post. The guard at the far end of the perimeter did not even seem awake, let alone alert. Sophia, mind spinning and heart sick, saw the revolver in the grass where Captain Marsh had dropped it in the night and forgotten it. She snatched it, released the safety catch and, on her knees, pointed the weapon, both hands fiercely gripping it. He was on the fence, hauling himself up, and her every emotion was frenzied. Only her country and the great final offensive counted now.

'Come back!' She screamed the words. Major Kirsten heard her. So did Elissa.

Captain Marsh was at the top. He turned his head for a last look at Sophia. He was poised for the jump. She fired. She fired mercilessly and compulsively. She had to. For Germany and for her father. Captain Marsh jerked, twisted and fell, inside the fence. His body thudded, and he lay very still. In the distance, Major Kirsten began to run, Elissa with him.

Sophia did not know how long it was before someone spoke to her.

'Sophia?' The voice was quiet but warm.

Lying on her face, shutting out the picture of what she had done, she lifted her head. Major Kirsten reached down and gently helped her to her feet. She swayed.

'Is he dead?' she asked, her face white, her eyes tragic.

'Sophia – '

'Have you looked at him? Is he dead?'

'Yes, I've looked at him.' Major Kirsten's face was drawn, his eyes tired. 'I'm sorry,' he said. 'An ambulance will be taking him away.'

Sophia closed her eyes. She shivered and her teeth chattered. She opened her eyes and looked. He was there, on the other side of the wire, not far from the runway. There was a blanket over his body, and a German soldier standing beside him. The Albatros was gone.

'Oh, dear God,' she said.

'Was it unavoidable in the end?' asked Major Kirsten.

'Yes. But he was a brave man, Major.'

'And an elusive one.'

'He did not harm me,' she whispered.

But he has left his mark on you, thought the major. The sadness on her face was heart-breaking.

'We worried a little,' he said.

'You have followed us all this time?' she said numbly.

'Yes.'

'He might have let you take him last night, for my sake.'

'I believe you,' said Major Kirsten gently. 'Sophia, there's some hot coffee on its way. Will you then permit me to take you to Head-quarters, to your father?'

'Yes.'

'I've no questions, except one. He was going for that plane?'

'Yes. And he would have informed the Allies about our troop movements. He would have had to, wouldn't he?'

'He would,' said Major Kirsten, and sighed. It was all he wanted to know for the moment, why

341

she had shot him. She had been desperately loyal to her country in the end. There would be no unpleasant questions now. He saw Elissa coming up. 'Sophia, this is Lieutenant Landsberg, with the coffee. If you wish to talk to her, you'll find her a person who will understand. I'll wait by the car.'

He delivered Sophia into Elissa's care. Elissa pressed a mug of coffee into her hands. Sophia sipped at it like a woman who had no idea what she was drinking or why.

'Sophia, will you allow me, please?' said Elissa, and put a German greatcoat around Sophia's shoulders, for Sophia's own coat seemed inadequate. She was shivering from head to foot. The greatcoat had been left by Captain Marsh. He and Sophia had shared it during the night.

'Thank you,' said Sophia. Elissa had never seen eyes so hugely tragic. 'You were with Major Kirsten, following us.'

'Yes,' said Elissa. 'We were so very worried, you see.'

'You saw us,' said Sophia, looking again at the blanket-covered body.

'I can't recall that,' said Elissa.

'Why did you do nothing?'

Elissa took the empty mug from the numb hands and said, 'I saw only your eyes, I did not see you. I beg you not to mention it to Major Kirsten.'

Sophia touched the hand of the woman who had understood.

She felt frozen. He had loved her and he was dead now. His motor garage would stand empty. Only his friend, a man called Simon Tukes, would make the horseshoes.

'I am so sad,' she said, and Elissa knew why General von Feldermann's daughter had turned about in her allegiance and gone freely with the British airman, and why it had been the most tragic moment of her life when she realized she had to shoot him.

A strong sleeping draught took Sophia out of her nightmare and into long rest. She lay in a room next to her father's in the chateau.

Headquarters was a hive of activity. Ludendorff had been and gone, leaving everything as near to planned perfection as it could be, with General von Feldermann quite clear about what was expected of him and his Corps. The general had had little time to spare for other things this morning, but he had talked to Sophia, and Sophia had said all she wanted to in the space of a minute. The essence of it was that she was willing to return to her mother, but that she would like the privilege of deciding her own future. He understood.

'One can learn, Sophia, even at my age,' he said. 'I'm aware now that your life is your own. It belongs to no one else, only to you.'

He also found time to talk to Major Kirsten. He did so in the major's own room. They spoke, of course, about Sophia and the RFC airman. At the end, the general asked whether the man would recover.

'Incredibly, he has a chance,' said Major Kirsten. 'I frankly thought him dead until the hospital telephoned to say that the ambulance orderly had detected the faintest pulse rate. He seems a man determined not to give in.'

'The situation is impossible, Josef, you realize that?'

'General, I think you'll find Sophia realizes it herself.'

'It would be better, then, for Sophia to still think him dead. For her sake, that would be infinitely better.'

Major Kirsten wondered if that really was for Sophia's sake.

'General—'

'Yes, I know what you're thinking. But consider it, Sophia imagining herself in love with a man so lacking in honour and decency that he was prepared to use her as a hostage.'

'If I'm to believe Lieutenant Landsberg, Sophia isn't imagining it. It's unfortunate, but stranger things have happened. I'd suggest—'

'I'd prefer no compromise,' said the general. 'I am, I assure you, putting Sophia's welfare first. Please leave things as they are. I'm old enough and you're wise enough for both of us to know she'll get over him. Does Lieutenant Landsberg know the man is still alive?'

'No. She's in her quarters getting a few hours' sleep.'

'Say nothing to her, Josef. If the man fully recovers, he's to be sent to a prisoner-of-war camp. That's all. No other action is to be taken.'

'None in respect of what might be termed his abduction of your daughter?'

'None.' General von Feldermann was crisp. 'Good God, can you imagine the new ordeal for Sophia when she's called to testify? And would she testify on coming face to face with him?'

'I agree, she should be spared any inquiry,' said Major Kirsten. 'But – '

'Yes?'

'We're not sparing her a worse ordeal, her sense of tragedy. Imagined or not, she was in love with him, but she stopped him escaping. She stopped him taking information to the Allies of our build-up. In doing that she thinks she killed him. It would mean a great deal to her peace of mind if she were given the news that he has a chance of recovery.'

'No. I know Sophia. She would fly to his bedside, never mind that his country is at war with ours.'

'I beg to disagree, General. I don't think she'd do that. She'd wait.'

'Wait?'

'Until the war is over.' Major Kirsten wondered

why he was fighting for Sophia and the airman. 'Your worries about her might be eased, for if she's going to get over her feelings, that would give her time to.'

'Josef, allow me to decide whether she's to be told or not.' The general grimaced in self-distaste. 'Her life is her own, but she needs a little help to find the right direction.'

'As you wish, General,' said Major Kirsten, though for once he was not in complete agreement with the Corps commander. 'But if he recovers, he may write to her.'

The general frowned.

'I hope there'll be no letters,' he said. 'Sophia should be allowed to forget the trauma of it all. Josef, if this man recovers, tell no one. And may I leave it to you to ensure there'll be no letters?'

'Ensure?'

'Yes. Thank you. Incidentally, some staff adjustments are being made to cope with divisional requirements during the offensive. These mainly concern our WAC personnel. Ten of them are being transferred.'

'I suppose they can be considered surplus to our requirements now that planning work is complete,' said Major Kirsten. His scarred eye looked blank, his sound eye looked tired. He guessed what was coming.

'Lieutenant Landsberg will be going to 51st Divisional Headquarters,' said the general. 'I think you can spare her now?'

'Frankly, General, she is not an assistant I can easily spare.'

'Quite understood, Josef, but there it is, and I'm grateful for all the cooperation I get from you.'

Major Kirsten's damaged eye ached. He had been advised to wear a patch, but could not bring himself to go about with a one-eyed look in addition to a one-armed state. He said, 'I think I'll opt for early retirement.'

General von Feldermann regarded him with a wry smile.

'You need some rest,' he said, 'and I need to convince myself I've made the right decision between what is fair and what is unavoidable. That's all for the moment, Josef. Get a few hours' sleep. Everything now concerns only the offensive.'

Four hours later, Elissa knocked on Major Kirsten's office door and entered. He had taken a rest himself, but still looked drawn. She looked freshened up, but unhappy.

'Major?'

He saw her unhappiness and said, 'Yes, not a very pleasant day, Lieutenant.'

Elissa drew a breath.

'I am being transferred,' she said.

'So I've been informed,' he said. He got up from his desk and walked to the window. The parkland of the chateau offered a misty green vista.

'I would prefer, Major, I would prefer – ' Elissa coloured.

'What would you prefer?' he asked, his back to her.

'To stay.'

'Yes, I'd prefer that too.'

'Am I to have no option?'

'Promotion sometimes has an option to it. The orders of a general concerning transfers and dispositions leave no options. That is the basis of efficiency and discipline in the German Army.'

'I have a feeling, Major, that I'm being transferred because – because – '

'Yes. You are. We are both an embarrassment to the general. We know, you see. But his position is understandable. You must recognize that.' He turned and smiled at her. It distressed him then, to see tears in her eyes. 'Are you as unhappy as that?'

'I am a little stupid, Major. It's of very small account, a transfer, when everything else means life and death to Germany.'

'I am ready myself for a quick end to the war. I also feel ready for retirement.'

'Retirement? But you're still young, Major.'

He laughed.

'My dear Lieutenant, I'm almost forty.'

'When a woman is forty, she's on the bridge of sighs,' said Elissa. 'When a man is forty, he's on the river of life.'

'Well, I think I've been swept out to sea. No, Elissa, I'm ready for the pastures. There's been too much war, and I'm depressed about Sophia. You're convinced she loved Captain Marsh?'

'I'm convinced the impossible happened,' said Elissa, hiding the full extent of her unhappiness.

Major Kirsten shook his head at the incomprehensibility of women.

'Elissa, we spent the night looking in all the wrong places. They were up against the wire fence, or almost so. I failed Sophia.'

'No,' said Elissa.

'Had we found them earlier, or had we at least managed to separate them in some way, we could have saved her from tragedy.'

Elissa's unhappiness deepened. She had known exactly where they were at one stage and done nothing. She had looked into Sophia's eyes and seen a woman desperately in love, and so she had said nothing and done nothing, and that at a moment when Major Kirsten, with the help of Sergeant Lugar, could have taken care of everything.

'You didn't fail her,' she said.

'I failed myself, then.' Major Kirsten thought of Sophia's deep sadness. 'I should have been less of an actor in that copse and more of a soldier. Well, at least you and I shared two very eventful days.' He smiled reminiscently. 'I count you as a very close friend, if I may. Elissa, we've real worries. For all my faith in General Ludendorff, I doubt our capacity to sustain the offensive long enough. There simply aren't enough reserves, and when the Americans arrive in force against us, we shall be at our weakest and most vulnerable. We shall hope, of course, but one way or another the war will be over this year. I shan't be too unhappy to commune with my vegetables.'

'But you love the army, and you've given so much of yourself,' said Elissa.

'Not as much as the millions who've died,' he said. 'I've no real complaints, so compose yourself.'

'I'm not in the mood to be rapturous,' said Elissa. Still sensitive in his presence, she coloured again under his concerned eyes. She was not to know he was wishing himself younger, with two arms. She drew another breath. 'I am to leave in the morning. I have a little work to finish this afternoon. You will then allow me to say goodbye to you?'

'Allow you? Good God, am I such a martinet?'

'Oh, no. No. Perhaps I should say goodbye now. Major, it has been so good, working here with you.' New tears came then and her weakness shocked her, for the tears spilled. Silently, Major Kirsten gave her his handkerchief. She dabbed her eyes. 'I'm so sorry – please forgive me for embarrassing you.'

'Permit me,' he said. He took her hand and raised it to his lips. 'That is to salute you and to convey the very deep regard I have for you. For you as much as myself and Germany, I wish victory and peace. Soldiers lose their lives in war, but it is women who endure the greater suffering. The peace must belong mainly to you, Elissa and all women.'

Elissa did not know how she was going to bear victory or peace with her emotions in the state they were.

'Major, please don't think me importunate, but on your estate, after the war – will you need someone? A secretary – someone to help you look after things? It would interest me very much, the business of an estate. Oh, I don't mean to imply you could not run it very well yourself, but if – ' She stopped. It was too difficult to make known to him exactly why she was so unhappy.

Major Kirsten's self-discipline cracked for a moment, and he looked painfully unsure of himself. Then he said lightly, 'You must allow me to write you about such an excellent idea. My place isn't huge – it can't compare with the great estates of Prussia, but the prospect of renewing our relationship in peacetime is very tempting. I'll let you know eventually how things stand and what kind of a post can be offered you.'

Elissa did not really know whether that was

a promise or not, whether it gave her hope or not.

'Thank you, Major,' she said.

'My dear Elissa – ' He checked himself. In not finding Sophia in time, he had failed her and also her father. He felt he had little to offer a woman to compensate for his many limitations. 'Until the war is over, then,' he said.

'Yes, Major,' said Elissa, and felt her heart was dying.

Ludendorff's offensive began with a massive attack south of Valenciennes, the purpose of which was to roll back the British on both sides of St Quentin. The British, caught off guard, reeled under the hammer blow. Outnumbered, outgunned, their lines broke, and for the first time in years the war on the Western Front became fluid in terms of ground gained, ground lost and the rapid movements of armies. Ludendorff won a well-planned and well-executed breakthrough. The Germans swept on, crossing the Somme to return to the territory they had won during their great advance in 1914. They turned on the French. This was the crucial stage of their offensive. With the British still staggering from the unexpected weight and fire of the assault, Ludendorff sought to smash the French and drive his huge wedge between them and the British. The French engaged, the British recovered, the Americans were in, and the battle produced a stalemate that was to prove fatal for Germany, although Ludendorff was not finished yet.

Chapter Twenty

The German soldier on guard outside the isolated sickroom saluted at the approach of an officer with one arm. Major Kirsten returned the salute, the soldier opened the door for him, and he went in. The patient looked up from his bed in which he lay on his back. Major Kirsten regarded him with a great deal of interest. He saw a man whose eyes were steady and whose mouth was firm. The patient, a little drawn, eyed his visitor with curiosity. He saw the empty left sleeve. He gave Major Kirsten a slight smile.

'Good afternoon, Captain Marsh,' said the major in English. He had not wanted this commission. It was one he disliked. But he had, by silent assent, promised General von Feldermann he would do what he could. 'May I enquire after your health?'

'You may. You're Major Kirsten.'

'I am.'

'I thought so.' Again a slight smile. 'My health? Improving, I think.'

'You should be dead, of course,' said Major Kirsten evenly.

'Have I disappointed anyone?' asked Captain Marsh. It had been three weeks since the incident.

'No. You have annoyed a few, however. I congratulate you on your resilience, but you're in serious trouble. Do you realize that?'

'What's going to happen?' asked Captain Marsh.

'Yes, there you have it,' said Major Kirsten. 'But I'm here to point the way to the best possible conclusion. A prisoner-of-war camp. However, I'd first like to know how you managed to be so elusive when you must have found your hostage a most awkward burden.'

Captain Marsh reflected. The request was aimed, of course, at Sophia's possible complicity and its extent.

'You'll understand,' he said, 'that having seen me hold up two of your soldiers, Miss von Feldermann knew I would use my revolver. Not on her, naturally, but on anyone who stood in my way, German or otherwise. She did not want to be responsible for someone getting a bullet. By not doing what I wanted her to, she would have felt responsible. She's a compassionate young lady. I'm sorry, of course, about all the inconvenience I put her to.'

'Are you?' Major Kirsten raised an eyebrow. 'Why did you need to keep her with you, except to use as a hostage? Since I imagine you know that would earn you the death penalty, I presume you'll deny you took her as a hostage. Why, after you abandoned the car, didn't you simply tie her up and leave her?'

'No rope,' said Captain Marsh, 'and I thought there was always a good chance of getting hold of another car.'

'Mine, as it turned out.'

'So sorry,' said Captain Marsh. 'Not that I was able to drive myself. I dislocated one finger and broke another when I crash-landed. Miss von Feldermann is a very good driver, and you'll appreciate, I know, the advantage of using a car instead of one's legs.'

Major Kirsten looked sceptical. The man, obviously, meant to protect Sophia against the slightest suspicion of collaboration.

'I must advise you that you've a difficult case to answer, Captain Marsh, and Miss von Feldermann an awkward one. I'm going to assume you have some respect for her, and would prefer the matter to be resolved in the simplest and quietest way. An inquiry leading to your being tried in a criminal court would mean the appearance of Miss von Feldermann on both occasions. You would have to explain your every action, and how you kept her under duress for the purposes of making your escape. She would have to explain all her own actions. She would be asked why she apparently made no attempt to get away from you. You spent a few hours in an inn at Lutargne with her, where the proprietor asked no questions of either of you, or so he said, and she made no protest to him or his family. Some people would feel that extraordinary.'

'Let some people declare if they'd call for help or make any protests in a situation where a gun might go off,' said Captain Marsh. 'As a uniformed combatant, I'm entitled to resist capture and promote my escape according to the rules of war.'

'Ah, rules,' said Major Kirsten. 'I'm not sure how they apply to Sophia von Feldermann, except to demand of her the actions of a patriot. Bear in mind that I should give evidence.'

'Yes, you were very close to us at times.'

'Very close. I was never sure, however, of how much of a real threat you were to her.'

'Major Kirsten?' said Captain Marsh, and felt worried for Sophia.

'Yes, very awkward,' said Major Kirsten. 'You can see why we prefer a quiet solution, those of us whose regard for her has no selfish motives.'

Captain Marsh, wincing, said, 'There was no easy way out, once I decided to commandeer her car and her services.'

'And there were other factors, of course,' said Major Kirsten, 'but there it is, we'll dispatch you to a prisoner-of-war camp providing you keep it all to yourself and make no attempt to communicate with her.'

'Why should I want to communicate with a young lady only too pleased to be free of me?'

'Yes, indeed,' said Major Kirsten thoughtfully, 'why should you?'

'You can have no doubts about her patriotism, since she was the one who shot me. Twice, I believe, and scored a hit each time.'

'You're prepared, then, to elect for an inquiry and a trial, and for her to be subjected to the ordeal of being questioned?'

'No, damn it, I'm not,' said Captain Marsh.

'Her father, General von Feldermann, will be most relieved you wish to spare her that. You are requested, of course, to forget her.'

Captain Marsh looked plainly out of temper with that. He was being asked to permanently sever his links with Sophia. He accepted they could have no real relationship until the war was over. But when peace came, he would need to make contact of some kind with her. He would want to tell her he understood why she shot him. At the very last, in that grey dawn, she had been as true to her country as she could be. She had been warm and loving during the night.

'Forget her for the time being, until the war is over, is that what you mean, Major Kirsten?'

'I mean forget her.' Major Kirsten was firm. 'She belongs to a very conservative Prussian family. Is it necessary for me to tell you more than that? You aren't getting a bad bargain, my friend – a prisoner-of-war camp instead of a trial and a possible execution.'

'Has Miss von Feldermann agreed to this?'

'You have my word that Miss von Feldermann would like to forget what happened,' said Major Kirsten, and knew that to be quite true in respect of her firing of the revolver.

Captain Marsh winced again.

'Yes, I can understand how she feels,' he said, 'but even so, I've reservations. I can keep quiet about her, and will, and I can promise not to communicate with her, especially if she wishes it, but I'm not sure it's a promise I can keep for ever.'

'I see.' Major Kirsten pondered on the problem of traumatic love. He was not prepared to take up a wholly unyielding attitude, only to do as much as he thought necessary to the immediate purpose. 'Will you give me your word you'll wait two years?'

'Two years? God Almighty,' said Captain Marsh.

'You know as well as I do, my friend, that even if the war ended tomorrow, no real reconciliation could be effected between your people and ours for quite two years. However, let us say a year after the end of the war. Do you agree?'

'That could still be a hell of a time,' said Captain Marsh. It could be a time of very painful waiting, giving Sophia every opportunity to forget him and to fall in love with one of her own countrymen, probably the most natural and helpful thing she could do for herself. But he had no alternative. 'I give you my word,' he said.

'I accept your word,' said Major Kirsten.

'I'd like her family address. Is that asking too much of you?'

'Yes,' said Major Kirsten, but made a gesture. Captain Marsh handed him a writing pad. Major Kirsten placed it on the bedside table and scribbled Sophia's family address in South Prussia. Captain Marsh thanked him. The major gave him a brief nod.

'Goodbye, Captain Marsh.'

'How is the war going?' asked the RFC man as the major walked to the door.

'Bloodily,' said Major Kirsten.

Ludendorff had launched another massive attack in an attempt to destroy the Ypres salient. Again the result was inconclusive. Further attacks were made in May and June, all brilliantly conceived and all taking heavy tolls of the Allies and disastrous tolls of the Germans. Ludendorff, short of reserves, made his final effort in July, a huge and desperate offensive on both sides of Rheims. It failed.

Germany, completely exhausted, could no longer plan for victory, only for a defence effective enough to secure tolerable peace terms. But the country was being reduced to a condition of near anarchy by the effects of the sea blockade, by the huge casualty lists and by revolutionaries dangerously infected by the Bolshevism which had overthrown Imperial Russia.

Germany asked for an armistice. The Kaiser abdicated. The war was lost.

Chapter Twenty-one

The bookshop in Munich was a treasure house of literature, and it seemed a pity, with so many excellent volumes on offer, that there was only one customer present. And the customer, ancient and shabby, was more likely to browse than to buy. But times were hard in Germany in June 1920, and few people were spending money on books.

There was another man in the shop, talking to Mr Meister, the proprietor. He, however, had only come to inquire about the assistant.

'At lunch, at lunch,' said Mr Meister, wispy-haired and testy. Despite his love of literature and his affinity with people who shared that love, he had to be testy or some people would stand in his shop all day, reading the finest works and buying not even a bookmark.

'When will she be back?' asked the caller.

'Back? Back?' Mr Meister peered irritably over his spectacles.

'Yes, when will Miss Landsberg be back from lunch?'

'Ah, from lunch? Why didn't you say so?' Mr Meister took his spectacles off and fussily polished them. 'She'll be back when she's finished her bread and cheese and her young man is ready to escort her.'

'I see.' The caller smiled resignedly. 'Does that mean she'll linger?'

'Linger? Linger?'

'Young women do linger with young men. What time is she due back?'

'One-thirty,' said Mr Meister.

The caller consulted his watch. It was just coming up to one.

'I'm sorry to have missed her,' he said. 'Will you be so good as to give her my regards?'

'With pleasure, but from whom?'

'Tell her Major Kirsten called to enquire after her welfare, having had occasion to be in Munich today.'

Mr Meister,' said Elissa in anguish, 'you didn't ask him to wait or come back?'

'Ah – no.' Mr Meister looked penitent.

'He didn't offer to wait?'

'I said you'd be back at one-thirty with your young man – '

'Oh, no, you didn't tell him that,' protested Elissa, 'how could you? Franz is not my young man.'

'But every day you go to the park with him and – '

'He's a friend, an ex-soldier,' said Elissa, 'and all ex-soldiers are special to me.'

'Ah,' said Mr Meister, peering at his charming assistant, who had gone off in 1917 in a state of nerves to join the Women's Army Corps and returned at the end of the war a far more self-assured young lady. Elissa, in a pale brown frock, polished shoes and shining rayon stockings, her braided hair immaculate, looked sorrowfully at her employer.

'Mr Meister, didn't Major Kirsten speak of coming back?'

'Coming back, coming back?' Mr Meister sounded as if her question had been plucked out of a tome of obscure Chinese riddles.

Elissa turned away to gaze at the street through the shop's bow window. The people passing by did not seem quick and vigorous with life. The peace had not improved things. Germany was broken and suffering, the Weimar Republic at desperate odds with the Allies over the huge reparations demanded, and 1920 was one more bitter and humiliating year for the Fatherland. Major Kirsten had never written. He had come to Munich without letting her know, and he had dropped into the bookshop and gone away. He had been told she had a young man. Her disappointment at missing him was unbearable.

'Mr Meister, how did he look?'

'An upright man. Ah, a war casualty, of course. A sad smile.'

'What do you mean, a sad smile?'

'When I told him of your young man, he seemed – '

'Mr Meister,' said Elissa, the light of decision in her eyes, 'I wish to give notice.'

'Notice, notice?' Mr Meister was querulous. Miss Landsberg was invaluable. She knew precisely where every book in the place was. 'But – '

'You've been the kindest man, but please accept my notice. I have to go to Saxony. I've something desperately important to do.'

Mr Meister muttered, but said she could take a week off. She need not give notice.

Major Kirsten, walking stick in his hand, swished off the head of a pernicious weed as he strode briskly along the path between shrubberies. To the left lay the sweep of meadows, lush and green under the bright sky of Saxony. There were two cows, a heifer and a bullock, and he had the greatest difficulty in retaining possession of even those few animals. Germany was full of people who, finding the Weimar government was not providing milk and honey in plenty, were ferociously helping themselves to what did not belong to them. Moral attitudes were in deplorable decline. He could only suppose that the people who made off with livestock at night had families with empty bellies.

Germany had all the portents of a country heading for civil strife. Anyone who had known the best of Germany, bursting with energy, enterprise and prosperity, and with colour and pride, could only contemplate its present state with sadness. A philosophical outlook was difficult to sustain.

June, however, was always a month of warm, bright hope. He walked up to his house. His housekeeper, Mrs Wessler, a war widow as comely as a full-bosomed opera star, addressed him as he wandered in through her kitchen. She was also his cook.

'Major, you have a visitor, a young lady.'

'A young lady?' Major Kirsten smiled. Young ladies blossomed in June. 'Who is she?'

'She's charming, but has given no name. She only said she wishes to see you and won't leave until she does.'

'Ah, so. We have a charming young lady visitor who is also mysterious.'

The housekeeper preceded him to the sitting room, square, comfortable and full of light from the open windows. Major Kirsten, discarding his hat and stick, walked in. The housekeeper closed the door and left him to the mercies of the visitor. The young lady, her back to the door, was gazing at a small framed

366

photograph on a little wall shelf. She turned.

Major Kirsten pulled up and stared.

'Major?' Elissa, in a delicate summer dress of cornflower blue, with a blue and white hat, and white gloves, came to his eyes like the spirit of Germany's bright yesterday.

'Elissa, my dear young lady, I'm delighted to see you,' he said. He took her hand and brought it lightly to his lips. For all her determination, Elissa's colour rose and a pulse beat in her throat. How well he looked, fit and lean and vigorous, though his damaged eye seemed very blank. It was blind.

'Major, you are a picture,' she said.

'A picture?'

'Of health.'

He laughed. Elissa, faithful to the love she had always had for him, felt a surge of pleasure in his masculinity.

'True, I'm fit enough, but I doubt I'm a picture. I see only a rusticating old soldier in my mirror. But you look splendidly young and very delightful. Do sit down. Let me order you some refreshment. What shall it be? The coffee can't be fully recommended. Dare I offer you tea?'

'I wish no refreshment at the moment, Major.' Elissa, nerves taut, orientated herself for immediate attack. 'I'd like to settle things first.'

'Settle things? Do you have some business to see to in Dresden, perhaps?' His modest estate was not far from Dresden.

'Not in Dresden, no,' said Elissa. 'Here. In your house. Why did you not wait for me when you called at the bookshop?'

'I had an appointment,' said Major Kirsten, 'and was already a little late for it.'

'Why did you not call back?' asked Elissa, desperation overriding palpitation.

'Ah, yes,' said Major Kirsten, and cast his eye at her summery hat.

'That is not an answer,' she said.

'Elissa, do sit down.'

'Very well,' she said, and seated herself. Her dress – her best – flowed silkily around her trim figure and firm breasts. The hemline, shorter than the wartime styles, revealed her shimmering calves. Elissa, at the crossroads, was not disposed to be coy. Major Kirsten sat down opposite her. She smiled at the distinct glimmer in his sound eye.

'You're sure you'll take no refreshment?' he said.

'Not yet, thank you,' said Elissa. 'Major, you haven't given me an answer to my question.'

'I'm at a loss to find one.'

'I can't believe you could come to Munich and make no real attempt to see me.'

'You mustn't think that,' he said. 'I had every intention of doing so, and went straight to your bookshop from the station. Not finding you there, I was disappointed, of course, but did not want to become a nuisance.'

'A nuisance? I'm expected to believe that?'

'One does what one thinks best.'

'Best for whom?' said Elissa.

'I thought your work, your friends – '

'Major, I've always thought you incapable of dissembling.'

'Dissembling?' Major Kirsten seemed out of his depth.

'You have, of course, always been discouraging.'

'Good God,' he said.

'You're afraid I'll get too close,' said Elissa, blood up in her determination. 'Well, you must prepare yourself for shocks, because I mean to get very close. Why did you not write as you promised?'

Major Kirsten, feeling outgunned, said, 'Ah, yes. Yes.'

'Yes? What kind of answer is that?'

'I mean things haven't been precisely promising. Money is losing its value, chickens becoming priceless and an estate a liability. I've a housekeeper and two gardeners, that's all, and if I weren't able to let them live in and feed them, they'd not stay on the wages I'm able to pay. There was no position I could offer you, Elissa.'

Elissa eyed him coolly and without any sign that her heart was thumping.

'I should not, of course, have wanted to be your housekeeper or one of your gardeners,' she said.

'One of my gardeners?' Major Kirsten came to and regarded her with something approaching delight. Ex-Lieutenant Landsberg had become a joy. 'One of my gardeners?' he said again.

'I've something quite different in mind,' she said.

'Name it,' he said. 'I'm sure it's going to surprise me.'

'It is.' Elissa summoned up the last remnants of her courage. 'I have in mind a far higher position – as your wife.'

'Dear God in heaven,' said Major Kirsten.

'You once said that in certain circumstances I might surprise myself. Well, now I think I've surprised both of us. But I am saying to myself "Courage, Elissa, courage, you are no longer in uniform and he cannot have you shot." I've waited eighteen months to hear from you, and it's making me thin.'

'Thin?' said Major Kirsten, beyond any other comment in his stunned conviction that what he was hearing she could not be saying. 'Thin?'

Elissa, trying to remain unaffected by his appraisal of her figure, said, 'Mr Meister, my employer, has remarked at times that I've looked quite peaky. I must tell you I've no desire to spend all my life waiting.' Wondering when her voice was going to fail her, she went quickly on. 'I want to be loved. I need to be loved. Josef, please advise me of the significance of this.' She rose and moved to the little shelf and pointed.

He let his eye travel. She was pointing at a photograph in a brown leather frame. It was a photograph of three WAC officers serving at General von Feldermann's Headquarters at Valenciennes in 1918. Elissa was in the middle of the little group.

'It's a constant reminder to me of a lovely young lady,' he said.

'I am someone lovely?' she said.

'You're not questioning my taste?'

'No. But I am questioning your courage. Josef, I want to care for you, and have you care for me. Things are going to get worse in Germany, and when they do we should face them together, because I believe that together we'll put up a very good fight and not go under. I believe myself capable of being a good wife. I will be. But of course, you must marry me first. Josef, are you in love with me?'

Major Kirsten coughed.

'Ah – '

'Josef!' Elissa, having survived the ordeal of the confrontation, was not going to be put off.

'Of course I love you, my dearest Elissa.'

'Then stand up, please,' said Elissa, swept by colour and bliss.

He came to his feet. She put her arms around

him, lifted her face and kissed him warmly on the lips.

'Elissa – '

'You have given me a terrible time, but I love you, you dear man, you know I love you, and yet you were afraid.'

'Not afraid, my dear, merely unsure of myself. You're not getting a very good bargain, you must see that.'

Elissa pressed close.

'I'm getting you and you're getting me,' she said. 'I would rather have you than any other man. My mother says I'm a discriminating woman, and I am, I know that, because you are the best of all men. I'm proud of you, and you're very good for reserved young ladies who need a special kind of understanding. You believed in me, and it made me love you very much. I would like to be married to you without wasting too much more time.'

'Today might be a little difficult to arrange,' said Major Kirsten, 'there are certain formalities which have to be considered.'

'Oh, I'll wait a few days, then.' She kissed him again, without reserve and without restraint, and melted at his warm, firm response. 'Josef, why did you come to Munich?'

'To see Sophia von Feldermann.'

'Josef?'

'And, with luck, to see you too, but you were out with your young man.'

'He isn't my young man, he's an ex-soldier. Miss von Feldermann is in Munich?'

'I heard from her father that she was. I telephoned her, spoke to a lady with a screaming voice – '

'Screaming?'

'It whistled in my ears. She went to fetch Sophia, Sophia spoke to me, said she was divinely blissed to hear from me – '

'Divinely blissed?'

'So she said.'

'You are not trying to make me jealous, are you?' said Elissa.

'Nothing of the kind, my dearest. She was frantically busy with people, she said, and begged me to come to lunch in two days' time. I was curious to see her, so I made the appointment.'

'Why?'

'Sit down,' he said. She sat down with him, on a very comfortable and cosy sofa where it was easy to be close to him. 'I wanted to find out if she had been cured of her attachment to Captain Marsh – the strangest attachment, considering the circumstances.'

'Josef, you of all men to be so insensitive – I'm sure that was the worst moment of her life, one she would have been desperate to forget. Josef, an attachment to a dead man, whom she herself killed – what were you thinking of?'

'It isn't quite like that,' said Major Kirsten. He put his strong right arm around her and Elissa cuddled up like an enchanted girl. 'Captain Marsh was not quite dead that morning. It was thought he was. There was no resident medical officer at that place, no one who might have proved the general opinion wrong. But in the ambulance, a corporal of the Medical Corps suspected the pulse was still beating. Captain Marsh was accordingly rushed to the hospital and there he made a complete recovery. He was eventually sent to a prisoner-of-war camp.'

'Oh, how relieved Miss von Feldermann must have been. And afterwards, when the war was over? Now I see why you – '

'Ah, not quite,' said Major Kirsten. 'Sophia wasn't told he'd recovered. Her father thought that the best way of ensuring an end to an unacceptable relationship. I understood his attitude to some extent, but it worried me. I couldn't forget Sophia's sense of tragedy. So, hearing she was in Munich, I couldn't resist making that appointment to have lunch with her. I'm afraid I wasted my time. Sophia has quite got over the man and his death, or what she assumed was his death. I had no real chance to talk to her. She has a palatial apartment and it was full of young people and some ex-servicemen, all stuffing themselves at a cold buffet. Sophia has become extremely vivacious and very involved, and I had no opportunity to talk privately to her. I confess I disliked the talk and the atmosphere. The talk was political and extreme, the atmosphere rather wild. The politics seemed to mainly concern a national revolutionary party violently opposed to Communism. There was little difference as far as I could make out. I left. Sophia gaily waved me goodbye. She was the spirit of postwar loudness and political adventurism, both unappealing to me. I felt there was no point at all in referring to something she had obviously succeeded in putting behind her. So I said nothing about Captain Marsh.'

Elissa looked doubtful.

'You didn't think she would have wanted to know she didn't kill him?'

'I felt the whole episode no longer interested her. Or Captain Marsh either. He obviously lost any urge he had to see her again. I felt, when I saw him in hospital, that he had some idea about marrying her. Time cured them both.'

'Do you think so?' said Elissa, remembering Sophia's haunting sadness.

'I think it seems so.'

'She was very vivacious?' enquired Elissa.

'She was a young woman of painted lips and constant laughter. Loud laughter.'

'Josef, I think you may have deceived yourself. I must go back to Munich, of course, to tell my parents about us. Will you please give me Sophia's address? I'd like to see her myself.'

'Why?'

'Painted lips and constant laughter, loud laughter, that's why, you dear man.'

Chapter Twenty-two

The caller offered a smile.

'Good morning,' she said.

Sophia stared uncomprehendingly at the young woman at her door. It was not a time when she was used to receiving visitors, for it was not yet eleven o'clock and she had only been up half an hour. But Elissa, wisely, had not wanted to choose a moment when she might find the apartment full of people and politics.

Sophia, suddenly recognizing her, flashed into a dazzling smile.

'I know you, of course I do,' she cried. 'Miss Landsberg – yes. First the deliciously distinguished Major Kirsten, and now you. Come in, do come in. You must forgive the mess, but I gave a little party last night and it was hopelessly late before everyone left.'

She brought Elissa into the living room. Picturesque and spacious, it was not at its best at the moment. It was, in fact, appallingly untidy, but Sophia presented its disorder to Elissa with a laugh and a wave. It looked as if a stampede had taken place. The polished floor was littered with cushions, pamphlets, glasses and cigarette ash. A large fireside rug was askew. A chair was on its side, and a table lamp, overturned, had not been righted. The odour of stale cigarette smoke permeated the room. On an elegant sideboard stood bottles, most of them empty.

'This was a little party?' said Elissa.

'Oh, everything does look a trifle chaotic, doesn't it?' Sophia threw a window open. 'Such dreadfully careless people, but all very sweet and earnest. We're planning a new Germany.' She laughed. 'Would you like a new Germany Miss Landsberg?'

'I'd like to be called Elissa.'

'Then I'm Sophia.' They shook hands. Sophia's smile radiated a new brilliance. Her teeth were a flashing white, her lips a gash of bright red. Her dress was a rich yellow, the bodice a flamboyance in the way it outlined her abundant breasts. Her hair, a pale and lustrous gold, was a careless flowing mass, her blue eyes large amid dusty blue shadows, and her face was rouged. Her beauty, thought Elissa, was gilded, but that was what many young women did to themselves these days with their paint.

'Josef – Major Kirsten – told me you were in Munich, and in very high spirits, so I thought I'd like to call. You don't mind?'

'Why, how could I mind? It's sweet of you,

and after all, we did meet somewhere special. How happy you look. Are you happy, Elissa?'

'I'm one of the few lucky ones,' said Elissa.

'Because you aren't dead, you mean?' Sophia's ready laugh echoed. 'Some say it's only the dead who are lucky. Some people talk that way, don't they? Why are you lucky, considering you're alive?'

'I'm in love,' said Elissa, deceptively demure.

'Oh, that isn't supposed to be lucky, but it is considered fashionable,' said Sophia with the sweetest of smiles.

'Fashionable?'

'But yes,' said Sophia. 'I mean, who is not in love? Everyone I know is in love with everyone else.'

'How confusing,' said Elissa. 'Is there no selective factor?'

'Darling, that has all gone. Love for everyone is the thing now. There was all that beastly hate during the war. Now there's only love. I can't count all those who are in love with me. Oh, rapture in its way, because one does so wish to be loved, doesn't one? But there can be little irritations. The jealousy, you have no idea. Will you drink coffee? Yes, you must. Stay there. Sit down, do sit down. I do have coffee, you know. Well, I have money, you see, and with money you can even get quite good coffee. I'll make some now, at once. Sit down.'

She was gone, a flash of yellow and gold, her

long legs gleaming in her short-skirted dress. Elissa moved about, righting furniture and picking up cushions and glasses. She emptied overflowing ashtrays into a pretty little basket already half-full of ash and butts and torn paper. From the floor beside an armchair she retrieved a dark red silk dress and a slip of crêpe de Chine. The slip was still faintly aromatic, the scent delicate and expensive. A little sigh escaped Elissa. She smoothed the garments and placed them neatly over the back of a chair. She opened another window and the warm air came to caress her and to sweeten the outraged room. Her heart was sad for Sophia, but singing for herself. Yes, she was lucky. How good life was to her, giving her Josef. And how cruel to others. Poor Sophia, dancing on brittle glass because she thought she had murdered Captain Marsh. That was how she would look at her action.

Sophia returned with a tray containing china and a coffee pot. She looked around the room, eyes opening theatrically wide.

'Forgive me,' said Elissa, 'but I've a terrible habit of straightening things, although I do try to avoid being fussy. A place must be lived in, and must look lived in, or it offers no welcome – but overturned chairs and crumpled rugs – '

'Oh, straightening things, yes, that is women's work by common consent,' laughed Sophia, setting the tray down on a table. Elissa noticed the attractive appearance of the laden tray, a pretty lace mat set diagonally over it, the china and the sugar bowl neatly arranged to complement the shining coffee pot. That was nothing to do with politics, thought Elissa, it was to do with a woman of simple feminine grace. 'Men disturb everything, Elissa, and women tidy up.'

'Well, women are more efficient at bringing order,' said Elissa. 'If we put the brooms into men's hands, all the dust would be swept under the carpets.'

'Oh, I'm trying to lose the ingrained habit of tidying up, as you've seen,' said Sophia, pouring coffee. 'I'd rather mend motor cars.'

'Mend motor cars?' said Elissa in astonishment.

Sophia's laugh was quick and brittle.

'Did I say something silly? I do, on occasion. But we all do, don't we? Even Bismarck had his moments. There.' She handed Elissa hot, fresh coffee.

'Thank you, Sophia,' said Elissa, and seated herself. Sophia perched on the arm of a chair, and it occurred to Elissa, from the way the yellow dress clung to her figure, that she was wearing very little beneath it.

'Who are you in love with, Elissa?'

'You are interested?' smiled Elissa.

'But of course.' Again the laugh. 'I'm always interested in who is in love with whom. Oh, did

I tell you that sweet and deliciously civilized Major Kirsten actually came to lunch with me and my friends? My girlfriends were smitten. I must tell you—'

'I don't think you'd better,' said Elissa.

'But, darling, why not?' said Sophia. She gulped thirstily at her coffee. 'I was holding a little political seminar here, over a cold lunch. Everyone was discussing the agonies of Germany until Major Kirsten appeared. There was a positive rush, would you believe. Well, he is so distinguished, isn't he, and a war hero. My girlfriends were so entranced there was a quite mesmerized consultation about who should have the privilege of sacrificing herself on the altar of spontaneous and unconditional love.'

'What is spontaneous and unconditional love?' asked Elissa.

'Oh, immediate bliss and an acceptance of all the risks,' said Sophia with vivacious candour.

'Who was the lady who ascended the altar?' asked Elissa, a mote in her eye.

'Oh, the let-down was disastrously humiliating,' said Sophia. 'He left before we'd finished drawing straws. We were shattered. He bowed to me, declared himself in the devil of a hurry and left. That, of course, was such an effective departure that we can't wait for him to come again, and I sent him a letter of sweet urgency only yesterday.'

'To discuss the altar arrangements?' said Elissa. 'Or something else?'

'Oh, you are deliciously quaint,' said Sophia, pouring more coffee. She was so brilliantly transparent that she seemed to Elissa like a fragile sparkling glass. 'It's all the thing, you know, to be madly in love with a war hero, especially as there are so few of them still alive. What do you think, darling? Do you think every thousand women should share one war hero?'

'You are talking about smothering them?'

Sophia's laughter pealed.

'Elissa, yes, you are delicious. You live in Munich?'

'Yes, with my parents.'

'Your parents?' Sophia looked very amused. 'Darling, how dull for you. Parents are fairly special, of course, as long as one doesn't have to live with them. You should come and live with me, yes, why not? You can do the tidying up and I will pay the rent. And you can join the Party.'

'Which Party?' asked Elissa, who had long since come to a conclusion that differed from Major Kirsten's.

'The German Workers' Party,' said Sophia with enthusiasm. 'There are other parties – oh, hundreds – but this is the one that will give us a new Germany as brave as the old one. The old one was rather lovely, wasn't it? All those parks and bandstands and music? I must tell you, a funny-looking little man called Anton Drexler comes here sometimes, and charges us all with fire and faith. And have you listened to Adolf Hitler of the Army's Political Department? Such a convincing nationalist. Well, one doesn't want Bolshevism, does one? That awful man Lenin, a walking horror. There'd be no fun, no beauty. Fritz Gerder, a dear friend of mine who survived the war, agrees that beauty is what we most desire.'

'Oh, beauty is very desirable,' said Elissa.

'And Major Kirsten must join too,' said Sophia. 'We must win him over.'

'You seem very interested in Major Kirsten,' said Elissa. 'Is that because he was so involved on the occasion when— Oh, that reminds me, did you know that the English airman, Captain Marsh recovered? You remember Captain Marsh and how—'

Sophia's cup and saucer fell from her hand. The china broke on the polished floor and the liquid spilled. Sophia's mouth was open, her eyes glazed, her body shaking. She looked at her empty hands and the smashed china. She slid from the arm of the chair on to her knees, her mouth working and her breathing convulsive.

'There's cognac – on the sideboard – could you – could you bring me some, please?'

Elissa found the cognac bottle on the littered sideboard. There was a little left. She also managed to find a clean glass. She poured the residue and took it to Sophia, who reached with shaking hands, clutched the glass and gulped a fiery mouthful. She gasped, coughed and shuddered.

'What is wrong?' asked Elissa gently.

'Nothing – only that I'm dying – oh, my God.'

'That's a little dramatic, isn't it?' Elissa smiled. Sophia looked up at her, mouth trembling, eyes huge. 'But Major Kirsten was wrong. He thought you'd got over Captain Marsh. But you haven't, have you?'

'He isn't dead? He's alive?'

'He made a complete recovery.'

'You are sure, you are really sure?' Sophia was still shaking.

'I discovered, after hearing the news myself, that he was repatriated to England with other British officers in December 1918.'

'Oh, dear God,' said Sophia. She came slowly to her feet and placed the glass back on the sideboard. She saw the sticky rings that stained the rosewood. They looked very ugly. 'This is a mess, isn't it?' she said in a peculiar high voice. 'It's a disgusting mess, isn't it? And look at me – I'm the worst mess of all. What would he think of me? Last night I danced on that chair with very little on, and the chair fell over and someone caught me, but no one picked the chair up, or my clothes. Oh, Elissa, I am such a mess.'

'Some women do worse things,' said Elissa.

'Yes. Yes. He's alive, Elissa, he's really alive?'

'Are you glad?' asked Elissa.

'Glad? Glad?' Sophia drew a shuddering breath. 'Oh, you can't know, no one can. You see, you see, there was no need to shoot him, was there? I needed only to fire that revolver in the air and the men would have come running from those aeroplane sheds. He fell, he fell from the top of the fence, and I knew as he hit the ground that it hadn't been necessary, that I'd killed him and destroyed myself in a moment of frenzy.'

'You mean you thought you'd killed him.'

'Yes. Yes.' Sophia wrapped her arms around her shaking body. 'Oh, thank you, thank you for telling me. Everyone else kept it from me, didn't they? They knew he hadn't died, my father knew, but they kept it from me.'

'They thought it for the best – '

'The best?' Sophia began to walk wildly about. 'Look at this place, look at me – is that for the best?'

'I think it was because he was English that it was all quite unacceptable, even for you. Sophia, so many people felt that had it not been for England and the British Navy, Germany could have won the war. Major Kirsten thought your father's view understandable.'

'Is one man to be blamed for what his country did? He saved my life, he saved me from falling into a canal, he risked his own life – '

'Was it gratitude, then?' asked Elissa. 'Was it gratitude rather than love?'

'Oh, Elissa, no – no. Elissa, all this time I thought him dead, and I've been dying myself.'

'You are sure you haven't been enjoying it after a fashion?' said Elissa, thinking dramatics of no use at all.

'Enjoying it?' Sophia's laugh was bitterly brittle. 'Do you know what it's like to feel you are dancing on a coffin containing the corpse of a man you loved and killed?'

'I'm sorry,' said Elissa.

'No – you have been so good, coming to see me and telling me. But I am a mess, aren't I?'

'Your lipstick is a little too gaudy, perhaps, and your attire a little risqué,' said Elissa candidly. 'You are wearing no slip and your legs can be seen through your dress. But you have a superb figure. I think, when you see Captain Marsh, you should wear something chic. I think men like the women they love to look elegant rather than risqué. They're very conventional.'

'See him?' Sophia began to shake again. 'Oh, my God, how can I? I've bags under my eyes and I don't even feel clean.'

'May I be your friend?' asked Elissa.

'Oh, yes, yes. You knew about my feelings, all that time ago – '

'That's in the past. Let's think about the future. First, we must give up high drama and theatricals, and thinking we can't look our men in the face. I'm sure men have far more on their consciences than we do. We must sit down together and enjoy a sensible discussion. That is, if you are quite sure you're still in love.'

'Please don't talk like my mother,' said Sophia. 'Oh, my poor mother, I have given her no peace. Elissa, please stay and discuss things with me – but how am I to see him without shaking like a leaf, even if I can look him in the face?'

Elissa laughed.

'Oh, I shook like a leaf too a few days ago. But women are more emotional than men, of course, and shake while men only cough. Josef – Major Kirsten – hardly batted an eyelash, but he did cough. I think all he suffered was astonishment.'

'Major Kirsten?' Sophia, every limb still weak, her emotions in turmoil, nevertheless smiled warmly at Elissa. 'What are you telling me?'

'That I don't think I can allow any ladies you know to engage in spontaneous and unconditional love with my future husband.'

'Elissa?' Crimson flooded Sophia. 'Oh, what must you think of me?'

'I'm simply very glad Josef saw the danger signals and departed. I'll tell him so.'

'No, please don't,' gasped Sophia, 'please don't. I should want the earth to open up and swallow me.'

Elissa smiled. Sophia, in an extravagance of

gratitude and warmth, swooped and kissed her on the cheek.

'You're very demonstrative,' said Elissa.

'I'm the odd one out in our family,' said Sophia. 'Oh you're going to be good for me, aren't you? You're going to help me feel clean again. You're going to help me tidy myself up. I'm so glad for you and Major Kirsten – you'll suit each other marvellously. But Captain Marsh – Elissa, what am I going to do?'

'Sit down and talk,' said Elissa. 'I'm still rather reserved, you know, but when one is desperate every effort must be made to slay one's dragons. You must be positive, even if you shake so much that your head falls off. First, of course, we must find out if Captain Marsh is married.'

'Oh, God,' said Sophia, and sat heavily down. 'Don't say things like that, don't. That isn't positive, Elissa, that's the way to new misery.'

'Where does Captain Marsh live?'

'In an English county called Wiltshire.'

'Wiltshire? That's all you know?'

'But Wiltshire is only a little county. He'll be known there, won't he? I've looked at it a thousand times on a map.'

'All this time, Sophia, you've been looking at a map?'

'He was dead to me, yes, but a place on a map kept him alive for me because he had a motor garage there – and his parents – and I thought one day I would go, and I would see the garage and perhaps his parents, and tell them I was the one who killed him.'

'Very dramatic,' said Elissa. 'All such morbid fancies must stop. We've some work to do.'

'Yes. You must help me think. I can't think for myself, not at the moment – except about him being alive. Isn't that wonderful, Elissa, isn't it?'

'The situation, perhaps, is better than it was,' said Elissa.

Sophia laughed. Shakily.

'Mama,' said Sophia over the telephone, 'dearest Mama, I want you to be very honest with me. There'll be no quarrel, I promise.'

'Sophia, where are you?'

'Still in Munich, Mama, and having such late nights over politics that I've bags under my eyes. Did you hear what I first said?'

'It's not a very good line, but yes, I heard you.'

'And you will be honest with me?'

'Sophia, that is not a question you should ask of either of your parents.'

'I know, Mama, but I am asking.'

'What is it you want?'

'Mama, I want you to tell me if you've ever received any letters for me which you haven't sent on. Will you tell me that, please?'

'Letters?'

'Mama, you receive letters for me sometimes

which you send on. Thank you for doing so. But
have there been any you haven't sent?'

A pause.

'What letters, my dear?'

'I am not to know that, am I, Mama, if I
haven't received them.'

'One doesn't always remember to send everything on. One hopes one's daughter will come
home sometimes and pick them up for herself.'

'Yes, but will you answer the question, please?'

'About certain letters? I'm not sure – very
well, I'll be frank. There was one. It arrived at
the end of November, I think.'

'Eight months ago? Eight?'

'And there was another in February.'

'Be my sweet and most dear Mama and tell
me who they were from.'

Another pause.

'I had hoped you would never hear from
him.'

'Yes, I know I was supposed to believe he was
dead, but I have found you out, Mama, you and
Papa. They were from Captain Marsh?'

'I regret, yes.'

'Mama, the war is over and you are very
caring and I understand why you have always
done what you thought best for me. Mama, did
you read the letters?'

A third pause.

'Yes. I was worried.'

'You have worried excessively, Mama, but I

understand that too. You knew the letters would tell me he was alive. What did he say in them?'

'I really can't remember.'

'I think you can, Mama. You must tell me. Do you still have them?'

'I burned them.'

'Yes, of course. So please tell me what was in them.'

'You are such a difficult girl.'

'I am not a girl, Mama.'

'The first – let me see – he asked questions.'

'About me, about my welfare, about what I was doing and so on?'

'Yes.'

'Mama, did he mention the shots I fired?'

'Really, Sophia.'

'Did he, Mama?'

'No. Not a word. He asked if you would let him know how you felt about him, whether he— I can't remember.'

'Yes, you can.'

'Whether he could come to see you, whether you would like him to.'

'Mama, did he say he loved me? Will you tell me that, please?'

A longer pause.

'I really don't know. I put it on the fire before I'd finished it.'

'Yes, Mama. And the second letter?'

'It was brief. It was about the fact that you hadn't replied. He said he understood. He

wished you happiness. He – I really can't remember everything.'

'He what, Mama?'

'He sent you his love.'

'Thank you, Mama. You're an angel. I'll see
you and Papa soon, I'm coming home for a
little while.'

'Sophia, my dear, I wish you would, I hope
you will.'

'Mama, you wish to be happy for me, don't
you?'

'Yes.'

'You are very wise, Mama, and must know
you can only be happy for me if I'm happy myself. While I'm home with you, I'd like you to
teach me a little English. You speak English, I
know.'

'Sophia, you aren't thinking of – you can't
possibly – '

'Mama, I love you.'

'Oh, my dear.'

Chapter Twenty-three

Pattie, the sole servant in the vicarage, answered the ring at the door. Outside on the gravelled drive stood a motor car, its yellow paintwork dusty. On the step stood a beautiful young woman in a summer costume of pastel blue, the long jacket perfectly tailored to her waist and bosom. Her shoes were blue, her hat navy and white, and her gloves were white. Her fair hair, where it escaped her hat, was softly looped over ears and forehead. Pattie stared in awe and admiration. The young woman, a phrase book in her hand and a slightly anxious smile on her face, said in heavily accented English, 'Please, to see the pastor, may I?'

'Pastor? You mean parson? There be the Reverend Howard Marsh, he be the parson, miss.'

'Marsh, yes.' Sophia's smile became warm with relief. 'If you please?'

She was so gracious and so elegant that Pattie, mesmerized, asked her to step in and went to fetch the vicar from his study. The Reverend Howard Marsh, tall, grey-headed and upright, arrived on a note of benign curiosity. In the vicarage parlour, Sophia greeted him a little nervously.

'Please, good morning,' she said.

'Good morning,' he said genially, thinking her as beautiful as the summer day.

Sophia, carefully precise because her vocabulary was limited, said, 'If you please, you are the pastor here?'

'The vicar. Please sit down.'

'Thank you, sir.' Sophia sat, her long legs modestly tucked back. 'I am come, please, to ask – ' She consulted the phrase book, as much to gather herself together as to find the right words. 'I am come to ask is it correct you are father to Captain Peter Marsh – if you please.' She had got it out, and the tall man in clerical grey and white dog collar was smiling at her.

'Yes, Peter is my younger son.'

'Good, yes,' said Sophia, and worried a little about the difficulty of articulate communication. 'The French or the German you do not speak?'

'I speak French. Would you prefer that?'

'Oh, yes,' said Sophia gratefully. The vicar, frankly dazzled, smiled again. In French she said, 'I have very few words in English. I have some like how much and which is the way to

395

Somerset House, London, but I'm proficient in French.'

'You're excellent,' said the vicar, taking up the conversation in the preferred language.

'It's beautiful here, isn't it?' she said. She had motored slowly through the village and seen the picturesque stone cottages, the little shops and an old-looking saddler's establishment. 'So many pretty gardens, and such a lovely day.'

'On such a day all God's creatures dwell in radiance,' said the Reverend Marsh, 'and we should give thanks for that.'

'And for His many wonders?' said Sophia, a lapsed Christian who had recently returned to the fold.

'For that which is before us,' smiled the vicar, a healthy admirer of beauty in women. He observed his intriguing visitor with new interest, a suspicion as to her identity forming in his mind. She seemed hesitant about explaining the reason why she was here, looking around as if seeking inspiration from the solid Victorian furniture, the multitude of ornaments and the roses on the wallpaper. 'May I ask if I can be of service to you?' he said. His French was not as well spoken as his son's, for his son had perfected his fluency and accent in France, but it was easily understood by Sophia.

Her gloved hands tightened around the phrase book in her lap.

'I – I would like very much to see Captain Marsh, if I may,' she said.

The vicar studied the pale gold of her hair and her blue eyes.

'My dear young lady,' he said, 'are you Sophia von Feldermann?'

Her face lit up.

'Oh, you know me, Monsieur le Curé? He has told you about me?'

'Indeed he has. A story of his transgression and your fortitude. The wrath of the Lord should have descended on him. He assured me it almost did.'

'Oh, no, it wasn't like that,' said Sophia. 'He was trying to avoid capture. He hated the thought of a prisoner-of-war camp, and there are rules which permit soldiers on the run to take desperate measures. I understood that.'

'It sounded to me as if he made his own rules.' The vicar's smile was thoughtful. 'Is it possible that the reason you're here is to tell him you've forgiven him? His story shocked me. I confess it did not affect my wife in quite the same way. She was enthralled. However, it did inspire a sermon of mine which I thought very good, but I'm not sure if my congregation fully appreciated it. Have you come all the way from Germany to visit us?'

'Yes.' Sophia's anxiety about her reception was changing to melting gratitude. She had shot this clergyman's son, but he had only kindness for her. 'But not to forgive Peter. How could I do that, when I am the one who should ask him to forgive me?'

'Upon my soul,' said the Reverend Marsh, 'you've arrived in sweet charity, my child. To speak of asking forgiveness of the transgressor is a gesture of true Christian humility. There's not too much of that about.'

'But I – ' Sophia's heartbeats were painful. 'Monsieur le Curé, I – '

'I think it's more suitable, even in French, to call me Reverend.' The vicar carefully enunciated the title.

'Yes. Reverend.' Sophia enunciated just as carefully. 'Please, may I see Peter?'

'You will have to go to Little Bassington.'

'Excuse me, please?' said Sophia, wondering how to get her tongue around that.

'Little Bassington.' Again the vicar enunciated with care.

'Yes, Leedle Bazzinkdonk,' said Sophia.

'That will do,' said the enchanted clergyman. 'It's a very small country town, and not too far.'

'Please, will you tell me, does he have a motor garage and forge there?'

'Yes, and a cottage in which he lives.'

Sophia radiated delight.

'Oh, that is wonderful, isn't it?'

'A motor garage?' The vicar seemed dubious. 'Has God really designed us for the purpose of mechanization?'

'I am sure the wheel was a gift from God,' said Sophia earnestly.

'Well, there it is,' said the vicar, 'a motor garage, although not very profitable. However, it isn't the profiteers who receive all the blessings.'

'I am very good myself with motors,' said Sophia.

'So Peter said.' The Reverend Marsh eased his long frame into a chair, the better to study this extraordinary and vital-looking German girl. German – alas, there would be a few frowns. 'My outrageous son was favoured by your aptitude at the wheel, I believe. He was also favoured in not dying when the sentry shot him.'

'The sentry?' said Sophia faintly.

'I have the story right? He was attempting to reach a German aeroplane, but was shot by the sentry. We received a hospital postcard from him when he was on the mend, but not until he arrived home did we hear exactly what had happened.'

'Oh, but—' Sophia stopped. She must confess to this man of God – except why had Peter said the sentry shot him? She must ask him before she confessed to his parents. Her whole body was melting because the answer might mean cherishing love.

The door opened and a plump lady in a dark brown dress came in, a lady with streaks of silver in her hair and a flush of garden warmth about her. In her hand was a pair of shears, and on her face was a look of homely exasperation.

'Howard, these shears— Oh, I beg your pardon.'

'My dear Mary,' said the vicar, rising from his chair, 'do you remember Peter's extraordinary story and its regrettable nature? Who do you think is here but none other than the young lady who showed such fortitude during the ordeal he forced on her?'

'Oh, my goodness!' gasped the astonished Mrs Marsh.

'Sophia – may I call you Sophia? – this is my wife, Mary. Mary, this is Sophia von Feldermann, an entirely forgiving young lady.' The vicar made the introduction on a highly intrigued note, and Sophia rose to her feet, nervous again.

'Oh, my dear goodness,' said Mrs Marsh, and turned her astonishment on the visitor. Astonishment became approval. It was impossible to fault Sophia's appearance. Her costume was chic. It bestowed elegance. Her hat was a delicious piquancy, and silk stockings graced her legs. Her eyes had the clarity of a cloudless summer sky. 'Was there ever such a surprise?' said the vicar's wife. 'How delightful of you, my dear. Of all things, this is the most intriguing. That dreadful son of mine. My husband was appalled at his infamy.' She had not been too appalled herself, and had told her husband not to forget that God helped those who helped themselves. The vicar, in words of many syllables, had pointed out the gracelessness of such a sentiment.

'Frau Marsh – ' said Sophia.

'Our son Peter ventured to suggest it was simply the only thing he could do at the time. Quite the most thoughtless thing, of course. A young lady. Her car. And you're so very young – oh, but it's all over, my dear, the war. You haven't come to have him arrested, I hope? I shouldn't blame you, although I felt perhaps he was more thoughtless than unprincipled. You must stay to lunch – '

'Please, you are speaking too quick,' said Sophia, 'I have only the little English.'

Mrs Marsh patted her arm and said, 'Well, never mind, we shall teach you a little more over lunch. If Pattie is on her toes, we shall eat in an hour at twelve-thirty. You have come to stay a while, I hope. Reconciliation is the peaceful child of time. You're really quite well known to us through Peter. I believe he wrote to you. Is that why you're here? But he lives in—'

'Please to excuse me?' begged Sophia. She knew she could not possibly wait until after lunch to be on her way to see Peter. If he had told his family so much about her, that was a good sign, surely. But, the letters, the letters to which he had received no reply. There might be someone else now. There were so many eligible women, and such a scarcity of eligible men. She must go, she must.

The Reverend Marsh, reading her wishes, said, 'We'll happily excuse you.' He continued in French. 'I understand from Pattie that you arrived in a car. If that means you have your luggage with you, then please leave it here. You must stay with us until you return to Germany, and we shall try to restore the family's credit. To get to Little Bassington, go through the village and turn right. Go on until you reach the Crown crossroads. You'll see the Crown Inn on the corner. Turn left and Little Bassington is fifteen miles on. The motor garage is on the right just before you enter the high street.'

'Oh, thank you, Reverend. You have been kindness itself. I am so grateful. You will not think too badly of me if I go at once?'

'I think you'll find my deplorable son will be delighted to see you.'

'Oh, thank you,' said Sophia again, and breathlessly.

'I'm only catching a little of what you're both saying,' said Mrs Marsh, 'but never mind. I'm sure Peter will accept that retribution in the shape of a visitation could only be delayed. It's now arrived.'

She smiled at Sophia in homely warmth.

Sophia faintly coloured. Peter's mother knew why she had come.

She drove through the village, the sun a caress and the air so soft. The cottage gardens were bursting with colour, and a boy and girl, standing at the gates of the little village school, looked at her as she passed by in the car she had driven all the way from Munich, accompanied by Elissa and Major Kirsten. They had seen her on to an early-morning ferry in Boulogne, and from Dover she had driven to a hotel in Salisbury, a cathedral city that entranced her. Elissa had been so helpful. So had Major Kirsten. So had her father. As a respected soldier he could still pull one or two strings, and had eventually come up with the address of Captain Marsh's family, together with the information that Captain Marsh was not married. Her mother, at last reconciled to the fact that Sophia must live her life her own way, saw her off affectionately, but not without a sigh.

Sophia had spent three weeks in Lissa reorientating herself and shedding the dusty blue rings around her eyes. Now she was here, in Wiltshire, turning on to the road that led to Little Bassington. What a strange name for a place.

Her engine was purring, behaving itself so well after such an arduous and lengthy journey. There had been looks from some people in the Salisbury hotel on discovering she was German.

She supposed she would have to accept that some English memories could be as long as German ones. But if she could come among the English, knowing they had been wrong and unfair in going to war with Germany, then they should be similarly tolerant of her, for Germany had no guilt. At the moment, of course, it was only important that she did not receive similar looks from Peter.

Her heart was at its most erratic and painful, her foot even trembling on the accelerator as the car steadily ate up the country road. The little hills were a dry hot green, the apple orchards laden, the hedgerows sprinkled with yellow honeysuckle and green blackberries. High in the seat of the car, Sophia travelled on fluttering wings of anxiety and hope, her motoring scarf whisking. The eyes of other travellers turned and stared and smiled. Chin up, mouth firm, hands tight, Sophia drew on her courage. Shake if you must, Elissa had said, but be positive.

There it was. Little Bassington. The sign said so. She saw the high street ahead, hazy and softly brown in the golden light of August. And the motor garage, that was there too, on the other side of the road. Her heart stopped beating, or seemed to. There was a farm cart outside the adjacent forge, one wheel off. Next door, on the garage forecourt, stood an old truck and two cars. Sophia turned in and came to a careful halt beside one of the cars. She sat there. No one was about. Her hands remained glued to the wheel. Her knees were shaking. Could she get out without buckling? She tried it. She did not fall down, although every limb was tremulous.

There was a name over the wide doors of the garage workshop: PETER MARSH – AUTOMOBILE REPAIRS. Inside, there were benches, tools and a pit that looked dreadfully oily. A lad was working at a bench, repairing the damaged wire spokes of a wheel. Absorbed, he did not see her as she passed in front of the open doors.

Over the entrance to the forge was another name, that of Joshua Henry, Blacksmith. It was very faded. She supposed that was the name of the previous owner. Expecting Peter to appear at any moment, she was charged with sensitive anticipation. She peeped into the forge. The fire was a glowing furnace. She saw two men, one thin and dark, the other stout and hearty. The thin man had iron in the fire, tongs grasping it. The stout man was talking to him. The fire and the heat reddened their faces.

Out came the white-hot iron to be laid on the anvil. Sophia gazed in fascination. The hammer smote. The iron rang. The sparks flew. The stout man shouted to make himself heard.

'That be it, then, Simon, that be what I want, fairish quick and mind what 'ee charges me.'

'Fairish quick be the best I can do, Tom.'

The stout man came out. He eyed Sophia out of a rugged, weatherbeaten face. He blinked and touched his hat to her.

'Be a fine marning, missy, I reckon,' he smiled.

Heavens, thought Sophia, what has he said?

'Good morning, sir,' she ventured, feeling that could not be a totally wrong response.

'I be zur? Well, I never did,' he said, and proceeded at a jaunty walk towards the high street.

Sophia put her head inside the forge door and said, 'If you please?'

The thin man turned. His eyes opened wide at the silhouetted figure at the door. He put the iron into the fire, shut off the draught for the moment, and came out, his leather apron blackened, his long-fingered hands sooty.

'Be you wanting me, miss?'

Sophia liked the look of him. His lean face was strong, his mop of curly black hair damp from the sweat at his temples, his eyes friendly and his smile shy.

'Good morning, sir,' she said.

'Marning to 'ee too,' he said.

'I speak the little English,' said Sophia.

'Ah,' he said.

'To ask you I wish – are you Simon Tukes?'

'That be I,' said Simon.

'Excuse me?' Sophia, nonplussed by the West

406

Country accent, was apologetic in her failure to understand.

'Simon Tukes, that be I,' said Simon, overwhelmed by the picture she presented.

'Please,' said Sophia, picking her words very carefully, 'I am asking to see Captain Peter Marsh.'

'Ah,' said Simon again. He brightened. 'Be your car knocked up?'

'Excuse me?'

He tried again.

'Be that your car, miss?' he said, pointing to the parked yellow Benz.

'Yes,' said Sophia, and smiled with relief at having established a beginning to communication. 'If you please, sir, where is Captain Marsh?'

'Captain Marsh be out, miss.'

Sophia understood that and her face fell.

'Oh,' she said.

'Say thirty minutes,' said Simon.

'Please?'

'He'll be back in thirty minutes, I reckon,' said Simon, finally recognizing he needed to explain himself a little better.

'Oh, yes.' Sophia smiled. Its radiance poured over Simon. He grinned very shyly. 'I will wait, may I, please? I wish to.'

Simon shuffled his feet and nodded.

'You be right welcome,' he said.

Sophia had a thought.

'Please,' she said, 'how wrong is that motor?'

She pointed to the car standing beside her own. It was a battered black Sunbeam.

'Ah, that be Mr Martin's little tiddler. Be his plugs again, I reckon. They dirty up fast.'

'Plugs?' Sophia had caught that. 'The spark plugs?'

'I reckon,' said Simon.

Sophia's eyes gleamed. Excitement rushed to displace palpitations.

'I may look?' she said.

'Miss?' Simon gaped.

'Thank you,' said Sophia.

'You be Swedish?' ventured Simon.

Sophia took the plunge.

'I am German,' she said.

'Ah.' Simon ruffled his dark mop. 'Well, miss, it be a real pleasure to meet you.' He gave her another shy grin and returned to his fire.

What had he said? Sophia thought from the smile he had given her that his words could not have been unfriendly.

She entered the garage workshop. She looked around. The young apprentice mechanic saw her and gaped.

'Oh, by tiddly gum,' he said.

'If you please, that,' said Sophia, smiling and pointing. Quivering, mesmerized, the lad handed her the plug spanner. Numbly, he watched her as she lifted a faded brown working coat from its hook and went back into the sunlight.

She had her hat off, the scarf covering her hair and the working coat on. The bonnet of the Sunbeam was up. Two plugs were dirty and needed cleaning, two were cracked and needed replacing. The awestruck apprentice gave her two new ones, while mumbling a hope that it wouldn't get him the sack. Sophia, not understanding a word, gave him a warm smile of thanks.

She worked while she waited. She was excited, apprehensive and nervous.

Thirty minutes, how long was thirty minutes if not another lifetime?

She heard him just as she had all four plugs tightly fitted. She heard his footsteps. That is, she heard footsteps which she was sure were his. A feeling almost akin to panic took hold of her. She could only pray he had not found someone else, and that their reunion would be one of instant reconciliation.

The footsteps stopped. Her every limb began to shake.

Hidden by the lifted bonnet, she slipped off the working coat and the scarf. Her gloves were ruined, but she had had to sacrifice some part of her chic look to let him see what she wanted to share with him. She fought her nerves and straightened up. She saw him as her head came above the bonnet. He was there, on the other side of the car. He was wearing an old tweed cap, an open-necked shirt and knockabout brown cord trousers. He was brown-faced and alive. Seeing her, he at once looked stunned and incredulous. Her heart hammered. She had to speak French. Her English would be totally inadequate. Be positive. Even if you are shaking to death, be positive. Elissa had been emphatic about that.

She drew a deep breath.

Quite lightly, she said, 'It was the sparking plugs – two were no good at all – I've had to fit new ones.'

'Oh, my God,' he said, transfixed by disbelief.

'Darling, I'm quite good with cars, you know. I would have come before, but my mother burned your letters. Shall I start the engine?'

'Sophia? Are you real?'

Sophia smiled. Tiny specks of golden summer dust danced in the soft air, and her face was drenched with light.

'Darling, of course I'm real. You're pleased to see me, aren't you?' Her voice became a little throaty. 'I shall be very upset if you aren't. I came so that I could be a help to you with your business, and to ask you why you told your family it was the sentry who shot you.'

Peter Marsh was still groping.

'The sentry?' he said.

'Yes. Why didn't you tell them I was the one?'

410

He came to.

'Because, in the first place, it wasn't important. What did it matter whether it was you or the sentry? You both belonged to Germany. Secondly, I had the future in mind. I didn't want people constantly pointing me out as the man who was shot by his wife.'

'Wife?' Sophia felt her limbs were melting.

'Yes. I never gave up that hope. With that in mind, it was better to say the sentry shot me. Otherwise, you and I would have been forever explaining. Can't you imagine how tiresome that would have been? Have things been bad in Germany, Sophia?'

'Yes. And especially bad for me. Because of you, and thinking I'd killed you.'

'However much it may upset your mother, will you tell her I'm going to marry you? You'll not get away, Sophia, not now you're here.'

She said huskily, 'It's beautiful here, where you live, isn't it?'

'Not as beautiful as you are.'

'Look.' She stripped off her ruined gloves, dropped them to the ground and put out her hands. 'Look how I'm shaking.'

He laughed. She rushed around the car and fell into his arms. She clung feverishly. He held her. Every trauma slipped away and she felt engulfed by peace.

'Will you say yes, Sophia, or must I run off with you again?'

411

She lifted her face, her moist eyes shining. She smiled.

'Darling, you don't think I've come all this way to be a sister to you, do you?' She pressed closer, oblivious to everything except the gift of warm and wonderful life. 'Isn't it heavenly, our motor garage and Monsieur Simon Tukes and the forge – oh, I can't understand a word he says, but you will teach me English, won't you? Where is our cottage, where is the home where we are going to love each other?'

'Just a ten minutes' walk. Sophia – '

'Oh,' she said breathlessly, 'you stayed alive for me – thank you, thank you.'

'Shall we talk or find a place where I can kiss you?'

'You can kiss me here,' said Sophia positively.

THE END

NURSE ANNA'S WAR
Mary Jane Staples

Brussels, 1915

It is a frosty April evening in occupied Belgium when a beautiful young woman finds herself on the run from the enemy. Also being pursued is Ned Scott, a British army major who has been badly injured. The pair find themselves at a hospital run by the famous Edith Cavell, who agrees to treat the major while offering them both refuge and a false identity – she names the young girl Anna.

However, it seems no one is safe, and as details of Anna's true identity emerge, the enemy's net tightens. Meanwhile, the major is torn between his desire to stand by the brave Edith and the knowledge that he must escape.

Closely watched wherever they go, is there anyone these three people can trust? And will love have the power to overcome the horrors of war?

NATASHA'S DREAM
Mary Jane Staples

Can the secrets of the past be forgotten?

1925, a damp wintry night in Berlin.
Englishman Philip Gibson, in Germany to
seek the answers to a tantalizing mystery
surrounding the Grand Duchess Anastasia,
witnesses an attack on Natasha, a young
woman who has fled from Russia.

When Philip takes the fragile, lonely Natasha
in to help her recuperate, she quickly falls for
his kind and caring nature. But when further
threats are made on her life, Philip finds
himself at the heart of another mystery.

What is it that links Natasha to the mystery
of the duchess? And will her love for Philip
survive the secrets that will be unearthed?

THE LONGEST WINTER
Mary Jane Staples

When Baroness Sophie von Korvacs meets
British painter James Fraser one hot summer's
day in Vienna, the attraction is instant. A
whirlwind romance follows, with Vienna
bathed in the brilliance of the last days of
the emperor. And when James proposes
to Sophie it seems a fitting end to that
wonderful, enchanting summer.

But darker days are on the horizon as Europe
teeters on the brink of war. James must make
the ultimate choice: love for King and Country
or love for Sophie. Before he knows it, his
difficult decision is made for him, and he and
Sophie are on opposite sides of a bloody
and devastating conflict.

Four bleak years of fighting and death roll by.
Will Sophie's long winter ever end and can
their love conquer all?